U0057155

澄清聲明

親愛的讀者：

倍斯特出版事業有限公司鄭重聲明，大陸中國紡織出版社與本社無業務往來。

近來發現本社之公司Logo，出現於中國紡織出版社之貝斯特英語系列書籍，該出版社自 2012年11月1日起之所有出版品與本社並無任何關係；鑑於此事件，懷疑有人利用本社之商業信譽，藉此誤導大眾，本社予以高度關注。特此聲明，以正視聽。

倍斯特出版事業有限公司　敬啟

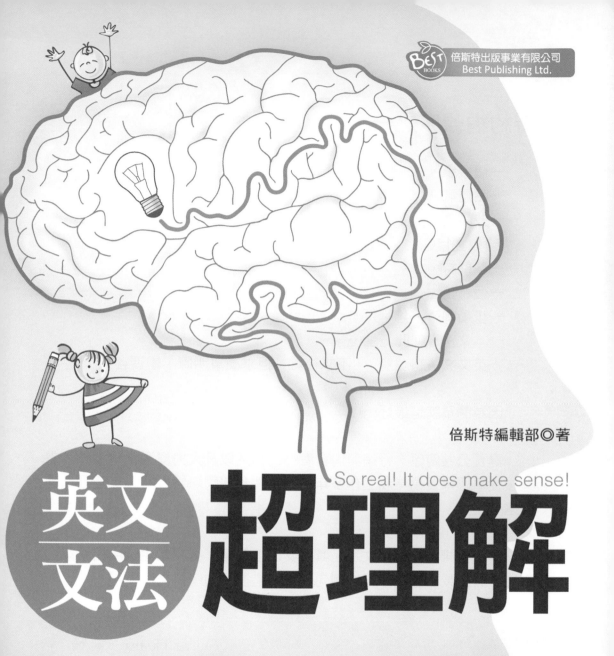

倍斯特出版事業有限公司
Best Publishing Ltd.

倍斯特編輯部◎著

So real! It does make sense!

英文文法 超理解

① 全書所有文法皆由**詳盡例句**做說明，文法
觀念學習透徹並且有效理解文法的架構。

② 全書中**英文達人文法小筆記**由教學經驗豐
富的老師們編寫文法重點，讓你短時間零
距離的學到切身需要的文法解析。

③ 學習文法不再是強記死背，本書強調**理解
式學習**，簡單明瞭的例句循序漸進掌握文
法重點。

④ 全篇文法皆由**電影經典文
學名著**或**名人金句**為引導，
讓學習充滿趣味與增進文
化素養和文學陶冶。

⑤ 特別收錄**超高頻率形容詞、
動詞、名詞**各五十個。使用
簡單的字彙清楚表達，不再
詞不達意。

特約編輯序之一

一個機緣，

一點運氣，

一些鼓勵，

一段掙扎，

一種堅持，

一個希望，

一步衝刺⋯⋯

一本文法書就此誕生⋯⋯

「英文文法超理解」，不求複雜，但求簡單明瞭，學習容易，

因為簡單就是最好⋯⋯

專長公共關係、行銷與消費者行為相關以及人力資源管理相關，畢業後從事國際貿易業務工作多年，經常性參與國際性展覽，英語是溝通的主要工具。

討厭硬梆梆的英文文法。其實文法很簡單，把平常生活中所接觸的電影、音樂或雜誌為學習的例句，也能是很好的學習文法。

Anlita Huang 黃梅芳

特約編者序之二

在英語教學多年的經驗裡，本人發現文法雖然是學校中英語教學的重點，但是許多學生還是對其領域抱有許多恐懼。其中問題癥結除了學生缺乏一系統性的概念，也是因為多數人採用死記死背的方式。在編寫本書的內容時，筆者構思的重點與靈感就是來自於不斷回想在教授文法課程時學生常見的問題，以及學生在遇到諸如問題時，如何解釋可以讓學生清楚明瞭。

在文法課時，本人常與學生介紹概念，也希望在此藉著這次機會與讀者分享。

我常問學生，如果今天你們有機會到一陌生城市去旅遊，譬如紐約，要拜訪想玩的景點以及到不同地方的方法，請問第一步應該是熟記路名還是抓清楚各景點東西南北的大方向。同學多認同應先認識大方向。我又再問，如果學習文法就跟旅遊一般，那應該是要先死記文法規則，還是應該先了解文法規則中的大方向呢？許多學生聽到此一比喻時就能了解為何在學習文法多年之後還是英文會講不出來或寫不出來，甚至會遇到卡住的現象。就像剛剛所舉之例，要到達觀光景點必須先至少知道由哪個方向出發，可以使用那些方法到達。而熟記路名是能讓你有辦法準確找到此一景點，就像只知道帝國大廈在第五大道 350 號，可以搭地鐵或公車時卻連它位於曼哈頓的那一區域都沒有概念，那這樣要如何知道往北往南或那一方向呢？透過這樣的說明，希望讀者能重新審視文法學習的重點與方法，可以讓文法觀念是在幫助各位能夠更快清晰表達溝通，而不是不斷的被文法規則所絆住或綁住。

在學校或在補習班，遇到形形色色的學生，都有著不同的要求與期許。但是我一直發現，不論任何背景與年紀的學生，他們都能感受出本人的認真與熱忱。自己要像每次要出場比賽的球員一樣，這也是我每次在上課前告訴自己的話，Be well prepared; be inspirational!

吳悠嘉

特約編輯序之三

　　英語已是世界通用的語言，也是被廣泛使用溝通的工具。學好英語已被列為求職者所必備條件之一。編者本人因旅居加拿大多年，深知學會基本句型和文法是與英語母語者溝通的必備條件。本書以一般生活中簡單句子為基礎，加入引用名人語句當做應用，以表達出如何將文法概念融入生活用語中，並知其文法的使用。以期讀者能在短時間內建立一些正確且簡易基本的文法觀念，運用於職場與考試中。

　　本書除了詳細的文法解說，並列出相似文法概念的相同與相異性，亦運用一些佳句讓讀者了解如何使用該句型，更加入一些測驗題以便讓讀者測試自己是否已了解該文法觀念。因本書設定是為希望學習到國中基本文法的讀者而編寫，故單字亦儘量以英語單字量為兩千單字量為基礎，而較深且複雜的文法亦不在本書編寫範圍內。若有不近詳細之處，敬請見諒。若有謬誤，敬請來信指正，以作修訂參考。

黃淑敏

編者序

　　「全球化」早已不再是新詞，全球化的事實也已發生在你我每天生活之間，從早上智慧手機設定的鬧鈴聲響起，盥洗、穿鞋襪、整理儀表、出門、工作、飲食、看電視、上網，直到夜晚熄燈就寢，看似平淡無奇，跟世界無關緊要，但其實都和全球化息息相關，因為幾乎各位從事這些活動所使用的器具多少都是來自台灣以外的國家，也就是説，在無意識中我們已經是這廣大意念中一部分，且幾乎是毫無退路的持續進行著。鑑於台灣之不可逆的全球化事實以及與世界各國頻繁聯繫之需要，台灣教育當局除了繼續在大學教育中鼓勵英語教育，也將英語教育往下扎根至國小低年級學生中，即便如此英文仍是很多人急欲逃離的對象，其中英文文法更被眾多學習者視為洪水猛獸，避之唯恐不及。

　　然而，真正想學好、自由揮灑英文，文法是重要關鍵，而文法觀念其實並不難，市面上文法書籍眾多，卻少有一本能將多數常用的文法觀念一網打盡，使用者常為了查詢一個文法概念，得在好幾本文法書中翻閱搜找，才能得到解答；且文法書對一般讀者文字抽象常不易閱讀，即為一解這些困擾，倍斯特編輯部企劃「英文文法超理解」，將書分為三大部分：句型文法、字詞文法、和英文單字不打結。句型文法談論英文句子的文法，字詞文法談論詞性與詞彙特性，此兩部分的章節中引用各媒體中實際被運用的例句或是名人語錄和其故事，為讀者導讀該文法單元重點，比如五大句型單元中的「S＋Vt＋O」(主詞＋及物動詞＋受詞) 以電影「征服情海」經典台詞：「You complete me.」(我的世界因你而完整。) 為例，讀者記住了英文例句，便能舉一反三；本書每單元都會提供數個實用例句，且在書末編有「英文單字不打結」，增進讀者對常用的英文字詞辨析能力，冀望如此規畫能為讀者帶來一些助力。

倍斯特編輯部

目 錄 CONTENTS

PART I 句型文法

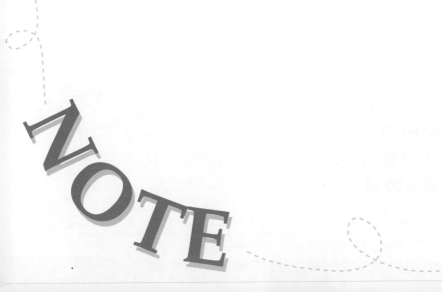

NOTE

Part Ⅰ
字詞文法

第1單元：五個基本句型

英文達人小筆記！

一個完整的英文句型是由主詞和動詞這二個基本元素所組成的句子，並且能完整表達語意。主詞，是一個句子中想要強調或凸顯的人、事、物；通常由單字詞類中的「名詞」扮演主詞的角色。動詞，則是主詞採取的行為或動作。所以，由主詞＋動詞作為基本原型，依動詞的特性，再加上受詞與補語，可延伸出英文簡單的五大基本句型。

句型一：**S + Vi**（主詞＋不及物動詞）Miracles happen every day!

句型二：**S + Vi + SC**（主詞＋不及物動詞＋主詞補語）

Time is money.

句型三：**S + Vt + O**（主詞＋及物動詞＋受詞）You complete me.

句型四：**S + Vt + O + OC**（主詞＋及物動詞＋受詞＋受詞補語）

People call me Forrest Gump!

句型五：**S + Vt + IO + DO**（主詞＋及物動詞＋間接受詞＋直接受詞）

（You）show me the money.

01 句型一：S + Vi（主詞＋不及物動詞）

名言範例：

Miracles happen every day. 奇蹟每天都在發生。

在電影《阿甘正傳》裡，在有著樂觀天性的母親，總是對著不是很聰明，並且經常遭到鄰居同學欺負的阿甘說出不少的名言，在往後的生活面臨各種困難時，阿甘總是會用母親對他説的話，安慰自己或他人。

句型文法概念解析

句型一中的動詞為不及物動詞，後面不需要有接受動作者（O 受詞），或者補充説明（C 補語）；也就是説，動詞本身的意念就很清楚，可以表達出完整的意思。

1. 觀念說明

a. 不及物動詞（Vi）：動作可以獨立發生，不牽涉到別的人或物，這種動詞就叫做「不及物」動詞。

Ex. Fishes *swim*.　魚兒游。

b. 沒有受詞或補語：動詞的後面不需要有動作接收者（O 受詞），也不需要補充説明（C 補語）。

Ex. It rained.　下雨了。

c. 可以有修飾語：主詞或是動詞都可以有修飾語。

Ex. *Most* students laughed *loudly*.　大部分的學生大聲地笑。

（most 修飾 students；loudly 修飾 laughed）

2. 延伸文法結構

a. S 主詞＋ Vi 動詞＋ Adv. 副詞

後面可以接副詞，副詞片語，或是副詞子句，用來修飾動詞。

Ex. I run fast.（fast 修飾 run）我跑步很快。

Ex. Nothing happened last night.（last night 時間副詞）昨晚沒事發生。

Ex. Baby laughed when she saw me.（when…副詞子句）寶寶一見我就笑了。

b. S 主詞＋Vi 動詞＋prep. 介系詞＋O 受詞

不及物動詞後面如有需要加上受詞（O）時，前面需加上介系詞。

Ex. Don't laugh at me. 要嘲笑我。

c. S 主詞＋Vi 動詞＋不定詞 or 不定詞片語

光是一個不及物動詞，有時可能無法表達完整意思，這時再後面加上不定詞片語，可以更完整傳達語意。

Ex. Will you come to see me? 你會來看我嗎？

3. 使用特點

a. 同樣一個動詞，可以作及物動詞（Vt）用，也可作不及物動詞用（Vi），但在句型一中的動詞，永遠只作不及物動詞（Vi）使用。

b. 常用於句型一的動詞有 arrive／bloom／come／cry／go／happen／rain／rise／run／sing／sit／sleep／smile…等。

 絕妙好例句

1. Nothing happened!（S＋Vi）無事發生！

2. Who knows?（S＋Vi）誰知道呢？

3. She sings loudly.（S＋Vi＋adv.）她大聲唱歌。

4. The handsome man smiled at me.（S＋Vi＋prep.＋O）

   那帥哥對我微笑

5. He ran to catch the bus.（S＋Vi＋不定詞片語）他跑去趕公車。

 換你寫寫看

1. Jane slept _____ last night.（badly／slept／Jane）

2. Time _____ .（to fly／flies）

3. The shop _____ March 17.（on／open）

4. Alex _____ desk.（A)is sitting (B)sat on (C)sits

5. Tom stopped to listen to her talking.（A)S＋Vi (B)S＋Vi＋to S＋Vi＋adv. (C)S＋Vi＋adv.

6. The sun _____ in the east and _____ in the west.（rise／set）

7. I believe.（A)S＋Vi (B)S＋Vi＋adv. (C)S＋Vi＋prep.＋O

8. She _____ a cup of tea.（A)is asking (B)asked (C)asked for

● 答案與中譯解析

1. 答：(B)（adly，S＋Vi＋adv.）昨晚 Jane 睡得不好。

2. 答：flies（S＋Vi）時間飛逝。

3. 答：opened、on（S＋Vi＋adv.）商店於三月十七日開幕。

4. 答：(B)（S＋Vi＋prep.＋O）Alex 坐在桌上。

5. 答：(B)（stopped 後面跟著表示原因的不定詞 to listen，S＋Vi＋to 不定詞片語）Tom 停下來聽她說話。

6. 答：rises、set（S＋Vi＋adv.）太陽東升西落。

7. 答：(A)（S＋Vi）我相信。

8. 答：(C)（S＋Vi＋prep.＋O）她要了一杯茶。

02 句型二：S＋Vi＋SC（主詞＋不及物動詞＋主詞補語）

Time is money. 時間就是金錢。

　　最早出自於美國著名政治家，科學家班傑明•法蘭克林（Benjamin Franklin，1706-1790），之後仍被廣泛引用在不同領域。近來，更有一部電影《IN TIME 鐘點戰》，便是因 Time is money 時間就是金錢這個概念而衍生而出的故事，影片中金錢被時間取代，人們賺得，花得，皆是以時間為計價單位，富有的人意味著有無窮的時間。

句型二：S 主詞＋Vi 不及物動詞＋SC 主詞補語文法概念解析

句型二中的動詞為不及物動詞，後面不需要有接受動作者（O 受詞），但是要加上對主詞的補充說明（即 SC 主詞補語）；也就是說，動詞本身不能表達完整的意義，需要主詞補語。

1. 觀念說明

　　a. 不及物動詞（Vi）：句型二的動詞為 Be 動詞或連綴動詞（Linking Verbs），是一種沒有動作的不及物動詞，主要是用來連接主詞與主詞補語，動作本身沒有辦法表達語意。

　　He *is*…他是…

　　He *looks*…他看起來…

　　b. 主詞補語（SC）：因為動詞本身沒有辦法完整表達語意，這時需要加些東西來補充說明、或描述主詞的情況，即稱為主詞補語（SC）。補語可以是名詞、形容詞、動名詞、名詞子句、代名詞、或是不定詞等。

　　Ex. He is *a teacher*.（名詞當 SC）他是老師。

　　Ex. He looks *happy*.（形容詞當 SC）他看起來很高興。

2. 使用特點

　　a. 常用的連綴動詞：

　　表示「感覺」的動詞：

　　smell／feel／taste／sound…等。

　　表示「似乎、變得、看起來」的動詞：

become ／ look ／ seem ／ appear ／ remain ／ stay ／ turn ／ fall⋯
等。

Ex. Coffee tastes bitter.. 咖啡嘗起來有苦味。

b. 區分（S ＋ Vi ＋⋯）與（S ＋ Vi ＋ SC）句型：

Ex. She appeared suddenly.（S ＋ Vi ＋⋯）她突然出現。

Ex. She appeared tired.（S ＋ Vi ＋ SC）她似乎累了。

Ex. He came to see me.（S ＋ Vi ＋⋯）他來看我。

Ex. Dream came true.（S ＋ Vi ＋ SC）夢想成真。

 絕妙好例句

1. I am Lisa.（Lisa ＝ SC，名詞 N.）我叫 Lisa。
2. Ryan looks shy.（shy ＝ SC，形容詞 Adj.）Ryan 看起來很害羞。
3. My favorite exercise is jogging.（jogging ＝ SC，動名詞 V-ing）
   我喜歡的運動慢跑。
4. An iPad was what she wanted for her birthday.
   （what⋯＝ SC 名詞子句）一台 iPad 正是她生日想要的。
5. To see is to believe.（to believe ＝ SC，不定詞）眼見為憑。

換你寫寫看

1. I ___ crazy.（am ／ crazy ／ I）
2. The pen _____ _____ .（mine ／ is ／ the pen）
3. The soup _____ _____ .（Taste ／ delicious ／ the soup）
4. He seems _____ .（A)the answer （B)to know the answer
5. The lovers _____ .（A)kiss （B)are kissing （C)to kiss

6. The toilet _____ . (A)is bad (B)is out of order (C)is out

7. The weather becomes warm. (A)S＋Vi＋adv. (B)S＋Vi＋SC (C)S＋Vi

8. Nancy is a housewife. (A)S＋Vi (B)S＋Vi＋adv. (C)S＋Vi＋SC

● 答案與中譯解析

1. 答：am（形容詞 crazy 修飾主詞）我瘋了。

2. 答：is mine（代名詞 mine 修飾主詞 The pen）這筆是我的。

3. 答：tastes、delicious（形容詞 delicious 說明主詞 The soup）
   這湯嚐起來很美味。

4. 答：(B)（不定詞 to know the answer 修飾主詞 He）他似乎知道答案。

5. 答：(B)（動名詞 kissing 修飾主詞 The lovers）情人正在接吻。

6. 答：(B)（片語 out of order 通常用於連綴動詞 be 之後做主詞補語）馬桶故障。

7. 答：(B)（形容詞 warm 補充說明主詞 The weather 的情況）天氣變暖。

8. 答：(C)（名詞 a housewife 補充說明主詞 Nancy）Nancy 是位家庭主婦。

---

03 句型三：S＋Vt＋O（主詞＋及物動詞＋受詞）

You complete me.　你使我完整。

　　這是在電影《征服情海》一段影史經典對白，Tom Curise 對 Renee 告白
"You complete me."，我的世界因你而完整；而這樣一句情人間深情對話
套用在電影《蝙蝠俠：黑暗騎士》的情節裡，當瘋狂的 Joker 對蝙蝠俠說出
"You complete me" 時，就又顯得荒唐又可怕。

句型三：S 主詞＋Vt 及物動詞＋O 受詞 文法概念解析
句型三中的動詞為及物動詞，要有接受動作者（O 受詞），不需要補語
（C）；也就是說，動詞本身需要一個受詞，才能表達完整的意義。

1. 觀念說明

a. 及物動詞（Vt）：句型三的動詞為及物動詞，後面通常必需跟著一個受詞來接受這個動作。

Ex. I *miss* you.　我想你。

b. 受詞（O）：受詞是指人、事、物用以承受動詞之動作者。跟主詞一樣，受詞都是由名詞類扮演，像是名詞、代名詞、名詞片語、動名詞、不定詞或名詞子句等，人、事、物來接收。

Ex. I know *you*.（O 是代名詞）我認識你。

Ex. Someone opened *the door*.（O 是名詞）有人開了門。

2. 使用特點

a. 常見的及物動詞：answer ∕ ask ∕ bring ∕ buy ∕ carry ∕ cook ∕ do ∕ eat ∕ enjoy ∕ hate ∕ hear ∕ know ∕ love ∕ make ∕ sell ∕ speak ∕ wash…等。

Ex. She *asked* a question.　她問了一個問題。

b. 大多數的動詞，可作及物動詞用，又可作不及物動詞用，但在這個句型中的動詞，永遠只作及物動詞使用。

Ex. We ate at home.（S ＋ Vi ＋ adv.）我們在家吃飯。

Ex. I ate lunch.（S ＋ Vt ＋ O）我吃了午飯。

 絕妙好例句

1. I love you.（you 代名詞；當受詞 O）我愛你。
2. Jack stopped drinking.（drinking 動名詞；當受詞 O）Jack 戒酒了。
3. We want to buy a house.（to…不定詞；當受詞 O）
　 我們想買一間房子。

4. You don't know what I think.（what…名詞子句；當受詞O）

你並不知道我怎麼想的。

5. I know how to swim.（how …名詞片語；當受詞O）

我知道如何游泳。

換你寫寫看

1. I _____ _____ .（beat／him／I）

2. _____ likes _____ the piano.（the piano／playing／likes／my friend）

3. I _____ _____ you this bad news.（to tell／hate）

4. _____ see _____ you mean.（what／I）

5. Everyone wants _____ .（A)go (B)to go (C)going

6. Father is fixing the car. (A)S＋Vt＋O (B)S＋Vi＋SC (C)S＋Vi

7. I wrote a letter. (A)S＋Vt＋O (B)S＋Vi＋SC (C)S＋Vi

8. Somebody wants _____ you. (A)see (B)saw (C)to see

● 答案與中譯解析

1. 答：(B) eat、him（O＝代名詞＝him）我打他。

2. 答：My friend、playing（O＝動名詞＝playing …）我朋友喜歡彈鋼琴。

3. 答：hate、to tell（O＝不定詞＝to tell…）我討厭告訴你這壞消息。

4. 答：I、what（O＝名詞子句＝what…）我瞭解你的意思。

5. 答：(B)（O＝不定詞＝to go）每個人都想去。

6. 答：(A)（O＝名詞＝the car）父親正在修車。

7. 答：(A)（O＝名詞＝the letter）我寫了封信。

8. 答：(C)（O＝不定詞＝to see…）有人想見你。

04 句型四：S＋Vt＋O＋OC（主詞＋及物動詞＋受詞＋受詞補語）

My name's Forrest Gump, People call me Forrest Gump.
我的名字是阿甘，人們叫我阿甘。

　　在《Forrest Gump 阿甘正傳》電影裡，每當阿甘認識新的朋友時，都會用這句話做自我介紹，這句話幾乎貫穿整部電影。

句型四：S 主詞＋Vt 及物動詞＋O 受詞＋OC 受詞補語文法概念解析

句型四中的動詞為及物動詞，除了要有接受動作者（O 受詞），還要加上對受詞的補充說明（即 OC 受詞補語）；也就是說，動詞本身除了一個受詞之外，還需要一個受詞補語，說明有關受詞（O）的情況，這樣句子意思才能完整。

1. 觀念說明

a. 及物動詞（Vt）：句型四的動詞為及物動詞，如果只跟著一個受詞來接受動作，整個句子意思感覺不會完整。
　　He makes you…（S＋Vt＋O）他使我………

b. 受詞補語（OC）：因為動詞本身沒有辦法完整表達語意，這時需要加些東西來補充說明、或描述有關受詞的情況，即稱為受詞補語（OC）。受詞補語可以是形容詞、名詞、不定詞片語（當名詞）、現在分詞（當形容詞）、過去分詞（當形容詞）。
　　Ex. He makes me happy.（S＋Vt＋O＋OC）他使我快樂。

2. 使用特點

● 常見的及物動詞：believe／call／consider／feel／find／keep／leave／name／prove／think／watch…等。
　　Ex. Father gave him a book.　父親給了他一本書。

絕妙好例句

1. We called him "007." ("007" ＝ OC，名詞，補充說明 him)
   我們叫他 007。

2. This move made me cry. (cry ＝ OC，名詞，補充說明 me)
   這部電影使我哭了。

   I found the box empty. (empty ＝ OC，形容詞，補充說明 the box)
   我發現這盒子是空的。

3. She kept her boyfriend waiting for hours. (waiting ＝ OC，現在分
   詞，補充說明 her boyfriend)她讓她男友等了幾個小時。

4. I must get this job done. (done ＝ OC，過去分詞，補充說明 this
   job)我必須要把這件事做完。

5. The teacher wants us to read this book. (to read… ＝ OC，不定詞
   片語，補充說明 us)老師要我們去讀這本書。

換你寫寫看

1. She asked ＿＿＿＿＿＿ ＿＿＿＿＿＿ . (his name／him／asked／she)

2. ＿＿＿＿＿＿ kept ＿＿＿＿＿＿ ＿＿＿＿＿＿ . (quiet／she／the child／kept)

3. I found this news ＿＿＿＿＿＿ . (interesting／this news／found／I)

4. I prefer ＿＿＿＿＿＿ ＿＿＿＿＿＿ . (I／the steak／well done)

5. Mother warned us ＿＿＿＿＿＿ . (A)late (B)not to be late (C)be late

6. He made me ＿＿＿＿＿＿ . (A)changed (B)changing (C)to change

7. Can you give me some advice?
   (A)S＋Vt＋O＋OC (B)S＋Vi＋SC (C)S＋Vt＋O

8. Boss wants you ＿＿＿＿＿＿ this document.
   (A)leave (B)leaving (C)to leave

● 答案與中譯解析

1. 答：him、his name（OC ＝名詞＝ his name）她問他的名字。
2. 答：She、the child、quiet（OC ＝形容詞＝ quiet）她讓小孩保持安靜。
3. 答：interesting（OC ＝形容詞＝ interesting）我發現這新聞有趣。
4. 答：the steak、well done（OC ＝過去分詞＝ done）我想要牛排全熟。
5. 答：(B)（OC ＝不定詞＝ not to…）母親警告我們別遲到了。
6. 答：(A)（OC ＝過去分詞當形容詞用＝ changed）他使我改變了。
7. 答：(A)（S＋Vt＋O＋OC，OC ＝名詞＝ some advice）
   你可以給我些建議嗎？
8. 答：(C)（O ＝不定詞＝ to leave…）老闆要你留下文件。

---

05 句型五：S ＋ Vt ＋ IO ＋ DO（主詞＋及物動詞＋間接受詞＋直接受詞）
（**You**）**show me the money**　你要讓我賺大錢。

　　《征服情海》情節中，當球員經紀人 Jerry 試圖說服一位脾氣很壞的二線球員 Rod 跟著他時，Rod 要求 Jerry 為他做一件事，就是跟著一起在電話中大喊 "Show me the money"。而後，這句話多被財經相關節目或文章所引用。

句型五：S 主詞＋ Vt 及物動詞＋ IO 直接受詞＋ DO 間接受詞文法概念解析
句型五中的動詞為及物動詞又稱為授與動詞，後面需要接兩個受詞（O），傳達「給某人某物」的句型；也就是說，動詞本身需要二個受詞，才能表達完整的意義。

1. 觀念說明

a. 及物動詞（Vt）：句型五的動詞為及物動詞又稱為授與動詞，後面通常必需跟著二個受詞：間接受詞（IO）與直接受詞（DO）。

b. 間接受詞（IO）：通常指人或動物，表示授與的對象；放在直接受詞（DO）前。

c. 直接受詞（DO）：通常指事或物，表是授與的東西；放在間接收詞（IO）後。直接受詞可以是名詞、不定 詞、名詞片語或名詞子句。

Ex. I gave you a book.（IO＝you，DO＝a book）我給你一本書。

2. 使用特點

a. 常見的授與動詞：bring ╱ give ╱ lend ╱ offer ╱ pay ╱ send ╱ show ╱ teach ╱ tell ╱ write⋯等。

Ex. She offered me a job. 她提供我一個工作。

b. 間接受詞（IO）和直接受詞（DO）的排列位置可以互換，但是中間必須要有介系詞，如 to、for 或 of 等介於兩者之間。

Ex. Chris sent me a letter.（S＋Vt＋IO＋DO）
Chris 寄給我一封信。

Ex. Chris sent a letter to me.（S＋Vt＋DO＋Prep.＋IO）
Chris 寄了一封信給我。

 絕妙好例句

1. Mother bought me a gift.（me＝IO；a gift＝DO，名詞）
母親給我買了禮物。

2. He showed her to her seat.（her＝IO；to her seat＝DO，不定詞）他把她帶到座位上。

3. Will you buy me a drink?（me＝IO；a drink＝DO，名詞）

你要不要請我喝杯酒？

4. I wish you luck.（you ＝ IO；luck ＝ DO 名詞）祝你好運。

5. John bought a coffee to me.（S ＋ Vt ＋ DO ＋ to ＋ IO，a coffee ＝ DO，名詞；me ＝ IO）約翰買了一杯咖啡給我。

✏️ 換你寫寫看

1. He passed me the ball. IO＝＿＿＿ ；DO＝＿＿＿＿

2. He passed the ball to me. IO＝＿＿＿＿ ；DO ＿＿＿＿

3. She showed us how to make a cake. IO＝＿＿＿＿ ；DO＝＿＿＿＿

4. He bought an iPad for his girlfriend. IO＝＿＿＿＿ ；DO＝＿＿＿＿

5. I told you not to do that. DO＝ (A)不定詞 (B)名詞 (C)名詞片語

6. He sent me a card. DO＝ (A)he (B)a card (C)me

7. John promised me that he would go. DO＝ (A)that…go (B)me (C)John

8. She asked a question of me. IO＝ (A)a question (B)she (C)me

● 答案與中譯解析

1. 答：IO ＝ me，DO ＝ the ball（S＋Vt＋IO＋DO）他傳給我球。

2. 答：IO ＝ me，DO ＝ the ball（S＋Vt＋DO＋prep.（to）＋IO）他傳球給我。

3. 答：IO ＝ us，DO ＝ how to make a cake（名詞片語）
   她教我們如何製作蛋糕。

4. 答：IO ＝ his girlfriend，DO ＝ an iPad（S＋Vt＋DO＋prep.（for）＋IO）
   他給她女友買了台 iPad。

5. 答：(A)，IO ＝ you，DO ＝ not to do that（不定詞）我告訴過你不要做此事。

6. 答：(B)，IO ＝ me，DO ＝ a card（名詞）他寄給我一張卡片。

7. 答：(A)，IO ＝ me，DO ＝ that…go（名詞子句）John 答應我他會去。

8. 答：(C)，IO ＝ me，DO ＝ a question（S＋Vt＋DO＋prep.（of）＋IO）
   她問我一個問題。

第2單元：時態

英文達人文法小筆記！

英文對時間的表示有三種，分別為過去（Past），現在（Present），未來（Future）。對狀態的表示有四種，分別為簡單式（Simple）、進行式（Progressive）、完成式（Perfect）以及完成進行式（Perfect Progressive）。透過狀態與時間的交叉組合，可形成英文的 12 種時態。

	過去（Past）	現在（Present）	未來（Future）
簡單式（Simple）	過去簡單式 Simple Past	現在簡單式 Simple Present	未來簡單式 Simple Future
進行式（Progressive）	過去進行式 Past Progressive	現在進行式 Present Progressive	未來進行式 Future Progressive
完成式（Perfect）	過去完成式 Past Perfect	現在完成式 Present Perfect	未來完成式 Future Perfect
完成進行式（Perfect Progressive）	過去完成進行式 Past Perfect Progressive	現在完成進行式 Present Perfect Progressive	未來完成進行式 Future Perfect Progressive

`01` 現在簡單式 Simple Present

名言範例：

You are beautiful. It's true! 你很美麗，是真的！

　　摘自於英國創作型歌手 James Blunt 的代表作品 You're Beautiful，收錄於專輯 Back to Bedlem。這首歌於 2005 年一推出，便攀升之英國流行歌曲排行榜的冠軍，並且停留 6 周；2006 年在美國 "Billboard Hot 100" 單曲排行榜上，排行榜首；隨後更橫掃全世界的流行排行榜。

1. 使用時機

a. 反覆性的動作或習慣：說明動作重覆或是習慣。

　　Ex. I drink a cup of coffee every morning.　我每天早上喝咖啡。

b. 一般性真理：說明普遍相信的真理事實。

　　Ex. The sun rises in the East.　旭日東昇。

c. 事實或狀態：陳述事實或表達現在的狀況。

　　Ex. She is a teacher.　她是老師。

2. 文法結構

主詞 S ＋助動詞（do ／ does）＋動詞 V（-s ／ -es）＋…
主詞 S ＋ Be 動詞（am ／ are ／ is）＋…

a. 肯定句

　　主詞 S ＋動詞 V ＋…

　　Ex. You drink coffee.　你喝咖啡。

　　主詞 S ＋ Be 動詞＋…

　　Ex. She is a teacher.　她是老師。

b. 否定句

　　主詞 S ＋助動詞＋ not ＋動詞 V ＋…

　　Ex. You do not（don't）drink coffee.　你不喝咖啡。

1
2
3
4
5
6
7
8
9
10

主詞 S ＋ Be 動詞＋ not ＋…

Ex. She is not（isn't）a teacher.　她不是老師。

c. 疑問句

助動詞＋主詞 S ＋動詞 V ＋…

Ex. Do you drink coffee?　你喝咖啡嗎？

Be 動詞＋主詞 S ＋…

Ex. Is she a teacher?　她是老師嗎？

3. 使用特點

a. 肯定句的動詞前不加助動詞。

b. 主詞 S 為第三人稱（he ／ she ／ it），動詞 V 字尾要加上 s ／ es；助動詞要用 does。

c. 否定句與疑問句的動詞不做變化，只有助動詞隨主詞變化。

d. 常使用於現在簡單式的時間副詞：every day ／ often ／ always ／ sometimes ／ never。

e. is not ＝ isn't；are not ＝ aren't；do not ＝ don't

 絕妙好例句

1. John walks to school every day.（V ＝ walks，現在式表重覆動作）
   John 每天走路去上學。

2. The Moon goes around the Earth.（V ＝ goes，現在式表真理）
   月亮繞著地球。

3. She is not here now.（is ＋ not，現在式表事實或狀態）
   她現在不在這裡。

4. The party starts at 7 o'clock.（V = starts，現在式表事實或狀態）
   舞會 7 點開始。

5. Do you collect stamp?（V = collect，現在式表習慣）你集郵嗎？

換你寫寫看

1. I _____（to live）in Taiwan now.

2. She _____（to think）she is right.

3. He _____（to love）his daughter.

4. The train _____（to leave）every morning at 8 o'clock.

5. Do you _____（to have）your passport with you?

6. Pet always _____（to forget）his wallet.

7. He _____（do，to like）dog.

8. Water _____（to boil）at 100 degrees Celsius.

● 答案與中譯解析

1. 答：V = live（表事實或狀態）我現在住在台灣。

2. 答：V = thinks（表事實或狀態；think 表示看法時，只能用現在簡單式）
   她認為她是對的。

3. 答：V = loves（表事實或狀態）他愛她女兒。

4. 答：V = leaves（表反覆性動作或習慣）火車每天早上八點離開。

5. 答：V = have（表事實或狀態）你有帶護照嗎？

6. 答：V = forgets（表反覆性動作或習慣）Pet 總是忘記他的皮夾。

7. 答：V = doesn't like（表事實或狀態）他不喜歡狗。

8. 答：V = boils（表真理）水在攝氏一百度下沸騰。

02 現在進行式 Present Progressive

名言範例：

No one is going to hurt you. 沒有人能傷害你。

摘自美劇影集 The Vampire Diaries《吸血鬼日記》，改編自作者 L.J. Smith 同名小說，2009 年於 CW 電台首播。很常出現的一句話，不論是 Damon 對著獵物進行催眠時，蠱惑的話語；還是 Stefan 安撫受驚嚇的 Elena 時，安慰的話語；很常用的一句話。

1. 使用時機

a. 動作正在進行或發生：強調「現在／當下」正在進行的動作，且這個動作有可能會繼續發展下去。

Ex. We are watching TV now.　我們正在看電視。

b. 計畫性的未來動作：現在進行式也可以用來表示已經計畫，並且即將發生的未來動作。後面通常會加上表示未來的時間副詞，如：tonight ／ tomorrow ／ next Friday ／ at noon…等。

Ex. I am going to the theatre tonight.　我晚上要去電影院。

2. 文法結構
主詞 S ＋助動詞（am ／ are ／ is）＋現在分詞（V-ing）＋…

a. 肯定句

主詞 S ＋（am ／ are ／ is）＋現在分詞（V-ing）＋…

Ex. They are eating dinner.　他們正在吃晚餐。

b. 否定句

主詞 S ＋（am ／ are ／ is）＋ not ＋現在分詞（V-ing）＋…

Ex. They are not（aren't）eating dinner. 他們沒再吃晚餐。

c. 疑問句

（Am ／ Are ／ Is）＋主詞 S ＋現在分詞（V-ing）＋…

Ex. Are they eating dinner? 他們正在吃晚餐嗎？

3. 使用特點

a. 用 Be 動詞（am ／ are ／ is）為助動詞

b. 動詞使用使用現在分詞，也就是在原形動詞字尾加上「-ing」

c. 常使用於現在進行式的時間副詞：now，right now，just now，at this moment…

 絕妙好例句

1. He is playing football now.（V ＝ play，進行式表動作正在進行／發生）他現在正在踢足球。

2. I am preparing for my exam.（V ＝ prepare，進行式表動作正在進行／發生）我正在準備考試。

3. She is going to Hong Kong next Friday.（V ＝ go，進行式表計畫性的未來動作）她下周五即將去香港。

4. Are you coming with us to that store?（V ＝ come，進行式表計畫性的未來動作）你要跟我們去那家店嗎？

5. Jane is not talking on the phone now.（V ＝ talk，進行式表動作正在進行／發生）Jane 現在沒有在講電話。

1

2

3

4

5

6

7

8

9

10

換你寫寫看

1. I _____ for London tomorrow morning.（to leave）

2. They _____ checking the printer.（to check）

3. She _____ to the park.（not／to walk）

4. _____ they _____ to help?（to try）

5. Look! They _____ !（to come）

6. My sister is _____ _____ with us.（not／to live）

7. _____ you _____ to party with us tonight?（to go）

8. This project is not ready. I _____ on it.（to work）

● 答案與中譯解析

1. 答：am leaving（表示計畫性的未來動作）我明早動身去英國。
2. 答：are checking（表示動作正在進行／發生）他們正在檢查印表機。
3. 答：is not walking（表示動作正在進行／發生）她沒有走去公園。
4. 答：are、trying（表示動作正在進行／發生）他們是想幫忙嗎？
5. 答：are coming（表示動作正在進行／發生）看！他們來了！
6. 答：is not living（表示動作正在進行／發生）我姊姊不和我們住在一起。
7. 答：are、going（表示計畫性的未來動作）你今晚要跟我們去舞會嗎？
8. 答：am working（表示動作正在進行／發生）這個案子還沒好，我正在處理。

---

03 現在完成式 Present Perfect

名言範例：

You have been the one for me. 你是我今生的唯一。

摘自於英國歌手 James Blunt，於 2004 年發行的首張專輯 Back to Bedlem 的其中一首 "Goodbye My Lover" 歌詞內容；這首歌一推出，隨即攀升至英國單曲排行榜第三名的位置。透過 James Blunt 獨特的嗓音，道出離別的悲傷，因為有關分手，所以歌詞內容運用了很多的現在完成式時態。

現在完成式 Present Perfect 文法解析

現在完成式（**Present Perfect**），強調的是過去與現在的關係，主要在表達動作在過去不確定的時間發生，持續一段時間直到現在的狀態，動作已完成／未完成、經驗與持續性的動作。

1. 使用時機

a. 動作已完成：強調某個動作／事件，已經完成、剛剛完成或者未完成的狀態。

Ex Pet has done this project.　Pet 已經完成這個案子。

b. 過去經驗：說明過去曾經歷的經驗。

Ex Pet has done this project before.　Pet 曾經做過這個案子。

c. 持續性的動作／事件：說明動作／事件從過去發生一直到現在，並且有可能還會繼續下去。

Ex Pet has done this project for one month.
Pet 做這個案子已經有一個月了。

2. 文法結構

主詞 S ＋助動詞（have ／ has）＋過去分詞（p.p.）＋…

a. 肯定句

主詞 S ＋助動詞（have ／ has）＋過去分詞（p.p.）＋…

Ex. She has fixed the problem. 她已經解決問題。

b. 否定句

主詞 S ＋助動詞（have ／ has）＋ not ＋過去分詞（p.p.）＋…

Ex. She has not（hasn't）fixed the problem. 她還沒解決問題。

c. 疑問句

助動詞（Have ／ Has）＋主詞 S ＋過去分詞（p.p.）＋…

Ex. Has she fixed the problem? 已經解決問題了嗎？

3. 使用特點

a. 不管肯定句、否定句或是疑問句，加上助動詞（have ／ has），依主詞選擇適合的助動詞，第三人稱助動詞選用 has，其餘用 have。

b. 動詞使用過去分詞；規則動詞字尾加上 "-ed"，不規則性動詞變化，則另參照列表。

c. 常使用於現在完成式的時間副詞：

just ／ yet ／ never ／ already ／ since ＋（過去某一時間到現在 or 過去式子句）／ for ＋（一段時間）。

d. have not ＝ haven't；has not ＝ hasn't

4. 區分（have ／ has）＋ been to 與（have ／ has）＋ gone to 用法

a. been to 表示某人曾經去過某地方且已經回來，人現在就在這裡。

Ex. He has been to London before. 他曾去過倫敦。

b. gone to 表示某人已經去某地方但是還沒回來，人現在不在這裡。

Ex. He has gone to London. 他已經去倫敦了。

絕妙好例句

1. He has played football for 2 hours.（V ＝ play，完成式表示持續性的動作／事件）他已經踢了 2 個小時的足球了。

2. I have prepared for my exam since last week.（V ＝ prepare，完成式表示持續性的動作／事件）從上週開始，我已經在準備考試了。

3. She has never been to Hong Kong.（been to，完成式表示過去經驗）她從未去過香港。

4. They have not come to the party.（V ＝ come，完成式表示動作已完成／未完成）他們還沒來到這個舞會

5. My mother has lived here for 20 years.（V ＝ live，完成式表示持續性的動作／事件）我的母親在這裡已經住了 20 年。

換你寫寫看

1. I _____ my brother for a long time.（not／to see）

2. She _____ her answers for 5 times.（to check）

3. _____ she _____ to the park?（to walk）

4. _____ you ever _____ that girl?（to see）

5. My sister _____ with us for 2 years.（to live）

6. How long _____ you____ there?（to stay）

7. John _____ his book.（to find）

8. I _____ on this project since last night.（to work）

● 答案與中譯解析

1. 答：have not seen（表示持續性的動作／事件）我已經很久沒有見到我哥了。

2. 答：has checked（表示動作已完成／未完成）她已經檢查她的答案 5 次了。

3. 答：Has、walked（表示動作已完成／未完成）她已經走到公園了嗎？
4. 答：Have、seen（表示過去經驗）你曾經見過那個女孩嗎？
5. 答：has lived（表示持續性的動作／事件）我姊姊和我們住在一起已經兩年了。
6. 答：have、stayed（表示過去經驗）你在那裡待了多久？
7. 答：has found（表示動作已完成／未完成）John 已經找到他的書了。
8. 答：have worked（表示持續性的動作／事件）我從昨晚開始一直處理這個案子。

04 現在完成進行式 Present Perfect Progressive

名言範例：

I have been waiting for you. 我一直都在等你。

摘自美國音樂創作歌手 Ben Harper 於 2006 年發行的專輯 Both Side of The Gun，歌曲名稱為 Waiting for you，整首歌詞大多是運用現在完成進行式的時態；這是一首甜蜜浪漫的情歌，特別適合在戀愛剛開始的階段。

現在完成進行式 Present Perfect Progressive 文法解析

現在完成進行式 **Present Perfect Progressive**，主要在表達動作在過去不確定的時間發生，一直到現在，動作還在持續進行，或者是剛剛結束；強調的是動作的持續性。

1. 使用時機

- 動作的持續性：說明動作在過去已經發生，說話的當下，動作還在持續進行中，或剛剛結束。

Ex. We have been standing here for 1 hour.

我們站在這裡已經一個小時了。

2. 文法結構

主詞 S ＋助動詞（have ／ has）＋助動詞 been ＋現在分詞（V-ing）＋…

a. 肯定句

主詞 S ＋助動詞（have ／ has）＋助動詞 been ＋現在分詞（V-ing）＋…

Ex. I have been sitting on a sofa for a while.

我已經坐在沙發上有段時間了。

b. 否定句

主詞 S ＋助動詞（have ／ has）＋ not ＋助動詞 been ＋現在分詞（V-ing）＋…

Ex. She has not been fixing the problem since last night.

自從昨晚，她都還沒解決問題。

c. 疑問句

助動詞（Have ／ Has）＋主詞 S ＋助動詞 been ＋現在分詞（V-ing）＋…

Ex. Has she been fixing the problem?　她已經在解決問題了嗎？

3. 使用特點

a. 有兩個助動詞（have ／ has）以及 been，只有助動詞（have ／ has）跟著主詞變化。

b. 用 "how long" 表示動作持續多長時間。

c. 常使用於現在完成式的時間副詞：

since ＋（過去某一時間到現在or 過去示子句）／ for ＋（一段時間）／ lately ／ recently。

4. 現在完成式 VS. 現在完成進行式

現在完成式與現在完成進行式兩者主要都在表示動作發生在過去，一直持續到現在，但是強調的重點不同。

a. 現在完成式，大多時候主要在表示動作已經完成，強調結果。

Ex. Pet has done this project.　Pet 已經完成這個計畫。

b. 現在完成進行式，大多時候主要在表示動作還在進行，強調動作的持續性。

Ex. Pet has been doing this project.　Pet 還在做這個計畫。

 絕妙好例句

1. He has been playing football for 2 hours.（V ＝ play，完成進行式表動作的持續性）。他已經連續踢了 2 個小時的足球。

2. I have been preparing for my exam since last week.
（V ＝ prepare，完成進行式表動作的持續性）。
從上週開始，我都在準備考試。

3. She has not felt well lately.（V ＝ feel，完成進行式表動作的持續性）。她最近一直覺得不舒服。

4. I have been watching you.（V ＝ watch，完成進行式表動作的持續性）。我一直在注意著你。

5. Mother has been living here for 20 years.（V ＝ live，完成進行式表動作的持續性）。母親一直在這裡住了 20 年。

換你寫寫看

1. I _____ my brother for a long time.（not／to see）

2. She _____ so hard.（to work）

3. We _____ since last month.（to date）

4. You _____ to the teacher for last 5 minutes?（not／to listen）

5. How long _____ you _____ here?（to stay）

6. Sandy _____ this book lately.（to read）

7. John _____ for his book for two days.（to look）

8. I _____ on this project since last night.（to work）

● 答案與中譯解析

1. 答：have not been seeing（表示動作的持續性）我已經很久沒有見到我哥了。

2. 答：has been working（表示動作的持續性）她一直努力工作。

3. 答：have been dating（表示動作的持續性）從上個月開始我們一直在約會。

4. 答：have not been listening（表示動作的持續性）
   從過去五分鐘到現在，你一直都沒有在聽課。

5. 答：have、been staying（表示動作的持續性）你在這裡待多久了。

6. 答：has been reading（表示動作的持續性）Sandy 最近一直在看這本書。

7. 答：has been looking（表示動作的持續性）John 已經找他的書找 2 天了。

8. 答：have been working（表示動作的持續性）
   我從昨晚開始一直都在處理這個案子。

05 過去簡單式 Simple Past

名言範例：

You found me. 你發現了我。

　　摘自美國鄉村音樂創作歌手 Tayler Swift 於 2012 年底發行的單曲
"I Knew you were a trouble"，收錄於專輯 Red，推出首週即排上美國
Billboard Hot 100 第三名，隨後更攀上冠軍行列。"I knew you were trouble
when you walked in."（當你走進來時，我就知道你會是個麻煩。），內容
主要有關失戀，大多用過去簡單式的時態敘事；You found me 很實用的句
子，可以應用到很多場合。

過去簡單式 Simple Past 文法解析

過去簡單式 Simple Past，主要在表達過去發生的動作、事實、習慣，並且
在過去的時間已經結束。簡單來說，就是強調「過去」跟「現在」沒有關係。

1. 使用時機

　　a. 過去的動作／狀態：表示動作發生在過去並且已經結束。

　　　Ex. He watched a football game yesterday. 昨天看了場足球賽。

　　b. 過去的習慣：表示過去的習慣，現在沒有這個習慣。

　　　Ex. I studied French when I was a child. 我小時候曾學過法文。

　　c. 過去的事實：表示過去發生的事實，現在已經停止。

　　　Ex. He liked onion before. 他以前喜歡洋蔥。

2. 文法結構

主詞 S ＋助動詞（did）＋動詞 V-ed（規則或不規則動詞）＋…

主詞 S ＋ Be 動詞（was ／ were）＋…

a. 肯定句

主詞 S ＋動詞 V-ed（規則或不規則動詞）＋…

Ex. She worked hard.　她過去努力工作。

主詞 S ＋ Be 動詞（was ／ were）＋…

Ex. She was a teacher.　她曾是老師。

b. 否定句

主詞 S ＋助動詞（did）＋ not ＋動詞 V ＋…

Ex. You didn't drink coffee.　你過去不喝咖啡。

主詞 S ＋ e 動詞（was ／ were）＋ not ＋…

Ex. She was not a teacher.　她以前不是老師。

c. 疑問句

助動詞（Did）＋主詞 S ＋動詞 V ＋…

Ex. Did you drink coffee?　你以前喝咖啡嗎？

Be 動詞（were ／ was）＋主詞 S ＋…

Ex. Was she a teacher?　她以前是老師嗎？

3. 使用特點

a. 肯定句的動詞前不加助動詞，規則動詞字尾加 "-ed"，不規則動詞則依動詞變化來使用。

b. 不管主詞 S 人稱，助動詞用都 "did"。Be 動詞（was ／ were），則依據主詞作變化；主詞為第一、三人稱時，使用 "was"，主詞第二人稱或複數，使用 "were"。

c. 否定句與疑問句的動詞，都用原形動詞。

d. 常使用於過去簡單式的時間副詞：yesterday，last ＋（week，night…），ago

 絕妙好例句

1. He played football before.（V ＝ play，過去式表過去的事實）
   他以前踢過足球。

2. I prepared for my exam last week.（V ＝ prepare，過去式表過去的動作狀態）我在上週為考試而做準備。

3. She did not feel well yesterday.（V ＝ feel，過去式表過去的動作狀態）她昨天覺得不舒服。

4. I loved you.（V ＝ love，過去式表過去的事實）我曾愛過你。

5. My mother lived here.（V ＝ live，過去式表過去的事實）
   我的母親以前住這。

換你寫寫看

1. I _____ to my brother.（not／to talk）

2. She _____ so hard long time ago.（to work）

3. We _____ last month.（to date）

4. You _____ your car yesterday.（not ／to wash）

5. _____ you _____ milk when you were a child?（to drink）

6. May _____ shy before.（were／was）

7. _____ it cold last night?（were／was）

8. We usually _____ to a pub many years ago.（to go）

● 答案與中譯解析

1. 答：did not talk（表示過去的動作／狀態）我沒和我哥說話。
2. 答：walked（表示過去的事實）她很久以前努力工作過。
3. 答：dated（過去的動作／狀態）從上個月我們曾約會過。
4. 答：did not wash（表示過去的動作／狀態）你昨天沒有洗車。
5. 答：Did、drink（表示過去的習慣）你小時候喝牛奶嗎？
6. 答：was（表示過去的事實）May 以前很害羞。
7. 答：Was（表示過去的事實）昨晚天氣冷嗎？
8. 答：went（表示過去的習慣）很多年前我們經常去 pub。

06 過去進行式 Past Progressive

名言範例：

I was dreaming of the past 我昨晚夢到過去
And my heart was beating fast. 而我的心跳地非常快

　　選自於約翰藍儂的歌曲 Jealous Guy（忌妒的男人）。約翰藍儂是一名英國音樂人、歌手及作曲，以身為披頭四團員揚名全球。與他的妻子小野洋子同為激進和平主義者與視覺藝術家，影響當今流行音樂深遠。

過去進行式 Past Progressive 文法解析

過去進行式 Past Progressive，主要在表達過去某個「特定」時間點上與「正在進行」的動作／狀態。

1. 使用時機

a. 過去正在發生的動作／狀態：表示在過去某特定時間點上，動作／狀態正在進行。

　　Ex. He was watching a football game at 10 p.m. last night.
　　　他昨晚 10 點正在看足球賽。

b. 兩個動作**同時**發生：表示過去某個特定時間點上，剛好兩個動作正在平行進行。

　　Ex. While he was watching a football game, she was talking on the phone.　當他看足球賽時，她正在講電話。

c. 經常搭配過去簡單式：主要表達兩個動作都發生在過去，一個進行中的動作，被另一個動作／事件介入。

　　Ex. He was watching a football game when she called.　當她來電時，他正在看足球賽。

2. 文法結構

主詞 S ＋助動詞（was／were）＋現在分詞（V-ing）＋…

a. 肯定句

　　主詞 S ＋助動詞（was／were）＋現在分詞（V-ing）＋…
　　Ex. She was watching TV at 7 p.m.　昨晚 7 點她正在看電視。

b. 否定句

　　主詞 S ＋助動詞（was／were）＋ not ＋現在分詞（V-ing）＋…
　　Ex. She wasn't watching TV at 7 p.m.　昨晚 7 點她沒有在看電視。

c. 疑問句

　　助動詞（Was／Were）＋主詞 S ＋現在分詞（V-ing）＋…
　　Ex. Was she watching TV at 7 pm.　昨晚 7 點的時候，她在看電視嗎？

3. 使用特點

a. Be 動詞（was ／ were）為助動詞，主要動詞字尾加 "-ing"。

b. 助動詞（was ／ were），則依據主詞 S 作變化；主詞為第一、三人稱時，使用 "was"，主詞第二人稱或複數，使用 "were"。

c. 常使用於過去簡單式的時間副詞：when，while

d. was not ＝ wasn't；were not ＝ weren't

 絕妙好例句

1. Andy was playing football when I arrived.（V ＝ play、arrive，搭配過去簡單式）當我到的時候，Andy 正在踢足球。

2. I was preparing for my exam at 7 p.m.（V ＝ prepare，過去正在進行的動作狀態）我在晚上 7 點時，準備著我的考試。

3. She was not cooking when I visited her.（V ＝ cook、visit，搭配過去簡單式）我昨天拜訪他時，她沒有在煮飯。

4. My mother was travelling to London last week, when I called her.
（V ＝ travel、call，搭配過去簡單式）
上週當我打給我媽時，她正好在倫敦旅遊。

5. Pet was sitting there while I was shopping at the store.（V ＝ sit、shop，兩個動作**同時**發生）當我在店裡購物時，Pet 就坐在那裏。

換你寫寫看

1. I _____ to my brother.（to talk）

2. When you _____ , I _____ to my brother.（to come／to talk）

3. We _____ at 7pm last night.（to date）

4. We _____ , while you _____ to party.（to date／to go）

5. Thomas _____ and I _____ , too.（not／to work）

6. _____ you _____ , when I called last night?（to sleep）

7. _____ you _____ all night?（to study）

8. While I _____ my email, my laptop went off suddenly.（to write）

● 答案與中譯解析

1. 答：was talking（過去正在進行的動作狀態）我正在跟我哥說話。

2. 答：(C) Came、was talking（搭配過去簡單式）
   當你來的時候，我正在和我哥說話。

3. 答：were dating、went（過去正在進行的動作狀態）我們昨晚 7 點正在約會。

4. 答：were dating、were going（兩個動作**同時**發生）
   你們去舞會的時候，我們在約會。

5. 答：was not working、was not working（兩個動作**同時**發生）
   Thomas 不用上班，我也不用上班。

6. 答：Were、sleep（搭配過去簡單式）昨晚我打給你時，你正好在睡覺嗎？

7. 答：Were、studying（過去正在進行的動作狀態）你整晚都在讀書嗎？

8. 答：was writing（搭配過去簡單式）當我正在寫郵件時，突然當機。

07 過去完成式 Past Perfect

名言範例：

You hid your skeletons when I had shown you mine.
當我向你展現自我時，你卻隱藏了自己的軀體。

You woke the devil that I thought you'd left behind.
你喚醒了那頭我以為你已經擺脫了的惡魔。

電影《吸血鬼獵人：林肯總統》Abraham Lincoln：Vampire Hunter 的主題曲，Linkin Park（聯合公園）為其量身訂做的歌名為 Powerless（無能為力），吸血鬼獵人是一部 2012 年美國電影，改編自 2010 年的同名小說，作者為 Seth Grahame Smith 為美國一位暢銷小說作家及電影監製。

過式完成式 Past Perfect 文法解析

過式完成式 **Past Perfect**，主要在表達動作／狀態在過去的時間開始，並且過去時間已經完成；簡單來說所有的動作與狀態，都在「過去」的時空背景下，開始、進行到結束。

1. 使用時機

a. 表達二個過去動作的先後順序，與過去簡單式 Simple Past 使用，第一個先發生的動作使用 "過式完成式 Perfect Past"，第二個則使用 "過去簡單式 Simple Past"；提供一個容易的記住的口訣「先完成後簡單」。

Ex. Pet had never cooked before he went to college.
　　Pet 上大學前，從未下過廚。

第一個動作：Pet had never cooked.（過去完成式）
第二個動作：He went to college.（過去簡單式）

2. 文法結構

主詞 S ＋助動詞（had）＋過去分詞（p.p.）＋…

a. 肯定句

主詞 S ＋助動詞（had）＋過去分詞（p.p.）…

Ex. I had lived in Taiwan before I moved to USA.

我搬去美國前，一直住在台灣。

b. 否定句

主詞 S ＋助動詞（had）＋ not ＋過去分詞（p.p.）＋…

Ex. I had not lived in Taiwan before I moved to USA.

我搬去美國前，不住在台灣。

c. 疑問句

助動詞（had）＋主詞 S ＋過去分詞（p.p.）＋…

Ex. Had you lived in Taiwan before you moved to USA.

你搬去美國前，是住在台灣嗎？

3. 使用特點

a. 用助動詞（has ／ have）的過去式 "had"，不隨著主詞 S 作變化。

b. 動詞使用過去分詞；規則動詞字尾加上 "-ed"，不規則性動詞變化，則另參照列表。

 絕妙好例句

1. Vicky was hungry; she had not eaten for 8 hours.（1st action 過去完成式，V ＝ eat）Vicky 餓了，她已經 8 個小時沒吃飯了。

2. John had had that mobile phone for 4 years before it broke down.
（1st action 過去完成式，V = have）
John 在他的手機壞掉前，已經使用它 4 年了。

3. Had Anne talked to Mother before she cooked dinner?（1st action
過去完成式，V = talk）Anne 煮晚餐前有跟母親說話嗎？

4. I had never visited London before I went there in 2010?（1st action
過去完成式，V = visit）我在 2010 年去倫敦的，之前從來沒去過。

5. I had worked all day before my friends came to pick me up.
（1st action 過去完成式，V = work）
我朋友來接我時，我之前已經工作一整天了。

換你寫寫看

1. Jane knew the movie because she _____ it before.（to see）
2. Before I ran to my sister's house, I _____ her.（to call）
3. By the time the rain began, she _____ .（to arrive）
4. I _____ Olivia for 2 years before I met her in France.（not／to see）
5. We _____ enough, so we lost the basketball game.（not／to practice）
6. _____ Frank _____ the instructions before they use this notebook?（to read）
7. _____ she _____ a house by that time?（to find）
8. When she arrived at the restaurant, Kevin _____ already _____ another cup of coffee.（to order）

- 答案與中譯解析

1. 答：had seen（1st action 過去完成式）

Jane 知道這部電影因為她之前已經看過了。

2. 答：had called（1st action 過去完成式）

在我跑去我姐姐家之前，我已經打過電話給她了。

3. 答：had arrived（1st action 過去完成式）雨開始下之前她已經抵達了。

4. 答：had not seen（1st action 過去完成式）

我在法國碰到 Olivia，在之前我已經有 2 年見過她了。

5. 答：had not practiced（1st action 過去完成式）

我們之前練習的不夠，所以我們才會輸了這場球賽。

6. 答：Had、read（1st action 過去完成式）

Frank 在使用手提電腦前，有先讀過使用說明嗎？

7. 答：Had、found（1st action 過去完成式）在那之前，他是否有找到房子。

8. 答：Had、ordered（1st action 過去完成式）

當她到餐廳時，Kevin 已經又點一杯咖啡。

---

08 過去完成進行式 Past Perfect Progressive

名言範例：

I had been trying to emulate Barbara Walters, since the start of my TV career.

Barbara Walters，她是我自電視生涯開始，就試圖模訪的對象。

　　脫口秀主持人、20 世紀最富有的美國黑人 Oprah（歐普拉）在史丹佛大學 2008 年畢業典禮的演講，Oprah 在演講裡分享 3 個人生經驗，是有關感覺、失敗、及尋找快樂。

過去完成進行式 Past Perfect Progressive 文法解析

過去完成進行式 Past Perfect Progressive，主要在表達動作／狀態在過去的時間開始，且持續一段時間；簡單來說所有的動作與狀態，都在「過去」的時空背景下，開始並且持續進行；強調「**過去動作的持續性**」。

1. 使用時機

- 表達二個過去動作的先後順序，與過去簡單式 simple Past 使用，第一個先發生的動作已經持續一段時間，用「過去完成進行式 Past Perfect Progressive」；第二個動作則使用「過去簡單式 Simple Past」；提供一個容易的記住的口訣「先完成進行後簡單」。

Ex. We had been standing here for over 1 hour when she finally arrived.　當她終於抵達的時候，我們站在這裡已經一個多小時了。

第一個動作：We had been standing here for over 1 hour.
　　　　　　（過去完成進行式）

第二個動作：when she finally arrived.（過去簡單式）

2. 文法結構

主詞 S ＋助動詞 had ＋助動詞 been ＋現在分詞（V-ing）＋⋯

a. 肯定句

主詞 S ＋助動詞（had）＋助動詞 been ＋現在分詞（V-ing）⋯

Ex. I had been waiting for him for a while when he showed up.
　　當他出現時，我已經等了一會了。

b. 否定句

主詞 S ＋助動詞（had）＋ not ＋助動詞 been ＋現在分詞（V-ing）⋯

Ex. I had not been waiting for him for a while when he showed up.
　　當他出現之前，我已有一會兒沒等他了。

c. 疑問句

助動詞（had）＋主詞 S ＋助動詞 been ＋現在分詞（V-ing）…

Ex. Had you been waiting for him for a while when he showed up?

當他出現之前，你已經等了一會了嗎？

3. 使用特點

a. 有兩個助動詞 had 以及 been，兩者都不隨著主詞 S 作變化。

b. 動詞使用現在分詞（V-ing）

c. 常使用於現在完成式的時間副詞：

for ／ since ／ the whole day ／ all day

 絕妙好例句

1. They had been talking for over hours before father came home.
   （1st action 過去完成進行式，V＝talk）
   當父親回家時，他們已經聊了好幾個小時。

2. John had been using that mobile phone for 4 years before it broke
   down.（1st action 過去完成進行式，V＝use）
   John 在他的手機壞掉前，已經使用它 4 年了。

3. Had Anne been eating for last few days? She lost a lot of weight.
   （1st action 過去完成進行式，V＝ear）
   Anne 過去幾天有吃東西嗎？她瘦了很多。

4. I had not been visiting London before I went there in 2010 again.
   （1st action 過去完成進行式，V＝visit）
   我在 2010 年再去倫敦的，之前已經很久沒有去過了。

5. I had been working all day before my friends came to pick me up.

（1st action 過去完成進行式，V＝work）

我朋友來接我時，我之前已經工作一整天了。

✏ 換你寫寫看

1. Jane knew the movie because she ＿＿＿＿＿ it several times.（to see）

2. Before I ran to my sister's house, I ＿＿＿＿＿ her for million times.（to call）

3. It ＿＿＿＿＿ all day , when she arrived.

4. I ＿＿＿＿＿ Olivia for 2 years before I met her in France.（not／to see）

5. We ＿＿＿＿＿ enough, so we lost the basketball game.（not／to practice）

6. ＿＿＿＿＿ Frank ＿＿＿＿＿ for 12 hours when I came home?（to sleep）

7. ＿＿＿＿＿ she ＿＿＿＿＿ for a house by that time?（to look）

8. When she arrived at the restaurant, Kevin ＿＿＿＿＿ already ＿＿＿＿＿ another cup of coffee.（to drink）

● 答案與中譯解析

1. 答：had been seeing（1st action 過去完成進行式）
   Jane 知道這部電影因為她之前已經看過很多遍了。

2. 答：had been calling（1st action 過去完成進行式）
   在我跑去我姊家之前，我已經打過電話無數次給她了。

3. 答：had been raining（1st action 過去完成進行式）
   當她已經抵達時，已經下了整天的雨了。

51

4. 答：had not been seeing（1st action 過去完成進行式）

　　我在法國碰到 Olivia，在之前我已經有 2 年沒見過她了。

5. 答：had not been practicing（1st action 過去完成進行式）

　　我們之前練習的不夠，所以我們才會輸了這場球賽。

6. 答：Had、been sleeping（1st action 過去完成進行式）

　　Frank 在我回家之前已經睡了 12 小時了嗎？

7. 答：Had、been looking（1st action 過去完成進行式）

　　在那之前，她一直在找房子嗎？

8. 答：Had、been drinking（1st action 過去完成進行式）

　　當她到餐廳時，Kevin 已經又喝一杯咖啡。

---

09 未來簡單式 Simple Future

名言範例：

Take a breath, I'll pull myself together… You'll never know….

深呼吸，我會振作起來……你永遠也不會知道……

　　摘自歌曲 Save You，收錄於 2008 年發行的同名專輯 Simple Plan 中。Simple Plan（簡單計劃樂團），是一支於 1999 年在加拿大魁北克地區成立的流行龐克樂團。

未來簡單式 Simple Future 文法解析

未來簡單式 Simple Future，說的是「未來」，主要在表達未來將會發生的動作或即將存在的狀態。

1. 使用時機

a. 未來的行動的意願：對未來行動的決定，説之前並沒有任何計畫與決定。

Ex. I will make dinner tonight.　我今晚會做晚餐。

b. 表達承諾：對未來的作出承諾。

Ex. I will be carefull.　Don't worry!　我會小心的，別擔心！

c. 對未來的預測／假設：預測未來可能會發生的事情。

Ex. She will win this game.　她會贏得這次比賽。

d. 未來成真／確認的事實：未來即將發生，成為不可改變的事實、確認的未來。

Ex. She will be 18 next month.　她下個月即將滿 18 歲。

2. 文法結構

主詞 S ＋助動詞（will）＋動詞 V ＋…

a. 肯定句

主詞 S ＋助動詞（will）＋動詞 V ＋…

Ex. I will call you this weekend.　我周末將會打電話給你。

b. 否定句

主詞 S ＋助動詞（will）＋ not ＋動詞 V ＋…

Ex. I will not call you this weekend.　我周末不會打電話給你。

c. 疑問句

助動詞（will）＋主詞 S ＋動詞 V ＋…

Ex. Will you call me this weekend? 你周末會打電話給我嗎？

3. 使用特點

a. 助動詞用 "will"，不隨著主詞 S 作變化。

b. 動詞使用原形動詞。

c. 常 使 用 於 現 在 完 成 式 的 時 間 副 詞：tomorrow ／ next ＋（hour，year）…etc.

4. 另一個表示未來的句型 "Be going to"

主詞 S ＋助動詞（am ／ are ／ is）＋ going to ＋動詞 V ＋…

a. 表示對未來的計畫、想法與打算，不管未來有沒有可能實現。

Ex. I am going to call you this weekend.（打算）我打算這週末打電話給你。

Ex. I will call you this weekend.（意願）我這週末會打給你。

b. 也可以用作「預測」未來跟 "will-furture" 的「預測未來」的作用相同。

Ex. She is going to win this game. 她將要贏得這次比賽。

Ex. She will win this game. 她將會贏得這次比賽。

c. 確定行動會在未來發生。

Ex. I am going to read this book tonight. 我今晚準備讀這本書。

 絕妙好例句

1. I will help you later.（V＝help，表示意願）我待會幫你。

2. It will rain tomorrow.（V＝rain，表示預測）明天預計會下雨。

3. I will take care of myself.（V＝take，表示承諾）我會照顧好我自己。

4. Kevin will return next week.（V = return，表示未來的事實）

   Kevin 下周將回來。

5. My boss is going to take few days off.（V = take，表示打算）

   我老闆打算放幾天假。

換你寫寫看

1. _____ you _____ me?（to marry）

2. I _____ in London tomorrow.（be）

3. Pet _____ this competition.（to win）

4. Will you meet May at coffee shop tomorrow.（to meet）

5. I _____ her.（not／going to／to help）

6. Ladies and gentlemen, tonight, we _____ Mr. President to show up.（to invite）

7. _____ you _____ to the party tonight?（to go）

8. She _____ the bus in time.（not／to catch）

● 答案與中譯解析

1. 答：Will、marry（表示意願、承諾）你願意嫁給我嗎？

2. 答：will be（表示未來的事實）明天我將會在倫敦。

3. 答：will not win（表示預測）Pet 不會贏得這個比賽的。

4. 答：Will、meet（表示意願）你明天將會和 May 在咖啡店碰面嗎？

5. 答：am not going to help（表示打算）我不打算幫她。

6. 答：will invite（表示未來的事實）各位先生女士，今晚我們請總統先生出場。

7. 答：will、go（表示意願）你今晚會去舞會嗎？

8. 答：will not catch（表示預測）她將會趕不上這班公車。

10 未來進行式 Future Progressive

名言範例：

I'll Be Missing You. 我會一直想你。

　　這首歌是 1997 年 Puff Daddy 寫給意外過世的好友 Notorious B.I.G 的曲子，參與和聲的有團體 112，以及 B.I.G. 的遺孀— Faith Evans。這首歌改編自 70 年代名曲 Every Breath You Take 原作者是警察合唱團（Police），吹牛老爹將這首歌改成輕快的嘻哈風，收錄在專輯 No Way Out 中。Puff Daddy 也曾經在黛安娜王妃的紀念音樂會上（2007 年 7 月 1 日），向全世界演唱這首歌。

未來進行式 Future Progressive 文法解析

未來進行式 Future Progressive，主要在表達在 "未來某一個特定時間點" 上，動作／事件即將進行或者還在持續進行中；強調未來動作的持續。

1. 使用時機

● 未來特定的時間點上，動作將會進行，或持續進行；通常動作／事件，已經事先被規劃，確認會在未來的某個特定時間發生。

　Ex. I will be making dinner at 8 o'clock tonight.

　　　今晚 8 點的時候，我將會在那時候做晚餐。

2. 文法結構

主詞 S ＋助動詞（will）＋助動詞（be）＋現在分詞（V-ing）＋…

　a. 肯定句

　　主詞 S ＋助動詞（will）＋助動詞（be）＋現在分詞（V-ing）＋…

　　Ex I will be calling you this Sunday. 我周日將會打電話給你。

b. 否定句

主詞 S ＋助動詞（will）＋ not ＋助動詞（be）＋現在分詞（V-ing）＋⋯

Ex. I will not be calling you this Sunday.　我周日將不會打電話給你。

c. 疑問句

助動詞（will）＋主詞 S ＋助動詞（be）＋現在分詞（V-ing）＋⋯

Ex. Will you be calling me this Sunday?　你周末將會打電話給我嗎？

3. 使用特點

a. 有二個助動詞 "will" 與 "be"，都不用隨著主詞 S 作變化。

b. 動詞使用現在分詞（V-ing）。

 絕妙好例句

1. We will be going to party this Friday night.（V = go，表示動作將進行中）這週五晚上，我們將會去舞會。

2　At this time tomorrow, we will be leaving for Taipei.（V = leave，表示動作將進行中）明天這個時候，我們將動身前往台北。

3. Next week, she will be working for her new boss .（V = work，表示動作將進行中）她下周即將替她新老闆工作。

4. Kevin will not be returning next Monday.（V = return，表示動作將進行中）Kevin 下周一將不會回來。

4. Will Mary be taking few days off from tomorrow?（V = take，表示動作將進行中）從明天開始，May 將會休幾天假嗎？

換你寫寫看

1. _____ she _____ him in one year?（to marry）

2. _____ Bill _____ lunch with us at 6pm tonight?（to eat）

3. The storm _____ soon.（to come）

4. Petty _____ to Italy this fall.（to go）

5. _____ you _____ the car tomorrow morning.（to use）

6. They _____ on the beach this time next week.（to sit）

7. _____ he _____ at 3 pm?（to leave）

8. She _____ this movie with Tom tonight.（not／to watch）

● 答案與中譯解析

1. 答：Will、be marrying（表示動作將進行中）她一年內會嫁給他嗎？

2. 答：Will、be eating（表示動作將進行中）Bill 今晚 6 點會和我們一起晚餐嗎？

3. 答：will be coming、表示動作將進行中）暴風雨即將來臨。

4. 答：will not be going，表示動作將進行中）Petty 今年秋天將不會去義大利。

5. 答：Will、be using（表示動作將進行中）你明早會用車嗎？

6. 答：will be sitting（表示動作將進行中)下週的這個時間，他們會坐在海灘上。

7. 答：Will、be leaving（表示動作將進行中）他下午 3 點會離開嗎？

8. 答：will not be watching（表示動作將進行中）她今晚將不跟 Tom 去看這個電影。

11 未來完成式 Future Perfect

名言範例：

When you learn to tap this source, you will truly have defeated age. 當你學會使用這個資源時，你將真的已經戰勝年老。

　　Sophia Loren（索非婭 · 羅蘭）為義大利著名女演員，以《兩婦人》電影，於 1961 年獲得奧斯卡最佳女主角。那一年，她與瑪麗蓮夢露、碧姬芭鐸一起，被封「世界上最性感的女人」。

未來完成式 Future Perfect 文法解析

未來完成式 Future Perfect，主要在表達在「未來某一個特定時間點」之前，動作／事件已經發生、結束或完成；簡單來說，預設在未來的時空下，動作已經發生、結束或完成的狀態。

1. 使用時機

- 預設在未來特定的時間點之前，動作／事件已經發生、結束或完成的狀態。

  Ex. I will have written this letter by tomorrow.

  　　我將會明天之前，寫完這封信。

2. 文法結構

主詞 S ＋助動詞（will）＋助動詞（have）＋過去分詞（p.p.）＋…

a. 肯定句

　　主詞 S ＋助動詞（will）＋助動詞（have）＋過去分詞（p.p.）＋…

　　Ex. I will have called you by this Sunday.　我周日前將會打電話給你。

b. 否定句

主詞 S ＋助動詞（will）＋ not ＋助動詞（have）＋過去分詞（p.p.）
＋…

Ex. I will not have called you by this Sunday.

我周日前將不會打電話給你。

c. 疑問句

助動詞（Will）＋主詞 S ＋助動詞（have）＋過去分詞（p.p.）＋…

Ex. Will you have called me by this Sunday?

你周末前將會打電話給我嗎？

3. 使用特點

a. 有二個助動詞 "will" 與 "have"，都不用隨著主詞 S 作變化。

b. 動詞使用過去分詞（p.p.）。

c. 使用的時間副詞片語或子句的動詞，要用「現在簡單式」。

 絕妙好例句

1. By 7pm, his wife will have cooked dinner.（V ＝ cook，表示動作預計已經完成）在 7 點之前，他太太將煮好飯了。

2. When you arrive, the bus will have left.（V ＝ leave，表示動作預計已經完成成）當你抵達的時候，巴士估計已經離開了。

3. She will have met for her new boss by next week.（V ＝ meet，表示動作預計已經完成）下周之前，她將會見過她的新老闆了。

4. Kevin will not have returned from his holiday next Monday.（V ＝ return，表示動作預計完成）Kevin 下周一還不會從休假中回來。

5. Will Mary have taken few days off by next month?（V＝take，表示動作預計已經完成）下個月之前，May 將會休幾天假嗎？

換你寫寫看

1. _____ she _____ him by next year?（to marry）
2. Bill _____ lunch when we come home at 1pm.（to eat）
3. May _____ at office by 9 am.（to arrive）
4. Petty _____ to Italy by next fall.（not／to go）
5. _____ you _____ the new car by next year?（to buy）
6. They _____ this project before the deadline.（to complete）
7. She _____ home by 10pm.（to go）
8. She _____ by the time John comes.（to sing）

● 答案與中譯解析

1. 答：Will、have married（表示動作預計已經完成）
   明年之前，她已經嫁給他了嗎？
2. 答：will have eaten（表示動作預計已經完成，時間副詞用現在簡單式）
   當我們下午 1 點回家時，Bill 將已經吃完午餐了。
3. 答：will have arrived（表示動作預計已經完成）
   9 點之前，May 將已經到辦公室了。
4. 答：will not have gone（表示動作預計已經完成）
   Petty 明年秋天之前，將不會去義大利。
5. 答：Will、have bought（表示動作預計已經完成）明年之前你已經買了車嗎？
6. 答：will have completed（表示動作預計已經完成）
   在截止日前，他們將已經完成這個案子。
7. 答：will have gone（表示動作預計已經完成）她 10 點之前要回到家。

8. 答：will have sung（表示動作預計已經完成，時間副詞用現在簡單式）John 來之前，她將已經唱完歌了。

---

11 未來完成進行式 Future Perfect Progressive

名言範例：

"Next July I will have been doing this for 50 years," Springsteen says.（2013.Aug.）

到明年 7 月，我的演唱生涯就要滿 50 年了。

　　Bruce Springsteen（布魯斯・史普林斯汀）是美國搖滾歌手、創作者與吉他手。創作出詩人般的歌詞常以家鄉新澤西為主軸。

未來完成進行式 Future Perfect Continuous 文法解析

未來完成進行式 Future Perfect Continuous，主要在表達動作／事件，在過去發生，一直持續到現在，並且延續到未來某一個特定時間點，動作／事件還可能會持續下去；也就是過去發生的動作／事件，橫跨現在與未來的時空，強調動作的持續。

1. 使用時機

- 動作的持續：在未來特定的時間點之前，動作／事件已經開始並且持續一段時間，有可能會繼續下去。

　Ex. Within 10 minutes, I will have been waiting 1 hour for bus.

　　　十分鐘之內，我將會已經等 1 小時公車了。

2. 文法結構

主詞 S ＋助動詞（will）＋助動詞（have）＋助動詞（been）＋現在分詞
（V-ing）＋…

a. 肯定句

主詞 S ＋助動詞（will）＋助動詞（have）＋助動詞（been）＋現在分
詞（V-ing）＋…

Ex. In 10 minutes, I will have been waiting 1 hour for bus.

再過十分鐘，我即將等公車 1 小時了。

b. 否定句

主詞 S ＋助動詞（will）＋ not ＋助動詞（have）＋助動詞（been）＋
現在分詞（V-ing）＋…

Ex. I will have not been studying for many years; it's time to go back
to school. 我將要已經很久沒有學習了，該是回學校進修的時候。

c. 疑問句

助動詞（will）＋主詞 S ＋助動詞（have）＋助動詞（been）＋現在分
詞（V-ing）＋…

Ex. Will you have been waiting 1 hour for bus in?

再過十分鐘，你們就將等了 1 小時公車了嗎？

3. 使用特點

a. 有三個助動詞 will、have 以及 been，都不用隨著主詞 S 作變化。

b. 動詞使用現在分詞（V-ing）。

c. 使用的時間副詞片語或子句的動詞，要用「現在簡單式」。

絕妙好例句

1. By 7 pm he comes home, his wife will have been cooking dinner.
   （V＝cook，表示動作的持續）
   在 7 點他回來之前，他太太將還在煮飯。

2. I will have been working here for 8 years next week.（V＝work，表示動作的持續）下星期我在這裡工作即將滿 8 年。

3. Pet will have been playing football all day long.（V＝play，表示動作的持續）Pet 將幾乎踢了一整天的足球了。

4. Kevin will not have been using the car.（V＝use，表示動作的持續）Kevin 將不會用車。

5. Will Mary have been taking her vacation for a month.（V＝take，表示動作的持續）May 下個月將會繼續休假嗎？

換你寫寫看

1. _____ she _____ him for 5 year by the end of next month?（to marry）

2. Bill _____ lunch when we come home.（to eat）

3. We _____ Wii for 12 hours by midnight.（to play）

4. Petty _____ to Italy by next fall.（not／to go）

5. _____ we _____ in USA long enough to get the citizenship next year?（to live）

6. They _____ for over an hour by the time Thomas arrives.（to talk）

7. You _____ TV all the time.（to watch）

8. She _____ for 10 years by the end of this year.（to sing）

● 答案與中譯解析

1. 答：Will、have been married（表示動作的持續）

   到下個月底，她嫁給他即將滿 5 年了嗎？

2. 答：will have been eating（表示動作的持續，副詞子句動詞用現在簡單式）

   當我們回家時，Bill 將繼續在吃午餐。

3. 答：will have been playing（表示動作的持續）

   到凌晨我們玩 Wii 即將持續了 12 小時。

4. 答：will not have been going（表示動作的持續）

   到明年秋季，Petty 將不會繼續待在義大利。

5. 答：will、have been living（表示動作的持續）我們是否在 USA 住得夠久，

   明年即將可以拿到公民身份嗎？

6. 答：will have been talking（表示動作的持續，副詞子句動詞用現在簡單式）

   他們在 Thomas 來之前，他們聊了即將超過一個小時。

7. 答：will have been watching（表示動作的持續）你持續一直在看電視。

8. 答：will have been singing（表示動作的持續）

   到今年底，她唱歌即將滿 10 年。

第3單元：祈使句

英文達人文法小筆記！

名言範例：

Run, Forrest! Run! 跑，阿甘，快跑！

在電影 Forest Gump《阿甘正傳》因為阿甘的個性，小時候遭受不少欺負，每回這時候青梅竹馬 Jenny 總是對著阿甘大喊 Run, Forrest! Run! 幫助阿甘躲過危險，不知是不是因為這樣長期的鍛鍊，造就阿甘之後美式足球輝煌的成績。其實，祈使句在電影的場景中，經常出現，尤其是動作片或者是警匪片呢！Don't move! 下回留意看看吧！

祈使句 Imperative Mood 文法解析

祈使句 Imperative Mood，主要是用來表達命令、請求、禁止、建議或勸告等等的句子。主詞 S 有時候會被省略。

1. 使用時機

a. 表示命令或要求：
   Ex. Stand Up! 起立 ➡ 一般動詞
   Ex. Be quiet! 安靜 ➡ Be 動詞

b. 表示禮貌委婉：通常加 "please" 或用附加問句表示如 will ／ won't you，would ／ could you…等。

Ex. Please stand up! 請起立 ➡ 一般動詞

Ex. Be quiet ,please! 請安靜 ➡ Be 動詞

c. 表示請求、允許或建議：通常用 "Let" 表示允許，用 "Let's"（＝Let us）表示建議。

Ex. Let him go! 讓他走！

Ex. Let's go to see the movie. 讓我們一起去看電影。

d. 表示條件：通常在祈使句後，加上 "and" 或 "or" 的子句，表示條件。

Ex. Study hard, and you will succeed.（and 表示正面）
努力學習然後你會成功。

Ex. Study hard, or you will fail.（or 表示負面）
努力學習要不然你會失敗。

2. 文法結構

a. 肯定句

● 原形動詞 V ＋…

Be 動詞＋….

Let ＋受詞 O ＋原形動詞 V

Let's ＋原形動詞 V ＋…

Ex. Let's play basketball! 我們一起去打籃球吧！

b. 否定句 可用以下幾種表示：

Don't（Do not）＋原形動詞 V ＋…

Don't ＋ be ＋…

Ex. Don't be so silly. 別傻了。

No ＋名詞 or 動名詞

Never ＋動詞原形

Don't ＋ Let ＋受詞 O ＋原形動詞 V

Let's ＋ not ＋原形動詞 V ＋…

Ex. Don't do that again.　不要再這樣做。

c. 疑問句附加問句字眼 will ／ won't you，can ／ could ／ would ／ you…
等字眼

Ex. Come here a moment, could you?　你到這裡一會兒，可以嗎？

Ex. Could you come here for a moment?　你能夠到這裡來一下嗎？

3. 使用特點

a. 祈使句的主詞 S 大部分時候會被省略，如要強調時「主詞 S」放句尾，
前面要加「逗號」。

Ex. Be quiet, Tom! 安靜 Tom ！

b. 表示禮貌委婉的字眼如 "please"，以及附加問句，都可以放在句首或
句尾，只是放句尾時前面要加上「逗號」。

Ex. Give me a book, would you?　你可以給我一本書嗎？

c. 肯定句前如加上 "Do" 可以強調語氣。

Ex. Do have another cup of coffee!　再喝杯咖啡吧！

 絕妙好例句

1. Let's go!（表示建議）我們走吧！

2. Take him home, Pet!（表示要求）帶他回家，Pet ！

3. Never do that again!（表示命令）別再做那種事了！

4. Be patient, kid!（表示勸告）有耐心，孩子！

5. Have a cup of tea, will you?（表示禮貌委婉）來杯茶嗎？

換你寫寫看

1. Marry me! _____ my wife, May!（to be）

2. _____ in, please!（to come）

3. Let's _____ open the window. It's raining now!

   （A）don't （B）not （C）isn't

4. _____ _____ it!（A）Don't touch （B）touching （C）Aren't touch

5. _____ yourself comfortable!

   （A）Do to make （B）To do make （C）Do make

6. Don't tell a lie, _____ the police will keep you here!

   （A）or （B）for （C）so

7. _____ a good boy, Kevin!（A）Be （B）Are （C）To be

8. _____ your steps!（A）Watching （B）To watch （C）Watch

- 答案與中譯解析

  1. 答：Be（表示請求）嫁給我，成為我的妻，May！
  2. 答：come（禮貌委婉）請進！！
  3. 答：(B)（表示建議，Let's not＋V）讓我們不要開窗，現在下雨了！
  4. 答：(A)（表示命令）別碰它！
  5. 答：(C)（表示禮貌委婉）請自便！！
  6. 答：(A)（表示條件、警告）別說謊，否則警察將留你在這裡！
  7. 答：(A)（表示警告、命令）當個乖小孩，Kevin！
  8. 答：(C)（表示警告）走路小心！！

第4單元：被動式

英文達人文法小筆記

名言範例：

Now life has killed the dream I dreamed.

如今現實的生活已經扼殺了我昔日的夢想。

聽起來很耳熟嗎？

　　I Dreamed a Dream 是一首來自音樂劇《悲慘世界》的歌曲，為劇中角色Fantine 於第一幕演唱的獨唱歌曲。這首歌曲是一首哀歌，演唱角色 Fantine 當時十分痛苦和貧窮，並回想起以往的美好時光。

現在完成式被動式文法解析

英文句子是由「主詞 S ＋動詞 V」為基本元素組成以及延伸，表達主詞執行／完成動作的概念，那麼，怎麼說？英文句子依主詞與動詞的互動關係，可以分為兩種語態：主動語態（Active Voice）與被動語態（Passive Voice）；主動或被動，主要是以動詞的角度來看主詞，是動詞的執行者或接受者？

主動式語態：主詞 S 是動詞 V 的執行者。

       I opened the door. 我開了門。

       S（執行者）＋ V ＋ O（接受者）

被動式語態：主詞 S 是動詞 V 的接受者。

       The door was opened by me. 門被我開了。

       S（接受者）＋ Be 動詞＋ p.p. ＋ *by* ＋ O（執行者）

如果，主詞（S）的角色是動作的執行者，那麼就是主動式語態，英文句子大部分的句型，都是以主動式語態呈現；然而有時候，為了強調動作接受者的重要性，主詞（S）的角色成為動作的接受者，就是被動式語態了。

被動式語態（Passive Voice）文法解析

被動式語態（Passive Voice）的概念，以動詞為出發點，可以理解為主詞是被動的承受動作的接受者，接受者可以是人、事物。

1. 使用時機

  a. 強調動詞的接收者：當執行者與接受者相比，更想要強調「接受者」。

    Ex. The last book was bought by him. 最後一本書被他買走了。

  b. 不知道誰是執行者，或是不願意說出執行者時：

    Ex. This book was bought. 最後一本書被買走了。

  c. 禮貌性修辭：有時用被動語氣更能表示禮貌委婉的語氣。

    Ex. Your application was rejected. 你的申請被拒。

2. 文法結構

主詞 S（接受者）＋助動詞（Be 動詞）＋過去分詞（p.p.）＋ *by* ＋受詞 O（執行者）＋…

a. 肯定句

主詞 S ＋助動詞（Be 動詞）＋過去分詞（p.p.）＋ by ＋受詞 O ＋…

Ex. The last book was bought.　最後一本書被買走了。

b. 否定句

主詞 S ＋助動詞（Be 動詞）＋ not ＋過去分詞（p.p.）＋ by ＋受詞 O ＋…

Ex. The last book was bought.　最後一本書被買走了。

c. 疑問句

助動詞（Be 動詞）＋主詞 S ＋過去分詞（p.p.）＋ by ＋受詞 O ＋…

Ex. Was the book bought by him?　最後一本書被他買走了嗎？

3. 使用特點

a. 在被動語態中，執行者被「降級」到受詞的地位，前面須加 "by" 有時可以省略，求其是在執行

者不重要、不知道或者是不方便提的情況下。

b. Be 動詞的單複數，隨主詞 S 變化。

c. 主要動詞用過去分詞形式，且只有及物動詞（Vt）才能形成被動語態。

4. 常用時態的被動式語態變化

a. 現在簡單式（Simple Present）

主詞 S ＋ Be 動詞＋過去分詞（p.p.）＋ by ＋受詞＋…

主動＝ Tom *takes out* the garbage every night.

　　　Tom 每天晚上都會倒垃圾。

被動＝ The garbage *is taken out by* Tom every night.

　　　垃圾每天晚上會被 Tom 拿出來倒。

b. 現在進行式（Present Progressive）

主詞 S ＋ Be 動詞＋ being ＋過去分詞（p.p.）by ＋受詞＋…

主動＝ Sara *is opening* the window now.　Sara 現在打開窗戶。

被動＝ The window *is being opened by* Sara now.

現在窗戶被 Sara 打開。

c. 現在完成式（Present Perfect）

主詞 S ＋ have ／ has ＋ been ＋過去分詞（p.p.）＋ by ＋受詞＋…

主動＝ He has taken these photos.　他已經拿到這些照片了。

被動＝ These photos has been taken by him.　這些照片是由他負責。

d. 現在完成進行式（Present Perfect Progressive）

主詞 S ＋ has ／ have ＋ been ＋ being ＋過去分詞（p.p.）＋ by ＋受詞＋…

主動＝ Recently, John *has been doing* the work.

最近，John 一直在工作。

被動＝ Recently, the work *has been being done* by John.

最近，工作都是由 John 負責。

e. 過去簡單式（Simple past）

主詞 S ＋ Be 動詞＋過去分詞（p.p.）＋ by ＋受詞＋…

主動＝ A car hit him.　車子撞了他。

被動＝ He was hit by a car.　他被車撞了。

f. 過去進行式（Past Progressive）

主詞 S ＋ was ／ were ＋ being ＋過去分詞（p.p.）＋ by ＋受詞＋…

主動＝ I *was teaching* Jane when you came.

你來的時候我正在教導 Jane。

被動＝ Jane *was being taught* by me when you came.

你來的時候，Jane 正在被我教導中。

g. 過去完成式（Past Perfect）

主詞 S ＋ had ＋ been ＋過去分詞（p.p.）＋ by ＋受詞＋…

主動＝ George *had repaired* many cars before he received his mechanic's license.

George 在修理許多汽車前就已取得他的技師執照了。

被動＝ Many cars *had been repaired* by George before he received his mechanic's license.

許多汽車是被 George 修理的，在 George 取得他的技師執照前。

h. 未來簡單式（Simple Future）

主詞 S ＋ will ＋ be ＋過去分詞（p.p.）＋ by ＋受詞＋…

主動＝ I will love you. 我會愛你。

被動＝ You will be loved（by me）. 你會被人愛。（被我）

i. 未來完成式（Future Perfect）

主詞 S ＋ will ＋ have ＋ been ＋過去分詞（p.p.）＋ by ＋受詞＋…

主動＝ Sue *will have completed* her new book before the deadline.

Sue 將在截止日期前完成了她的新書。

被動＝ Sue's new book *will have been completed*（by her）before the deadline.

Sue 的新書已在截止日期前完成了。

換你寫寫看

1. The dog bit the old lady.（Active Passive）

_____ .

2. Will you accept my apology?（Active Passive）

_____ .

3. Both parties have signed the contract.（Active Passive）

_____ .

4. People will not steal this car. It's too old.（Active Passive）

_____ .

5. Your application _____ .（to receive, Simple Past）

6. Pet _____ to give up this job.（to compel, Simple Past）

7. Swimming _____ here.（not／to allow, Simple Present）

● 答案與中譯解析

1. 答：The old lady was bitten by the dog.（V ＝ bit 強調接受者＝ the old lady）
   狗咬了老婦人 ➡ 老婦人被狗咬了。

2. 答：Will my apology be accepted（by you）?（V ＝ accept，強調接受者＝
   my apology）你接受我的道歉嗎？ ➡ 我的道歉被接受嗎？

3. 答：The contract has been signed by both parties.（V ＝ sign，強調接受者
   ＝ the contract）雙方已簽署合同。 ➡ 合同已被雙方簽署。

4. 答：This car will not be stolen.（V ＝ steal 執行者未知）
   不會有人偷這輛車，太舊了。 ➡ 這輛車不會被偷，太舊了。

5. 答：was received（禮貌委婉）您的申請已收到。

6. 答：was compelled（執行者未知）Pet 被迫離職。

7. 答：is not allowed（禮貌委婉）這裡禁止游泳。

第5單元：比較句

名言範例：

Walking with a friend in the dark is better than walking alone in the light.

在黑暗中有朋友相伴行走比在光亮中獨自而行還要好。

　　海倫凱勒（Helen Keller），知名的美國作家，也是一名教育家、慈善家與社會運動人士。最為人所知的就是她克服自我本身的殘疾，激勵許多人心的人生歷程。本單元的標題出自看不見這個世界的海倫凱勒更是能貼切的讓讀者感受到這光明與黑暗的比較。單元標題的例句，是在比較 "walking with a friend in the dark" 在黑暗中有朋友相伴行走與 "walking alone in the light" 在光亮裡獨自而行這兩件事情，句型為 A is better than B。雖然一般人都會比較偏好走在光亮的地方，但是即使如此，一個人走在光亮處但是沒有人陪伴還是不為大多數人的選擇。另外一方面，那些走在黑暗裡卻有朋友陪伴的人其實是多了安全感甚至是安慰。個人的延伸解讀是人在成功耀眼的時候，如果身旁沒有人可以分享光榮，還比不起在低潮的時候，在黑暗中有人拉你一把。

英文達人文法小筆記！

01 表達相似與不同的單字

1. 表達相似的單字

These oranges are *the same*.　這些橘子都一樣。

These oranges are *alike*.　這些橘子很像。

These oranges are *similar*.　這些橘子很類似。

These oranges smell *similarly*.　這些橘子聞起來差不多。

This orange is *like* that orange.　這顆橘子很像那顆橘子。

2. 表達不同的單字

The pen and the pencil are *different*. 這筆與鉛筆不同。

The pen and the pencil are *unalike ／ not alike*.　這筆與鉛筆不一樣。

The pen and the pencil are *dissimilar*.　這筆與鉛筆不相似。

The pen and the pencil look *differently*.　這筆與鉛筆看起來不一樣。

The pen is *unlike* the pencil.　這筆是不像鉛筆。

02 表達相似與不同的片語

1. 使用 as…as，the same…as，like 等表達相似

This pear is *as* big *as* that pear.　這顆梨子跟那顆梨子一樣大。

This pear has *the same* flavor *as* that pear.

這顆梨跟那顆梨有一樣的味道。

This pear *looks like* that pear.　這顆梨看起來像那顆梨。

This pear is *similar to* that pear.　這顆梨跟那顆梨很相似。

This pear is *like* that pear.　這顆梨像那顆梨。

2. 使用 not as…as，different…from，unlike 表達不同

The peach is **_different from_ ／ _than_** the pear.　這桃子跟梨不同。

This peach is **_not as_** sweet **_as_** this pear.　這桃子不像這梨一樣甜。

The peach is **_more_** flavorful **_than_** the pear.　這桃子比梨更有味道。

The peach is **_more like_** an apple **_than_** the pear.

這桃子比較像蘋果不像梨。

The peach **_in contrast to_** the pear is sweet.　這桃子比較起梨是甜的。

03 表達相似與不同的連接副詞

1. 連接副詞表達相似

This van is big. **_Similarly_**, that car is also spacey.

這個箱型車很大。相似地，那台車也是空間大。

This van is big. **_In the same way_**, that car is also spacey.

這個箱型車很大。同樣地，那台車也是空間大。

This steak is delicious. **_Likewise_**, that lamb is very flavorful.

這塊牛排很美味。一樣地，那塊羊肉很有味道。

This steak is delicious. **_Equally_**, that lamb is very flavorful.

這塊牛排很美味。相同地，那塊羊肉很有味道。

This steak is flavorful. **_In a similar manner_**, that lamb is very tasty.

這塊牛排很有味道。相似地，那塊羊肉非常好吃。

2. 連接副詞表達不同

The house is big. **_In contrast_**, the apartment is small.

這房子很大。相反地，這公寓很小。

Some people think a tomato is vegetable. **On the contrary**, others think a tomato is fruit.

有些人認為番茄是蔬菜。相對地，其他人認為番茄是水果。

While ／ Whereas potato is high in nutrition, French fries are not.

雖然馬鈴薯營養很高，薯條卻不是。

Potato is high in nutrition. **However**, French fries are not.

馬鈴薯營養很高。然而，薯條卻不是。

On the one hand potato is high in nutrition; **on the other hand,** it takes much time to cook.

馬鈴薯一方面營養很高。另一方面卻要花很多時間調理。

04 形容詞比較級

1. 比較形容詞（－ er）

This peach is **better** than that one.　這顆桃子比那一顆好。

This peach is **redder** than the other one.　這顆桃子比那一顆紅。

2. 比較形容詞（more）

This pear is **more beautiful** than that one.　這顆梨比那一顆漂亮。

This pear is **more flavorful** than the other one. 這顆梨比另外一顆有味道。

 絕妙好例句

1. The more…the more…

   The more we find out the truth, **the more** we feel terrified.

   我們知道越多真相時，我們感到越害怕。

   The more the wave rose, **the faster** we ran.

   這浪升得越高，我們跑得越快。

The more he talked to the witness, ***the less*** he believed her.

他跟這證人談得越多，他就越不相信她。

The more time we have spent on the project, ***the fewer*** obstacles we find in the process.

我們在這計畫中花得時間越多，我們就會在過程中找到越少阻礙。

2. Prefer & Would rather

先注意 prefer 的用法

I prefer ***coffee*** to ***tea***.

我喜歡咖啡勝於茶。

→ coffee 跟 tea 是單純兩個名詞

I prefer ***drinking coffee*** to ***drinking tea***.

我喜歡喝咖啡勝於喝茶。

→ drinking coffee 跟 drinking tea 是動名詞所形成的兩件事，跟比較上一句兩個名詞是相同觀念

I prefer ***to drink coffee*** rather than（***drink***）***tea***.

我喜歡喝咖啡勝於喝茶。

→ 這一句子則是比較兩個動作 drink coffee 與 drink tea

prefer to…than…與 would rather…than…是同樣的句型，所接的都是原形動詞

I'd rather stay at home tonight than go to the cinema.

我寧願帶在家裡勝於去電影院。

＝ I prefer to stay at home than go to the cinema.

3. …as many ／ much as…

Linda has ***as many shoes as*** her older sister does.

Linda 跟她姐姐有一樣多的鞋。

➡ as many…as 接可數名詞

I drink **as much tea as** I drink coffee every day.

我每天喝一樣多的茶跟咖啡。

➡ as much…as 接不可數名詞

The living cost here is not **as high as** in the city.

這裡的物價沒有像城市那麼高。

➡ as…as 中間可加形容詞作比較

The senior employee doesn't work **as hard as** the newcomer.

這資深員工沒像新進人員工作一樣努力。

➡ as…as 中間也可加副詞作比較

As many as（**up to**）5 people were missing in this incident.

多達五人在這意外中失蹤。

➡ as many／much as ＋數量＝up to ＋數量，表示有多達…之多

4. 倍數＋ adj／adv ＋ than

The man weighs **three times heavier than** his wife.

這男人體重是他太太三倍。

➡ 倍數＋ adj. 比較級＋ than

＝ The man weighs **three times as much as** his wife.

＝ The man weighs **three times his wife's weight**.

I work twice harder than you do.

我工作比你雙倍地努力

➡ 倍數＋ adv. 比較級＋ than

＝ I work twice as much as you do.

5. A is to B as C is to D

Water is to plants as reading is to me.

閱讀對我來說就跟水對植物一樣重要。

→ 這是在比喻 water is to plants 水對植物來說就像 reading is to me 閱讀對我一樣重要。

= Water is to plants what reading is to me.

= As water is to plants, so is reading to me.

= Reading to me is like water to plants.

換你寫寫看

1. The language spoken in Brazil is different _____ the language spoken in Argentina.（than／from）

2. The lesson we had yesterday was similar _____ the today's lesson.（as／to）

3. The climates in these two places are _____ .（like／alike）

4. The dress she buys from that store is _____ than the one from this store.（beautifuller／more beautiful）

5. The car has the same color _____ the truck.（as／than）

6. I prefer _____（drive a car／driving a car）to _____（ride a bike ／riding a bike）.

7. We'd rather _____（invite／to invite）the guests over for dinner than _____（take／to take）them to a restaurant.

8. The more time I spend on practicing my English, _____（the better／ the well）I become in speaking and listening.

9. Sylvia doesn't do _____（as much／as many）exercise as her

doctor tells her to do.

10. She makes three times _____（more／much）than she used to.

● 答案與中譯解析

1. 答：from，在巴西所使用的語言在阿根廷使用的語言不同。

2. 答：to，我們昨天上的課跟今天的課很類似。

3. 答：alike，這兩個地方的天氣很像。

4. 答：more beautiful，她在那一家店買的洋裝比這一家店買的好看。

5. 答：as，這車子跟卡車的顏色一樣。

6. 答：driving a car; riding a bike，我喜歡開車勝於騎腳踏車。

7. 答：invite、take，我們寧願要請客人過來吃飯勝於帶他們去餐廳。

8. 答：the better，我花越多時間在練習我的英文上，我在口說與聽力上就變得越好。

9. 答：as much，Sylvia 並沒有做跟她醫生叫她做的運動一樣多。

10. 答：more，她賺三倍以前她所賺的薪水。

第6單元：附屬子句

名言範例：

The World is a book, and those who do not travel read only a page. 這個世界就像一本書，而那些不旅行的人只讀了一頁。

　　聖奧古斯丁（St. Augustine）（354 − 430）是早期西方的神學家與哲學家。在許多年前，旅遊還是極度不方便的年代，將足跡踏遍各地的渴望已存在人們的心中。在中文，也有非常相似的句子，「行萬里路勝讀萬卷書」，所以不論在東西方的思想裡，都認同旅行是想要了解這個世界，認識各地的風俗民情的最好方法。單元標題裡使用到的文法觀念是本單元所要介紹的附屬子句，其中 "who do not travel" 為一形容詞子句在修飾 those（people）。

英文達人文法小筆記！

附屬子句文法解析

在深入了解附屬子句的各種結構之前，了解附屬子句本身與其餘子句的定義差別將對於文法裡的許多句型結構與句子的連接將有更清楚的觀念。

01 獨立子句與非獨立子句（Independent and Dependent Clauses）
首先，就讓我們先來了解子句的定義。一個子句是由一組字所組合而成，其中有名詞或代名詞所代表的主詞，也有動詞或其他詞性的單字。那甚麼時候一個子句可以形成一個完整的句子呢？

讓我們看一下下面兩個例句：

When I studied in the library yesterday

I studied in the library yesterday

這兩個句子都有主詞（I）、動詞（studied）、介系詞（in）、當作介系詞受詞的名詞（the library）與時間副詞（yesterday）。但很明顯的第一個例句的意思尚未完整的表達完畢（當我昨天在圖書館念書的時候），而第二個句子相對地已經有完整的意思（我昨天在圖書館念書）。一個完整可獨立存在的句子（sentence）又稱做獨立子句（**dependent clause**），就像上面所舉出的第二個例句。而像第一個例句，意思尚未表達完整，無法單獨獨立構成一個句子，所以又稱做非獨立子句（**independent clause**）。加上標點符號會更清楚看出兩者的差別：

When I studied in the library yesterday,

I studied in the library yesterday.

而非獨立子句要如何形成一個句子呢？它必須要連結一個獨立子句來讓它的意思完整。如以下例句：

> Ex. When I studied in the library yesterday, I found that I left the notes at home.
>
> 當我昨天在圖書館念書的時候，我發現我把筆記放在家裡。

而因為非獨立子句無法單獨存在，必須與一個獨立子句連接，所以又稱做為附屬子句（Subordinate Clause），而所連接的獨立子句則又為主要子句（Main Clause）。連接附屬子句與主要子句的連接詞則稱為從屬連接詞（Subordinating Conjunction）。

02 附屬子句（Subordinate Clause）

根據附屬子句在句子中的使用，可分成三大類，形容詞子句、副詞子句與名詞子句。形容詞、副詞、與名詞子句的功能與性質就與形容詞、副詞、與名詞本身相同。

1. 副詞子句（Adverb Clause）

就跟副詞的功能一般，副詞子句（Adverb Clause）可修飾動詞、形容詞或副詞，或者是一個片語或子句。副詞子句跟副詞一樣可能出現在句子中的任何位置。

After the meeting was over, John decided to meet with his teammates to discuss the report.

在會議結束之後，John 決定跟他的組員碰面討論這份報告。

→ 副詞子句After the meeting was over 在這裡也為時間子句，在介紹John decided⋯這件事情發生的時間點。

a. 副詞子句的種類與所使用的從屬連接詞

時間	因果	對比	條件
after, before, when, while, as, once, by the time（that）, as soon as, since, until, whenever, the first time（that）, the next time（that）, the last time（that）, every time（that）	because, since, as, as long as, so long as, due to the fact that, now that	Although ＝ though ＝ even though, whereas, while	if, even if, only if, unless, in case（that）, providing（that）, provided（that）, in the event（that）, as long as

目的	讓步	限制	狀態
so that, in order that, lest	whether, no matter, no matter wh- = wh-ever（whenever, whoever, wherever, whatever, whichever, however）	as far as, in that	as, as if

b. When VS. While

Ex. The phone rang **when** Cindy opened the door.

Cindy 開門時電話響了。

→ When 連接的句子裡如果都是簡單式，when 之後的動作先發生。在這個例句中，Cindy opened the door 先發生，the phone rang 在之後發生。

Ex. **When** my friend called, we were having dinner.

當我朋友打電話來時，我們正在吃晚餐。

Ex. **While** we were having dinner, my friend called.

當我們正在吃晚餐時，我朋友打電話來。

→ 這裡以兩個不同的時態來表示兩個事件的時間關係。進行式代表持續進行的動作（we were having dinner），而在進行的當中，發生了另一件事件（my friend called）。

這時候在連接詞的選擇上，when 習慣接在簡單句之前，而 while 則是大多數放在進行式之前。

Ex. *While* she was studying hard for the test, her friends were having a party in the house.

當她正在努力念書準備考試的時候，她的朋友正在房子裡開派對。

➝ While 在這裡則是連接兩個進行式。

Ex. *While* some people are suffering from hunger, others are wasting much food.

當有些人受到飢餓的折磨，其他人卻在浪費許多食物。

➝ 這裡的 while 也當作直接對比的連接詞。

c. 標點符號的使用

Ex. We all went to bed early *because* we were all exhausted.

我們都很早睡因為我們都累壞了。

Ex. *Because* we were all exhausted, we went to bed early.

因為我們都累壞了，我們都很早睡。

➝ 在字義解釋上就可以看出附屬子句 because we were all exhausted 與主要子句 we all went to bed early 之間主與從的關係。而這個主從關係，也可以在之前獨立與非獨立子句的解釋了解到，因為非獨立子句無法單獨存在，必須依附另一獨立子句。所以在標點符號的使用上，如果附屬子句在主要子句之前，兩個子句需用逗號隔開。如是主要子句開始的句子，中間則不需要逗號隔開。

Ex. David buys it anyway *although* the suit is pricey.

David 還是買了雖然這西裝很貴。

= *Although* the suit is pricey, David buys it anyway.

雖然這西裝很貴，David 還是買了。

比較：The suit is pricey, **but** David buys it anyway.

這西裝很貴，但是 David 還是買了。

→ 之前說明了附屬子句裡標點符號的使用必須參照附屬子句與主要子句的位置。但 but 屬於對等連接詞（請參照連接詞單元），中間一定需用逗號分開，而對等連接詞與從屬連接詞不同的是對等連接詞所連接的為兩個獨立子句，其中並沒有主與從的關係。

d. 副詞子句中的時態使用

Ex. **After** I finish this project, I will take a short trip to Tainan.

在我完成這個專案後，我將到台南做短暫的旅遊。

Ex. We are going to give them a tour of our house first **when** the guests arrive tonight.

我們將先帶他們參觀我們的房子當客人今天晚上抵達的時候。

→ 當句子中表達不同未來時間發生的動作時，時間子句需使用現在時態。

Ex. I will walk to work **if** it doesn't rain tomorrow.

我將會走路上班如果明天不下雨的話。

= I will walk to work **unless** it rains tomorrow.

我將會走路上班除非明天下雨的話。

Ex. He will get the job done **as long as** he stops chatting and texting to his friends. 他將會把事情做好只要他停止傳簡訊跟朋友聊天。

Ex. **In case** you（should）need to have a discussion with me, I'll give you my office number.

萬一你需要跟我討論一下，我將會給你我的辦公室號碼。

→ If，as long as，in case（that）所引導的副詞子句又稱為條件子句。使用可能的條件的副詞子句中使用的是現在時態，主要子句則是表達將會發生的結果，使用的是未來時態。關於條件子句的用法，請參考假設語氣的單元。

2. 形容詞子句（Adjective Clause）

a. 形容詞子句（Adjective Clause）（關係子句 Relative Clause）修飾名詞或代名詞。為了讓形容詞子句與所修飾的名詞或代名詞關係明確，形容詞子句總是跟在所修飾的名詞或代名詞之後。

Ex. Our meeting, ***which starts at two in the afternoon***, discusses the importance of the budget cut.

我們在下午兩點的會議，討論預算縮減的重要性。

→ 形容詞子句 which starts at two in the afternoon 用來修飾 our meeting

b. 形容詞子句功能即為像形容詞，作用在修飾名詞。形容詞子句的位置一定是放在所修飾的名詞之後。而連接形容詞子句的連接詞又稱做關係代名詞（Relative Pronoun）。使用何種關係代名詞決定在之前所修飾的名詞為人、地方、時間或事物。首先先來認識關係代名詞的種類：

關係代名詞	例句
which → 事物	The ***food which*** we ate yesterday was delicious. 我們昨天吃的食物美味極了。
that → 人或事物	I've never talked to ***the man that*** is standing there. 我從來沒跟正站在那裡的男人說過話。
who(m) → 人	She is ***the teacher who(m)*** I told you about. 她就是我之前跟你提過的老師。

where → 地方	This is ***the school where*** I studied before. 這是我之前念書的學校。
when → 時間	It's so hard to find ***a day when*** everyone has time available. 很難去找到一天每個人都有空的時間。
whose → 所有	I know ***the student whose*** painting won the competition. 我認識這個贏繪畫比賽的學生。

c. 使用形容詞子句來結合句子

方法：首先在不同句子裡找出同為討論的名詞 然後再決定哪一句為主。

The teacher is nice.

He is in the classroom.

the teacher 跟 he 兩者是同一事物，所以在合併這兩個句子的時候，the teacher 即為句子中的主角，即是句子的主詞。再來就是決定要以哪一句子為主。

如果是以第一句為主要子句，第二句則是要變成形容詞子句跟在修飾的名詞之後：

Ex. The teacher ***who is in the classroom*** is nice.

那個在教室的老師很和善。

如果第二句為主要子句，則是將第一句變成形容詞子句跟在修飾的名詞之後：

Ex. The teacher ***who is nice*** is in the classroom.

那個很和善的老師在教室裡。

3. 名詞子句（Noun Clause）

a. 名詞子句（Noun Clause）擔任句子中主詞、受詞或補語的角色。許多時候名詞子句用於非直接或稱間接引用句（indirect speech or reported speech）。

Ex. Who is your favorite author? 你最喜歡的作者是誰？

Ex. Could you tell me *who your favorite author is*? 你可以告訴我你最喜歡的作者是誰嗎？

→ 第二句將第一句的問句引用在句子中，並將其改為一名詞子句，作為 tell 的間接受詞

b. 名詞在句中可能為主詞或受詞（請參照名詞子句）。相同的觀念可想見形容詞子句所修飾的 名詞可能在句子中是擔任主詞、動詞的受詞、或介系詞的受詞。這中間的差別將會決定其中的關係代名詞是否可以省略：

c. 所修飾的名詞作為主詞時，關係代名詞不可省略：

The dress is red.

It is in the closet.（it = the dress 在此為句子的主詞）

→ The dress *which* is in the closet is red.

→ The dress *that* is in the closet is red.

d. 所修飾的名詞作為動詞的受詞時，關係代名詞可省略：

The woman was my classmate.

I saw *her*.（her = the woman 在此為動詞 saw 的受詞）

→ The woman *who(m) I* saw was my classmate.（因修飾的名詞作為受詞時，關係代名詞 who 可用受格型式 whom 或是 that）

→ The woman *that* I saw was my classmate.

→ The woman(X) I saw was my classmate.（省略關係代名詞）

e. 所修飾的名詞作為介系詞的受詞時，關係代名詞可省略：

The bicycle is on sale.

I am looking at *it*.（it＝the bicycle 在此為介系詞 at 的受詞）

➔ The bicycle *at which* I am looking is on sale.

（介系詞放置於形容詞子句之前為較為正式的英語用法）

➔ The bicycle *which I* am looking at is on sale.

➔ The bicycle *that I* am looking at is on sale.

➔ The bicycle(X) I am looking at is on sale.（省略關係代名詞）

f. 英文基本句型：S＋V＋O（主詞＋動詞＋受詞），其中除了動詞 V 之外，其餘主詞 S 與受詞 O 為名詞或代名詞。

在了解英文基本句型與其中構成要素之後，各位還記得之前介紹子句的觀念中，一個子句包含了主詞、動詞以及其他可能詞性的單字。主詞在動詞（包含 Be 動詞與助動詞）之前形成了一般句，包括肯定與疑問句。而將動詞（包含 Be 動詞與助動詞）放置與主詞之前，則是形成了疑問句或是倒裝句。

What should we do?

疑問句：我們該怎麼做？

I wonder *what we should do?*

➔ 因為這疑問句要放在句中擔任動詞 wonder 的受詞，所以將疑問句 What should we do? 改成一般句 what we should do 為一名詞子句，就像名詞一般作 wonder 的受詞。

g. 名詞子句在句中的位置。

Where is he?　➔　問句（將在句子中變成名詞子句）

● 名詞子句為動詞的受詞

I don't know *where he is*. 我不知道他在哪裡。

● 名詞子句為介系詞的受詞

We never ask about *where he is*. 我們從來不去問他在哪裡。

● 名詞子句為主詞

Where he is remains a mystery. 他在哪裡仍然是個謎。

Ex. Where the bus station is?

→ Can you tell me where the bus station is?

你可以跟我講車站在哪裡嗎？

Ex. When does the next train come?

Do you know when the next train comes?

你知道下一班火車什麼時後到嗎？

注意：改成名詞子句之後即變成一般句。現在簡單式單數的第三人稱主詞（非單數的我或你）動詞人需加 s 或 es。

Ex. Where did you go last night.

→ You should tell me *where you went last night*.

你應該告訴我你昨晚去哪裡了？

注意：改成名詞子句時時態需保持一致。do ╱ does ╱ did 這三個助動詞先去掉，再將主詞放置與動詞之前。其餘助動詞與 Be 動詞則放置在主詞之後。

Ex. Can she finish the project on time.

→ We really need to know if ╱ whether she can finish the project on time.

我們真的需要知道她是否可以如期完成這個專案。

注意：疑問句如果是 Yes ╱ No 問句，也就是 Be 動詞或助動詞為首的疑問句，名詞子句則是以 if 或 whether 作連接。

換你寫寫看

1. I got a birthday present from my family. _____（When／While）I opened it, I _____（found／was finding）a surprise.

2. _____（Because／Although）the weather condition was so bad, I didn't go to school.

3. You'll feel tried at work tomorrow _____（if／unless）you stay up all night.

請填入適當的關係代名詞

4. Catherine is the lawyer _____ handled my case.

5. The teacher _____ class is 2A has much patience to her students.

6. The drink _____ you gave me is not a soda.

請將兩個句子合併，並以第一句為主要子句，第二句為形容詞子句。請寫出所有可以使用的關係代名詞：

7. The man comes from France. He is talking to me.

8. The story is fantastic. I have read it.

9. Everyone liked the pie. I made it.

請將以下疑問句改成名詞子句放在句中

10. Which one does she like? Let's ask her _____ .

11. Why did Lisa quit the job? _____ is a secret.

12. Are you leaving soon? Let me know _____ .

● 答案與中譯解析

1. 答：When、found（when 之後接簡單式，所接的動作 I opened it 先開始，再來是 I found a surprise）我收到一個我家人給我的生日禮物。當我打開時，我發現一個驚喜。

2. 答：Because（because 在句子中表達正確意思）因為天氣狀況如此地糟，我沒有去學校。

3. 答：if（if 在句子中表達正確意思）你明天上班將會覺得很累，如果你整晚熬夜的話。）

4. 答：who，Catherine 是之前處理我案子的律師。

5. 答：whose，那老師是 2A 的老師她對學生很有耐心。

6. 答：which or that，你之前給我的飲料不是汽水。

7. 答：The man who ／ that is talking to me comes from France.
   正在跟我說話的那個男人是從法國來的。

8. 答：The story that ／ which ／（X）I have read is fantastic.
   那我曾經讀過的故事很引人入勝。

9. 答：Everyone liked the pie that ／ which ／（X）I made.
   每個人都喜歡我做的派。

10. 答：Let's ask her which one she likes.　讓我們來問她她喜歡哪一個。

11. 答：Why Lisa quit the job is a secret.　Lisa 為何辭掉工作是個秘密。

12. 答：Let me know if ／ whether you are leaving soon.
   讓我知道你是否要很快離開了。

文法加油站

1. 句子中逗號使用方法

在英語中，只要是用逗號隔開的子句，放在句子中間，功能就是在做補充說明，這個觀念就像同位語的觀念。

Tokyo, **which is the capital of Japan,** is a very modern city.

（which is the capital of Japan 是一非限定形容詞子句。Tokyo 已經是一特定的城市，其後的形容詞子句只是在補充說明，不需再作限定縮小範圍。）

Tokyo, ***the capital of Japan,*** is a very modern city.

（the capital of Japan 是同位語也是在補充說明 Tokyo。）

東京，日本的首都，是一個很現代化的城市

重點：在使用逗號時，不可使用關係代名詞 that，也不可省略關係代名詞

> Ex. The man ***who(m)*** ／ ***that*** ／（***X***）***I met yesterday*** works at this company. 我昨天遇到的那個男人在這個公司上班。
>
> → 限定用法

> Ex. Mr. Thompson, ***who(m) I met yesterday,*** works at this company. Mr. Thompson，我昨天遇到的人，在這家公司上班。
>
> → 非限定，有逗號時，不可使用 that，也不可省略關係代名詞

2. 限定與非限定用法

（Restrictive and Nonrestrictive Adjective Clause）

關於限定與非限定的差別，首先先來看一下這兩個句子句義的差別：

There are 30 students in this class. 20 students passed the test. For those 20 students, they can get a certificate.

班上有 30 個學生，其中 20 個有通過考試。那 20 個通過的學生可以得到證書。

> Ex. The students ***who passed the test*** can get a certificate. → 這是限定的用法。首先 the students 是指這班上 30 個學生，利用形容詞子句 who passed the test 來限定縮小範圍到通過考試的那 20 個學生

> Ex. The students, ***who passed the test,*** can get a certificate. → 這是非限定的用法。the students 在此已經是指通過考試的那 20 個學生，形容詞子句 who passed the test 只是在做補充說明，並不會改變前面 the students 的範圍

3. 以 **that** 連接的名詞子句

句型	例句	其它
動詞＋that （that 可省略）	I believe that I can make it. ＝ I believe I can make it. 我相信我可以辦到。	think, feel, hope, know, understand, agree, decide, discover, hear, notice, remember
S ＋ Be ＋ adj. ＋ that（可省略）	I'm glad that you've found your wallet. ＝ I'm glad you've found your wallet. 我很慶幸你找到你的錢包。	sorry, happy, sure, surprised, worried, aware, afraid, angry, certain, disappointed, proud
It ＋ Be ＋ adj. ＋ that（可省略）	It's obvious that Oscar doesn't like his new teacher. ＝ It's obvious Oscar doesn't like his new teacher. 很明顯地 Oscar 不喜歡他的新老師。	clear, possible, strange, true, wonderful, important, strange
That －名詞子句作為主詞	（接上句）＝ That Oscar doesn't like his new teacher is oblivious.	

第7單元：假設語氣

名言範例：

Hold fast to dreams, for if dreams die, life is a broken-winged bird that cannot fly.

緊抓住你的夢想，不要讓它們流走或消失，因為如果夢想熄滅或死去的話，生命就像一隻折翼的鳥，無法在天空中飛翔。

這是一篇美國詩人Langston Hughes寫的短詩。這首短詩非常有詩意的但卻有力地比喻出夢想對人們的重要。不論年齡或背景，對於這個世界的好奇與新鮮都是啟發我們對於更多事物的想像力，也是我們不侷限自我勇於夢想以及追求實現的原動力。

英文文法達人小筆記！

假設法文法解析

假設語氣裡主要句型為 If 條件子句所形成的不同條件狀況，以下是四種不同的條件子句所構成的假設句型：

1. Conditional 0

If I am late, I take the taxi to work.

如果我遲到的話，我搭計程車上班。

→ 這是指經常發生的事件。If- 子句與主要子句皆為現在時態。在這種情況下，if 可以用 when 取代。

→ When I am late, I take taxi to work.

當我遲到的時候，我搭計程車上班。

2. Conditional 1

If it rains, we will stay at home.

如果下雨的話，我們將會待在家裡。

→ 這是在指可能會發生的事件，只要達到 if- 子句裡的條件，主要子句裡的事情就會成真。這裡的 if- 子句使用現在簡單式，而主要子句則是使用未來簡單式，或是使用助動詞 shall ／ can ／ may。

3. Conditional 2

If he worked harder, he would get the raise.

如果他工作更認真的話，他會得到加薪。

→ He doesn't get the raise.

→ 這是與現在或未來事實相反的假設，if- 子句中使用過去簡單式，而主要子句裡則根據句子的意思使用 would ／ should ／ could ／ might + V。

4. Conditional 3

If I had known the truth, I would have chosen to believe him.

如果我知道事實的話，我會選擇相信他。

＝ I didn't know the truth so I didn't believe him.

這是與過去事實相反的假設，if- 子句中使用過去完成式（had + p.p.），而主要子句裡則根據句子的意思使用 would ／ should ／ could ／ might + have + p.p.。

01 使用時機：

1.「萬一」的假設

2. 有可能成為事實的假設

3. 與現在事實相反

4. 與過去事實相反

5. 過去事實相反與現在事實混用

6. If 省略

7. Hope VS. Wish

02 使用特點：

1.「萬一」的假設

a. Should 在 if- 子句的用法：以 should 作假設的語氣，作萬一解釋。

Ex. If anyone should visit the company, please make an appointment in advance.

＝ If anyone visits the company, please make an appointment in advance.

萬一任何人要參觀公司，請事先預約。

Ex. If she should be here tomorrow, I will explain the whole thing to her. 萬一她明天在這裡，我會跟她解釋全部的事情。

比較 ➡ If she is here tomorrow, I will explain the whole thing to her. 如果她明天在這裡，我會跟她解釋全部的事情。

使用 should 在 if- 子句（If she should be here tomorrow）比較起使用現在時態（If she is here tomorrow）發生的機率較低。

b.「萬一」的其他用法：

Ex. ***In case***（that）the little baby（should）see a doctor, the parents will take a day off tomorrow.

萬一小嬰兒要看醫生，這父母明天將會請假。

Ex. ***What should I do if*** I forget to bring my passport?

萬一我忘記帶護照，我該怎麼辦？

= ***What if*** I forget to bring my passport?

2. 有可能成為事實的假設

平常或未來可能會發生的用法 Real Conditional

比較 Condition 0 與 Condition 1：

a. Conditional 0

If- 子句現在式＋主要子句現在式

Ex. If I have time, I usually walk the dog in the park.

如果我有時間，我通常會帶狗去公園散步。

→ 平常經常性會發生的事件。

b. Conditional 1

If- 子句現在式＋主要子句未來式或使用 shall ／ can ／ may

Ex. If I have time, I will walk the dog in the park ***tomorrow***.

如果我有時間，我明天會帶狗去公園散步。

→ 必須符合 if- 子句裡的條件才會發生。

 換你寫寫看

1. If it's cold, what _____ you usually wear?（A）are（B）did（C）do（D）X

2. If it's cold, what _____ you going to usually wear?（A)do（B)X（C) is（D)are

3. If you like the book, you _____ keep it.

（A)will（B)would（C)may（D)usually

4. If the train _____ , I will miss the seminar.（A)should be delayed（B) should be delaying（C)is delaying（D)delayed

● 答案與中譯解析

1. 答：(C) 如果很冷時，你通常會穿什麼？

2. 答：(D) 如果很冷的話，你將會穿什麼？

3. 答：(C) 如果你喜歡這書的話，你可以留著。

4. 答：(A) 萬一火車誤點的話，我將會錯過研討會。

3. 與現在事實相反

與現在或未來事實相反 Unreal Conditional（Conditional 2）：

If- 子句過去式＋主要子句 would ／ should ／ could ／ might ＋ V

注意：If- 子句過去式中的 Be 動詞一律使用 were

Ex. If I **had** wings, I **would** fly to anywhere that I wanted to be.

如果我有翅膀的話，我會飛到任何我想到的地方。

這一類的句子時常在做不可能的假設。人類不可能有翅膀，所以用這個假設語氣來代表與現實相反的情形。

＝ I don't have wings so I won't fly to any where that I want to be.

我沒有翅膀，所以我不會飛到任何我想到的地方。

Ex. I **would** give everyone more vacation days if I **were** the boss.

我會給每個人更多有薪假如果我是老闆的話。

103

→ 這是與現在事實完全相反的的假設，代表我不是老闆，也不會給每個人有薪假。

= I won't give everyone more vacation days since I'm not the boss.　我不會給每個人更多有薪假既然不我是老闆。

Ex. If I won the lottery, I *would* buy a house.
如果我中樂透的話，我將會去買房子。

→ If I won the lottery, I *could* buy a house.
如果我中樂透的話，我就可以去買房子。

這兩個句子的差別為 would 代表期望與想做的事，而 could 為 could be able to 表示達到某種能力。

 換你寫寫看

請將提供的句子改寫成與事實相反的假設句

e.g. She is very busy, that's why she doesn't go out very often.

→ If she weren't so busy she would go out more often.

1. Joe doesn't take any exercise, that's why he is so fat.

　→ _____ .

2. Amy is very shy, so she doesn't go to parties.

　→ _____ .

3. I don't know his email address so I can't write to him.

　→ _____ .

4. People drives very fast so there are many car accidents.

　→ _____ .

5. I don't have a dog so I'm often scared of walking at night.

　→ _____ .

● 答案與中譯解析

1. 答：Joe doesn't take any exercise, that's why he is so fat.

   Joe 不做任何運動，那就是他為何如此的胖。

   ➜ If Joe took any exercise, he wouldn't be so fat!

   如果 Joe 做任何運動，他就不會如此的胖了！

2. 答：Amy is very shy, so she doesn't go to parties.

   Amy 非常害羞，所以她不去參加派對。

   ➜ If Amy weren't very shy, she would go to parties.

   如果 Amy 不是非常害羞，她會去參加派對。

3. 答：I don't know his email address so I can't write to him.

   我不知道他的 email 住址所以我沒辦法寫信給他。

   ➜ If I knew his email address, I could write to him!

   如果我知道他的 email 住址，我就可以寫信給他了！

4. 答：People drive fast so there are many car accidents.

   人們開車很快所以造成很多的車禍。

   ➜ If people drove more slowly, there wouldn't ／ shouldn't ／ might not many car accidents.

   如果人們開車慢一點，就不會／應該不會／可能不會許多車禍。

5. 答：I don't have a dog, so I'm often scared of walking at night.

   我沒有狗，所以我常常害怕在晚上走路。

   ➜ If I had a dog, I wouldn't be often scared of walking at night.

   如果我有狗，我就不會害怕在晚上走路。

4. 與過去事實相反

I should have known better（*1964*）*by The Beatles*

a. 與過去事實相反 Past Conditional（Conditional 3）：

If- 子句過去完成式（had ＋ p.p.）＋主要子句 would ／ should ／ could

／ might ＋ have ＋ p.p.

Ex. I **wouldn't have gone** to the meeting if you had told me that it was cancelled.　我就不會去那會議如果你跟我說它取消的話。

真實情況　➡　I went to the meeting because you didn't tell me that it was cancelled.　我去了那會議因為你沒跟我說它取消了。

Ex. We **would have shopped** at that store if the salesperson had been nice to us.　我們會在那一間店消費如果店員對我們好的話。

真實情況　➡　We didn't shop at that store because the salesperson wasn't nice to us.　我們沒在那一間店消費因為店員對我們不好。

b. 過去式助動詞 should，could，would 加 have p.p. 可表示對過去曾經或不曾發生的事情一個相反的假設，表達後悔之意。

should have ／ could have ／ would have ＋ p.p.

Ex. I **should have applied** for the job.　我應該要申請那工作。

真實情況　➡　I didn't apply for the job.　我沒有申請那工作。

*should have 代表這件事是一個好主意，但是卻沒有做。

Ex. I **shouldn't have missed** the deadline.　我不應該錯過期限。

真實情況　➡　I missed the deadline.　我錯過了期限。

*shouldn't have 表示這件事不應該去做，但是卻去做了。

Ex. I **could have taken** the opportunity.　我其實可以把握這機會。

真實情況　➡　I didn't take the opportunity.　我沒有把握這機會。

*could have 代表本來可能可以做的選擇，但是沒有去做。

Ex. I **would have helped** you.　我本來會幫你的。

真實情況　➡　You didn't ask me for help　你沒有請求我的幫忙。

注意：would have 表示本來願意或將會發生的事情。

注意：should have，could have，would have 在句子中經常以縮寫型式 should've，could've，would've 出現，在口語中則是念成 shoulda，coulda，woulda。

換你寫寫看

請使用以下動詞，配合句子意思，搭配填入 should have／could have／would have＋p.p.

1. We _____ so much money on shopping last week.（spend）

2. I didn't know you were going to school. I _____ you there.（drive）

3. I _____ to the movies last night, but I was tired, so I just stayed home.（go）

4. Andy failed the test yesterday. He _____ more before he took the test.（study）

5. That was a terrible idea. Kathy _____ at the teacher like that.（yell）

6. I _____ hello to you in the cafeteria, but I didn't see you there.（say）

7. The manager is upset because the team didn't do well at the presentation. They really _____ more in advance.（prepare）

● 答案與中譯解析

1. 答：We **shouldn't have spent** so much money on shopping last week.
   我們上星期不應該花這麼多錢在血拼上。

2. 答：I didn't know you were going to school. I **would have driven** you there.

我不知道你要去上學。我本來可以載你過去的。

3. 答：I **could have gone** to the movies last night, but I was tired, so I just stayed home.

我昨天晚上其實可以去看電影，不過我很累，所以我待在家裡。

4. 答：Andy failed the test yesterday. He **should have studied** more before he took the test.

Andy 昨天考試沒通過。他應該在他考試前更認真念書。

5. 答：That was a terrible idea. Kathy **shouldn't have yelled** at the teacher like that.

那真是糟糕的主意。Kathy 不應該像那樣對老師大叫。

6. 答：I **would have said** hello to you in the cafeteria, but I didn't see you there.

我本來會在自助餐廳跟你打招呼的，但是我沒看到你。

7. 答：The manager is upset because the team didn't do well at the presentation. They really **should have prepared** more in advance.

這經理正在生氣因為這團隊在報告時表現不好。他們事先應該要多準備。

5. 過去事實相反與現在事實混用

a. 先與過去事實相反後與現在事實相反

I didn't eat breakfast this morning. ➡ 過去 （我今天早上沒有吃早餐。）

I feel hungry now! ➡ 現在（我現在感到餓了！）

➡ If I ***had eaten*** breakfast this morning, I ***would not feel*** hungry now.

如果我今天早上有吃早餐的話，我現在就不會感到餓了。

這個句子是在結合與過去事實相反 If- 子句過去完成式（had + p.p.）

I didn't eat breakfast this morning

➡ If I ***had eaten*** breakfast this morning.

以及與現在事實相反 主要子句 would ／ should ／ could ／ might + V

I feel hungry now ➡ I ***would not feel*** hungry now

b. 先與現在事實相反後與過去事實相反

He is not a responsible employee. ➡ 現在(他不是一個負責的員工。)

He did not finish the work on time. ➡ 過去（他沒有準時完成工作。）

➡ If he ***were*** a responsible employee, he ***would have finished*** the work on time. 他如果是個好員工的話，他之前就會把工作準時完成。

這個句子是在結合與現在事實相反 If- 子句過去式

He is not a responsible employee

➡ If he ***were*** a responsible employee

以及與過去事實相反主要子句 would ／ should ／ could ／ might + have + p.p.

He did not finish the work on time

➡ he ***would have finished*** the work on time

換你寫寫看

請以第一個句子為If- 子句結合題目中兩個句子

1. I stayed up all night last night. I am tired now.

    ➡ _____ .

2. I don't know how to speak Italian. I didn't talk to the man.

    ➡ _____ .

3. You didn't open the window.The room is so hot.

    ➡ _____ .

● 答案與中譯解析

　1. 答：If I had not stayed up all night last night, I would not be tired now.
　　　　如果我昨晚沒有整晚熬夜的話，我現在就不會累了。

　2. 答：If I knew how to speak Italian, I would have talked to the man.
　　　　如果我會講義大利文的話，我之前就會跟那男人講話。

　3. 答：If you had opened the window, the room would not be so hot.
　　　　如果你之前有開窗戶的話，房間也不會那麼熱了。

6. If 省略

If- 子句中如有出現 *should*，*were*，*had*，可省略 if，再將 *should*，*were*，*had* 倒裝至主詞之前

　　Ex. *Should* it rain tomorrow, we will cancel the company picnic.

　　　= If it should rain tomorrow, we will cancel the company picnic.

　　　　萬一下雨的話，我們將會取消公司野餐。

Ex. **Were** your father here, he would be so proud of you.

　= If your father were here, he would be so proud of you.

　　如果你父親在這裡，他會為你感到非常地驕傲。

Ex. **Had** you been in the same situation, you would have also told the truth.

　= If you had been in the same situation, you would have also told the truth.　如果你之前在同樣的情況下，你也會說實話的。

7. Hope VS. Wish

a. Hope（針對過去的事情，使用過去簡單式）

　Ex. I hope she **found** the company.　我希望她有找到那公司。

　Ex. I hope he **passed** the driving test.　我希望他有通過駕駛考試。

b. Hope（針對現在的事情，使用現在簡單或現在進行式）

　Ex. I hope everyone is alright.　我希望每個人都沒事。

　Ex. I hope my friends **are having fun** at the party.

　　我希望我的朋友都正在派對上玩的開心。

c. Hope（針對未來的事情，較常用現在簡單，但也可以使用未來簡單式）

　Ex. I hope she **comes** to visit us next year.

　　我希望她明年可以來拜訪我們。

　= I hope she **will come** to visit us next year.

　　重點：Wish 的用法跟假設語氣是一樣的觀念

d. Wish（針對過去的事情，使用過去完成式）

　Ex. He wishes he **had passed** the driving test.　他但願他有通過考試。

　➡ He didn't pass the driving test.（與過去事實相反）

111

e. Wish（針對現在的事情，使用過去簡單式）

Ex. I wish I *had* a million dollars.　我但願我有一百萬。

→ I don't have a million dollars.（與現在事實相反）

f. Wish（針對未來的事情，使用 would）

Ex. I wish he *would* quit smoking soon.　我但願他會盡早戒菸。

→ Maybe he will quit smoking soon.（對未來事件的假設）

換你寫寫看

1. I wish I _____ a bigger house. I can't have a party here.（have）

2. I hope she _____ a good job soon.（get）

3. I hope you _____ at the party last night.（have a good time）

4. I hope she _____ the restaurant tonight.（find）

5. I wish I _____ the singer when he came to my city two years ago.
（meet）

6. I wish doctors _____ the cure for cancer in the near future.（have）

● 答案與中譯解析

1. 答：I wish I *had* a bigger house. I can't have a party here.
　　我但願我有一個更大的房子。我現在這邊沒辦法辦派對。

2. 答：I hope she *gets*／*will* get a good job soon.　我希望她能盡快找到工作。

3. 答：I hope you *had a good time* last night.　我希望你昨天晚上玩得開心。

4. 答：I hope she *finds*／*will* find the restaurant tonight.
　　我希望她今天晚上會找到這餐廳。

5. 答：I wish I *had met* the singer when he came to my city two years ago.
　　我但願我在那歌手兩年前來我的城市時我有遇見他。

6. 答：I wish doctors *would have the* cure for cancer in the near future.
　　我但願醫生能在不久的將來找到癌症的解藥。

第8單元：疑問句

名言範例：

Student："Dr. Einstein, aren't these the same questions as last years'."

Dr. Einstein："Yes. But this year the answers are different."

學生：「愛因斯坦教授，這不是去年的考卷嗎？」

愛因斯坦：「對，但是答案跟去年的不一樣。」

　　愛因斯坦是二十世紀偉大的科學家。他一直思考與世界有關的物理問題。有一天他在他所任教的大學給學生出期末考考卷，學生質疑反應題目與去年期末考考題相同，愛因斯坦回答說：是的，但答案與去年不同。愛因斯坦意在告訴學生不要拘泥於固有的框架與答案，要跳脫出來，才有新視野。

英文達人文法小筆記！

英文疑問句分為三種：

（一）以Be動詞為句首（二）以助動詞為句首（三）以疑問詞為句首。

1. 以Be動詞為句首

a. 中文翻譯為「是」的動詞為英文的Be動詞。例如：is，am，are，was，were。有這些動詞的句子，移動Be動詞到句首成為疑問句。Be動詞與主詞一致表如下：

I 我	am ／ was	we 我們	are ／ were
You 你	are ／ were	you 你們	are ／ were
he ／ she ／ it 他／她／它	is	they 他們	are ／ were

Ex. He is a good student. ➙ Is he a good student.

是一位好學生。 ➙ 他是一位好學生嗎？

2. 以助動詞為句首句子若有一般動詞，變成疑問句時，助動詞放在句首，主詞後面的動詞變成原形動詞，成為疑問句。

a. 當主詞為第三人稱單數時，助動詞為 does。第三人稱單數： he（他）、she（她）、it（它）。

Ex. He has a new book. ➙ Does he have a new book.

他有一本新書。 ➙ 他有一本新書嗎？

b. 第一人稱單數、複數和第二人稱單數、複數，第三人稱複數，助動詞為 do。第一人稱： I（我）、we（我們）。第二人稱： you（你）、you（你們）、they（他們）。

Ex. You finish your homework. ➙ Do you finish your homework.

你完成你的家庭作業。 ➙ 你完成你的家庭作業了嗎？

c. 過去式的助動詞一律用 did。

Ex. He went to school yesterday. ➙ Did he go to school yesterday.

他昨天去學校。 ➙ 他昨天去學校了嗎？

3. 以情態助動詞為句首：情態助動詞為 may〈可以／祝願〉，can〈能夠／可以〉，must〈必須〉，should〈應該〉，could〈能夠〉，would〈會／願意〉，will〈將〉，might〈可以〉，這些情態助動詞

有其特定的意義以表達特定的態度和意見。而這些情態助動詞不能單獨存在，必須和原形動詞一起使用，不會因主詞人稱或數量不同而有所不同。在疑問句中，情態助動詞當句首。

Ex He can speak English. ➡ Can he speak English.

他可以說英語。 ➡ 他可以說英語嗎？

Ex He should tell the truth. ➡ Should he tell the truth.

他應該說實話。 ➡ 他應該說實話嗎？

4. 以疑問詞為句首：英文有五大疑問詞當疑問句句首為 where，when，what，who 和 how。助動詞和主詞一致，其句型為：

a. 疑問詞＋Be 動詞＋主詞？

Ex Where is my book? 我的書在哪裡？

b. 疑問詞＋助動詞＋主詞＋原形動詞？

Ex What do you think? 你在想什麼？

特例！以 Which one 為疑問詞句首，用於人或事的二選一選擇。

Ex Which one do you like, Jenny or Jean?

你喜歡哪一人，Jenny 還是 Jean ？

 絕妙好例句

1. Are they new students?（Be 動詞當句首）他們是新學生嗎？

2. Does John walk to school every day?（現在式助動詞 does 當句首，第三人稱單數當主詞）John 每天走路學校嗎？

3. Do they have a good time?（現在式助動詞 do 當句首，第三人稱複數當主詞）他們玩的愉快嗎？

4. Did he eat his lunch?（過去式助動詞 did 當句首）他吃過午餐嗎？

5. How are you?（疑問詞當句首）你好嗎？

6. Which one do you like? Coffee or tea?（疑問詞當句首，有兩個選項）你喜歡哪一個？咖啡還是茶？

換你寫寫看

1. _____ he a good teacher?

2. _____ they like your book?

3. _____ he take a bus to school every day?

4. _____ do they come from?

● 答案與中譯解析

1. 答：Is（第三人稱單數 he 當主詞，疑問句以 Be 動詞當句首，he 的 Be 動詞為 is）他是一位好老師嗎？

2. 答：Do（第三人稱複數 they 當主詞，疑問句以助動詞當句首，they 的助動詞為 do）他們喜歡你的書嗎？

3. 答：Does（第三人稱單數 he 當主詞，疑問句以助動詞當句首，he 的助動詞為 does）他每天搭公車上學嗎？

4. 答：Where（疑問詞 where 當句首，第二人稱單數 you 當主詞，助動詞放在主詞前面）他們來自哪裡？

第9單元：附加問句

名言範例：

A toothbrush is a non-lethal object, isn't it?

牙刷是一支非致命的東西，不是嗎？

　　此句話出自美國電影《刺激 1995》（The Shawshank Redemption）是一部 1994 年上映的美國電影，電影中的男主角安迪由提姆 • 羅賓斯飾演，男配角由摩根 • 費里曼飾演，劇情主要圍繞著安迪在獄中的生活，闡述希望、自由、體制化等概念。此句話為摩根 • 費里曼給劇中男主角一把牙刷的一句話：牙刷是一支非致命的東西，不是嗎？

英語達人文法小筆記！

附加問句文法解析

附加問句是放在直述句後的問句，表示「（不）是嗎？」、「是嗎？」、「對嗎？」。直述句是肯定句時，附加問句為否定。直述句是否定句時，附加問句為肯定。附加問句的主詞需與直述句主詞的人稱代名詞一致。

01 使用方法

1. Be 動詞的附加問句

直述句的動詞為 Be 動詞時，句型如下：

a. 主詞＋肯定句，Be 動詞否定式縮寫＋主詞之代名詞？

b. 主詞＋否定句，Be 動詞肯定式＋主詞之代名詞？

　　Ex. Angela is smart, isn't she?　Angela 很聰明，不是嗎？

　　Ex. The school isn't big, is it?　這所學校不大，對吧？

2. 一般動詞的附加問句

直述句的動詞為一般動詞時，句型如下：

a. 主詞＋一般動詞肯定句，助動詞否定式縮寫＋主詞之代名詞？

b. 主詞＋一般動詞否定句，助動詞肯定式＋主詞之代名詞？

　　Ex. He likes jogging in the park, doesn't he?

　　　　他喜歡在公園裡慢跑，不是嗎？

　　Ex. You didn't believe me, did you? 你不相信我，對吧？

02 文法重點

1. 主詞是 I 時，附加問句為 am I not, am not 不能縮寫，口語常用代替 aren't I 代替。

　　Ex. I am beautiful, am I not?（我是漂亮的，不是嗎？）

2. 情態助動詞 will ／ can ／ should 的附加問句與完成式助動詞 have 的附加問句

a. 主詞＋有助動詞肯定句，助動詞否定式縮寫＋主詞之代名詞？

b. 主詞＋有助動詞否定句，助動詞肯定式＋主詞之代名詞？

　　Ex. You can't ride a bicycle, can you?　你不會騎腳踏車，不是嗎？

　　Ex. She has gone to Japan, hasn't she?　她已經去日本，不是嗎？

119

3. 直述句有 **have ／ has to** 時，附加問助動詞為 **do ／ does**。

> Ex. They have to go to school quickly, don't they?
>
> 他們必須快速回學校，不是嗎？

4. 若直述句的主詞為 **there**，附加問句主詞為 **there**。若直述句的主詞為 **this** 和 **that**，附加問句主詞為 **it**。若直述句的主詞為 **these** 和 **those**，附加問句主詞為 **they**。

> Ex. There is a bank near here, isn't there?
>
> 附近有一間銀行，不是嗎？

> Ex. This is a good book, isn't it?　這是一本好書，不是嗎？

> Ex. Those are your pencils, aren't they?　那些是你的鉛筆，不是嗎？

5. 若直述句有否定意味的字，如 **no**、**no one**、**nobody**、**nothing**、**few**（很少，用於可數名詞）、**little**（很少，用於不可數名詞）、**seldom**（不常）、**never**（從不）等，附加問句為肯定句。

> Ex. He never plays basketball with you, does he?
>
> 他從沒與你打籃球，對吧？

> Ex. Few students were present yesterday, were they?
>
> 昨天很少學生出席，不是嗎？

03 延伸文法結構

1. 若直述句的主詞為 **something**、**everything**、**nothing**、**anything**、虛主詞 **it**、不定詞、動名詞，附加問句主詞為 **it**。

> Ex. Everything is perfect, isn't?　每件事都完美，不是嗎？

> Ex. It is wonderful to meet you here, isn't it?
>
> 在這裡遇見你真棒，不是嗎？

Ex. Eating less doesn't make you healthy, does it?

吃少一點並不會使你健康，對吧？

2. 若直述句的主詞為 **everyone**、**everybody**、**no one**、**nobody**，主要子句動詞用單數動詞，附加問句的主詞用複數代名詞 **they**，動詞用複數動詞。

Ex. Everybody looks happy, don't they?

每個人看起來快樂，不是嗎？

3. 祈使句的附加問句一律為 **will you**。

Ex. Please open the window, will you? 請打開窗戶，好嗎？

4. 有邀請意味的祈使句，附加問句為 **won't you**。

Ex. Have some tea, won't you? 喝些茶，好嗎？

5. **Let's not** 的附加問句為 **OK** 或 **all right**。**Let's** … 的附加問句為 **shall we**。

Ex. Let's go back home, shall we? 讓我們回家去，好嗎？

6. **too**…**to**…的附加問句為否定式。

Ex. He is too short to play basketball, isn't he?

他太矮以致於不能打籃球，不是嗎？

 絕妙好例句

1. Your parents are always here for you, aren't they?（Be 動詞的否定式附加問句）你的父母親永遠在你身邊，不是嗎？

2. You have never been to Canada, have you?（有否定意味字詞 never 的附加問句）你從未去過加拿大，不是嗎？

121

3. Everyone has to finish one project, don't they?（直述句有 have ／ has to 時，附加問句助動詞為 do ／ does）每個人必須完成一個計畫，對吧？

4. I am your best friend, am I not?（主詞是 I 時，附加問句為 am I not）我是你最好的朋友，不是嗎？

5. Don't lie to us, will you?（祈使句的附加問句一律為 will you）不要對我們說謊，好嗎？

6. Andy wants to be a scientist in the future, doesn't he?（一般動詞的否定式附加問句）Andy 想要在將來成為一位科學家，是嗎？

7. Going to bed early is good for your health, isn't it?（動名詞當直述句的主詞）早睡有益你的健康，不是嗎？

換你寫寫看

1. Joe is not a teacher, _____ ?

2. Rachel likes to drink a cup of coffee after lunch, _____ ?

3. Playing computer games is interesting, _____ ?

4. You have to arrive at the train station before 6 pm, _____ ?

5. There will be a show on TV tomorrow, _____ ?
   (A)will it (B)won't it (C)will there (D)won't there

6. Have some coffee, _____ ?
   (A)is it (B)won't you (C)isn't it (D)will you

7. He is tired because he worked very late last night, _____ ?
   (A)didn't he (B)isn't he (C)did he (D)is he

● 答案與中譯解析

1. 答：isn't he（有 Be 動詞的肯定句，附加問句為否定式，主詞為 Joe 人稱代名詞）

2. 答：doesn't she（有一般動詞的肯定句，附加問句為助動詞否定式縮寫，主詞為 Rachel 人稱代名詞）

3. 答：isn't it（動名詞當直述句的主詞，附加問句主詞為 it）

4. 答：don't you（直述句有 have ／ has to 時，附加問助動詞為 do ／ does）

5. 答：(D)（直述句的主詞為 there，附加問句主詞為 there。附加問句為助動詞否定式縮寫）

6. 答：(B)（有邀請意味的祈使句，附加問句為 won't you）

7. 答：(B)（附加問句依主要子句來造問句）

1
2
3
4
5
6
7
8
9
10

第10單元：間接問句

名言範例：

I can see how it might be possible for a man to look down upon the earth and be an atheist, but I cannot conceive how a man could look up into the heavens and say there is no God.

我可以了解當一個人從天上看地球時那一個人可能是無神論者。但我不認為當一個人抬頭看上天時，會說沒有上帝的存在。

　　Abraham Lincoln 亞伯拉罕‧林肯是美國最偉大的總統其中之一。他在 1861 年當選美國總統，當時美國因應否解放黑奴問題，南北發生衝突，引發了南北戰爭。

英文達人文法小筆記！

間接問句文法解析

當一個問句放入句子中間，而非句首，則成為間接問句，當「名詞子句」，當作其前面動詞或介系詞的受詞。間接問句後面的標點符號視主要子句決定。疑問句成為間接問句。疑問句中的主詞、助動詞與動詞的位置將會有變化。其變化如下：

01 使用時機：

1. 有 be 動詞的間接問句

間接問句的動詞為 Be 動詞時，句型如下：

主要子句＋疑問詞＋主詞＋Be 動詞

要訣：只要將疑問句中的 Be 動詞與主詞對調，成為直述句句型。

> Ex. I don't know that.
>
> Who is he?
>
> → I don't know who he is.（間接問句中，Be 動詞與主詞對調）
>
> 我不知道他是誰。

2. 有一般動詞的間接問句

間接問句的動詞為一般動詞時，句型如下：

主要子句＋疑問詞＋主詞＋一般動詞

要訣：一定要將疑問句中的助動詞去掉，動詞恢復成原來的時態，成為直述句句型。也就是如果去掉的助動詞為過去式，則動詞就必須恢復成為過去式。若去掉的助動詞為 does，間接問句的動詞就必須加 s 或 es。

> Ex. I don't know that.
>
> Where did he go?
>
> → I don't know where he went.（去掉的助動詞為過去式，動詞 go 恢復成為過去式 went）
>
> 我不知道他去哪裡。

3. 沒有疑問詞的疑問句沒有疑問詞的 **yes-no** 疑問句，分為三種

a. 以 Be 動詞為句首的 yes-no 疑問句，句型如下：

主要子句＋ if ／ whether ＋主詞＋ Be 動詞

要訣：將 yes-no 疑問句中的 Be 動詞與主詞對調，成為直述句句型，在

間接問句前面加 if ／ whether（是否）。

Ex. I don't know that.

Is she a good teacher?

→ I don't know if ／ whether she is a good teacher.

（Be 動詞與主詞對調，在間接問句前面加 if ／ whether）

我不知道她是否是一位好老師。

b. 以 do、did、does 助動詞為句首的 yes-no 疑問句，句型如下：

主要子句＋ if ／ whether ＋主詞＋原來時態的動詞

要訣：將 yes-no 疑問句中的 do、did、does 助動詞去掉，成為直述句句型

在間接問句前面加 if ／ whether（是否）。

Ex Please tell me.

Did he finish his homework?

→ Please tell me if ／ whether he finished his homework.

（did 助動詞去掉，在間接問句前面加 if ／ whether，動詞變成原時態）

請告訴我他是否完成他的家庭作業。

c. 以 can、will 等情態助動詞為句首的 yes-no 疑問句，句型如下：

主要子句＋ if ／ whether ＋主詞＋情態助動詞＋原形動詞

要訣：將 yes-no 疑問句中的 can、will 等情態助動詞移到主詞後面，成為直述句句型，在間接問句前面加 if ／ whether（是否）。

Ex. He didn't tell me.

Could I eat my breakfast there?

→ He didn't tell me if ／ whether I could eat my breakfast there.

（將情態助動詞移到主詞後面，在間接問句前面加if／whether）

他沒告訴我是否可以在那裏吃早餐。

d. 若間接問句句首字詞為when ／ if，則須注意是否為副詞子句，則時態須注意。間接問句的時間若為未來式，則須用現在式代替未來式。當 when 和if 意思是（何時）和（是否），則該間接問句為名詞子句，其後動詞的時態與一般用法相同，亦即若時間為未來，則仍用未來式。若 when 和if意思是（當…的時後）和（假如），則該間接問句為副詞子句，且時態為未來式時，其動詞的時態則須現在式代替未來式。

Ex. Please tell me.

When will he come back tomorrow?

→ Please tell me when he will come back tomorrow.

（when 的意思為「何時」，間接問句，為名詞子句用未來式。）

請告訴我明天他何時回來。

Ex. Please tell me the truth.

When will he come back tomorrow?

→ Please tell me the truth when he comes back tomorrow.

（when 的意思為「當…的時候」，間接問句為副詞子句，用現在式代替未來式。）

請告訴我實情，當他明天回來的時候。

特例！！

有些間接問句本身是主詞或修飾主詞，此類問句原本就沒有「倒裝」，故不用恢復成直述句。

Ex. Do you know?

What made him so happy?

→ Do you know what made him so happy?

你知道什麼使得他如此快樂？

 絕妙好例句

1. Do you know how he goes to school?（間接問句中助動詞 does 去掉，變成直述句，主詞為第三人稱單數，動詞 go + es。）

   你知道他如何上學的嗎？

2. He forgot how many students there were in the classroom.（間接問句中 were there 改成 there were，變成直述句。）

   他忘記有多少學生在教室裡。

3. Do you know what he did at his birthday party?（間接問句中助動詞 did 去掉，變成直述句，動詞 do 變成過去式 did。）

   你知道他在他的生日派對做了什麼？

4. Tell me if ／ whether he can speak English.（yes-no 疑問句變成間接問句，將情態助動詞 can 到間接問句主詞後面，變成直述句，間接問句句首加 if ／ whether。）告訴我他是否會說英文。

5. Do you remember how old he is?（間接問句中 Be 動詞與主詞對調。）你記得他年紀多大了？

6. Do you know what is wrong with him?（間接問句 what 本身是主詞，此類問句原本就沒有倒裝）你知道他怎麼了嗎？

換你寫寫看

1. Do you know? What did Jane do yesterday?

   ➡ _____ .

2. I don't remember. Has he ever been to Japan?

   ➡ _____ .

3. I don't know. Where should I go?

   ➡ _____ .

4. When is the TV show? Do you know?

   ➡ _____ .

5. Do you know _____ ？（A)what is the matter with him （B)what the matter is with him （C)who is he （D)where he go

---

● 答案與中譯解析

1. 答：Do you know what he did yesterday?（間接問句中助動詞 did 去掉，變成直述句，動詞 do 變成過去式 did。）你知道他昨天做什麼嗎？

2. 答：I don't remember whether ／ if he has ever been to Japan.（Yes-no 疑問句變成間接問句，將現在完成式助動詞 has 移到間接問句主詞後面，變成直述句，間接問句句首加 if ／ whether。）我不記得他是否去過日本。

3. 答：I don't know where I should go.（間接問句中，將情態助動詞 should 移到間接問句主詞後面，變成直述句，間接問句句首加 If ／ whether。）我不知道我應該去哪裡。

4. 答：Do you know when the TV show is?（間接問句中 Be 動詞與主詞對調）你知道電視表演是什麼時候？

5. 答：(A)（間接問句 what 本身是主詞，此類問句原本就沒有倒裝）你知道他怎麼了？

第11單元：分詞構句

名句範例

A kind heart is a fountain of gladness, making everything in its vicinity freshen into smile.

一顆善良的心就像欣喜的噴泉，使周遭的每一件事都顯出清新的笑容。

　　華盛頓・歐文（Washington Irving）（1783-1859），是美國著名作家、短篇小說家、也是一名律師，曾當過政府官員，是對西班牙與英國的外交官。句子中原本有一形容詞子句 "which makes everything in its vicinity freshen into smiles" 來修飾 A kind heart。這一句形容詞子句省略 which 以及將 makes 改成 making 形成了一分詞構句。

英文達人文法小筆記！

分詞構句文法解析：

分詞構句可以由形容詞子句或副詞子句簡化，或將兩個句子合併，將其中一主詞省略（形容詞子句的用法請參照第六單元附屬子句）

01 簡化形容詞子句

1. 省略關係代名詞與 Be 動詞

　　Ex. I've never talked to the man ~~that is~~ standing there.

我從來沒跟正站在那裡的男人說過話。

→ I've never talked to the man standing there.

The topics ~~which are~~ discussed in class are related to the current events. 上課討論的話題與時事相關。

→ The topics discussed in class are related to the current events.

2. 省略關係代名詞並將一般動詞改成 V-ing

The singer ~~who made~~ his debut album a big hit has created more popular songs. 這位初張專輯就造成轟動的歌手一直推出受人歡迎的歌曲。

→ The singer making his debut album a big hit has created more popular songs.

Anyone ~~who wants~~ to attend the conference has to sign up early. 所有想參加這個研討會的人必須及早登記。

→ Anyone wanting to attend the conference has to sign up early.

3. 形容詞子句若是有其他主詞則無法簡化

The woman who I saw was my classmate. 我看到那女人是我以前的同學。

→ The woman I saw was my classmate.（只可省略關係代名詞）

Everyone liked the pie that I made.（每個人都喜歡我做的派。）

→ Everyone liked the pie I made.

4. 非限定形容詞子句簡化時變成同位語

We visited Penghu, ~~which are~~ islands located in the Taiwan Strait. 我們之前拜訪澎湖，是位於台灣海峽的島。

→ We visited Penghu, islands located in the Taiwan Strait.

（Penghu = islands located in the Taiwan Strait.）

換你寫寫看

請將以下形容詞子句簡化

1. The girl who is talking on the phone is my best friend.

2. His company, which was based in New York, filed bankruptcy last week.

3. Something that smells bad may be rotten.

4. I met Cindy, who was Jack's wife, when I stopped by their place.

5. Have you read the crime novel which is written by J.K. Rowling?

● 答案與中譯解析

1. 答：The girl talking on the phone is my best friend.
   這個正在講電話的女生是我最好的朋友。

2. 答：His company, based in New York, filed bankruptcy last week.
   他的公司，設立於紐約，上星期宣佈破產。

3. 答：Something smelling bad may be rotten!
   聞起來很糟的東西有可能就是壞掉了！

4. 答：I met Cindy, Jack's wife, when I stopped by their place.
   我遇到Cindy，Jack 的老婆，當我去他們家拜訪的時候。

5. 答：Have you read the crime novel written by J.K. Rowling?
   你有讀過J.K. Rowling 寫的犯罪小說嗎？

---

02 簡化副詞子句

（副詞子句的用法請參照第六單元附屬子句）

1. 如何簡化副詞子句

確定副詞子句與主要子句兩個主詞是同一主詞才可簡化。

a. 省略副詞子句中的主詞與 Be 動詞

Ex. While I was having dinner, I heard the phone ring.

當我在吃晚餐時，我聽到電話響。

→ While having dinner, I heard the phone ring.

b. 省略副詞子句中的主詞並將一般動詞改成 V-ing

Ex. After I finished the assignment, I went to the party.

在做完這工作後，我去了派對。

→ After finishing the assignment, I went to the party.

2. 不同的種類的副詞子句的簡化

a. 表達時間關係的副詞子句 after，before，since，when，while

Ex. Before I came to Taiwan, I lived in the United States.

我來台灣之前，我住在美國。

→ Before coming to Taiwan, I lived in the United States.

b. while 連接的句子，while 也可省略

Ex. While I was having dinner, I heard the phone ring.

當我在吃晚餐時，我聽到電話響。

→ While having dinner, I heard the phone ring.

→ Having dinner, I heard the phone ring.

c. 表達因果關係的副詞子句 because 也可省略

Ex. Because he wants to make more money, he's looking for a second

job.　因為他想要多賺些錢，他正在找第二份工作。

→ Wanting to make more money, he's looking for a second job.

Ex. Because I didn't want to hurt her feeling, I didn't tell her the truth.

因為我不想傷害她的感受，我沒有告訴她實話。

133

→ Not wanting to hurt her feeling, I didn't tell her the truth.

Ex. ~~Because I have lived~~ in that city before, I have many friends there.

因為我之前住過那城市，我有很多朋友在那。

→ Having lived in that city before, I have many friends there.

Ex. ~~Because I had read~~ the book, I didn't want to read it again.

因為我之前已經讀過那本書了，我不想再讀一遍。

→ Having read the book, I didn't want to read it again.

Ex. ~~Because she was~~ nervous about flying, she couldn't sleep that night. 因為她對搭飛機很緊張，她那一晚都睡不著。

→ Being nervous about flying, she couldn't sleep that night.

→ Nervous about flying, she couldn't sleep that night.

（Be 動詞可省略）

d. when 所形成的副詞子句，簡化的子句前可加 upon 或 on

Ex. ~~When she heard~~ the news, she was so surprised!

當她聽到這消息時，她十分的驚訝！

→ When hearing the news, she was so surprised.

→ Upon hearing the news, she was so surprised.

→ On hearing the news, she was so surprised.

03 合併句子再簡化

要合併句子再簡化時，首先要確定兩個句子的主詞一樣。再來決定那一個主要子句。

1. 省略主詞與 Be 動詞

Ex. ~~I was~~ watching a horror movie last night.

I didn't feel scared at all. → 主要子句

→ Watching a horror movie last night, I didn't feel scared at all.

昨晚看恐怖電影，我一點都不覺得害怕。

Ex. ~~The teacher was~~ interrupted by the students all the time.

He finally got upset. → 主要子句

→ Interrupted by the students all the time, the teacher finally got upset. 一直被學生打斷，這老師終於生氣了。

（合併之後主詞只出現過一次，所以不用代名詞。）

Ex. ~~The car is~~ the fastest car in the world.

Needless to say, it's very expensive. → 主要子句

→ Being the fastest car in the world, needless to say, the car is very expensive. 做為世界上最快的車，不用說，這一定很貴。

（如過 Be 動詞之後是說明主詞的補語，Be 動詞不可省略，改成 being）

2. 省略主詞並將一般動詞改成 V-ing

Ex. ~~Richard has~~ eaten too much.

He feels sick. → 主要子句

Having eaten too much, Richard feels sick. Richard 吃太多東西感覺想吐。

Ex. Judy comes from a small town.

She is fascinated with the interesting nightlife in Taipei. → 主要子句

→ Coming from a small town, Judy is fascinated with the interesting nightlife in Taipei.

來自小鎮的 Judy 對台北有趣的夜生活很嚮往。

3. 簡化後的句子可以放在不同的位置

Ex. Judy comes from a small town.

She is fascinated with the interesting nightlife in Taipei. ➡ 主要子句

➡ Coming from a small town, Judy is fascinated with the interesting nightlife in Taipei.

➡ Judy, coming from a small town, is fascinated with the interesting nightlife in Taipei.

➡ Judy is fascinated with the interesting nightlife in Taipei, coming from a small town.

 換你寫寫看

請合併以下兩個句子

1. Chris was severely injured in the car crash.

He has stayed in hospital for three months.

➡ _____ .

2. The student didn't catch the topic.

He didn't know what to say in the discussion.

➡ _____ .

● 答案與中譯解析

1. 答：Severely injured in the car crash, Chris stayed in hospital for three months.　在車禍中嚴重受傷，Chris 在醫院待了三個月。

2. 答：Not catching the topic, the student didn't know what to say in the discussion?　沒有聽到主題，學生不知道要在討論中說甚麼？

第12單元：倒裝句

名言範例：

Seldom, very seldom, does complete truth belong to any human disclosure; seldom can it happen that something is not a little disguised or a little mistaken.
完整的真相很少被揭露出來，偽裝與誤認是常發生的。

　　珍‧奧斯（Jane Austen），（1775 - 1817），19 世紀英國小說家，世界文學史上最具影響力的女性文學家之一，其最著名的作品是《傲慢與偏見》和《理性與感性》，以細緻入微的觀察和活潑文字描述十九世紀的女性生活著稱。

英文達人文法小筆記！

否定副詞倒裝／地方副詞倒裝文法解析
在英文中為了強調句子的某一部分，將一般敘述句的主詞與動詞位置改變，成為倒裝句。本書將討論副詞倒裝句與地方副詞倒裝句。

01　否定副詞倒裝
當句首是否定詞，其後面句子則用倒裝句，句型如下：
have ／ has ／ had ＋主詞＋ p.p.
否定副詞＋ Be 動詞＋主詞＋形容詞／名詞

137

助動詞＋主詞＋原形動詞

常用否定副詞與片語如下

1	never ＝ not at all ＝ by no means ＝ in no way ＝ on no account 絕不
2	hardly ＝ scarcely ＝ rarely 幾乎不
3	few ／ little 幾乎沒有，seldom 很少
4	not until 直到…才… no sooner…than… 一…就… not only…but（also）不但…而且…

Ex. Hardly did anyone know the secret.

幾乎沒有任何一個人知道那個秘密。

Ex. Never have they seen such a situation.

他們從未看過如此這種情況。

Ex. By no means would you help him pay back the money.

你絕不會幫他還那筆錢。

Ex. Not until the age of forty did he make his dream come true.

直到四十歲他才完成他的夢想。

Ex. Not only did he come, but he saw her.

他不只是來，而且看到她。

02 Only 的倒裝句型

當 only 當句子的句首時，主要子句用倒裝句。句型如下：

Only ＋副詞子句／副詞片語… ＋倒裝句

Ex. Only by working hard did he finish his project.

只有藉由努力工作他完成他的計畫。

03 表也／也不的倒裝句，句型如下：

> 肯定句，and 主詞＋Be 動詞／助動詞，too.
> ＝肯定句，and so ＋倒裝句
> ＝肯定句，So ＋倒裝句

> 否定句，and ＋主詞＋Be 動詞／助動詞＋not，either.
> ＝否定句，$\left\{ \begin{array}{l} \text{nor} \\ \text{and neither} \end{array} \right\}$ ＋倒裝句
> ＝否定句. $\left\{ \begin{array}{l} \text{Nor} \\ \text{Neither} \end{array} \right\}$ ＋倒裝句

Ex. I am a student, and he is, too.

　＝ I am a student, and so is he.

　＝ I am a student.　So is he.

　我是一個學生，他也是。

Ex. I am not a teacher, and he is not, either.

　＝ I am not a teacher, nor is he.

　＝ I am not a teacher, and neither is he.

　＝ I am not a teacher.　Neither is he.

　我不是一位老師，他也不是。

Ex. He likes music, and I do, too.

　＝ He likes music, and so do I.

　＝ He likes music.　So do I.

　他喜歡音樂，我也是。

Ex. He didn't finish his homework, and I didn't, either.

= He didn't finish his homework, nor did I.

= He didn't finish his homework, and neither did I.

= He didn't finish his homework.　Nor did I.

= He didn't finish his homework.　Neither did I.

他沒完成他的家庭作業，我也沒有。

特例！！So 之後的句子如果不倒裝，則表示同意。

　　Ex. Helen is a good student.　So she is.

　　　Helen 是一位好學生。她的確是。

04 強調地方副詞的倒裝句

1. 當句首是（1）地方副詞 There ／ Here（2）表地方的介副詞，（3）表位置的副詞片語時，其後面的主要子句須為倒裝句。

句型如下

There ／ Here ＋ Be 動詞／一般動詞＋主詞（名詞）

There ／ Here ＋主詞（代名詞）＋ Be 動詞／一般動詞

請注意當主詞是名詞與代名詞時，句子排列方式的差異性。而 Be 動詞／一般動詞單複數形式依主詞決定。

2. 表地方介副詞，如 up，down，off，away….

3. 表位置的副詞片語，如 at the door，on the table…

　　Ex. Here comes the bus.　公車來了。

　　Ex. Up flies the balloon.　汽球往上飛。

05 表讓步的倒裝句型

1. 當一般句子句首為 Although，為了語氣強調，亦可用倒裝句。

其句型如下

Although ＋主詞 ＋ Be 動詞 ＋ 形容詞／名詞＋主要子句
＝形容詞／名詞／副詞 ＋ as ／ though ＋主詞 ＋ Be 動詞＋主要子句

Ex. Although he is poor, he is happy.

　＝ Poor as ／ though he is, he is happy.

　雖然他是貧窮的，他是快樂的。

2. 當名詞放句首，冠詞要省略

Ex. Although he is a child, he acts like an adult.

　＝ Child as ／ though he is, he acts like an adult.

　雖然他是一個小孩，他舉止像大人。

 絕妙好例句

1. Here you are.（There ／ Here ＋主詞（代名詞）＋Be 動詞／一般動詞）給你。

2. Out rushed the students.（表位置的副詞片語時＋Be 動詞／一般動詞 ＋主詞（名詞））學生們衝出去。

3. You do not feel comfortable, and I don't, either.（否定句，and ＋主詞＋Be 動詞／助動詞＋not，either）你覺得不舒服，我也是。

4. Not until Jenny visited him did she realize how ill he was.（Not until ＋…助動詞＋主詞＋原形動詞）

　直到 Jenny 探望他，她才了解他病得多重。

5. Seldom did I go shopping in the supermarket on Saturdays.（否定副詞 ＋助動詞＋主詞 ＋原形動詞）我很少星期六到超級市場購物。

✏️ 換你寫寫看

1. Only when one is away from home _____ . (A)one realize how home is nice (B)one can realize how nice home is (C)does one realize how nice is home (D)does one realize how nice home is

2. Jane can hardly eat it, _____ . (A)May can, too. (B)neither can't May (C)nor can May (D)so can May

3. Sick _____ he was, he went to the meeting as usual. (A)in spite (B)despite (C)although (D)though

4. _____ she left the house than it began to snow. (A)Sooner no had (B)Sooner had no (C)No sooner had (D)Had no sooner

---

● 答案與中譯解析

1. 答：(D)（Only 當句首，主要主子句須倒裝。倒裝句句型為助動詞＋主詞＋原形動詞）只有當一個人離開家，才了解家是多麼好。

2. 答：(C)（hardly 為有否定意味的字詞，「也不」的倒裝句型為 nor ／ neither＋助動詞＋主詞）Jane 幾乎不吃它，may 也不是。

3. 答：(D)（表讓步子句的倒裝句型，形容詞／名詞／副詞＋as ／ though＋主詞＋Be 動詞＋主要子句
他雖然生病，他一如往常去參加會議。

4. 答：(C)（no sooner＋had＋主詞＋p.p. …than＋子句）
她一離開房子天氣就下雪。

NOTE

第13單元：虛主詞句型

名言範例：

It is not enough to win a war; it is more important to organize the peace.

贏得戰爭是不夠的，組織和平才是更重要的。

　　亞里斯多德是古希臘哲學家，柏拉圖的學生。他的著作包含許多學科，包括了物理學、形上學、詩歌（包括戲劇）、邏輯學、政治、政府、以及倫理學等。和柏拉圖、蘇格拉底一起被譽為西方哲學的奠基者。

英文達人文法小筆記！

01 It takes ＋人＋時間＋ to V…＝人＋ spend ＋時間＋ V-ing
　　　　　　　　　　　　　　　＝人＋ take(s) ＋時間＋ to V

take 在此句型中文意思為「花…多少時間」，其後接不定詞片語。

虛主詞 it 代表句子中的不定詞片語。

　　Ex. It took me five hours to read this book.

　　　＝ I spent five hours reading this book.

　　　＝ I took five hours to read this book.

　　　我花了五小時讀這本書。

02 It is ＋ adj.（修飾事物的形容詞）＋ for ＋人＋ to V

It is ＋ adj.（修飾人的形容詞）＋ of ＋人＋ to V

It is ＋ adj.（必要、緊要、重要等形容詞＋ that ＋ S ＋（should）＋原V

1. 虛主詞 it 代表句子中的不定詞片語。

It is adj. ＋ of ＋人＋ to V 的句型用於讚美或責備某人。

此類形容詞如下：nice、kind 、honest 、polite 、impolite 、wrong bad 、foolish 、stupid 、generous 、wise …等

Ex. It is really kind of you to help the poor girl.

＝ You are so kind to help the poor girl.

你真是仁慈來幫忙這位貧窮的女孩。

2. 虛主詞 it 代表句子中的不定詞片語。

It is adj. ＋ for ＋人＋ to V 的句型，其中文涵意為「…事對某人是…」。

此 類 形 容 詞 如 下：difficult 、easy 、possible 、necessary 、enough unnecessary 、convenient 、inconvenient 、polite…等

Ex. It is impossible for him to finish the project.

完成這個計劃對他而言是不可能的。

3. It is ＋ adj.（必要、緊要、重要等形容詞）＋ that ＋ S ＋（should）＋原V

虛主詞 it 代表句子中的 that 子句，此類形容詞如下：necessary 、important 、essential 、urgent …等

Ex. It is important that you（should）follow the directions.

遵守指示對你們而言是重要的。

03 It is no wonder + that 子句，中文意思為「…一點也不為奇；難怪」，此句型中的 it is 和 that 常被省略。

Ex. It is no wonder that he didn't want to come back.

= No wonder he didn't want to come back.

難怪他不想回來。

 絕妙好例句

1. It is difficult for me to speak in public.（It is + adj.「修飾事物的形容詞」+ for + 人 + to V）對我而言，在公開場合演講是困難的。

2. It is wise of you to answer this hard question.（It is + adj.「修飾人的形容詞」+ of + 人 + to V）你是有智慧能回答這個困難的問題。

3. It is no wonder that he wanted to stay at home.（It is no wonder + that 子句，中文意思為「…一點也不為奇;難怪」）難怪他想待在家。

4. It took him fifty minutes to arrive at the train station.（It takes + 人 + 時間 + to V…，虛主詞 it 代表句子中的不定詞片語。）他花五十分鐘到達火車站。

5. It is important that Jane passed the final exam.（It is + adj.「必要、緊要、重要等形容詞」+ that + S +（should）+ 原 V，虛主詞 it 代表句子中的 that 子句）對 Jane 而言通過期末考試是重要的。

6. It is good for you to take a walk for thirty minutes every day.（It is adj. + for + 人 + to V 的句型，其中文涵意為「…事對某人是…」。）每天散步三十分鐘對你是好的。

 換你寫寫看

1. _____ is impossible to run as fast as the light.

2. _____ _____ him one day to clean his room.

3. _____ is no _____ that you want to go to Canada with me.

4. _____ is necessary _____ you _____ finish your homework on time.

5. _____ is generous _____ you _____ send me such a valuable present.

6. It _____ me three days _____ for the test. （A)spent; preparing （B) takes; to prepare （C)took; to prepare （D)cost; to prepare

7. _____ is very important that you go to the meeting on time. （A) That （B)This （C)It （D)There

---

● 答案與中譯解析

1. 答：It（It is＋adj.「修飾事物的形容詞」＋to V）
   要跑得像光一樣快是不可能的。

2. 答：It、took（It takes＋人＋時間＋to V…，虛主詞 it 代表句子中的不定詞片語）他花一天時間打掃他的房間。

3. 答：It、wonder（It is no wonder＋that 子句，中文意思為「…一點也不為奇；難怪」）難怪你想跟我一起去加拿大。

4. 答：It、for、to（It is adj.＋for＋人＋to V 的句型，其中文涵意為「…事對某人是…」。）準時完成功課對你來說是必要的。

5. 答：It、of、to （It is＋adj.「修飾人的形容詞」＋of＋人＋to V）
   你真慷慨送我如此貴重的禮物。

6. 答：（C）（It takes＋人＋時間＋to V…），我花三天準備這場考試。

7. 答：（C）（It is＋adj.「必要／緊要／重要等形容詞」＋that＋S＋（should）＋原 V，虛主詞 it 代表句子中的 that 子句）你準時去開會是很重要的。

第14單元：強調語氣句型

名言範例：

The glory of friendship is not the outstretched hand, not the kindly smile, nor the joy of companionship; it is the spiritual inspiration that comes to one when you discover that someone else believes in you and is willing to trust you with a friendship.

友誼不是伸展開的手，不是仁慈的微笑，不是陪伴的喜悅；而是心靈的激勵，此激勵是來自於你發現有人願意以友誼之情來相信你、信賴你。

　　拉爾夫·沃爾多·愛默生（Ralph Waldo Emerson，1803 － 1882），生於波士頓，為美國著名思想家、文學家。愛默生的作品，是以其日記中對針對事物觀察後的意見為主。

01 句型：It is ＋強調部份＋ that ＋其餘部分

說明：that 子句用於說明前面強調部份，為真主詞，it 為形式主詞。

　　　Ex It was yesterday that my car was stolen. 就是昨天我的車子被偷了。

02 句型：主詞＋動詞＋ it ＋受詞補語 ＋ { to 原形動詞 / that ＋主詞＋動詞

說明：it 為形式受詞，代表後面的不定詞片語或 that 子句，受詞補語補充說明 it，受詞補語為形容詞或名詞。It 前面的動詞有 "make，take，think，find，believe，consider…"

Ex. We consider it difficult to finish this big project on time.

我們認為如期完成這個計劃是困難的。

03 含 it 的慣用語：

1. take it for granted that ＋子句　　視…為理所當然

Ex. We take it for granted that parents take care of their children.

我們視父母親照顧小孩為理所當然。

2. make it a rule to ＋動詞　　習慣於…

Ex. They make it a rule to go to the library every Sunday.

他們習慣於每週日去圖書館。

3. 否定字 not 放在不定詞之前，not to ＋原形動詞

Ex. He thinks it hard not to get on the Internet.

他認為不上網是困難的。

換你寫寫看

1. It is I that _____ about to head for Taipei.

2. They found _____ easy to make cupcakes by themselves.

● 答案與中譯解析

1. 答：am（that 子句主詞為子句前面的 I，所以 Be 動詞為 am）

就是我打算要前往台北。

2. 答：it（it 為形式受詞，代表後面的不定詞片語或 that 子句）

他們發現靠自己做杯子蛋糕是容易的。

第15單元：特殊句型

名言範例：

I was too absorbed to be responsive. 我太投入以致於無法回應。

　　《大亨小傳》（The Great Gatsby）是美國作家費茲傑羅於 1925 所寫的一部以 1920 年代美國為背景的小說。蓋茲比生活於紙醉金迷的奢侈毫豪門世界中，一心追求自己的浪漫愛情夢想，卻也為自己帶來悲劇的命運。

英文達人文法小筆記！

01 …too…to

1. 句型如下

S ＋ Be 動詞＋ too ＋形容詞＋ to ＋原形動詞

S ＋一般動詞＋ too ＋副詞＋ to ＋原形動詞

2. 中文意思為「…太…以致於不能…」，當句子的動詞為 Be 動詞時，too 後面接形容詞，to 後面接原形動詞。當句子的動詞為一般動詞時，too 後面接副詞，to 後面接原形動詞。此句型有否定的意思。

3.…too…to ＋原形 V ＝ so…that…can't

　　Ex. He is too short to play basketball　他太矮以致於不能打籃球。

　　Ex. He is too young to go to school.　他太小以致於不能上學.

02 so…that…

1. 句型如下

S ＋ Be 動詞＋ so ＋形容詞＋（a ／ an ＋ N）＋ that 子句

S ＋一般動詞＋ so ＋副詞＋ that 子句

2. 中文意思為「如此…以致於…」，當句子的動詞為 Be 動詞時，so 後面接形容詞，that 後面接子句。當句子的動詞為一般動詞時，so 後面接副詞，that 後面接子句。

> Ex. She is so beautiful（a girl）that everyone likes her.
> 她是如此美麗的（一個女孩）以致於每個人喜歡她。

> Ex. He runs so fast that nobody can catch up with him.
> 他跑得如此快以致沒有人可以趕上他。

03 Why not ＋原形動詞

中文意思為有兩種：（一）「為何不可」（二）「為什麼不行」。

1.「為何不可」，表示同意。從下面的例子可知

A：Do you mind my borrowing your book?

B：Why not?

A：你介意我借你的書嗎？

B：為何不可？

2.「為什麼不行」，表示疑問。從下面的例子可知

A：He can't go to the meeting with you.

B：Why not?

A：他不能和你去參加會議？

B：為什麼不行？

此處的 why not 和 why 可互換，表疑問。

04 How come ＋子句

1. 中文意思是「為什麼；怎麼回事」。但 How come 是表驚訝，不需要對方的回答，但 Why 是需要對方的回答。

2. How come 和 why 的中文意思一樣，但 How come 比較口語化。How come 後接名詞子句。

> Ex A：I am sorry for being late.
>
> B：How come you are late?
>
> A：我很抱歉遲到了。
>
> B：咦，你怎麼遲到了。

05 What do you think ＋子句

當主要子句為 Do you think（guess，believe）表達自我主觀判斷的動詞，則疑問詞置於句首，do you think（guess，believe）置於其後。助動詞 do，did，does 去掉，動詞恢復為原來時態。

> Ex. What did he do last night? Do you think?
>
> → What do you think he did last night?　你認為他昨晚作了什麼？

✎ 換你寫寫看

1. _____ do you think he is? I think he is our new teacher.

2. A：Please keep quiet. B：_____ we need to keep quiet?

3. _____ come with us? The activity is very interesting.

4. He walked _____ fast _____ nobody wanted to be with him.

    (A)so…that (B)too…to (C)so… as to (D)very…that

5. The game is _____ dangerous for us _____ it again.

(A)so…that… (B)too…to playing (C)too …to play (D)so….as to

● 答案與中譯解析

1. 答：Who （當主要子句為do you think 表達自我主觀判斷的動詞，則疑問詞置於句首，do you think 置於其後。）你想他是誰？

2. 答：How come（How come＋子句）A: 請保持安靜。 B：為什麼要保持安靜？

3. 答：Why not（Why not＋原形動詞）為什麼不跟我們一起去？那活動很有趣。

4. 答：(A)（so…that＋子句，如此…以致於…）
   他走得如此快以至於沒人想要和他再一起。

5. 答：(C)（too＋adj.…to＋原形動詞，太…以致於不能…）
   這比賽對我們而言太危險了以致於不能再比一次。

NOTE

Part II
字詞文法

第16單元：名詞

名言範例：

I honestly have no idea how to live without you.

沒有你，我真地不知如何活下去。

　　新月是美國作家 Stephenie Meyer 所著《暮光之城》系列小說的第二集，描寫女主角貝拉、吸血鬼愛德華與狼人雅各之間的愛情故事。此句的意思是「沒有你，我真的不知如何活下去。」

英文達人文法小筆記！

可數／不可數名詞／集合名詞／名詞片語 文法解析

名詞為人、事、時、地、物等。分為「可數」與「不可數名詞」。集合名詞是由單數或複數人或項目所組成，有時為單複數同行的名詞 依語意來決定其單複數。名詞片語則由兩個字詞以上組成的名詞片語，有名詞之功能。

01 可數名詞

有固體形體，可用 1、2、3…數字計算，可數名詞可為：規則名詞與不規則名詞。

● **規則名詞**

單數名詞成為複數名詞，其規則分為三種：（一）字尾加 s（二）單數名詞字尾為"子音＋y"，去 y 加 ies。（三）單數名詞字尾為"母音＋y"，則直接加s。（四）單數名詞字尾為"s，x，z，sh，ch"，字尾加 es。（五）單數名詞字尾為"f，fe" 則去f／fe字尾加ves。（六）單數名詞字尾為"子音＋o"字尾加es。（七）單數名詞尾為"母音＋o"字尾加s。

例子如下：

（一）字尾加s

book	books	書
girl	girls	女孩
road	roads	道路
hour	hours	小時

（二）單數名詞字尾為"子音＋y"，去y加ies，例子如下：

party	parties	派對
city	cities	城市
body	bodies	身體
library	libraries	圖書館

（三）單數名詞字尾為"母音＋y"，則直接加s，例子如下：

key	keys	鑰匙
day	days	天
holiday	holidays	假日

（四）單數名詞字尾為"s，x，z，sh，ch"，字尾加 es，例子如下：

watch	watches	手錶
box	boxes	箱子
glass	glasses	玻璃

（五）單數名詞字尾為"f，fe"則去f／fe字尾加ves，例子如下：

half	halves	一半
wife	wives	妻子
knife	knives	刀子

（六）單數名詞字尾為"子音＋o"字尾加es，例子如下：

tomato	tomatoes	番茄
hero	heroes	英雄

（七）單數名詞尾為"母音＋o"字尾加s，例子如下：

radio	radios	收音機
zoo	zoos	動物園

特例！！有些名詞單複數變化不規則例子如下：

foot	feet	腳
tooth	teeth	牙齒
goose	geese	鵝
child	children	小孩
mouse	mice	老鼠
woman	women	女人
man	men	男人
ox	oxen	公牛

02 不可數名詞

不可數名詞分三種**（一）抽象名詞**（如：happiness 快樂，love 愛，friendship 友誼）、**（二）專有名詞**（如：Taiwan 台灣，September 九月，

The Great Wall 萬里長城）、（三）**物質名詞**（如：coffee 咖啡，air 空氣，water 水）。不可數名詞之前通常不加冠詞，也沒有複數形。動詞需用單數形動詞或 Be 動詞。

03 集合名詞

由單數或複數人或項目所組成，有時為單複數同型的名詞 依語意來決定其單複數。例子如下：

the police	警方（複數集合名詞）
Chinese	中國人（單複數同形）
cattle	牛群（複數集合名詞）
family	家庭、家人
class	班級、班上同學、課程

Ex. The cattle are gazing in the field. 牛群正在牧場吃草。

Ex. My family is a big family. 我的家庭是一個大家庭。

Ex. My class is made up of fifty students. 我的班是由五十位學生組成。

04 名詞片語

由兩個字詞以上組成有名詞之功能，但不含主詞與動詞的的片語，既為名詞片語。如所有格加名詞、複合名詞既為其中之的例子，例子如下：

a girl's bicycle	名詞的所有格＋名詞	一位女孩的腳踏車
Tom and Jane's father	共同所有格＋名詞	湯姆和珍的父親
the legs of the table	無生物所有格＋名詞	桌子的腳
a friend of mine	雙重所有格＋名詞	我的一位朋友
a good student	形容詞＋名詞	一位好學生

flashlight	名詞＋名詞	手電筒
toothpaste	名詞＋名詞	牙膏
seat belt	名詞 名詞	座位安全帶
full moon	名詞 名詞	滿月
mother-in-law	名詞＋介系詞＋名詞	岳母、婆婆

 絕妙好例句

1. Mr. Wang is a friend of my father's.（名詞片語 a friend of mine）
   王先生是我父親的一位朋友。

2. My family are all teachers.（family 在本句是家人為複數，動詞用複
   數動詞 are）我的家人都是老師。

3. There are five geese on the pond.（goose 鵝，複數為不規則變化
   geese）有五隻鵝在池塘上。

4. Sam is drinking some water.（水為不可數名詞，為單數名詞）
   Sam 正在喝一些水。

5. I am a Chinese.（中國人 Chinese 單複數同型）我是一位中國人。

6. For most people，love is very important in the world.（愛 love 是不
   可數名詞，用單數動詞 is）
   對多數人來說，愛是世界上一件非常重要的東西。

7. My dad bought two deer last month.（deer 為單複數同型的名詞，
   不用加 s）我父親上個月買了兩隻鹿。

8. There are six knives in the kitchen.（knife 複數為不規則變化
   knives）有六把刀在廚房裡。

換你寫寫看

1. He ate too much _____.

2. This desk is made up of _____ .

3. There are three _____ in the university.

4. My class _____ smaller than John's. There are only ten students in my class.

5. The air in the mountain _____ very fresh.

6. The police _____ trying to find the lost boy.

7. He likes to eat _____ . (A)fries potatos (B)fishes ad beefs (C)grilled meat (D)boiling egg

8. _____ are asked to clean their _____ before going to bed. (A)Child，tooth (B)Child，teeth (C)Children，tooth (D)Children，teeth

---

● 答案與中譯解析

1. 答：fruit（水果為不可數名詞，複數不可加s。）他吃太多水果了。

2. 答：wood（木頭為不可數名詞，複數不可加s。）這張桌子是由木頭做成的。

3. 答：libraries（library 字尾為子音＋y"，複數要子去y加ies。）
   有三間圖書館在這所大學裡。

4. 答：is（class 意思為班級，單數名詞。）
   我的班比 John 的班小。只有 10個學生在我的班。

5. 答：is（air 為不可數名詞，需單數 Be 動詞is。）山上的空氣非常的清新。

6. 答：are（the police 警方，為複數集合名詞，故 Be 動詞用複數動詞are。）
   警方正努力尋找那名失蹤的男童。

7. 答：(C)（(A) potato 複數為 potatoes；(B) fish 和beef 都為不可數名詞，不可加es 或s；(D) egg 為可數名詞，複數要加s。）他喜歡吃烤肉。

8. 答：(D)（child 為不規則變化的名詞，複數為children；tooth 為不規則變化的名詞，複數為teeth。）孩子們被要求床前要刷牙。

第17單元：動詞

英文達人文法小筆記！

Be 動詞

名言範例：

You are beautiful.　你是美麗的。

　　上尉詩人James Blunt，一曲成名的一首歌 "You are beautiful"。這首歌成為 2005年最熱門單曲之，風靡全球；除了在英國流行歌曲榜，停留了 6週的冠軍；另外更奪得美國Billboard TOP100的冠軍寶座，以及各國音樂排行榜上交出漂亮成績單，創下驚人銷量。歌詞開頭的兩句 "My life is brilliant. My love is pure." 是基本的 Be 動詞句型，簡單好學。

Be 動詞文法解析

Be 動詞在英文裡的身分很特殊，它可以當主要動詞，也可以當助動詞用。

01 Be 動詞為主要動詞（Main Verb）

1. 用法

a. Be 動詞跟一般的動詞不同，它不表現任何動作，而是表達一種存在、狀態、情境、或是地位。

　　Ex. I am a teacher.　我是一位教師。

b. Be 動 詞 總 共 有 8個 ， 分 別 為 ***am*** ／ are ／ is ， was ／ were ， be ／ being ／ been。

- 原形＝be，不隨主詞變化

  Be 動詞為主要動詞使用時，如句型有助動詞時，要用原形。

  Ex. I ***will Be*** with you.

- 現在式＝am ／ are ／ is，隨主詞變化

  單數＝I am，you are，she ／ he ／ it is

  複數＝we are，you are，they are

- 過去式＝was ／ were，隨主詞變化

  單數＝I was，you were，she ／ he ／ it was

  複數＝we were，you were，they were

- 進行式＝現在分詞（動名詞 Be＋ing）＝being，不隨主詞變化

  單 數 ＝I am ／ was＋being，you are ／ were＋being，she ／ he ／ it＋is ／ was＋being

  複數＝we are ／ were＋being，you are ／ were＋being，they are ／ were＋being

- 完成式＝過去分詞＝been，不隨主詞變化

  單數＝I have ／ had＋been，you have ／ had＋been，she ／ he ／ it has ／ had＋been

  複數＝（we，you，they）＋have＋been

c. Be 動詞主要表達的是中文的「是」或「很」的意思，若 Be 動詞表達的「很」的意思，那麼主詞補語（SC）後面要接形容詞。

  Ex. You are beautiful.（S＋Be 動詞＋SC）

2. 文法結構

a. 肯定句：主詞 S ＋ Be 動詞＋受詞補語 SC

Ex. You are a teacher. 你是一位教師。

b. 否定句：主詞 S ＋ Be 動詞＋ not ＋主詞補語 SC

Ex. You are not a teacher. 你不是一位教師。

c. 疑問句：Be 動詞＋主詞 S ＋主詞補語 SC

Ex. Are you a teacher? 你是一位教師嗎？

02 Be 動詞為助動詞（Auxiliary Verb）

1. 協助主要動詞形成進行式，包括現在、過去、與未來進行式

a. 現在進行式：主詞 S ＋助動詞 Be（am ／ are ／ is）＋現在分詞（V-ing）

Ex. I *am reading* a book. 我正在看書。

b. 過去進行式主詞 S ＋助動詞 Be（was ／ were）＋現在分詞（V-ing）

Ex. I *was reading* a book 我當時正在看書。

c. 未來進行式主詞 S ＋助動詞（will）＋助動詞 Be ＋現在分詞（V-ing）

Ex. The world *will be watching* the World Cup.

2 協助主要動詞形成被動語態

a. 主詞＋助動詞 Be ＋過去分詞（p.p.）

Ex. The book was written by John. 這本書是 John 寫的。

絕妙好例句：

1. Am I bothering you?（Be 動詞＝助動詞）我打擾你了嗎？
2. Phillip is known as great actor.（Be 動詞＝助動詞，被動式）Phillip 是位知名的演員。
3. It was a nice day yesterday.（Be 動詞＝主要動詞）昨天是美好的一天。
4. I will Be a college student soon.（Be 動詞＝主要動詞）我很快將會是大學生。
5. She is in the library.（Be 動詞＝主要動詞）她在圖書館。

 換你寫寫看

1. The baby _____ .（be，to sleep）寶寶正在睡覺。
2. Tom _____ a singer.（not／ be）Tom不是歌手。
3. The door _____ .（has，to open，被動）門已經被打開了。
4 Kitty _____ bad again.（A)was being (B)be (C)are being
5. She _____ very cute.（A)am   (B)is   (C)are

●答案與中譯解析

1. 答：is sleeping（Be 動詞＝助動詞，現在進行式）
2. 答：is not（Be 動詞＝主要動詞）
3. 答：has been opened（Be 動詞＝助動詞，現在完成式）
4. 答：(A)（was ＝助動詞，being ＝主要動詞）Kitty 又不乖了。
5. 答：(B)（Be 動詞＝主要動詞）她很可愛。

一般動詞 Ordinary Verb

You had a bad day. 你有一個糟糕的一天。

　　城市琴人 Daniel Powter，第一首鋼琴流行單曲 Bad Day，曲風因符合現代大眾的口味，而且歌的內容又有鼓勵的作用，廣受大眾喜愛。這首歌最早出於 2005 年華納唱片公司為可口可樂選曲，作為在歐洲市場的廣告歌曲，很輕鬆簡單易學的英文歌曲。

一般動詞指的是除了 Be 動詞或是助動詞以外的動詞型態。

01 不及物動詞 VS. 及物動詞

1. 不及物動詞（Intransitive Verbs ＝ Vi）
動詞本身可以獨立表達完整意思，後面不需要受詞。

　a. 完全不及物動詞：動詞後面完全不需要受詞（O）與任何補語
　　Ex. A funny thing happened.　一件好笑的事發生了。

　b. 不完全及物動詞：不需要受詞（O），但是需要補語（C），才能完整表達意思
　　Ex. She looks pretty.　她看起來很漂亮。

2. 及物動詞（Transitive Verbs ＝ Vt）
動詞後面須要有受詞，接受動作。

　a. 完全及物動詞：動詞後面需要受詞 O，承受動作，但是不須要補語 C
　　Ex. I love you.　我愛你。

　b. 不完全及物動詞：動詞後面不但要有受詞 O，還要有受詞補語（OC）。
　　Ex. I asked him a question. 我向他問了一個問題。

c. 授與動詞：動詞須要有 2 個受詞 O，間接受詞（IO 通常指人）與直接受詞（DO 通常只事物）才能完整表達意思，常見的授與動詞為 give，buy。

Ex. I gave you a book. 我給你一本書。

12

02 一般動詞變化

1. 規則動詞 VS. 不規則動詞

a. 規則動詞（Regular Verbs）

動詞在原式、過去式與過去分詞的時態變化上有規則可循。

● 最常見的是在動詞後面加 "ed"

Ex. 原形＝ work，過去式＝ work*ed*，過去分詞＝ work*ed*

● 動詞字尾已有 e 時，直接加 "d" 即可

Ex. 原形＝ move，過去式＝ move*d*，過去分詞＝ move*d*

● 字尾是「子音＋y」時，須先去掉 y，再加 "ied"

Ex. 原形＝ study，過去式＝ stud*ied*，過去分詞＝ stud*ied*

● 字尾是「短母音＋子音」時，須重覆字尾，再加 "ed"

Ex. 原形＝ stop，過去式＝ stop*ped*，過去分詞＝ stop*ped*

b. 不規則動詞（Irregular Verbs）

動詞的原形、過去式與過去分詞的時態變化無規則可循，但仍有幾種形態：

● 三種時態全部相同

Ex. 原形＝ hit，過去式＝ hit，過去分詞＝ hit

● 過去式與過去分詞相同

Ex. 原形＝ bring，過去式＝ bought，過去分詞＝ bought

18

● 原形與過去分詞相同

Ex. 原形＝come，過去式＝came，過去分詞＝come

● 三種時態全部不相同

Ex. 原形＝begin，過去式＝began，過去分詞＝begun

2. 動詞的變化

一般動詞的單複變化，須隨主詞變化。單數主詞，搭配單數動詞；複數主詞
搭配複數動詞。

a. 現在式：第三人稱以及單數主詞，後面動詞字尾須＋s／＋es／-y＋
   ies

   Ex. 原形＝work，單數＝work**s** ➡ She works at home.

   原形＝go，單數＝go**es** ➡ She goes to school.

   原形＝try，單數＝tr**ies** ➡ She tries her best.

b. 過去式的單複數：無論何種人稱，單、複數都用同型。

c. 不管否定句或疑問句，一般動詞的人稱，單、複數都是用原形，只有助
   動詞隨主詞變化。

d. 一般動詞在現在分詞與進行式的變化上，一般在動詞字尾加上"ing"。

   Ex. 原形＝work，現在分詞＝working

 絕妙好例句

1. Tommy read a good article last week.（Vt＝read，read，read，不
   規則變化，過去式read。）Tommy 上週讀了一篇好文章。

   註：read 屬不規則動詞變化，雖是拼法一樣，但是讀音不同。

2. Sue has worked in the restaurant for 2 years.（Vi ＝ work，worked，worked，規則變化，過去分詞，單複數由助動詞變化。）Sue 在餐廳工作已經有 2年了。

3. The doctor is saving the child's life.（Vt ＝ save，saved，saved，saving，規則變化，現在分詞，單複數由助動詞變化。）醫生正在拯救小孩的生命。

4. She picks me a good book.（Vt. ＝ pick，picked，picked，兩個受詞，規則變化，單數動詞加 "-s"。）她為我挑了一本好書。

5. Birds flew across the blue sky.（Vi ＝ fly，flew，flown，不規則變化，過去式 flew。）鳥群飛過湛藍的天空。

換你寫寫看

1. The baby was _____ when I _____ in.（to sleep／to go）
2. The bus _____ .（to stop）
3. He _____ the ball.（not／to catch）
4. She _____ for a help at midnight.（A）cried（B）crying（C）was cried
5. Mother _____ right now.（A）cooked（B）is cooking（C）is cooked

● 答案與中譯解析

1. 答：sleeping、went（Vi ＝ sleeping，過去進行式，第三人稱單數助動詞變化；Vi ＝ go，went，gone，不規則變化，過去式）我走進去時寶寶正在睡覺。

2. 答：stopped（Vi ＝ stop，stopped，stopped，規則變化，過去式，單複數不變）公車停了

3. 答：didn't catch（Vt ＝ catch，caught，caught，不規則變化，過去式，第三人稱單數助動詞變化）

169

4. 答：(A)（Vi＝cry，cried，cried，規則動詞，過去式，單複數不變。）
   她在深夜哭喊求幫助。

5. 答：(B)（Vi.＝cook，cooked，cooked，現在進行式cooking，第三人稱單數
   助動詞變化。）母親正在煮飯

動詞片語 Verb Phrase

名言範例：

I can't help feeling. We could have had it all. 我不禁心生感觸，
我們本該擁有一切。

　　摘自於歌曲Rolling In The Deep，為英國創作行女歌手Adele於2011
年發行的專輯《21》的歌曲。這首歌一推出即在美國Billboard100（告示牌
100）上連續7週持續在冠軍寶座。這首歌集結多種曲風，搭配上Adele渾
厚的嗓子，在全球創下驚人銷量，並拿下多項獎項。

動詞片語 Verb Phrase（V.P.）文法解析
動詞片語（Verb Phrase）主要是一個主要動詞與一個或一個以上的助動詞
所形成，主要用來表時態、語態、疑問、或否定。

01 一個或一個以上的助動詞結構

1. 一個助動詞
動詞片語＝助動詞＋主要動詞
　　Ex. They **are talking** loudly.（V.P. ＝ are talking，現在進行式）

Ex. My car *is broken* by my brother.（V.P. = is broken，被動式語態）

2. 二個助動詞

動詞片語＝助動詞＋助動詞＋主要動詞

Ex. He *has been working* hard.（V.P. = has been working，現在完成進行式）

3 三個助動詞

動詞片語＝助動詞＋助動詞＋助動詞＋主要動詞

Ex. I *will have been waiting* for him.（V.P. = will have been waiting，未來完成進行式）

02 動詞片語有時會被隔離

1. 肯定句

動詞片語＝主詞＋副詞＋主要動詞

Ex. I *will* always *love* you.（V.P. = will love，被副詞 always 隔離）

2. 疑問句

動詞片語＝助動詞＋主詞＋主要動詞

Ex. *Have* you *done* your homework?（V.P. = have done，被主詞 you 隔離）

3. 否定句

動詞片語＝主詞＋助動詞＋ not ＋主要動詞

Ex. I don't care.（V.P. = do care，被 not 隔離）

絕妙好例句

1. Mike must eat my cake.（V.P. = must eat）

   Mike 一定吃了我的蛋糕。

2. Am I bothering you?（V.P. = am bothering）我打擾你了嗎？

3. She has not finished this project.（V.P. = has finished）

   她還沒完成這個案子。

4. Will Mary have taken few days off by next month?（V.P. = will

   have taken）下個月之前，May 將會休幾天假嗎？

5. The same joke has been heard twice by me.（V.P. = has been

   heard）同樣的笑話我已經聽過 2 次了。

 換你寫寫看

1. Don't buy that house. V.P. = _____　 (A)don't buy　(B)do buy　(C)buy

2. He is reading the book. V.P. = _____　 (A)is reading　(B)read　(C)is

3. We will Be going to party this Friday night. V.P. = _____

   (A)will be　(B)be going　(C)will Be going

4. Your application was rejected. V.P. = _____

   (A)was rejected　(B)was　(C)rejected

5. I had not lived in Taiwan before I moved to USA. V.P. = _____

   (A)had not lived　(B)had lived　(C)lived

● 答案與中譯解析

1. 答：(B)（V.P. = do buy）別買那棟房子。

2. 答：(A)（V.P. = is reading）他正在看書。

3. 答：(C)（V.P. = will Be going）這週五晚上，我們將會去舞會。

4. 答：(A)（V.P. = was rejected，被動式）您的申請被拒。

5. 答：(B)（V.P. = had lived）我搬去美國前，不住在台灣。

感官動詞 Sense Verb

名言範例：

I can't breathe! I feel dizzy...　我無法呼吸！我感到頭暈……

　　這天，Sally 突然抽走 Linus 的毯子，Linus 無法忍受形影不離的毯子離開身邊，像毒癮發作似的不斷顫抖。My blanket! I gotta have that blanket! I can't breathe!

　　Peanuts《花生漫畫》是一部美國報紙連環漫畫，作者是查爾斯・舒爾茨（Charles M. Schulz）《花生漫畫》是漫畫發展史上首部多角色系列漫畫，從 1950 年 10 月 2 日開始發行，到 2000 年 2 月 13 日作者病逝之時為止。漫畫以小孩生活為題材，觀察這個簡單又複雜的世界。漫畫的主要角色為小狗史努比（Snoopy）和查理・布朗（Charlie Brown）、莎莉（Sally Brown）、奈勒斯（Linus Van Pelt）、露西（Lucy Van Pelt）、謝勒德（Schroeder）等。

感官動詞 Sense Verb 文法解析

感官動詞 Sense Verb 主要描述視覺（see）、聽覺（hear）、知覺（feel）等等的感受與動作。

01 用法

感官動詞有：see ／ hear ／ feel ／ notice ／ watch ／ look at ／ listen to ／ observe ／ perceive

1. 強調事實完整過程，用原形動詞（V）

a. 句型：感官動詞＋受詞 O ＋原形動詞 V

b. 使用主動語態

c. 強調動作的完整性、真實性，如看見了或聽見了某事。
   Ex. He *saw* a bird *fly.*（他看到鳥在飛。）

2. 強調動作正在進行，用現在分詞（V-ing）

a. 句型：感官動詞＋受詞＋現在分詞（V-ing）

b. 使用主動語態

c. 強調動作的連續性、進行性，看到或聽見某事時，動作正在進行。
   Ex. He *saw* a bird *flying*.（他看到鳥正在飛。）

3. 表示被動語態的用法

a. 用過去分詞表示：感官動詞＋受詞＋過去分詞（p.p.）
   Ex. The boy's parents *see* him *pushed* away.
   （那男孩的父母看到他被推開。）

b. 感官動詞用被動式表示：感官動詞（被動式）＋現在分詞（V-ing）
   Ex. The boy *was seen pushing* away.

c. 用不定詞 to 表示：感官動詞（被動式）＋ *to* ＋原形動詞 V
   Ex. The boy *was seen to push away.*

 絕妙好例句

1. I hear someone knocking on the door.（強調動作正進行，主動）我
   聽到有人正在敲門。

2. He saw the girl fall down.（強調事實，主動）他看到這女孩跌倒。

3. I felt the wind blowing.（強調動作正進行，主動）我感覺風在吹。

4. She looked at him leave.（強調事實，主動）她注視著他離開。

5. I did not perceive anyone come in.（強調事實，主動）我沒有察覺到任何人進來。

換你寫寫看

1. Did you see a strange man _____ there five minutes ago?（to sit）

2. They were seen _____.（to arrive）

3. David didn't notice baby _____ .（to cry）

4. When I mentioned Amy, I noticed _____. (A)him smiling (B)he to smile (C)he smiling

5. He was seen _____ Tom's house. (A)enter (B)to enter (C)entered

● 答案與中譯解析

1. 答：sit（強調事實，主動）五分鐘前，你有看到一位陌生男人坐在那裡嗎？

2. 答：to arrive（被動式語態，用 to 表示）他們被看見到來了。

3. 答：crying（強調動作正進行，主動）David 沒有注意到寶寶正在哭。

4. 答：(A)（強調動作正進行，主動）當我提到 Amy 時，我注意到他正露出微笑。

5. 答：(B)（被動式語態，用 to 表示）他被看到進到 Tom 的房間。

11
12
13
14
15
16
17
18
19
20

情緒動詞 Emotional Verb

名言範例：

I'm tired of trying.　我懶得再去嘗試了。

　　歌曲 "Tired" 收錄於《19》首張專輯，發行於 2008年，是以 Adele 當時的年齡命名，在這專輯裡，她寫了很多歌曲，入選《英國排行榜》第一位。《泰晤士報》將這首歌喻為「重要的藍眼睛靈魂」的記錄。這首歌詞的意境其實是很讓人心碎的，但是卻搭配俏皮輕快的節奏。

情緒動詞 Emotional Verb 文法解析

情緒動詞 Emotional Verb，主要用來表達人或物的喜怒哀樂。

01 情緒動詞

1. 常用情緒動詞及動詞變化

情緒動詞（原形）	現在分詞（-ing） 當形容詞用（令人感到）	過去分詞（-ed） 當形容詞用（某人感到）
interest（使有趣）	interesting	interested（in）
bore（使無聊）	boring	bored（with，by）
excite（使興奮）	exciting	excited（about）
tire（使疲累）	tiring	tired（of，with）
surprise（使驚訝）	surprising	surprised（at）
confuse（使困惑）	confusing	confused（about）
satisfy（使滿意）	satisfying	satisfied（with）

amuse（使有趣）	amusing	amused（at）
worry（使擔憂）	worrying	worried（about）
disappoint（使失望）	disappointing	disappointed（at,with,about）

02 句型用法

1. 一般動詞用法

a. 主詞S（事／物）＋情緒（V）＋受詞O（人）

b. 意思：使某人感到

　　Ex. This movie interests me.　這電影使我感到興趣

2. 現在分詞用法

a. 主詞S（事／物）＋Be 動詞＋情緒（V-ing）＋to ＋受詞O（人）

b. 意思：令人感到或者「事物」對我而言

　　Ex. This is movie is interesting to me.　這電影使我感到有興趣

3. 過去分詞用法

a. 主詞S（人）＋Be 動詞＋情緒（-ed）＋介係詞＋受詞O（人／事／物）

b. 意思：人對某人／事感到…

c. 受詞可以是名詞、動名詞（Ving）

　　Ex. I am interested in this movie.　我對這部電影有興趣

　　　I am interested in jogging.　我對慢跑有興趣

4. 情緒動詞當形容詞用

a. 過去分詞（V-ed）當形容詞使用，用來修飾人

Ex. This movie made me interested.　這部電影令我感到有興趣。

b. 現在分詞（V-ing）當形容詞使用，用來修飾物

Ex. This is an interesting movie.　這是部有趣的電影。

 絕妙好例句

1. The World Cup excited all people.（一般動詞用法）
   世界杯賽事令所有人興奮。

2. People are satisfied with the new President.（過去分詞用法）
   人們對新總統感到滿意。

3. The news was surprising to me.（現在分詞用法）
   這新聞令人感到驚訝。

4. Pet is bored with reading this book.（過去分詞用法）
   Pet 對讀這本書感到無聊。

5. How did Sue feel about the music concert? She was disappointed.
   （當形容詞用，修飾人 V-ed）Sue 覺得這音樂會如何？她很失望。

換你寫寫看

1. We are _____ his reaction.（to confuse）

2. Math is a _____ subject.（to bore）

3. May is _____ her child.（to worry）

4. Tom was _____ football.

   (A)interested in playing　(B)interesting　(C)interested

5. They are _____ the _____NBA game last night.

(A)excited，excited　(B)excited about，excited　(C)excited about，exciting

---

● 答案與中譯解析

1. 答：confused about（過去分詞用法）我們對他的反應感到困惑。

2. 答：boring（修飾物，當形容詞用）數學是門很無聊的課程。

3. 答：worried about（過去分詞用法）May 擔心他小孩。

4. 答：(A)（過去分詞用法）Tom 對踢足球感興趣。

5. 答：(C)（過去分詞用法，exciting 當形容詞用，修飾NBA）
　　　他們對昨晚興奮的 NBA 球賽感到興奮。

使役動詞 Causative Verbs

名言範例：

Let it be! 算了吧！

　　Let it be 的歌詞簡單但是很有寓意，這首歌曲收錄於 1970年在英國發行的 Let It Be 專輯，是英國搖滾樂團 The Beatles（披頭四）發行第十二張錄音室專輯。披頭四樂團被公認為英國音樂在 1960年代「英國入侵」美國的代表樂團。其音樂風格源自 1950年代的搖滾，之後開拓了各種曲風，其音樂性之創新深深影響了之後的歐美樂壇發展，尤其是藍儂與麥卡尼這一對搭檔更是音樂樂史上最佳唱作搭檔之一。

使役動詞 Causative Verbs 文法解析

使役動詞 Causative Verbs 是表示主詞要求或強迫某人（受詞 O）去做事情，有使、令、讓、幫、叫、允許等意義。

01 使役動詞包括

常用使役動詞有：make，let，have，get，want，permit，allow，order，help 等

02 使役動詞的用法

1. 表示主動，第二動詞用原形（V）

a. 主詞 S ＋使役動詞＋受詞 O ＋（not）＋動詞 **V**

b. make、has ／ have、let

c. 有主動意味，讓受詞（O）去

   Ex. He made me laugh.　他使我笑了。

2. 表示主動，後加不定詞 to

a. 主詞 S ＋使役動詞＋受詞 O ＋（not）＋ to ＋動詞（V）

b. get、want、permit、allow、order、help

c. 有主動意味，讓受詞（O）去

   Ex. I got Tom to go home early.　我讓 Tom 早點回家。

3. 表示被動，第二動詞用過去分詞（p.p.）

a. 主詞 S ＋使役動詞＋受詞 O ＋（not）＋過去分詞（p.p.）

b. make、has ／ have、get

c. 有被動意味，讓受詞（O）被

Ex. I have my car washed.　我叫人洗車。

絕妙好例句

1. The manager makes me wait here.（動詞原形）經理讓我在這裡等。
2. Mother let me not enter.（動詞原形，否定句）母親讓我不要進來。
3. I get him to stay.（加不定詞）我要他留下。
4. I'll have your luggage sent to your room.（過去分詞，被動）我會將您的行李送到你房間。
5. Sue let me use her kitchen.（動詞原形）Sue 讓我使用她的廚房。

換你寫寫看

1. The teacher ordered him_____.（not／to go）
2. The news make me_____.（to excite）
3. She got her hand_____.（to burn）
4. My mom_____me finish my homework.

   (A)making　(B)need　(C)makes
5. Father helped me _____ the car.　(A)to fix　(B)fixing　(C)fixed

---

● 答案與中譯解析

1. 答：not to go（動詞原形，否定）老師命令他不要走。
2. 答：excited（過去分詞，被動）這則新聞讓我很興奮。
3. 答：burned（過去分詞，被動）她讓她的手被燒到。
4. 答：(C)（動詞原形，主動）我媽要我做完家庭作業。
5. 答：(A)（加不定詞，主動）父親幫我修車。

連綴動詞 Linking Verbs

名言範例：

Life is a tragedy when seen in close-up,but a comedy in long-shot. 從特寫鏡頭看人生是悲劇，從遠鏡頭看人生是喜劇。

　　卓別林（1889-1977）是一位英國喜劇演員及反戰人士，後來也成為一名非常出色的導演，尤其在好萊塢電影的早期和中期他非常成功和活躍。他奠定了現代喜劇電影的基礎。

連綴動詞 Linking Verbs 文法解析

連綴動詞（Linking Verbs）本身的意思不完全，主要用來連接、補充説明主詞（補語），後面不需要受詞，即是五大句型主詞（S ＋動詞 V ＋主詞補語 SC）。主詞補語可以是形容詞、名詞或介系詞片語來説明主詞的的情況，讓整個句子的意思變得完整。

01 常見連綴動詞

1. Be 動詞類（狀態）：am ／ are ／ is、was ／ were、be ／ being ／ been

2. 感官動詞類：look ／ sound ／ smell ／ taste ／ feel

3. 轉變動詞類：become ／ get ／ grow ／ turn

02 連綴動詞用法

1. 主詞 S ＋連綴動詞（L.V.）＋形容詞（Adj.）

　a. Be 動詞類（狀態）

- am ／ are ／ is、was ／ were、be ／ being ／ been
- 沒有進行式、被動式

Ex. You are beautiful.　你很漂亮。

b. 感官動詞類：表示（…起來／變成…）

- look ／ sound ／ smell ／ taste ／ feel
- 沒有進行式、被動式

Ex. You look beautiful.（你看起來很漂亮）

c. 轉變動詞類：表示「漸漸…；愈來愈…」。

- become ／ get ／ grow ／ turn
- 可用進行式，常用 Be ＋ Ving 的用法

Ex. Her face turns red.　她的臉變紅。

2. 主詞 S ＋連綴動詞（L.V.）＋ like（像）＋名詞（N）

a. Like 為介系詞，表示「像…」之意

b. 用於感官動詞類 look ／ sound ／ smell ／ taste ／ feel

c. 意思為看起來像、聽起來、聞起來像、吃起來像、感覺起來像

Ex. It *looks like* pizza.　它看起來像披薩。

3. 問答句：How & What

a. 問：How ＋助動詞＋主詞（S）＋連綴動詞（L.V.）？
答：主詞（S）＋連綴動詞（L.V.）＋形容詞（Adj）

Ex. How do you feel? I feel very good.　你感覺如何？我覺得很好。

b. 問：What ＋助動詞＋主詞（S）＋連綴動詞（L.V.）＋ like?
答：主詞（S）＋連綴動詞（L.V.）＋ like ＋名詞（N）

Ex. What does it look like? It looks like pizza. 它看起來像甚麼？ 它看起來像披薩。

 絕妙好例句

1. The steak tastes delicious.（S ＋ L.V. ＋ Adj.）這牛排吃起來美味。

2. Sue doesn't look like her mother.（S ＋ L.V. ＋ like ＋ N）
   Sue 看起來不像她媽媽。

3. Playing tennis sounds fun.（S ＋ L.V. ＋ Adj.）打網球聽起來好玩。

4. Father is getting old.（S ＋ Be ＋ L.V.-ing ＋ Adj.，進行式）父親漸漸變老。

5. What does the drink taste like? It tastes like tea.（S ＋ L.V. ＋ like ＋ N.）這飲料喝起來像甚麼？ 它喝起來像茶。

換你寫寫看

1. The weather _____ warm this morning.（to become）

2. Her voice _____ a duck.（to sound）

3. How do I look? You _____ .（awful）

4. Her voice _____ happy.（A）smalls （B）becomes （C）sounds

5. Do you feel better? No, I don't. My headache _____ .
   （A）get better （B）is getting worse （C）got worse

● 答案與中譯解析

1. 答：became（表示轉變，S＋L.V.＋Adj.）今天早上天氣變溫暖了。

2. 答：sounds like（感官連綴動詞，S＋L.V.＋like＋N）她的聲音聽起來像隻鴨子。

3. 答：look awful（感官連綴動詞，S＋L.V.＋Adj.）

　　我看起來如何？你看起來很糟糕。

4. 答：(C)（感官連綴動詞，S＋L.V.＋Adj.）她的聲音聽起來高興。

5. 答：(B)（轉變連綴動詞，進行式）

　　你覺得好些了嗎？沒有，我的頭痛愈來愈嚴重了。

11

12

13

14

15

16

17

18

19

20

第18單元：形容詞

名言範例：

Imagination is more important than knowledge.

想像力比知識還要重要。

　　愛因斯坦（Albert Einstein）對於宇宙萬物擁有許多知識，他的科學研究可以說影響了我們對時間與空間的了解。他告訴世人「想像力比知識還要重要」。因為知識將我們限制在我們現在所了解的事情上，而想像力卻讓人們想要知道的更多。

英文達人文法小筆記！

01 形容詞的位置

1. 形容詞一般來說用來形容名詞，放置於名詞之前

Ex. She is a woman. ➡ She is a beautiful woman.

　　她是一個女人。 ➡ 她是個美麗的女人。

Ex. They are students. ➡ They are diligent students.

　　他們是學生。 ➡ 他們是勤奮的學生。

Ex. We need some food. ➡ We need some flavorful food.

　　我們需要些食物。 ➡ 我們需要些美味的食物。

放在形容詞之前的 a 或 an 由形容詞的字首字母決定。子音開頭的字前加 a，母音開頭的字前加 an。

至於 the 在子音開頭的字前發音為／ðə／，在母音開頭的字前為／ðɪ／。

> Ex. She is a woman. ➡ She is a nice woman. ➡ She is an interesting woman.

> Ex. We like the room. ➡ We like the ／ðə／ red room. ➡ We like the ／ðɪ／ empty room.

2. 形容詞也可以放在主詞與 Be 動詞之後來補充說明主詞當補語

> Ex. The movie was boring.

> Ex. The actress is tall and elegant.

> Ex. He has been very helpful.

3. 形容詞除了可以放在 Be 動詞之後，也可以放在一般動詞之後，而這一類的動詞稱為連綴動詞（Linking Verbs）

a. 關於感覺或感官：feel，taste，look，smell，appear，seem，sound

> Ex. They seem happy.　他們似乎很開心。

> Ex. The idea sounds good.　這個想法聽起來很好。

b. 表示改變狀態，變成：become，turn，go，get，grow；證實：prove

> Ex. I get worried easily.　我很容易緊張。

> Ex. The food has gone bad.　食物已經壞了。

c. 表示保持，維持：remain，keep，stay

> Ex. Please stay calm.　請保持冷靜。

> Ex. We'll not keep silent in this case.　我們不會在這件事上保持沉默。

d. 有一些形容詞會接在動詞與受詞的後面來補充說明受詞當受詞補語

> Ex. I've never found this class interesting.
> 我永遠不會覺得這門課很有趣。

187

Ex. You can't leave the children hungry. 你不可以任由孩子們飢餓。

e. 有一些形容詞只接在動詞之後

Ex. He never likes to Be alone. 他從來就不喜歡單獨一個人。

Ex. They really look alike. 他們真的長很像。

02 比較級 & 最高級形容詞

1. 變化方法

a. 單音節形容詞
- 比較級：加 *er*（cheaper）
- 最高級：加 *est*（the cheapest）

b. 單音節形容詞 *"e"* 結尾
- 比較級：加 *r*（nicer）
- 最高級：加 *st*（the nicest）

c. 單音節形容詞 "子音－母音－子音" 結尾
- 比較級：重複子音結尾＋ *er*（hotter）
- 最高級：重複子音結尾＋ *est*（the hottest）

d. 雙音節形容詞 *"y"* 結尾
- 比較級：把 "y" 去掉＋ *ier*（happier）
- 最高級：把 "y" 去掉＋ *iest*（the happiest）

e. 多音節形容詞
- 比較級：加 *more* ／ *less*（more ／ less beautiful）
- 最高級：加 *the most* ／ *the least*（the most ／ least beautiful）

f. 不規則形容詞

- good - better - the best
- bad - worse - the worst
- far - further - the furthest

2. 使用時機

a. 使用比較級形容詞比較兩件事物（比較級形容詞＋than）

Ex Jane is ***thinner than*** Billie.　Jane 比 Billie 還要瘦。

Ex It's ***more expensive*** to travel by train ***than*** by bus.
搭火車旅遊比搭公車旅遊還要貴。

Ex My house is ***smaller than*** my friend's house.
我家的房子比我朋友家的房子還要小。

b. 使用最高級容詞來比較一件與其他同種類的事物

Ex Jane is ***the tallest*** in the class.　Jane 是班上最高的。

Ex He's ***the best*** baseball player in the team.
他是球隊裡最厲害的球員。

Ex This is ***the most expensive*** hotel I've ever stayed in.
這是我待過最貴的旅館。

c. 使用 as ＋ adj ＋ as 來敘述兩件事物相同之處

Ex He's ***as tall as*** me.　他跟我一樣高。

Ex Joe's car is ***as fast as*** mine.　Joe 的車子像我的車子一樣快。

d. 使用 not as ＋ adjective ＋ as 來敘述兩件事物不盡相同之處

Ex Joe's car is ***not as fast as*** mine.　Joe 的車子不像我的車子一樣快。

e. 重複比較級形容詞來敘述在改變的狀態

Ex. These exams are getting **harder and harder** every year.

考試每年變得越來越難。

Ex. She gets **more and more** beautiful every time I see her.

我每次看到她，她都變得越來越美。

f. 修飾 **more or less**

不可數名詞	可數名詞
There is **more** traffic.	There are **more** cars.
There is **much** more traffic.	There are **many** more cars.
There is **a lot ／ a little** more traffic.	There are **a lot ／ a little** more cars.
There is **more and more** traffic.	There are **more and more** cars.
There is **less** traffic.	There are **fewer** cars.
There is **far less** traffic.	There are **far fewer** cars.
There is **less and less** traffic.	There are **fewer and fewer** cars.

g. 使用 much，a lot，far，a little，a bit，slightly 修飾比較級形容詞

Ex. He is much richer than I am.　他比我有錢許多。

Ex. My sister's hair is slightly longer than mine.

我姐姐的頭髮比我的長一點。

h. 使用 by far，easily，nearly 修飾最高級形容詞

Ex. It is by far the best restaurant in town.　這是目前鎮上最好的餐廳。

Ex. Michael is nearly the oldest in the class.

Michael 幾乎是班上最老的。

i. 最高級形容詞前若是所有格則不加 the

Ex. His strongest point is his diligence.　他最大的優點是他的勤勉。

換你寫寫看

請根據句子的意思將所提示的形容詞作比較級或最高級的變化

1. This chair is _____ than the old one.（comfortable）

2. This is the _____ movie they have ever seen.（exciting）

3. Linda is _____ than Kate.（pretty）

4. You are _____ here than there.（safe）

5. Annie is the _____ child in the family.（young）

6. That TV set is the _____ of all.（cheap）

7. Tommy is _____ than Casey.（talented）

8. I pay for the _____ meal I have ever had.（expensive）

9. Trains are _____ than airplanes.（slow）

10. There are _____ girls than boys in this classroom.（many）

● 答案與中譯解析

1. 答：This chair is **more comfortable** than the old one.
   這張椅子比舊的那一張更舒服。

2. 答：This is the **most exciting** movie they have ever seen.
   這是他們看過最刺激的電影。

3. 答：Linda is **prettier** than Kate.　Linda 比 Kate 更漂亮。

4. 答：You are **safer** here than there.　你在這裡會比在那裡更安全。

5. 答：Annie is the **youngest** child in the family.　Annie 是家中最小的小孩。

6. 答：That TV set is the **cheapest** of all.　那電視組是裡面最便宜的。

7. 答：Tommy is **more talented** than Casey.　Tommy 比 Casey 更有才能。

8. 答：I pay for the **most expensive** meal I have ever had.
   我付了這餐我吃過最貴的一餐。

9. 答：Trains are **slower** than airplanes.　火車比飛機慢。

10. There are *more* girls than boys in this classroom.　教室裡的女生比男生多。

---

03 特殊形容詞

1. 所有格形容詞 Possessive Adjectives

單／複數	人稱	所有格形容詞	例句
單數	第一	my	This is my book.
	第二	your	I like your hair.
	第三	his ／ her ／ its	His name is Joseph.
複數	第一	we	We have sold our car.
	第二	your	Your children are lovely.
	第三	their	The students thanked their teacher.
單／複數		whose	Whose phone did you use?

在聽力中，以下是容易混淆的字

your ＝你或你們的

you're ＝ you are

its ＝它的

it's ＝ it is 或 it has

their ＝他們的

they're ＝ they are

there ＝地方副詞

whose ＝誰的

who's ＝ who is 或 who has

換你寫寫看

請填入適當的所有格形容詞

1. I have a car. _____ color is red.

2. The students didn't do _____ homework.

3. Sophia loves _____ grandmother.

4. Marco is from Italy. _____ wife is from France.

5. I like shopping. _____ friends usually go shopping with me.

6. We like to invite people to stay overnight in _____ house.

7. _____ book is this?

8. You shouldn't tell _____ own secrets to everyone.

9. We go to college together. _____ school is not very far.

10. Love is something every child needs from _____ parents.

● 答案與中譯解析

1. 答：I have a car. **Its** color is red.　我有一台車。它的顏色是紅色。

2. 答：The students didn't do **their** homework.　學生們沒有做他們的回家作業。

3. 答：Sophia loves **her** grandmother.　Sophia 很愛她的祖母。

4. 答：Marco is from Italy. **His** wife is from France.
   Marco 是從義大利來的。他的太太是從法國來的。

5. 答：I like shopping. **My** friends usually go shopping with me.
   我喜歡購物。我的朋友經常跟我去買東西。

6. 答：We like to invite people to stay overnight in **our** house.
   我們喜歡邀請人來我們家過夜。

7. 答：**Whose** book is this?　這是誰的書呢？

8. 答：You shouldn't tell **your** own secrets to everyone.
   你不應該告訴每個人你自己的秘密。

9. 答：We go to college together. **_Our_** school is not very far.

　　　我們一起上大學。我們的學校不會很遠。

10. 答：Love is something every child needs from **_their_** parents.

　　　愛是每個小孩從他們的父母身上需要的東西。

2. 數量形容詞

常見的數量形容詞有

	可數	不可數
任何	any	any
一些	some; a few	some; a little
所有	all	all
沒有	no	no
足夠	enough	enough
很多	a lot of; many	a lot of; much
很少	few; not many	little; not much

some 與 any 的用法

some 一般使用在肯定句，可用於可數與不可數名詞之前

　　Ex. I have some friends.　我有一些朋友。

　　Ex. They are looking for some furniture.　他們再找一些家俱。

any 一般使用在否定句與疑問句，可用於可數與不可數名詞之前

　　Ex. Karen hasn't bought any shoes lately.

　　　Karen 最近還沒買任何鞋子。

　　Ex. Do we have any water left in the house?　家裡還有殘留任何水嗎？

注意：some 也可以用在疑問句中，當作請求（request）或提供（offer）

Ex. Could I have some water?（request）我可以喝一些水嗎？

Ex. Would you like some bread?（offer）你需要一些麵包嗎？

換你寫寫看

請填入some或any

1. Is there _____ juice in the fridge?

2. I'm afraid I don't have _____ answers to life's problems.

3. Could I have _____ coke?

4. Would you like _____ water to drink?

5. Please have _____ more cake.

● 答案與中譯解析

1. 答：Is there **any** juice in the fridge?　冰箱裡還有任何果汁嗎？

2. 答：I'm afraid I don't have **any** answers to life's problems.
   我恐怕我對人生的問題沒有任何的答案。

3. 答：Could I have **some** coke?　我可以喝一些可樂嗎？

4. 答：Would you like **some** water to drink?　你想要喝一些水嗎？

5. 答：Please have **some** more cake.　請多吃一些蛋糕。

3. 分詞形容詞

動詞加上 -ing 與 -ed 形成分詞形容詞

	過去分詞（Vpp）用於描述感覺與接受動作的經驗者	現在分詞（Ving）用於描述造成動作的人與事
The lesson interests Anne.	Anne is very interested in the lesson.	The lesson is interesting（to Anne）.
The movie bored Bob.	Bob was bored by the movie.	Bob didn't enjoy the movie because it was boring.

常見的分詞形容詞

amazed	amazing	exhausted	exhausting
amused	amusing	fascinated	fascinating
annoyed	annoying	frightened	frightening
bored	boring	frustrated	frustrating
charmed	charming	interested	interesting
confused	confusing	puzzled	puzzling
convincing	convincing	relaxed	relaxing
damaged	damaging	satisfied	satisfying
depressed	depressing	shocked	shocking
disappointed	disappointing	terrified	terrifying
embarrassed	embarrassing	tired	tiring
excited	exciting	thrilled	thrilling

換你寫寫看

請填入適當的分詞形容詞

1. The manger has never been _____（satisfying／satisfied）with her work.

2. The news was so _____（shocking／shocked）that they all burst into tears.

3. Cleaning the house is so _____（tiring／tired）. I think I need to take a break.

4. He gets really _____（frustrating／frustrated）sometimes when he doesn't reach the sales target.

5. Bob is being so _____（annoying／annoyed）to his neighbors. He doesn't want to turn down the loud music.

● 答案與中譯解析

1. 答：The manger has never been **satisfied** with her work.
   經理從來對她的工作沒有滿意過。

2. 答：The news was so **shocking** that they all burst into tears.
   這消息如此的震驚他們全都哭了。

3. 答：Cleaning the house is so **tiring**. I think I need to take a break.
   打掃房子如此地累人。我想我需要休息一下。

4. 答：He gets really **frustrated** sometimes when he doesn't reach the sales target.
   他感到非常地沮喪當他沒有達到業績的目標。

5. 答：Bob is being so **annoying**. He doesn't want to turn down the loud music.
   Bob 很煩人。他不想把音樂關小聲。

4. 複合形容詞

a. 主動語態的句子將動詞改成現在分詞（V.ing）

Ex. The woman looks good. ➞ She is a good-looking woman.

（adj. ＋ Ving）她是個長相好看的女人。

Ex. The car runs fast. ➞ It is a fast-running car.

（adv. ＋ Ving）這是一台跑很快的車。

Ex. The project consumes time. ➞ It is a time-consuming project.

（N. ＋ Ving）這是一個耗時的計畫。

b. 被動語態的句子將動詞改成過去分詞（p.p.）

Ex. The house is painted red. ➞ It is a red-painted house.

（adj. ＋ p.p.）這是一個漆成紅色的房子。

Ex. The passengers were seriously injured in the accident.

➞ There were seriously-injured passengers in the accident.

（adv. ＋ p.p.）這些在事故中受傷嚴重的乘客。

Ex. This machine is operated by coins. ➞ It is a coin-operated

machine.（N ＋ Vpp） 這是一台投幣式的機器。

c. 特殊複合形容詞：形容詞後加上名詞加 -ed（adj. ＋ Ned）

Ex. He was a cold-blooded person and showed no emotion.

他是一個冷血的人且不帶任何情緒。

Ex. I wish you could Be more open-minded.　It's so hard to

communicate with you.

我希望你可以更心胸開闊點。跟你溝通真的很困難。

5. 相似單字比較

Ex. We have two dependent children.（需要依靠的）

Ex. We have two dependable children.（可以依靠的）

Ex. He is a loving teacher.（會付出愛的）

Ex. He is a lovable teacher.（讓人喜愛的）

Ex. She is a sensible person.（講理的）

Ex. She is a sensitive person.（敏感的）

Ex. Henry is a worthy team member.（有價值的）

Ex. Henry is a worthless team member.（沒有價值的）

Ex. We had a fun time at the movies.（有趣的）

Ex. We saw a funny movie.（好笑的）

第19單元：副詞

名言範例：

Money can add very much to one's ability to lead a constructive life, not only pleasant for oneself, but, hopefully, beneficial to others.

金錢可以增加一個人的能力去過著有意義的生活，不只是個人的享受，但是，希望對他人有助益。

　　大衛・洛克斐勒（David Rockefeller）來自於一個富可敵國的家族企業，身負著強烈的社會責任感。一生投入慈善事業。這個句子裡使用了副詞 hopefully 來修飾形容詞 beneficial。而兩個形容詞所形成的片語 pleasant for oneself 與 beneficial to others 則是用 not only…but…來做連接。

英文達人文法小筆記！

01 副詞的功能

1. 修飾動詞

Ex. The cars moved slowly in traffic.　車子在車陣中緩慢地行駛。

Ex. I can't even remember his name.　我甚至不記得他的名字。

Ex. She has handled the case carefully.　她仔細地處理這件事。

2. 修飾形容詞

Ex. The food is very good here.　這裡的食物非常好。

Ex. The man said, "I feel completely fine."

那男人說：「說我覺得徹底地好。」

Ex. It's never too late to Be who you want to be.

這永遠不會太晚去成為你想成為的人。

3. 修飾副詞

Ex. They speak German pretty well.　他們說德文挺好的。

Ex. The Taiwanese have worked too hard.　臺灣人工作太認真。

Ex. I took the test fairly confidently.　我相當有自信地參與這考試。

4. 修飾句子

Ex. Unfortunately, we couldn't find the answer.

不幸地，我們沒有找到答案。

Ex. Surprisingly, he didn't show up on time.

驚訝地，他並沒有準時出現。

Ex. Indeed, we all make mistakes sometimes.

的確，我們有時會犯錯。

02 副詞的種類

1. 情狀副詞

a. 情狀副詞用來修飾動詞，說明這動作是如何發生的或發生的情形

Ex. He reads slowly.　他看得很慢。

Ex. How does he read?　他看書看得如何？　→ slowly

Ex. She sings beautifully.　她唱地很優美。

Ex. How does she sing?　她唱歌唱得如何？　→ beautifully

b. 情狀副詞一般放在動詞後面，如果是放在動詞前面則是在作副詞的強調

　　Ex. My aunt calmly told everyone about her illness.　我的阿姨很冷靜地告訴大家她生病了。

　　Ex. She quickly finished her project.　她很快地完成她的計畫。

c. 有些特定的狀態副詞則一定放在動詞的後面（well、badly、hard）

　　Ex. Wilson did badly on the test.　Wilson 考試考得不好。

　　Ex. The only path to success is working hard.　成功的唯一途徑是努力地工作。

d. 動詞後面如果有受詞，狀態副詞一般放在動詞與受詞的後面

　　Ex. We celebrated cheerfully his birthday.（X）

　　　→ We celebrated his birthday cheerfully.　我們很愉快地慶祝他的生日。

e. 如果是放在動詞前面，同樣地是在作動作的強調

　　Ex. He surprisingly opened the present.　他很驚喜地打開了禮物。

f. 如果句子中不只一個動詞，那麼副詞的位置會影響到句子的意思

　　Ex. Lisa immediately decided to leave the party.

　　　→ immediately 修飾 decided

　　Lisa 很快地決定要離開派對。

　　Ex. Lisa decided to leave the party immediately.

　　　→ immediately 修飾 to leave the party

　　Lisa 決定要趕緊地離開派對。

　　Ex. The teacher quietly asked the students to finish the assignments.

　　老師小聲地請學生完成作業。

　　　→ quietly 修飾 asked

Ex. The teacher asked the students to finish the assignments quietly.

老師請學生安靜地完成作業。

→ quietly 修飾 to finish the assignments

換你寫寫看

請填入適當的副詞

1. Sylvia can type _____ .（fast）
2. He looked _____（careful）inside the room.
3. She ran away _____ .（nervous）
4. The teacher explained the lesson _____ .（slow）
5. They meet _____ .（regular）

● 答案與中譯解析

1. 答：Sylvia can type **fast**.　Sylvia 可以打字很快。
2. 答：He looked **carefully** inside the room.　他小心地看著房間裡面。
3. 答：She ran away **nervously**.　她緊張地跑掉了。
4. 答：The teacher explained the lesson **slowly**.　老師慢慢地解釋課程。
5. 答：They meet **regularly**.　他們定期地開會。

2. 地方副詞

a. 描述動作發生的地方，一般放在動詞或受詞之後

　　Ex. I looked everywhere ∕ around ∕ up ∕ down ∕ away.

　　Ex. John is going in ∕ out ∕ back ∕ home.

b. 單純描述一地方的地方副詞前面不需加介系詞

We need to get some fresh air inside ／ outside.

Please put it here ／ there ／ upstairs ／ downstairs.

c. here 跟 there 的用法

here 跟 there 常與一些介系詞連用來確切表達一個地方的位置

down here，down there；over here，over there；under here，under there；up here，up there

Here 跟 There 可作倒裝來強調地方，注意如果主詞是代名詞時則不能倒裝

Ex. Here comes the bus.　公車來了。

Ex. There she goes.　她走了。

d. 同時表達方向與地方的副詞 ahead、abroad、overseas、sideways、indoors、outdoors

Ex. I will run ahead and stop them.　我會跑向前並且阻止他們。

Ex. I used to study and work abroad.　我曾經在海外讀書與工作過。

 換你寫寫看

重組句子

1. is ／ over there ／ the department store.

_____

2. she ／ not ／ been ／ here ／ has.

_____

3. were ／ everywhere ／ we ／ for ／ looking ／ you.

_____

4. ？／there／a post office／nearby／is.

_____

5. must／we／walk／back home.

_____

● 答案與中譯解析

1. 答：The department store is over there. 百貨公司就在那裡。

2. 答：She has not been here. 她沒有來過這裡。

3. 答：We were looking for you everywhere. 我們之前在四處找你。

4. 答：Is there a post office nearby? 這附近有郵局嗎？

5. 答：We must walk back home. 我們必須走路回家。

3. 時間副詞

時間副詞分成三大類

- 何時發生：today ／ later ／ now ／ last year ／ next month ／ many years ago
- 發生多久：all day ／ not long ／ for a while ／ since last year
- 多久發生一次：sometimes ／ frequently ／ never ／ often ／ yearly

a. 何時發生的時間副詞一般放在句子最後。問句使用 When。

Ex. When did they go to Japan?　他們什麼時候去日本？

→ They went to Japan two years ago.　他們兩年前去日本。

Ex. When are you going to see the movie?　你什麼時候要去看電影？

→ I'm going to see the movie tomorrow.　我明天會去看電影。

但不同的位置的時間副詞則是在作不同的強調

EX. Later, Gloria will have some coffee. → 強調時間副詞 later

EX. Gloria will later have some coffee. → 這是用在較正式的寫作中

EX. Gloria will have some coffee later. → 一般用法，沒有特殊強調

b. 發生多久的時間副詞一般放在句子最後。問句使用 How long。

EX. How long did you watch TV? 你們看電視看多久？

→ We watched TV all day. 我們看電視看了一整天。

EX. How long will she Be staying in Paris? 她將在巴黎待多久？

→ Sue will Be staying in Paris for a while. 她將在巴黎待一陣子。

for 跟 since 與完成式連用。for 後是加一段時間，since 則是動作開始的時間點。

EX. She has been a chef for ten years. 她已經擔任主廚有十年了。

EX. She has been a chef since 2003. 她自從 2003 年擔任主廚。

c. 多久發生一次的時間副詞，一般為頻率副詞，位置為 Be 動詞或助動詞之後，一般動詞之前。問句使用 How often。

EX. How often do you eat fast food? 你多久吃一次速食？

→ I rarely eat fast food. 我很少吃速食。

EX. He never drinks coffee.（一般動詞之前）他從不喝咖啡。

EX. She is never late for work.（Be 動詞之後）她上班從不遲到。

EX. You must always fasten your seat belt.（助動詞之後）
你必須每次都繫好安全帶。

EX. I have never forgotten my first trip to the United States.（助動詞之後，一般動詞之前）我永遠都不會忘記我第一次去美國旅行。

d. 常見的頻率副詞

always → 100%

almost always → 95%

usually → 80%

often；frequently → 70%

sometimes → 50%

seldom；occasionally；rarely → 20%

hardly ever → 5%

never → 0%

e. 有些頻率副詞可放在句首或句尾。例如 usually 可以放在句首，而 sometimes 可以放在句首或句尾。

Ex. Usually she goes to dinner alone.　她經常自己去吃晚餐。

Ex. I email my friends in Japan sometimes. = Sometimes I email my friends in Japan.　有時候我會發電子郵件給我在日本的朋友。

帶有否定意義的頻率副詞如 seldom、occasionally、rarely、hardly ever、never 可放在句首，但句子需倒裝。

Ex. I have never read such an inspiring book. = Never have I read such an inspiring book.　我從來沒看過這麼啟發人的書。

Ex. He is rarely noticed. = Rarely is he noticed.　他幾乎很少被注意。

一些頻率副詞如 often，frequently 可放在句尾，前面再加上表達程度的副詞如 very，pretty，quite。

Ex. I talk to her at work very often.　我在工作時常常與她交談。

Ex. They have disagreement with each other quite frequently. 他們常常意見相左。

a lot 可放在句尾與 **often** 或 **frequently** 是相同意思。**not much** 否定句則是 **not often** 或 **not frequently**

Ex. I go to Tainan *a lot*. ＝ I often go to Tainan. 我常常去台南。

Ex. We don't go out *much*. ＝ We don't often go out. 我們不常出去。確切說明多久發生一次的時間副詞一般放在句子最後

Ex. He visits his family once a week. 他拜訪他的家人一周一次。

Ex. The magazine is published weekly. 這本雜誌一周發行一次。

f. daily、weekly、monthly、quarterly、yearly（＝ annual）也可以當成形容詞使用。

Ex. Where is the weekly sales report? 每周特價報在哪裡？

Ex. I've got the daily news updates by email. 我信箱有每日新聞更新。

g. yet & still

yet 表示仍未，尚未完成的動作，經常使用在完成式，放置於句尾。still 表示仍然，一般用在肯定與疑問句中，位置為 Be 動詞或助動詞之後，一般動詞之前。

Ex. A: Have you finished your work yet? B: Not yet.

A: 你完成你的工作了嗎？ B: 還沒。

Ex. She hasn't met the manager yet. 她還沒見到經理。

Ex. The professor still thinks it's your fault. 教授仍然覺得這是你的錯。

Ex. She is still waiting at the school. 她還在學校等。

h. 如果有不同種類的時間副詞，則使用以下順序排列

1. 發生多久

2. 多久發生一次

3. 何時發生

Ex. They work for *five hours every day*. ➡ 1＋2

Ex. He had to see the doctor *once a week last month*. ➡ 2＋3

Ex. The meeting will last *90 minutes tomorrow*. ➡ 1＋3

Ex. She went to a program for *six hours every weekend last year*. ➡ 1＋2＋3

換你寫寫看

請填入never、ago、yet、still、for、since

1. He said he has known you _____ a long time.

2. They moved away from here many years _____ .

3. I have _____ tried to cover the truth.

4. Is Natasha _____ here? I need to speak to her.

5. I haven't seen my family _____ last month.

6. We haven't had any problems _____ .

● 答案與中譯解析

1. 答：He said he has known you *for* a long time.
   他說他已經認識你很久一段時間了。

2. 答：They moved away from here many years *ago*.
   他們很多年前從這裏搬走。

3. 答：I have *never* tried to cover the truth. 我從來沒有試著掩蓋真相。

4. 答：Is Natasha *still* here? I need to speak to her.
   Natasha 還在這裡嗎？我需要跟她談一下。

5. 答：I haven't seen my family *since* last month.
   我自從上個月就沒有見到我的家人。

6. 答：We haven't had any problems *yet*. 我們還沒有任何的問題。

4. 程度副詞

a. 程度副詞可用來修飾動詞、形容詞與另一副詞，常見的程度副詞有 almost、nearly、quite、just、too、enough、hardly、scarcely、completely、very、extremely、especially、particularly、pretty、quite、fairly

程度副詞的位置一般是放在所修飾的單字前

Ex. The weather was extremely cold.（修飾形容詞 cold）
天氣非常地冷。

Ex. He said, "Thank you very much."（修飾副詞 much）
他說：「非常謝謝你。」

b. enough 表示足夠，放在形容詞或副詞之後

Ex. Is your coffee hot enough?（修飾形容詞 hot）
你的咖啡夠熱嗎？

Ex. Monty didn't work hard enough.（修飾副詞 hard）
Monty 工作沒有很努力。

enough 如果放在名詞前，為限定詞（determiner），可修飾可數與不可數名詞

Ex. We have enough books.（修飾可數名詞 books）
我們有足夠的書。

Ex. He doesn't have enough food.（修飾不可數名詞 food）
他沒有足夠的食物。

c. too 代表太過，放在形容詞或副詞之前

Ex. This coffee is too hot.（修飾形容詞 hot） 這咖啡太燙了。

Ex. He works too hard.（修飾副詞 hard） 他工作太認真了。

enough 與 too 修飾形容詞之後可加 for 某人或某事

Ex. The new secretary is not experienced enough for the job.
新任的秘書不夠有經驗去勝任這工作。

Ex. The sweater was too big for her. 這件毛衣對她而言太大。

not adj ／ adv ＋ enough to V 表示不夠程度去做某件事。

too adj. ＋ to V 意思為太…以致無法…

Ex. He didn't study hard enough to pass the test.
他沒有足夠努力讀書以致不能通過考試。

Ex. The girl was not old enough to get married. = The girl was too young to get married. 那女孩年紀還不夠大，以致於不能結婚。

d. very 表示非常，放在形容詞或副詞之前

Ex. The lady is very elegant.（修飾形容詞 elegant）
這女士非常地優雅。

Ex. He worked very quickly.（修飾副詞 quickly） 他工作非常地快。

not very 可與另一相反意義形容詞或副詞同義

Ex. He worked slowly. = He didn't work very quickly.
他工作慢。＝ 他工作沒有很快。

e. very 表達事實，too 則是陳述問題

Ex. They walk very fast. 他們走很快。

Ex. They walk too fast! 他們走太快！

5. 表示可能性的副詞

常見可能性的副詞有：certainly、definitely、maybe、possibly、clearly、obviously、perhaps、probably

a. maybe 與 perhaps 一般放在句首

Ex Perhaps the weather will Be fine.　或許天氣會變好。

Ex Maybe it won't rain. 或許不會下雨。

b. 其它常見表示可能性的副詞放在動詞之前，Be 動詞之後

Ex He is certainly coming to the meeting.　他一定會來參加這個會議。

Ex He will possibly go to England next year.　他有可能明年去英國。

Ex They are definitely at school.　他們絕對在學校。

Ex She was obviously very surprised.　她明顯地非常驚訝。

6. 地方與位置的副詞

a. 用介係詞表示位置

Ex He was standing at the door.　他站在門口。

Ex I can't find it in the drawer.　我在抽屜找不到那東西。

b. 表示方向

Ex Walk past the park and keep going.　穿過公園然後繼續走。

Ex Go straight ahead and turn left.　往前直走然後左轉。

c. 表示距離

Ex Hsinchu is 65 kilometers from Taipei.　新竹距離台北 65 公里。

Ex Hsinchu is not far away from Taipei.　新竹距離台北不遠。

7. 連接副詞

a. 連接副詞一般是用在句子間的轉折詞，常見的連接副詞有

時間	對比	增加	結果
then meanwhile henceforth afterward later soon	however nevertheless still on the other hand instead rather otherwise	likewise moreover furthermore besides in addition	consequently hence then therefore thus accordingly as a result

b. 連接副詞連接句子時可以出現在句子中不同的位置。句子間可以使用句號或分號，使用句號時句首字母需大寫，分號時則不用。連接副詞在句子中必須用逗號隔開。

Ex. My sister likes chocolate cookies; however, she doesn't eat many of them.

Ex. My sister likes chocolate cookies; she doesn't, however, eat many of them.

Ex. My sister likes chocolate cookies; she doesn't eat many of them, however.

 換你寫寫看

請填入in addition、therefore、on the other hand、however、otherwise

1. You have to stop smoking; _____ , you'll die early.

2. Golf is a very fun sport; _____ , it's very expensive.

3. Tony never watches what he eats; _____ , he gets really heavy.

4. This is a very useful tool; _____ , it's easy to carry around.

5. I would like to see the new movie this weekend; _____ , I might not have enough time to do that.

● 答案與中譯解析

1. 答：You have to stop smoking; *otherwise*, you'll die early.
   你必須要戒菸；不然你會很早死掉。

2. 答：Golf is a very fun sport; *on the other hand*, it's very expensive.
   高爾夫是很有趣的運動；另一方面它相當的貴。

3. 答：Tony never watches what he eats; *therefore*, he gets really heavy.
   Tony 從來沒有注意他吃的食物；所以他變得很胖。

4. 答：This is a very useful tool; *in addition*, it's easy to carry around.
   這是一個很實用的工具；除此之外它還攜帶方便。

5. 答：I would like to see the new movie this weekend; *however*, I might not have enough time to do that.
   我想要這周末看那新的電影；然而我可能會沒有時間去做那件事。

03 副詞的比較級

1. -ly 副詞

形容詞	副詞	比較級	最高級
quiet	quietly	more quietly	the most quietly
careful	carefully	more carefully	the most carefully
happy	happily	more happily	the most happily

Ex. Mary drives more carefully than John does.

Mary 開車比 John 還要小心。

Ex. Of all the drivers, Mary drives the most carefully.

在這麼多駕駛人中，Mary 開車最小心。

2. 形容詞與副詞同形

形容詞	副詞	比較級	最高級
hard	hard	harder	the hardest
fast	fast	faster	the fastest
early	early	earlier	the earliest

Ex. My brother gets up earlier than I do.

我哥哥起床比我早。

Ex. My brother gets up the earliest of all the family.

我的哥哥是家裡起床最早的。

3. 不規則副詞

形容詞	副詞	比較級	最高級
good	well	better	the best
bad	badly	worse	the worst
far	far	farther／further	the farthest／furthest

Ex. I did worse on the test than Leo did.

我考試考得比 Leo 差。

Ex. On that test, I did the worst in the class.

那次考試，我考得全班最差。

第20單元：動名詞

名言範例：

I just can't stop loving you. 我就是無法停止愛你。

　　這張單曲發行於1987年，收錄於專輯《Bad》，由 Michael Jackson 和歌手 Siedah Garret 合唱的情歌。在《Bad》這張專輯中，Michael 發行了7張單曲，其中有5首登上美國 Billboard Top 100的冠軍寶座，可以說是成果輝煌的一張專輯。"I just can't stop loving you" 是其中的一首冠軍歌曲，這首歌曾於2012年於美國著名影集 Glee 的「麥克傑克森特輯」中，由 Finn 與 Rachel 再度演唱。

英文達人文法小筆記！

動名詞（Gerunds）文法解析

動名詞（Gerunds）是由「動詞＋ing」組成，是具有動詞性質的「名詞」；已經轉為名詞的動名詞可以當句子的主詞（S）、受詞（O）、或補語（C）。而和現在分詞（V-ing）不同的地方，現在分詞是帶有形容詞的性質，而動名詞則為具有名詞的功用。

01 動名詞的特性

1.組成：動詞原形＋ing，將原本的動詞轉化為名詞
　　Ex. Read ＝ Reading，look ＝ looking，am ／ are ／ is ＝ being

2. 保有動詞的特性：動名詞後面可加受詞、補語、副詞修飾語、時態
　 與被動式。

a. 動名詞＋受詞

　　Ex. ***Playing basketball*** is good for you.　打籃球對你很好。

b. 動名詞＋補語

　　Ex. ***Being idle*** is the cause of his failure.　懶惰是造成失敗的原因。

c. 動名詞＋副詞

　　Ex. ***Dancing every*** day makes me healthy.　每天跳舞使我健康。

d. 動名詞的時態

　　● 簡單式動名詞（doing，being）：與主要動詞時間一致，或是表示未
　　　來。

　　Ex. I am sure of his ***coming***.　＝ I am sure that he ***will come***.
　　　（表示未來）我確定他會來。

　　● 完成式動名詞（having ＋ p.p.）：表示動名詞的時間比主要句子的動
　　　詞更早發生的事件。

　　Ex. Excuse me for not ***having answered*** your letter at once.
　　　很抱歉未能即刻回覆您信件。

e. 動名詞被動式

　　● 簡單被動式動名詞（being ＋ p.p.）。

　　Ex. I don't like ***being treated*** like that.　我不喜歡被這樣對待。

　　● 完成被動式動名詞（having been ＋ p.p.）。

　　Ex. I remember ***having been told*** that story.　我記得聽過這個故事。

3. 具有名詞的性質

a. 名詞前可放的詞類也適用於動名詞前。

Ex. I hate all *this arguing*.　我討厭這爭論。

b. 動名詞的單複數（純名詞）。

- 動名詞若只表示單一事件時，則後面接單數動詞。

Ex. Reading book is my hobby.　閱讀是我的嗜好。

- 動名詞有兩個以上時，主詞視為複數，和複數動詞連用。

Ex. *Reading and cooking are* my *hobbies*.　閱讀與下廚是我的嗜好。

c. 動名詞前可加「所有格」，仍帶有動詞特性。

Ex. Please excuse *my coming* late.　抱歉我來晚了。

02 動名詞的用法

1. 當主詞（S）：主詞（動名詞V-ing）＋動詞（V）＋形容詞Adj. ／名詞N

a. 動名詞當主詞時，後面接單數動詞。

b. 兩個動名詞當主詞，使用複數動詞。

Ex. *Getting up* early is good for healthy.　早起有益健康。

Ex. *Reading and cooking make* me happy.　閱讀與下廚讓我快樂。

2. 當主詞補語（SC）：主詞（S）＋Be 動詞（V）＋動名詞（V-ing）

- 動名詞放在 Be 動詞的後面，代表與主詞是同一件事。

Ex. My job *is solving* problem.　我的工作是解決問題。

3. 當受詞（O）：主詞（S）＋動詞（V）＋受詞（O ＝ V-ing）

a. 當動詞的受詞

- 多為及物動詞（V.t）

- 接動名詞的動詞

Mind 介意	Practice 練習	Begin 開始	Suggest 建議
Finish 完成	Enjoy 喜愛	Risk 風險	Admit 承認
Suggest 建議	Avoid 避免	Deny 否認	Resist 抵抗
Delay 延遲	Stop 停止	Postpone 延遲	Keep 保持
Imagine 想像	Consider 考慮	Escape 逃避	Catch 抓住
Quit 離開	Regret 遺憾	Complete 完成	Miss 錯過
Appreciate 感激	Resume 繼續	Spend 花費	Find 發現

Ex. I must *avoid doing* that again.（V.t ＋ V-ing）

我一定要避免再這麼做了。

Ex. I don't *mind staying* here alone.（V.t ＋ V-ing）

我不介意單獨待在這裡。

Ex. She admits having a crush on him.（V.t ＋ V-ing）

她承認對她有好感了。

b. 當介係詞的受詞

- 主詞（S）＋動詞（V）＋介係詞＋受詞（O ＝動名詞V-ing）

- 介係詞後接動名詞

● 接動名詞的片語

be afraid of 恐怕	be good at 擅長	be interested in 興趣	be worried about 擔心
worry about 擔心	dream of／about 夢想	talk about 談論	be careful about 小心
be fond of 喜歡	be responsible for 負責	be capable of 能力	be tired of 疲倦
believe in 相信	object to 反對	thanks for 感謝	be used to 習慣

Ex. He *is fond of* mountain *climbing*.（V ＋ of ＋ V-ing）他喜歡爬山。

Ex. *I am good at playing* the piano.（V ＋ at ＋ V-ing）我擅長彈琴。

03 常見慣用語

1. There is no V-ing ＝ It's impossible to ＋ V（…是不可能的…）

Ex. There is no smoking in this area.

＝ It's impossible to smoke in this area.　這裡不能抽菸。

2. It is no use ＋ V-ing ＝ It's of no use to ＋ V.（…是沒有用的…）

Ex. There is no use crying over spilt milk.

＝ It's of no use to cry over spilt milk.　覆水難收。

3. can't help ＋ V-ing ＝ can't but ＋原形V.（…不得不…）

Ex. I can't help falling in love with you.

＝ I can't but fall in love with you.　情不自禁愛上你。

4. On + V-ing… , S + V-ed… = As soon as S + V-ed, S + Ved…（一…就…）

> Ex. On hearing the bad news, she burst into tears. = As soon as she heard the bad news, she burst into tears.
>
> 一聽到這壞消息，她的眼淚就流出來了。

5. feel like + V-ing = would like +不定詞（想要…）

> Ex. I feel like buying a new car. = I would like to buy a new car.
>
> 我有想要買部新車。

6. 省略介系詞：be busy（in）+ V-ing…（忙於…）

be worth（of）+ Ving…（值得…）

> Ex. This movie is worth（of）seeing. 這部電影值得看。

7. go + V-ing…（去做…），一般用於戶外運動或休閒活動

> Ex. They go（shopping，swimming，dancing…）every Sunday.
>
> 他們每周日去（逛街、游泳、跳舞…）。

8. do + V-ing…（做…）

> Ex. She does the（cooking，cleaning，traveling…）
>
> 她（下廚、打掃、旅行…）。

9. how／what about + V-ing…（你認為…如何？）

> Ex. What／How about playing tennis together this afternoon?
>
> 今天下午一起打網球你認為如何呢？

10. What do you say to + V（…意下如何？）

> Ex. What do you say to join me for dinner?
>
> 跟我一起吃晚餐意下如何？

絕妙好例句

1. Seeing is believing.（believing ＝主詞補語 SC）眼見為憑。

2. Swimming is a good exercise.（Gerunds ＝ Swimming ＝主詞 S）
   游泳是個好運動。

3. Meggie enjoys riding her bike.（Gerunds ＝ riding ＝動詞的受詞）
   Meggie 喜歡騎腳踏車。

4. You just keep on going straight.（Gerunds ＝ going ＝介詞 on 的受
   詞）你只要繼續一直往前走。

5. I don't like being disturbed while reading.（Gerunds ＝ being
   disturbed ＝動詞的受詞，被動式）我不喜歡在讀書時被打擾。

換你寫寫看

1. I can't help _____ asleep during that boring speech.（to fall）

2. _____ something to eat _____better than nothing.（to have）

3. I look forward to_____ you soon.（to see）

4. Do you mind _____ on the air conditioner? It's hot in here.
   (A)to turn (B)turn (C)turning

5. It's no use _____ .
   (A)of complaining (B)their complaining (C)complaining

● 答案與中譯解析

1. 答：falling（Gerunds ＝動詞 help 的受詞，常見慣用語 can't help ＋V-ing）在
   聽無聊的演講時，我忍不住睡著了。

2. 答：Having（is；Gerunds ＝主詞，單數）有吃總比沒得吃好。

3. 答：seeing（Gerunds ＝介詞 to 的受詞）期待再相見。

4. 答：(C)（Gerunds ＝動詞 mind 的受詞）你介意開冷氣嗎？這裡好熱。
5. 答：(A)（It is no use ＋of ＋V-ing 常用慣用語。）抱怨是沒有用的。

20

第21單元：不定詞

名言範例：

I love to travel, but hate to arrive.

我喜歡旅行，但不喜歡到達目的地。

　　摘自愛因斯坦（Albert Einstein）是 20世紀猶太裔理論物理學家，創立了相對論；被譽為是「現代物理學之父」及二十世紀世界最重要科學家之一。他卓越的科學成就和原創性使得「愛因斯坦」一詞成為「天才」的同義詞。這句話可以表達顯示出愛因斯坦非常喜愛於研究的過程。

英文達人文法小筆記！

不定詞文法解析

不定詞（Infinitives）由「to＋原形動詞」組成，因是動詞演變而來，所以具有動詞特性，也扮演著名詞（N）、形容詞（Adj.）、（Adv.）的角色。因此 定詞可以拿來當主詞（S）、受詞（O）、或補語（C）。

01 不定詞的特性

1. 組成：to＋動詞原形（V）

　a. 否定在 to 前加 not＝not to＋V

　　Ex. I decide ***not to speak*** to Tom.　我決定不跟 Tom 講話了。

b. 有時會將 "to" 省略 所以會分為兩類 "有 to 不定詞" 與 "無 to 不定詞"。

- 感官動詞（如：see，hear，feel…）

Ex. I saw him（**to**）**swim** yesterday.

- 使役動詞（如：make，let，have…）

Ex. I let him（**to**）**go**.

2. 保有動詞的特性： 不定詞後面可加受詞、補語、副詞修飾語。也有時態與被動式。

a. 不定詞＋受詞

Ex. **To learn English** is difficult for me.　學英語對我來說是困難的。

b. 不定詞＋補語

Ex. **To Be honest**, I like you.　老實說，我喜歡你。

c. 不定詞＋副詞

Ex. I want you to **come early**.　我希望你能早點來。

d. 不定詞的時態

- 簡單式（to V）：不定詞與主要動詞時間一致。

Ex. I decide to learn English.　我決定學英文。

- 進行式（to be＋V-ing）：在主要動詞時間中，動作正在進行。

Ex. It's nice **to Be sitting** here with you.　跟你一起坐在這真好。

- 完成式（to have＋p.p.）：不定詞的時間比主要動詞更早發生的事件。

Ex. He seems **to have missed** the train.　他好像沒有趕上火 。

e. 不定詞的被動式

- 簡單式：（not）＋to **be**＋**p.p.**

Ex. No one likes **to Be found** faults with.　沒有人喜歡被人找缺點。

225

- 完成式：（not）＋ to have ＋ p.p.

Ex. Something seems **to have been forgotten**. 好像有東西被忘掉。

02 不定詞的用法

1. 當名詞（N）

a. 當主詞（S）

- 不定詞當主詞時，後面接單數動詞
- 兩個以上不定詞當主詞，使用複數動詞
- 可用「虛主詞it」作替代，把真正的主詞放在句尾：

  句型＝ It is ＋ adj ＋（for ／ of）＋ N ＋ to-V

Ex. **It** is difficult **for** me **to learn English**.（S ＝ to learn…）

　　＝ **To learn English** is difficult（for me）.

　　學英語對我來說是困難的。

b. 當受詞（O）

- 當一般動詞的受詞
- S ＋ V ＋（受詞O）＋（not）＋ to-V

Ex. He asked me **to mail the letter**.（S ＋ V ＋ O ＋ to-V）

　　他叫我去寄那封信。

Ex. I plan **to visit Paris**.（S ＋ V ＋ to-V）我計畫去巴黎。

- 可用「虛受詞it」作替代，把真正的受詞放在句尾

  句型＝ S ＋ V ＋ **it** ＋（adj，N）＋ to-V

Ex. I think **it** is better **to leave**.（O ＝ it ＝ to leave）

　　我認為離開比較好。

c. 當補語（C）

- 主詞補語（S.C）

Ex His dream is **to become a scientist**. 他夢想做一個科學家。

- 受詞補語（O.C）

Ex He taught me **to speak English**. 他教我說英語。

2. 當形容詞（Adj.）

a. 用來修飾名詞的不定詞，一定要放在被修飾名詞的後面

- 及物動詞（Vt）用法＝（代）名詞＋to-Vt.

Ex I want some water **to drink**.（adj. = to drink）我要一些喝的水。

- 不及物動詞（Vi）用法＝（代）名詞＋to -Vi ＋介詞

Ex He needs a chair **to sit on**. 他需要一張椅子坐。

3. 當副詞（Adv.）可以修飾動詞、形容詞、其它副詞、或一整個子句

a. 表目的，修飾動詞：

- （not）to ＋V ＝ so as（not）to ＋V ＝ in order（not）to ＋V

Ex I came **to buy a book** = I came **in order to buy a book**.（to-V 修飾動詞come）他來買一本書。

b. 表結果，修飾形容詞與副詞

- 表正面結果：（如此／太…以致於…）

so ＋（adj. ／ adv.）＋ as to ＋V ＝（adj. ／ adv.）＋ enough ＋ to ＋ V

Ex He studied hard **enough to pass the exam**.

= He studied **so** hard **as to pass the exam**.

（to-V 修飾副詞 hard）他很用功以致於能通過考試。

21 22 23 24 25 26 27 附錄1 附錄2 附錄3

● 表負面結果：（太怎樣…以致於不能…）

too ＋（adj. ／ adv.）＋ to V ＝（太…以致於不能…）

＝ not ＋（adj. ／ adv.）＋ enough ＋ to ＋ V

Ex. He is **too** weak **to stand up**.

＝ He is **not** strong **enough to stand up**.

（to-V 修飾形容詞 weak，strong）他太虛弱了以致於沒法站立。

c. 表原因／理由

● 主詞（人）＋ Be 動詞＋ adj ＋ to-V

● 表示情緒（喜怒哀樂等）或態度的形容詞之後加上不定詞（to-V），可以表達情感的原因，主要以人為主詞。

Ex. I am sorry **to give** you trouble.　抱歉給您添麻煩。

● **常見後面接不定詞的形容詞**

be pleased to 高興	be ready to 樂意	be sorry to 抱歉
be delighted to 高興	be prepared to 準備	be afraid to 恐怕
be lucky to 幸運	be anxious to 焦慮	be likely to 可能
be upset to 心煩	be eager to 渴望	be certain to 確信
be disappointed to 失望	be willing to 願意	be surprised to 驚訝
be proud to 驕傲	be careful to 小心	be excited to 興奮

d. 修飾整個子句（又叫做獨立不定詞）

Ex. To tell you the truth, I don't like you at all.　說實話，我並不喜歡你。

4. 不定詞的疑問句

a. 疑問句（Wh-）＋ to-V ＝名詞片語

b. 疑問句＝ how、when、what、where、whom

c. 名詞片語有「名詞」的性質，可以做主詞、受詞或補語

> Ex. I don't know **what to say**.（當受詞）我不知道該說甚麼。
>
> My question is **how to make coffee**.（主詞補語）
>
> 我的問題是如何煮咖啡。

5. 常接不定詞的動詞

a. 動詞 V ＋ to-V

Afford 負擔	Consent 同意	Manage 管理	Refuse 拒絕
Agree 同意	Decide 決定	Mean 意欲	Seem 似乎
Appear 顯露	Demand 要求	Need 需要	Struggle 掙扎
Arrange 安排	Deserve 值得	Offer 提供	Swear 發誓
Ask 詢問	Expect 期待	Plan 計畫	Threaten 威脅
Beg 乞求	Fail 失敗	Prepare 準備	Volunteer 自願
care 想要	Hesitate 猶豫	Promise 承諾	Wait 等待
Claim 主張	Hope 希望	Pretend 假裝	Want 希望

> Ex. I decide **to go**.（to-V 當 N 受詞）我決定去。

b. 動詞 V ＋名詞或代名詞＋ to-V

Allow 允許	Dare 膽敢	Instruct 指式	Remind 提醒
Ask 詢問	Encourage 鼓勵	Invite 邀請	Require 要求
Beg 乞求	Expect 期待	Need 需要	Teach 指導
Cause 導致	Forbid 禁止	Order 命令	Tell 告訴
Challenge 挑戰	Force 強迫	Permit 允許	Urge 催促
Convince 説服	Hire 雇用	Persuade 説服	Want 想要

Ex. I allow him **to come in**.（to-V 當 N 受詞補語）我允許他進來。

 絕妙好例句

1. I am very happy to meet you.（to-V 當副詞）很高興遇見你。

2. I expect to be invited to the part.

（to-V 被動式）我期待被邀請參加舞會。

3. Where to go is up to you?

（Wh 疑問句名詞片語，當主詞）隨你想去哪？

4. It is important to be on time.

（主詞＝ it ＝ to be on time）準時是很重要的。

5. The story is easy enough for a kid to read.

（to-V 當副詞，表結果）這故事夠簡單，小孩也能讀。

換你寫寫看

1. _____is one thing; _____is another.（to know，to do）
2. She seemed _____ out of her mind.（to be）
3. I don't have a key _____ his door.（to unlock）
4. My pocket is too small _____ my wallet.（A)to insert（B)insert（C)
   inserting
5. He promised _____ late again.（A)does not be（B)not Be（C)not to
   be

● 答案與中譯解析

1. 答：To know、to do（to-V ＝名詞＝主詞）知道是一回事，做是另一回事。
2. 答：to be（to-V ＝主詞補語）她似乎神經錯亂了。
3. 答：to unlock（to-V ＝形容詞 V，修飾 a key）我沒有開這扇門的鑰匙。
4. 答：(A)（to-V ＝副詞修飾形容詞 adj.）我的口袋太小以致於無法放入我的皮夾。
5. 答：(C)（否定句 not 放在 to-V 前）他答應不會再遲到。

第22單元：動名詞與不定詞的比較

名言範例：

To Be or not to be, that is a question.

存在或不存在，這真是一個問題。

　　莎士比亞（William Shakespeare）著作中名句很多，相信最多被人引用的算是這句了，在Hamlet《哈姆雷特》中第三幕主角的獨白。哈姆雷特一直在煩惱要不要殺了他的母親和繼父，心中充滿矛盾，不知如何處理這錯綜複雜關係的情況下，用這句獨白道出了哈姆雷特的悲傷、矛盾和無奈，猶豫掙扎。

英文達人文法小筆記！

動名詞（Gerund）與不定詞（Infinitives）的比較文法解析

動名詞（Gerund）與不定詞（Infinitives）都是由動詞轉換而來，在句子中雖具有動詞的特性，卻扮演著名詞、形容詞、或副詞的角色。

01 動名詞與不定詞的比較

1. 用法特性比較表

用法	動名詞（V-ing）	不定詞（to-V）
名詞 （N）	作主詞（S） 作受詞（O）：動詞後、介係詞後 作補語（C）：主詞補語（SC）	作主詞（S） 作受詞（O）：動詞後 作補語（C）：主詞補語（SC） 　受詞補語（OC）
形容詞 （adj）	N／A	可用來修飾名詞
副詞 （adv）	N／A	修飾動詞（V） 修飾形容詞（adj.） 修飾其它副詞（adv.） 修飾整個子句

Ex. Seeing is believing. = To see is to believe.　眼見為憑。

2. 虛主詞（it）與動名詞、不定詞的互換

a. 動名詞當主詞可以用可以用不定詞虛主詞代替

Ex: **Learning English** is difficult.

= **To learn English** is difficult.

= **It** is difficult **to learn English**.　學英語是困難的。

3. 動名詞與不定詞的時態

時態	動名詞（V-ing）	不定詞（to-V）
簡單式	V-ing	to V
進行式	N／A	to be ＋ V-ing
完成式	having ＋ p.p.	to have ＋ p.p.

233

4 動名詞與不定詞的被動語態

時態	動名詞（V-ing）	不定詞（to-V）
簡單被動式	being ＋ p.p.	to be ＋ p.p.
完成被動式	having been ＋ p.p.	to have been ＋ p.p.

02 動詞後加動名詞還是不定詞

1. 動詞可用動名詞或不定詞，句子意義相同

Like 喜歡	Begin 開始	Intent 意圖
Love 愛	Start 開始	Neglect 忽略
Hate 討厭	Cease 停止	Learn 學習
Dislike 不喜歡	Continue 繼續	Plan 計畫
Prefer 較喜歡	Can't stand 不能忍受	Can't bear 無法忍受

Ex. I like *to listen* to jazz. ＝ I like *listening* to jazz.　我喜歡聽爵士。

2. 動詞可用動名詞或不定詞，句子意義不同

	說明	例句
Stop 停止	V-ing 停下做某件事 To- V 停下來去做某事	He stops smoking. 他停止抽菸（戒菸）。 He stops to smoke. 他停下來抽菸。
Remember 記得	V-ing 記得已做的事情 To- V 記得未做的事情	I remember mailing the letter. 我記得寄過那封信。 I remember to mail the letter. 我要記得去寄那封信。

Forget 忘記	V-ing 忘記已做過的事情 To- V 忘記要去做的事情	He forgot doing his homework. 他忘記做過了功課。 He forgot to do his homework. 他忘記要做功課了。
Regret 遺憾	V-ing 後悔做過的事情 To- V 抱歉要去做的事情	I regret telling you these. 我後悔告訴你這些。 I regret to tell you these. 我很遺憾要告訴你這些。

換你寫寫看

1. I save some money so as to buy a new car.

   ＝I save some money _____ a new car.

2. My sister is good at _____（to cook）

3. He is too stubborn _____ with you.

   (A)agree　(B)agreeing　(C)to agree

4. Are you interested_____ tennis?　(A)in playing　(B)to play　(C)play

---

● 答案與中譯解析

  1. 答：in order to buy（to-V ＝副詞用法修飾動詞，表目的）我存錢為了買新車。

  2. 答：cooking（V-ing ＝介係詞的受詞）我姐姐很會煮飯。

  3. 答：(C)（too...to-V ＝副詞修飾形容詞 stubborn）

     他太頑固了以致於無法同意你。

  4. 答：(A)（V-ing ＝介係詞 in 的受詞）你對打網球有興趣嗎？

第23單元：語態助動詞

名言範例：

I Can't Catch You. 我抓不住你。

　　出處於嘟噹六便士合唱團（Sixpence None The Richer）的歌曲 I Can't Catch you。講出這個團名的時候，知道的人並不太多，但說結婚典禮熱門曲 Kiss Me 就是他們唱的，不少人就會露出恍然大悟的表情。此樂團以輕快甜美的歌曲熱播全球。

英文達人文法小筆記！

01 Can

1. 表達可能或能力

> Ex. John can speak Spanish. → 能力
>
> John 可以說西班牙文。
>
> Ex. I cannot hear you. → 能力
>
> ＝ I can't hear you. 我聽不到你。
>
> Ex. Can you talk to me? → 可能
>
> 你可以跟我說嗎？

2. can 一般用在現在式或未來式

> Ex. A: Can you help me with my homework? → 現在
>
> A: 你可以幫我做功課嗎？

Ex. B: Sorry. I'm busy now. I can help you tomorrow. ➡ 未來

B: 對不起。我現在在忙。我明天可以幫你。

3. 表達要求與命令

通常 can 在表達要求或命令時為問句的型式，但這並非一個真正的問句，而是一種較為強烈的要求的語氣。

Ex. Can you make some coffee, please? 可以給我咖啡嗎？

Ex. Can you Be here in a minute? 你可以現在就到嗎？

4. can 可用於徵詢或給予允許

Ex. A: Can I smoke in this room?

A: 我可以在這房間抽菸嗎？

Ex. B: You can't smoke here, but you can smoke in the garden.

B: 你不可以在這裡抽菸，但是你可以在花園抽菸。

注意：在詢問是否可以做一件事時，may，could，can 表達不同的正式與禮貌的程度

Ex. May I help you?

➡ 最正式與最有禮貌的用法

請問我可以幫你嗎？

Ex. Could I talk to you for a second?

➡ 禮貌的請求。could 在此沒有代表過去的時態

請問可以借一下跟你說話？

Ex. Can I see what you're making?

➡ 一般與朋友或認識的人所使用的語氣

可以讓我看你做在什麼嗎？

5. could 表達過去的能力

Ex. My grandmother could speak five languages.

我祖母過去可以說五種語言。

Ex. When we arrived home, we *could not* open the door.

= When we arrived home, we *couldn't* open the door.

當我們到家時，我們不能打開門。

Ex. Could you understand what he was saying?

你可以理解他當時在說甚麼嗎？

6. could 表達請求。相較 can 之下較為正式與禮貌

Ex. Could you tell me where the bank is, please?

請問你可否告訴我銀行在哪裡嗎？

Ex. Could you send me an email, please?

請問你可否寄 email 給我？

7. can ／ could ／ be able to

a. be able to 一樣表達有能力去做某件事情，但可以運用在不同的時態中。而 can 一般則只使用現在與未來時態的表達，could 則是用在過去時態。

Ex. I was able to fly an airplane. ➡（過去式） 我之前就能夠開飛機了。

Ex. I will Be able to fly an airplane very soon.

➡（未來式） 我很快將可以開飛機。

Ex. I have been able to fly an airplane since I was at college.

➡（完成式） 我自從大學的時候我就可以開飛機。

b. be able to 後面可加不定詞

Ex. I would like to Be able to fly an airplane. 我想要能夠開飛機。

🖊 換你寫寫看

請選擇最適當的答案

1. We _____ go to the party. We're going to a wedding.

(A)won't Be able to　(B)couldn't　(C)can't Be able to　(D)won't can

2. A: Can you lend me some money? B: Sorry. I _____. I haven't got any

either.　(A)can't　(B)won't　(C)'m not able to　(D)couldn't

3. You'll Be able to find the answer, _____?

(A)can't you　(B)couldn't you　(C)aren't you　(D)won't you

4. I didn't hear what you said. _____ repeat it again?

(A)Can I　(B)Can you　(C)May I　(D)Did you

5. I've left my wallet at my place. _____ borrow some money?

(A)Do you　(B)Can you　(C)Could I　(D)Will I

● 答案與中譯解析

1. 答：(A) 我們沒辦法去參加派對。我們要去一場婚禮。

2. 答：(A) 回答時根據問句使用一樣的助動詞

　　A: 你可以借我一些錢嗎？ B: 抱歉，我不行。我也沒有任何錢。

3. 答：(D) won't you → （附加問句保持與前面句子相同時態與助動詞，再將肯定句變成否定的疑問句）你有辦法找到答案，不是嗎？

4. 答：(B) Can you 我之前沒聽到你說甚麼。你可以再說一遍嗎？

5. 答：(C) 我把錢包放在家裡了。我可以借一些錢嗎？

02 *will & would*

1.will 表未來式，would 則是過去以為會發生的事

Ex. We'll Be there soon. 我們很快就會到那裡。

Ex. I thought we would Be there soon. 我原本以為我們會很快到那裡。

2.will 可以表示提供承諾

Ex. I will think of you all the time when I leave here.

我離開後我將會常常想你。

Ex. We will come and see you next week.

我下星期將會去看你。

3.will 表達意願，would 則是用在過去時態

Ex. I will do it if you want me to. 我會幫你做這些只要你希望我做。

Ex. The baby wouldn't stop crying last night. 嬰兒昨晚哭得不停。

4.will 與 would 都可以作為請求的問句，would 比 will 更有禮貌

Ex. Will you do me a favor? 你可以幫我個忙嗎？

Ex. Would you pass me the pepper? 可以請你幫我傳一下胡椒嗎？

5.would 的相關片語

a. would you mind（not）＋ Ving…是有禮貌的請求別人做某件事。如果是願意的，回答時則是用否定語氣來表示不介意

Ex. A: Would you mind opening the window?

A: 請問你介意我打開窗嗎？

Ex. B: No, I wouldn't. ／ Of course not. ／ Not at all. ／ No problem. ／ Sure

B: Would you mind not telling the teacher?

B: 不，不會介意。／當然不會介意。／沒關係。／沒問題。／當然可以。

B: 你介意不告訴老師嗎？

b. would you mind if I ＋過去式…

請求允許。准許時也是用否定語氣來表示不介意

Ex. Would you mind if I opened the window? 請問你介意我開窗嗎？

Ex. Would you mind if we used the restroom?
請問你介意我用化妝室嗎？

c. would you like…或 would you like to…

表達提供某件事情或邀請

Ex. Would you like to come visit us? 請問你可以拜訪我嗎？

Ex. Would you like another drink? 請問你還要其他飲料嗎？

d. I would like…或 I would like to…

表示想要的事物或想做的事＝I want 或 I want to

Ex. I'd like that one please. 我想要這個，謝謝。

Ex. I'd like to go home now. 我現在想要回家。

e. I would rather 表示偏好

Ex. I'd rather have some tea. 我比較想要茶。

Ex. I'd rather ask him to leave now. 我寧願請他走。

f. I would think 或 I would imagine 是在提供想法或意見

Ex. It's very difficult I would imagine. 我可以想見這很困難。

Ex. I would think that's the right answer. 我想這是正確的答案。

換你寫寫看

1. It's so hot! Would you _____ to drink some water?

(A)care (B)mind (C)like(D)think

2. A: Do you want to go out for a drink?   B: Actually, I'd _____ , if you don't mind. (A)prefer not (B)rather not (C)don't want (D)like to

3. I really need to go now. Would you mind _____ early? (A)leaving (B)if I leaving (C)if I would leave (D)if I left

4. A: Do you want to see a movie tonight?   B: That'd Be great! I'd _____.

(A)rather not (B)love to (C)prefer to (D)imagine

5. A: Would you mind saying that again?

B: _____. (A)Yes, I wouldn't. (B)No, I would. (C)No, of course. (D)No, of course not.

● 答案與中譯解析

1.(C) 好熱喔！你想要喝一些水嗎？

2.(B) A：你想出去喝一杯嗎？ B：我寧願不要，如果你不介意的話。

3.(D) 我真的需要走了。你介意我先離開嗎？

4.(B) A：你今天晚上想看電影嗎？ B：那太好了！我願意。

5.(D) A：你介意再説一遍嗎？ B：不，當然不會。

---

03 *may & might*

1.may 使用在我們不是很確定一件事情的時候

Ex. There may not be many people for today's class.

今天的課可能不會有很多人。

Ex We may be late for the meeting.　我們可能今天議會遲到。

2. 比較 maybe

→ Maybe we're late for the meeting.

maybe 為表示可能性的副詞，一般放在句首

Ex He is coming to see us tomorrow.

　→ Maybe he is coming to see us tomorrow.
　　他或許明天會來看我們。

3. may 可用來表達很有禮貌的請求

Ex May I borrow the car tomorrow?　我明天可以借用你的車嗎？

Ex May we come a little later?　我們可以晚一點到嗎？

4. may not 可用在表達強烈的拒絕

Ex A: May I borrow the car tomorrow?　A：我明天可以跟你借書嗎？

Ex B: You may not borrow the car until you can be more careful.

　　B：你不能借車直到你開車能更小心一點。

Ex A: May we come a little later?　A：我們可以晚一點到嗎？

Ex B: You may not!　B：不行！

5. might 使用在不是很確定一件事情的時候，跟 may 一樣可以使用在現在式中。

Ex I might see you tomorrow.　我可能明天會去看你。

Ex The tie looks nice, but it might be very expensive.

　　這領帶看起來很好，但是可能太貴。

6. 用在禮貌請求 may 的過去式

Ex He asked if he might borrow the car.　他想請問他是否可以借車。

243

Ex. They wanted to know if they might come later.

他們想知道是否可以晚一點到。

7. 非常有禮貌的請求

Ex. Might I ask you a question?　請問我可以問一個問題嗎？

Ex. Might we just interrupt for a second?　請問我們可以打擾一下嗎？

8. may have 與 might have 表是對已發生的事情的推測，而事情有持續的狀態

Ex. It's ten o'clock.　They might have arrived now.

現在十點了。他們可能已經到了。

Ex. Olivia wasn't in class today.　She may have been sick.

Olivia 今天沒有來上課。她可能生病了。

注意：might have 也用在假設語氣中與過去事實相反的假設。

Ex. He might have been here if you had asked him to come.

他本來可以在這如果你有叫他來的話。

→ You didn't ask him to come and he wasn't here.

你沒有叫他所以他不在這。

换你寫寫看

請填入may或might

1. _____ I have your attention, please?（禮貌請求）

2. Polly wondered if she _____ borrow some money.（禮貌請求過去式）

3. They _____ come see me this weekend.（不確定）

4. No one _____ not read my diary.（強烈的拒絕）

5. He _____ have forgotten all about the incident.（事情的推測）

● 答案與中譯解析

1. 答：**May** I have your attention, please?　請問大家可以注意一下嗎？

2. 答：Polly wondered if she **might** borrow some money.

   Polly 不確定她是否能借一些錢。

3. 答：They **may** come see me this weekend.　他們這星期也許會來看我。

4. 答：No one **may** not read my diary.　沒有人可以讀我的日記。

5. 答：He **may ／ might** have forgotten all about the incident.

   他可能已經忘了事件所有經過。

04 *shall & should*

1. shall 用在問句中表示一禮貌的問句

Ex Shall we dance? 我們跳舞好嗎？

Ex Shall I go now? 我該現在走嗎？

Ex Let's go, shall we? 走吧，好嗎？

2. shall 正式用法裡代表要求與義務

Ex Everyone shall obey the law.　每個人都該遵守法律。

Ex There shall Be no trespassing on this property.

我們不能非法入侵他人的土地。

Ex Visitors shall not enter this room.　旅客不能進入這間房間。

3. should 表示意見、建議、偏好、或想法

Ex You should stay home and rest today.　你今天該待在家裡休息。

Ex I should take a taxi this time.　我這次應該要搭計程車。

Ex He should Be more careful in the process.

他在流程中應該要更小心。

245

**4. 表示對過去曾經或不曾發生的事情一個相反的假設（should +
have + p.p.）**

Ex. You should have seen it. It was really beautiful.

→ You didn't see it.

你應該要去看。這真的很漂亮。 → 你沒有去看。

Ex. I should have completed it earlier to meet the deadline.

→ I didn't complete it early.

我應該在期限之前要早點做完。 → 你沒有早點做完。

Ex. We should have visited the place on the way. → We didn't visit the
place on the way.

我們在途中應該要參觀那地方的。 → 我們在途中沒有參觀那地方。

5. 詢問意見

Ex. What should we do now? 我們現在應該怎麼做好？

Ex. Should we continue our meeting? 我們應該繼續我們的會議嗎？

Ex. Should we go this way? 我們應該這樣做嗎？

6. 表達期望發生或預期正確的事情

Ex. There should be an old building here.

這應該會有一個老舊的建築。

Ex. Everybody should arrive by 6 p.m. 大家應該在六點抵達。

Ex. We should be there this evening. 我們今天下午應該要在那。

05 *must & have to*

1. must 表示基於合理的推測與充分的證據而做確定的推論

Ex. There's no air conditioning on. You must be hot.

這裡沒有空調。你一定很熱。

Ex. You must be proud of yourself that you've gotten this far.

你一定很自豪你自己已經堅持這麼久。

Ex. I can't remember when I did it.I must be getting old.

我不記得我什麼時候做的。我一定在變老的。

對於過去的推論則使用 must have

Ex. Sue was working nonstop on the assignment.　She must have been tired.　Sue 一直沒有休息地執行計劃。她一定很累了。

2. must 表示必須的義務與必須去做的事情

Ex. I must go to bed earlier.　我必須早點睡覺。

Ex. They must do something about it.　他們必須在這件事上做點什麼。

Ex. You must come and see us some time.　你必須早時間來看我們。

3. have to 在肯定時與 must 意思相同，但 have to 可作時態的變化

Ex. He has to arrive at work at 9 am.

→（現在式）　他必須在 9 am 上班。

Ex. They'll have to do something about it.

→（未來式）　他們將必須在這件事上做點什麼。

Ex. I had to send a report to the head office every week last year.

→（過去式）　我去年必須要每個禮拜寄報告到總公司。

4. have got to ＝ have to

Ex. I've got to take this book back to the library today.

我今天必須要把這本書還給圖書館。

Ex. We've got to finish the preparation for the dinner soon.

我們必須盡快完成晚餐的準備。

在口語中，have ／ has 經常會省略，got to 合併成 gotta

> Ex. I gotta go now.　= I've got to go now.　= I have to go now.
>
> 我們必須要走了。
>
> 注意：have to 與 must 在肯定句裡時意思相同，但注意在否定句中代表不同解釋。

5. must not（mustn't）表示必須的義務為一定不能做的事情

> Ex. We mustn't talk about our salaries.　They are confidential.
>
> 我們絕不能討論薪水。這是保密的。

> Ex. I mustn't eat too much sweet.　It's bad for my teeth.
>
> 我絕不能吃太多甜食。這對我的牙齒不好。

> Ex. They mustn't see us talking or they'll suspect something.
>
> 他們絕對不能看到我們對談；不然他們會懷疑我們。

6. don't ／ doesn't have to 表示不一定需要去做的事

> Ex. We don't have to get there on time.　我們不必準時到那裡。

> Ex. You don't have to come if you don't want to.　你不需要來如果你不想要來的話。

> Ex. He doesn't have to sign anything.　他不需要簽任何東西。

換你寫寫看

請填入 must、must not、have to、don't have to

1. I've finished my work, so I _____ stay up late again tonight.

2. You _____ try the shoes on, but it might be a good idea.

3. This appliance _____ be used in the bathroom. It's dangerous.

4. You _____ have a passport to travel to a foreign country.

5. Baggage _____ be left unattended.

● 答案與中譯解析

1. 答：I've finished my work, so I **don't have to** stay up late again tonight.
   我已經做完我的工作，所以我今天晚上不用再熬夜了。

2. 答：You **don't have to** try the shoes on, but it might be a good idea.
   你不一定要試穿這鞋子，但是這可能是個好主意。

3. 答：This appliance **must not** be used in the bathroom. It's dangerous.
   這個電氣絕對不能在浴室使用。這很危險。

4. 答：You **must ╱ have to** have a passport to travel to a foreign country.
   你必須要有護照去到別的國家旅遊。

5. 答：Baggage **must not** be left unattended.　行李絕對禁止無人看管。

---

06 *need*

1. need 當作必須解釋

可當作一般動詞使用，後面加不定詞 to

　　Ex. He needs to see a doctor.　他需要去看醫生。

　　Ex. Do you need to go to work tomorrow?　你明天需要上班嗎？

　　Ex. You don't need to be here.　你不需要在這裡。

2. need 也可當助動詞

一般用在否定句與疑問句，表示不必要的動作或詢問是否有此必要

　　Ex. You needn't do the dishes.　I'll wash them later.
　　你不需要洗碗。我待會會洗。

Ex. A: Need I lock the door when I leave the office?

A：我離開辦公室之前需要鎖門嗎？

Ex. B: No, you needn't.　Sarah will be back soon.

B：不，你不用。Sarah 待會就會回來。

3. needn't 與 don't need to 的差別

Ex. You needn't come if you don't want to.　➡ 不用當成一個義務

Ex. You don't need to be a genius to understand this.　➡ 不一定需要是

07 had better

1. had better & should

had better 比較起 should 是給予更強烈的建議，已經有警告的語氣。

had better 並不是一過去式的使用，主要是現在或未來的建議。

Ex. You'd better tell her everything.　你最好跟她坦白。

Ex. I'd better get back to work.　我最好回去工作。

Ex. We'd better meet early in the morning.

我們最好早點在早上時相見。

注意：使用 had better 後不需加 to

2. 否定型式 had better not

Ex. You'd better not say anything.　你最好不要說任何話。

Ex. I'd better not come.　我最好不要去。

Ex. We'd better not miss the beginning of the presentation.

我們最好不要錯過報告的開頭。

3. 一般狀況的建議則使用 should

Ex. You shouldn't say anything.

你不應該說任何話的。

Ex. He should dress more appropriately for work.

他應該上班穿正式一點。

4. had better 建議一件事情如未照此情形發生，另一相反狀況則會發生

Ex. You'd better do what I say or else you will get into trouble.

你最好找我的話做不然你會有麻煩。

Ex. I'd better get back to work or my boss will be angry with me.

我最好回去上班不然我的老闆會對我生氣。

Ex. We'd better get to the airport by five or else we may miss the flight.

我們最好在五點之前到機場不然我們會錯過航班。

第24單元：連接詞

名言範例：

I have frequently experienced myself the mood in which I felt that all is vanity , I have emerged from it not by means of any philosophy , but owing to some imperative necessity of action.

羅素（Russell）英國哲學家、數學家和邏輯學家，致力於哲學的大眾化、普及化。1921年羅素曾於中國講學，對中國學術界有相當影響。

英文達人文法小筆記！

01 連接詞的種類

1. 連接獨立子句（關於獨立子句定義請參照第六單元附屬子句）

a. 對等連接詞

對等連接詞連接文法性質相同的單字、片語、子句等。對等連接詞有 and、but、or、yet、nor、for、and so。

Ex. I will eat a sandwich and some chocolate. ➡ 連接名詞
我會吃一個三明治和一些巧克力。

Ex. I did not call nor email my mother. ➡ 連接動詞
我沒有打電話也沒有寄信給我的母親。

Ex. The man was nice but weird. ➡ 連接形容詞
這個男人很好但是很奇怪。

Ex. Today is Tuesday, and my projects due Thursday. ➡ 連接獨立子句中間需有逗號。

今天是星期二，而我的計畫截止日期是星期四。

b. 連接副詞（關於連接副詞的使用請參照第十九單元副詞）

Ex. I need to study for my test; in fact, I am going to the library now.

我需要準備我的考試；事實上，我現在正要去圖書館。

c. 相關連接詞

相關連接詞為一組或一對的連接詞，其中包含 both…and，not…but，not only…but also，either…or，neither…nor，although…yet，whether…or。與對等連接詞相同的是，**相關連接詞**連接文法性質相同的單字、片語、子句等。

Ex. The name of the book is not New Moon but Breaking Dawn.

➡ 連接名詞

這本書的書名不是新月而是破曉。

Ex. You should feel both excited and proud of your new achievement. ➡ 連接形容詞

你應該為你的成就感到興奮與驕傲。

Ex. You can either make the payment online or make a wire transfer at a bank. ➡ 連接動詞

你可以線上付款或者線上銀行轉帳。

Ex. Peggy not only finished her paper on time, but she also got an A.

➡ 連接獨立子句時中間需有逗號

Peggy 不只準時完成他的報告也得到了 A。

2. 連接非獨立子句（關於非獨立子句定義請參照第六單元附屬子句）

a. 形容詞子句

形容詞子句位於所修飾的名詞之後，由關係代名詞作連接，常見的關係代名詞有 which、that、who、whom、whose、where、when。形容詞子句其中又分作限定與非限定用法。

Ex. The woman whom I talked to was my best friend at high school.

→ whom I talked to 修飾 the woman

跟我說話的女人是我高中最好的朋友。

Ex. The class, which meets once a week, discusses the importance and use of grammar.

→ which meets once a week 修飾 the class。

前後逗號代表形容詞子句為非限定

這個班，每周一次課，課程內容是研討文法的重要與使用方法。

b. 副詞子句

副詞子句可以修飾定詞、形容詞、副詞、片語或整個句子。副詞子句由從屬連接詞連接。其中分成時間、假設、條件等。副詞子句在主要子句之前中間需用逗號隔開。

Ex. When she called, he had already eaten lunch.

→ when she called 在說明前後兩個事件的時間關係。

當她打過來時，他剛吃完他的午餐。

Ex. I wouldn't take that job offer if I were you. → if I were you 在此作一條件的假設，此條件句在做與現在事實相反的假設。

我不會接受這份工作，如果我是你的話。

c. 名詞子句

名詞子句可作為句子中的主詞，動詞或介系詞的動詞。一般名詞子句的連接詞為 wh 疑問詞、if／whether、或 wh 疑問詞加 ever

Ex. Whoever wins the competition will receive the reward.

→ whoever wins the competition 名詞子句在此作為句子的主詞

任何贏得比賽的人會得到獎品。

Ex. I don't know where the car key is.

→ where the car key is 名詞子句在此作為動詞 know 的受詞

我不知道車鑰匙在哪。

02 連接詞的比較

1. 對等連接詞可用分號取代

Ex. Jill didn't want any money.

Ex. She didn't ask for it.

→ Jill didn't want any money, nor did she ask for it.

Jill 不想要任何錢，她也沒有去追求。

注意：nor 用來連接兩個否定句。使用時將第二句倒裝，並將否定字 not 去掉

→ Jill didn't want any money; she didn't ask for it

→ 直接使用分號連接兩個句子

Jill 不想要任何錢；她沒有去追求。

2. 比較 but（對等連接詞），although（從屬連接詞），however（連接副詞）

Ex. The typhoon warning has been issued.　颱風警報已經發佈。

Ex. There are people go to the beaches.　有人去海邊。

a. but（對等連接詞）

Ex. The typhoon warning has been issued, but there are people go to the beaches.　颱風警報已經發佈，但是還是有人去海邊。

→ but 對等連接詞連接兩個獨立的子句，but 一定放在句子中間，中間用逗號隔開。兩個獨立子句可互換位置

= There are people go to the beaches, but the typhoon warning has been issued.　還是有人去海邊，但是颱風警報已經發佈。

b. although（從屬連接詞）

Ex. Although the typhoon warning has been issued, there are people go to the beaches.　雖然颱風警報已經發佈，還是有人去海邊。

→ 此句 there are people go to the beaches 是主要子句，although 一定要放在副詞子句 the typhoon warning has been issued

= There are people go to the beaches although the typhoon warning has been issued.　還是有人去海邊，雖然颱風警報已經發佈。

→ 主要子句在前中間不需加逗號

c. however（連接副詞）

Ex. The typhoon warning has been issued; however, there are people go to the beaches. 颱風警報已經發佈；然而，還是有人去海邊。

→ however 作為兩句子的轉折詞，可出現在不同的位置

= The typhoon warning has been issued; there are people, however, go to the beaches.

= The typhoon warning has been issued; there are people go to the beaches, however.

換你寫寫看

請填入but，although，或however

1. I asked everybody to calm down, _____ they still seemed to Be
   angry.

2. I asked everybody to calm down; _____, they still seemed to Be
   angry.

3. I asked everybody to calm down _____ they still seemed to Be
   angry.

4. I was so tired, _____ I still finished my work anyway.

5. _____ I was so tired, I still finished my work anyway.

● 答案與中譯解析

1. 答：I asked everybody to calm down, **but** they still seemed to Be angry.
   我要求每個人鎮靜下來，不過他們依然看起來很生氣。

2. 答：I asked everybody to calm down; **however**, they still seemed to Be
   angry.
   我要求每個人鎮靜下來；然而他們依然看起來很生氣。

3. 答：I asked everybody to calm down **although** they still seemed to Be
   angry.
   我要求每個人鎮靜下來，雖然他們依然看起來很生氣。

4. 答：I was so tired, **but** I still finished my work anyway.
   我覺得好累，但是我還是把我的工作完成了。

5. 答：**Although** I was so tired, I still finished my work anyway.
   雖然我覺得好累，我還是把我的工作完成了。

第25單元：介系詞與介系詞片語

名言範例：

I'd just Be the catcher in the rye and all. I know it's crazy, but that's the only thing I'd really like to be. I know it's crazy.

我就只是麥田裡的捕手罷了，我知道這很瘋狂，但是這是我唯一想做的事，我知道這很瘋狂。

The Catcher in the Rye 是為美國作家沙林格於 1951年發表的長篇小說，中文書名為《麥田捕手》。該書以主角霍爾頓‧考爾菲德（Holden Caulfield）講述自己被學校開除後在紐約城遊盪，企圖在成人世界去尋求純潔與真理的經歷。

英文達人文法小筆記！

介系詞與介系詞片語文法解析

介系詞為一個有語意連接功能的字，介係詞之後一定要接受詞。若介系詞後接動詞，則動詞需變成動名詞，若介系詞後面的受詞省略，則介系詞應跟著省略。介系詞分五類：1. 表時間的介系詞 2. 表地方的介系詞 3. 表相關位置的介系詞 4. 表位置移動的介系詞 5. 其他介系詞。介系詞片語是由介系詞與其後面的名詞片語組成，通常表「時間」或「地點」。

01 表時間的介系詞

in	年代、季節、月份、早上、下午、晚上
on	日期、星期、某特定日子
at	時刻、at noon、at night
for	表一段時間
during	在…期間

Ex. She was born in 2000.　她生於 2000年。

Ex. School starts on August 29th.　學校開學於八月二十九日。

Ex. Classes begin at 7:30 every morning.
課程開始於每天早上七點三十分。

Ex. During the summer vacation, people usually have a trip abroad.
在暑假期間人們通常去國外旅遊。

02 表地方的介系詞

in	用於大地方，如國家、城市等。
at	用於小地方，如在學校。

Ex. They live in Canada.　他們住在加拿大。

Ex. Joe will meet you at school in the afternoon.
下午Joe 將於學校與你碰面。

03 表相關位置的介系詞

in	在…範圍之內	over	在…正上方
on	在…之上	under	在…正下方
at	在…正前方	below	在…下方

outside of	在…的外面	off	脫離…
inside of	在…的裡面	in front of	在…前面
between	在…之間	in back of	在…後面
behind	在…後面		

Ex. Tom's mother is standing at the door.　Tom 的媽媽正站在門前。

Ex. There is a red bridge over the river.　有一座紅橋在河的正上方。

Ex. A cat is sleeping under the table.　有一隻貓正睡在桌下。

Ex. Let's go inside of the classroom.　讓我們進到教室裡面。

Ex. Mary is sitting between John and Jack.

　　Mary 正坐在 John 和 Jack 之間。

Ex. There is a beautiful garden behind the house.

　　一座美麗花園在房子後面。

Ex. Please take off your shoes before entering the room.

　　進房前請脫掉你的鞋子。

04 表位置移動的介系詞

from	從…	out of	從…出來
to	到…	through	穿越
into	進入	across	橫越
along	沿著	around	環繞

Ex. How long is it from your home to school?

　　從你家到學校要花多少時間？

Ex. Along the street, you will see a bank next to the post office.

　　沿著這條街，你將看到一間銀行在郵局隔壁。

Ex. He usually walks through a park to take a bus.

他通常走路穿越過一座公園去搭公車。

Ex. Be careful when you walk across the road.

當你走路橫越馬路時要小心。

05 其他介系詞

with	和、用、有
without	沒有
in	在…方面、過一段時間、在…氣候中
for	給、交換、為了…、總價
about	關於、大約
of	…的、在…之中

Ex. Rachel is the girl with long hair.　Rachel 是那位留長髮的女孩。

Ex. I bought the bag for two thousand dollars.　我花兩千元買這個袋子。

Ex. It is about five o'clock.　大約五點。

Ex. One of my friends is a doctor.　我的朋友之中有一位是醫生。

06 介系詞片語

功能	說明
主詞補語	主詞的位置
副詞	動作的地點和時間
形容詞	修飾名詞

1. 當主詞補語

Ex. Those chairs are in the living room.　那些椅子在客廳。

2. 當副詞

Ex. Joan is swimming in the swimming pool.　Joan 正在游泳池游泳。

3. 當形容詞

Ex. The doll on the sofa is mine.　在沙發的洋娃娃是我的。

 絕妙好例句

1. Drive along the road and you'll see the bank.（表位置移動的介系詞 along）沿著路一直開，你就可以看到銀行。

2. Remember to pick me up at 10 o'clock.（十點鐘是小時間介系詞用at）記得在十點來載我。

3. Next week we'll have a test on English.（特定某一科的考試用on）下週我們將有英文考試。

4. They ran out of the house when they heard their father's voice.（從…跑出來介系詞用out of）當他們聽到爸爸的聲音，他們從房裡跑出來。

5. Snow White is a beautiful princess with a kind heart.（有…介系詞用 with）白雪公主是一位有仁慈心腸的美麗公主。

 換你寫寫看

1. Our teacher asked us not to write _____ green pens?

2. He was born _____ the morning of June 26th , 1997.

3. I am sorry _____ my being late.

4. He saw a cat jumping _____ the window.

5. We saw some boats _____ the bridge.

6. _____ autumn, the leaves of trees turned yellow.

　　(A)On　(B)In　(C)After　(D)At

7. There are some cars running _____ the road.

　　(A)in　(B)at　(C)on　(D)behind

8. He opened the door _____ curiosity.　(A)in　(B)for　(C)out of　(D)with

9. His mother bought a house _____ twenty million dollars.

　　(A)by　(B)for　(C)with　(D)in

10. The earth goes _____ the sun.　(A)near　(B)about　(C)for　(D)around

● 答案與中譯解析

　1. 答：with（用…，介系詞用 with）我們老師要求我們不要用綠筆寫字。

　2. 答：on（某特定日子的早上、下午、晚上，介系詞用 on）
　　　　他生於 1997 六月二十六日早上。

　3. 答：for（be sorry for＋N／V-ing，為了…感到抱歉，穿過）
　　　　我為我的遲到感到抱歉。

　4. 答：through（穿越過，介系詞用 through）他看到一隻貓跳著穿過窗戶。

　5. 答：below（在…下方，介系詞用 below）我們在橋下看到一些船。

　6. 答：(B)（在…季節，介系詞用 in）在秋天，樹葉變黃色。

　7. 答：(C)（在…表面上，介系詞用 on）有一些車在路上跑。

　8. 答：(C)（出於…，介系詞用 out of）他打開門是出於好奇。

　9. 答：(B)（用…總價，介系詞用 for）他媽媽用兩千萬買這間房子。

　10. 答：(D)（環繞，介系詞用 around）地球繞著太陽運轉。

21

22

23

24

25

26

27

附錄一

附錄2

附錄3

第26單元：代名詞

名言範例：

You see I usually find myself among strangers because I drift here and there trying to forget the sad things that happened to me.

你瞧我經常總是在陌生人之中找到我自己，因我在此漂泊並試圖忘記發生在自己身上的悲傷之事。

　　《大亨小傳》（The Great Gatsby）是美國作家費茲傑羅於 1925所寫的一部以 1920年代的紐約市及長島為背景的短篇小説。本書從一位畢業生尼克（Nick）口中來敘述男主角蓋茲比一生的故事。蓋茲比生活於紙醉金迷的奢侈毫豪門世界中，一心追求自己的浪漫愛情夢想，故事一直圍繞蓋茲心中的執著，卻也為自己帶來悲劇的命運。此段為男主角蓋茲感嘆自己飄浮於陌生人中，試圖忘記發生在自己身上的悲傷之事。而蓋茲比的發跡的故事也代表了美國夢。

英文達人文法小筆記！

代名詞／反身代名詞／不定代名詞／數量代名詞 文法解析

代名詞用於代替前面的名詞，以避免同一名詞於句中連續使用，造成文字的累贅，並有承接的作用。代名詞分為六大類：人稱代名詞、指示代名詞、不定代名詞、疑問代名詞、數量代名詞、關係代名詞。本章將就代名詞、反身代名詞、不定代名詞以及數量代名詞加以說明。

01 人稱代名詞的分類

		單數形			複數形		
		所有格	主格	受格	主格	所有格	受格
第一人稱		I	my	me	we	our	us
第二人稱		you	your	you	you	your	you
第三人稱	男性	he	his	him	they	their	them
	女性	she	her	her			
	中性	it	its	it			

人稱代名詞主格其用法為當主詞和主詞補語。受格為當及物動詞與介系詞的受詞。所有格當形容詞用，後面接名詞。要注意的是兩個以上的人稱代名詞並用其順序為：單數：2、3、1（you、he ／ she、I）。複數：1、2、3（we，you，they）。

Ex. **She** likes his clothes.（she 主格當主詞）她喜歡他的衣服。

Ex. I was often taken to Be **he**.（he 主格當主詞補語） 我經常被誤認為是他。

Ex. He is afraid of **her**.（her 受格當介系詞的受詞）他害怕她。

Ex. You know **them**.（them 受格當及物動詞的受詞）你認識他們。

Ex. My dad bought **my brother** a bicycle.（my 所有格當形容詞用，後面接名詞 bicycle）我父親買給我弟弟一輛腳踏車。

Ex. You，she and I are in the same class.（單數人稱代名詞順序為 2,3，1）你、她和我在同一班。

Ex. We, you and they will go to the same university.（複數人稱代名詞順序為 1，2，3）我們、你們、他們將去同一所大學。

02 人稱代名詞 "it" 的用法

1. 可用於表示「時間、天氣、距離」

Ex. What time is it? It is three o'clock. 幾點了？三點了。

2. 當形式主詞和形式受詞，代替後面的不定詞片語或 that 子句

It is impossible to master math in one month.

→ It 當形式主詞代替後面的不定詞片語 to master math in one month）

一個月內精通數學是不可能的。

I found it difficult to catch up with him.

→ It 當形式受詞代替後面的不定詞片語 to catch up with him

我發現趕上他是困難的。

03 所有代名詞

所有代名詞用於避免重複，所有代名詞＝所有格＋名詞，其用法如下

mine ＝ my ＋名詞 我的

yours ＝ your ＋名詞 你的

his ＝ his ＋名詞 他的

hers ＝ her ＋名詞 她的

ours ＝ our ＋名詞 我們的

yours ＝ your ＋名詞 你們的

theirs ＝ their ＋名詞 他們的

Ex. This is my car; that is his.　這是我的車；那是他的。

Ex. His house is red, and mine is white.

他的房子是紅色的，而我的是白色的。

Ex. Their parents want them join the swimming team. Ours don't want us to do it.

他們的父母要他們加入游泳隊。而我們的父母卻不要。

04 反身代名詞

當主詞與受詞同一人或物時，則需用反身代名詞。語氣強調時亦用反身代名詞。反身代名詞沒有所有格，故用 one's own ＋名詞。反身代名詞有單複數之分，列表如下：

	單數	複數
第一人稱	myself	ourselves
第二人稱	yourself	yourselves
第三人稱	himself herself itself	themselves

Ex. He finished the project by himself. 他自己完成這個計劃。

Ex. We ourselves walk home. 我們自己走路回家。

Ex. I have my own house in Taipei.（反身代名詞沒有所有格，故用 one's own ＋名詞）我在台北有自己的房子。

05 不定代名詞

不定代名詞有兩部份：

（一）	both，all，neither，none，either，any	（二）	One…the other… 一個…另一個… One…the others… 一個…其餘…
			One…another…the other… 一個…另一個…另一個… One…another…the others… 一個…另一個…其餘…
			Some…some… 有些…有些… Some…，some…and still others… 有些…有些…還有些…

1. both，all，neither，none，either，any 的比較用法如下：

	肯定句	否定句	任何一個
二者	both	neither	either
三者 或三者以上	all	none	any

2. some（一些）用於肯定句；any（任一個）用於否定句、疑問句、條件句。

3. another，others，the others 和 the others 的分辨

	單數	複數
不特定	another	others
特定	the other	the others

Ex. I know neither of the two students. 這兩位學生我都不認識。

Ex. I know both of the students. 這兩位學生我都認識。

Ex. None of us can get into the classroom.

我們沒有任何一個可以進入教室。

Ex. Do you have any money?　你有任何錢嗎？

Ex. I have three sisters; one is a teacher, another is a doctor and the other is a nurse.

我有三個姐妹；一位是老師，一位是醫生，另一位是護士。

Ex. Lots of people are in the park in the morning.　Some are dancing. Some are jogging.　And still others are walking.

早上有很多人在公園。有些正在跳舞。有些正在慢跑。還有些正在散步。

06 數量代名詞

數量代名詞有 many，much，most，both，several，lot of，lots of，some，any，(a) few，(a) little,⋯等。有些「數量代名詞」用於可數名詞，有些用於不可屬名詞。

many 很多 several 幾個 both 兩者皆 a few 一些 few 一點點、幾乎沒有	＋可數名詞
much 很多 a little 一些 little 一點點、幾乎沒有	＋不可數名詞
all 全部 most 大部分 a lot of 很多 lots of 很多 some 一些 any 任何一個	＋可數名詞 或 ＋不可數名詞

Ex. Many people want to join the club. 很多人想要加入這家俱樂部。

Ex. I only have little money. 我只有一點點錢。

Ex. Some money is from John. 有些錢是來自約翰。

Ex. I didn't know any of the students. 這些學生中任何一個我都不認識。

 絕妙好例句

1. To say is one thing; but to do is another.（不特定單一其他 another）
   說是一回事；做又是一回事。

2. None of the students was present yesterday.（三者以上沒有任何一人 none）昨天這些學生沒有任何一個人出席。

3. Don't speak ill of others behind their backs.
   （不特定複數的其他人 others）不要在別人背後說壞話。

4. He used to refresh himself with a cup of coffee.
   （he 的反身代名詞為 himself）他過去習慣用一杯咖啡來提神。

5. Any of us can't get in the library.（沒有任何一個人 any of…not）
   我們之中沒有任何一個人可以進入圖書館。

6. Gold is much more valuable than iron.
   （金子和鐵是不可數名詞，沒有複數型不可加 s）金子比鐵更值錢。

7. If you have any left, please give me some.（any 用於 if 條件子句）
   如果你有任何留下來請給我一些。

 換你寫寫看

1. Five people were present in the meeting. One was a doctor and
   _____ were engineers.

2. The cars left one after _____ .

3. Which of the four books does he want? _____ will do.

4. Danny hurt _____ with a knife.

5. We should love_____ family.

(A)our own　(B)ours　(C)ourselves　(D)hers

6. Whose car is it? It is _____ . (A)my　(B)him　(C)myself　(D)theirs

7. He went his own way and I went _____ . We already separated.

(A)my own　(B)mine　(C)that　(D)my

● 答案與中譯解析

1. 答：the others（特定複數的其他人 the others）五個人出席會議一位是醫生，
　　其他人是工程師。

2. 答：another（one after another 一個接一個）車子一輛接一輛離開。

3. 答：Any（任何一個 any）那四本書之中他要哪一本？任何一本都可以。

4. 答：himself（傷到自己 he 的反身代名詞為 himself）Danny 用刀子傷到自己。

5. 答：(A)（one's own＋名詞，自己的…）我們應該愛自己的家人。

6. 答：(D)（他們的，所有格代名詞 theirs）車是誰的？他們的。

7. 答：(B)（my own way ＝ mine）
　　他走他的路，我走自己的路。我們已經分手了。

第27單元：量詞

名言範例：

You must not lose faith in humanity. Humanity is like an ocean; if a few drops of the ocean are dirty, the ocean does not become dirty.

你不需要對人性失去信心。人性就像大海，來自大海的一些水滴是髒的，但大海仍然不會變髒的。

　　此句話是印度聖雄甘地（Gandhi）所說的，甘地是印度民族主義運動領袖。他帶領印度邁向獨立，脫離英國的殖民統治。他的「非暴力」的哲學思想，影響了全世界的民族主義者和那些爭取和平變革的國際運動。此句話的意思是「你不需要對人性失去信心。人性就像大海，來自大海的一些水滴是髒的，但大海仍然不會變髒的。」

英文達人文法小筆記！

01 量詞

英文有許多量詞，可用於可數名詞與不可數名詞，大部份是慣用語，所有必須努力記之。本書將舉出部份常用的。

A can of soup	一罐湯	A group of students	一群學生
A bag of flour	一袋麵粉	A herd of elephants	一群大象
A bottle of soda	一瓶蘇打水	A school of fish	一群魚
A glass of water	一杯水	A pack of noodles	一包麵
A carton of milk	一紙盒的牛奶	A basket of apples	一籃蘋果
A cup of coffee	一杯咖啡	A bundle of flowers	一捆花
A spoon of sugar	一湯匙的糖	A piece of cake	一塊蛋糕
A jar of jam	一罐的果醬	A loaf of bread	一條麵包
A pair of shoes	一雙鞋	A bar of soap	一塊香皂
A dozen of eggs	一打蛋	A pile of paper	一堆紙

切記：當有形容詞來修飾名詞時，形容詞須放在量詞的前面，冠詞後面。既使不可數名詞前面用量詞修飾，不可數名詞仍不可加 s，可數名詞則須加 s。

　　Ex. I drank a glass of water.　我喝了一杯水。

　　Ex. There is a school of fish in the pond.　有一群魚在池裡。

　　Ex. My father bought a basket of apples.　我的父親買了一籃的蘋果。

　　Ex. He needs a new pair of shoes.　他需要一雙新鞋子。

　　Ex. She used a dozen of eggs to make a big piece of cake.　她用了一打的蛋來做一塊大蛋糕。

02 修飾可數量詞／修飾不可數量詞／修飾可數與不可數量詞與數量代名詞的差別

英文中有一些修飾量詞來修飾名詞，如：many、much、most、both、several、a lot of、lots of、some、any、（a）few、（a）little、…等。有些修飾量詞用於可數名詞、有些用於不可屬名詞。而有些則可同時用於修飾可數與不可數名詞，列表如下：

many 很多 several 幾個 both 兩者皆 a few 一些 few 一點點、幾乎沒有	＋可數名詞
much 很多 a little 一些 little 一點點、幾乎沒有	＋不可數名詞
all 全部 most 大部分 a lot of 很多 lots of 很多 some 一些 any 任何一個	＋可數名詞 或 ＋不可數名詞

Ex. I have lots of pencils.

我有很多筆。

Ex. He borrowed a few books from the library.

他從圖書館借了一些書。

Ex. Most students like to get on the Internet while they stay at home.

當大部份的學生待在家時，他們喜歡上網。

Ex. Some rice is white; some rice is black.

有些米是白色的；有些是黑色的。

Ex. Some people like to go to the movies; some like to go to the concert.

有些人喜歡去看電影；有些人喜歡去音樂會。

換你寫寫看

1. He has nothing to put on but _____ of pants.

2. You did give your teacher _____ trouble when you entered the school.

3. The mailman gave me _____ letters.

4. A _____ of elephants are coming to us.

5. My mother bought two _____ of bread yesterday.

6. He added _____ sugar to the coffee.

   (A)a few (B)many (C)a little (D)a lot

7. He read _____ news for his grandmother.

   (A)a (B)a pack of (C)a piece of (D)X

● 答案與中譯解析

1. 答：a pair（一條褲子，單位為 a pair）他沒有東西可穿除了一條褲子。

2. 答：a little（trouble 不可數名詞，用 a little 修飾）
   當你入學時，你的確給你老師帶來一些麻煩。

3. 答：a bundle of（一捆信單位為 a bundle of）郵差給我一捆信。

4. 答：herb（一群象單位為 a herb of）一群大象正朝我們來。

5. 答：loaves（一條麵包為 a loaf of，兩條麵包為 two loaves of）
   我母親昨天買了兩條麵包。

6. 答：(C)（sugar 糖為不可數名詞，一些為 a little）他加一些糖到咖啡裡。

7. 答：(C)（一則新聞為 a piece of news）他為他祖母讀一則新聞。

NOTE

附錄

附錄一：動詞50個

1. agree [əˋgri] 贊同，應允

英解：to accept others' opinion, feeling, or purpose
動詞變形：agreed, agreed, agreeing
類義詞：consent, approve

及物動詞的用法	不及物動詞的用法
1. agree＋to＋v 同意 She agreed to marry him. 她同意嫁給他了。 **2. agree＋that** 承認 I agreed that George was competent for this job. 我承認喬治有能力勝任這份工作。 **3. agree** 接受，對……達成協議 He has agreed the unequal pay offer. 他接受了不平等的工資待遇。	**1. agree＋with ／ about ／ on** 意見一致 Jessie doesn't agree with Ann on the new trend of the times. Jessie 與 Ann 在新的時代潮流上意見相左。 **2. agree＋with** 相符 This evidence doesn't agree with the fact. 證據和事實不符。 **3. agree＋with** 相宜，適合 This dress doesn't agree with me. 我不適合這條裙子。

同義辨析：consent，approve

He **consents** to work for Houston Rocket. 他**答應**效力於休斯頓火箭隊。

The association **approved** of the proposal. 協會**贊成**了這項提議。

2. ask [æsk] 詢問，請求

英解：to request, to question to sb
動詞變形：asked, asked, asking
類義詞：inquire, request

及物動詞的用法

1. ask + that ╱ ask sb to do 請求，要求

Jim asked Susan to lend him some money.
Jim 請求 Susan 借給他一些錢。

Miss Wang asked that her students (should) copy all the words twice.
王老師要求學生把所有單詞抄兩遍。

2. ask 邀請

Simon asked all his classmates to come to his birthday party.
Simon 邀請了他所有的同學參加他的生日派對。

不及物動詞的用法

1. ask + about 詢問，問候

Please tell your parents she asked about them.
請轉告你的父母她向他們問好。

I have nothing to ask about.
我沒什麼可問的了。

2. ask + for 要求，請求

They're asking for your help.
他們在向你求助。

同義辨析：inquire, request

Please tell your parents she **inquired after** them.　請轉告你的父母她向他們**問好**。

Obama **requested** civilians support in his speech.　歐巴馬在他的演講中**要求**民眾的支持。

3. become [bɪˋkʌm] 變成，適合

英解：to turn to be; to be suitable
動詞變形：became become becoming
類義詞：turn; go

及物動詞的用法

● **become** 適合，同……相稱

Please behave yourself. That doesn't become you.
請管好您的言行。那樣的行為與您不相稱。

連綴動詞的用法

● **become** 變成，成為，開始變得

After a short time, Sarah became acquainted with her new friends.
過了不一會，薩拉就和她的新朋友熟絡起來。

同義辨析：turn, go

Once the autumn came, all the leaves **turned** yellow.　秋天到了，樹葉**變**黃了。

After that accident, he **went** nuts.　經過那場意外，他**瘋**了。

4. believe [bɪˋliv] 相信，認為

英解：to regard sth or sb true or real
動詞變形：believed, believed, 無進行時態
類義詞：trust, deem

及物動詞用法	不及物動詞用法
1. believe, believe + that 相信，認為 Villagers didn't believe what the boy said any more. 村民們再也不相信那個男孩說的話了。 **2. believe + that** 認為，猜想，料想 I didn't believe he is the criminal. 我認為他不是兇手。	**1. believe + in** 相信，信任，信仰 He believes in the wizard school. 他相信有魔法學校。 **2. believe** 信教 My family go to the church every week, because we believe. 我們家人每週都去教堂，因為我們信教。

同義辨析：trust, deem

I don't **trust** him. 我不信他。

Dora **deemed** he should be responsible for this loss.
Dora **認為**他應該為這次的損失負責。

5. bring [brɪŋ] 帶來，促使，引起

英解：to carry; to cause
動詞變形：brought, brought, bringing
類義詞：take, fetch

及物動詞用法	不及物動詞用法
1. bring 帶來，拿來 My mother always brings an umbrella with her. 我媽媽總是隨身帶著一把雨傘。	**1. bring + about** 產生導致 The accident brought about a series of butterfly effect. 此次事故產生了一系列蝴蝶效應。

2. bring 是產生，導致

The nuclear burst brought unpredictable damage to the village. 這場核爆炸給小村莊帶來了不可預料的危害。

2. bring + down 降低，打倒

The peasant farmers' uprising brought down the landowners. 農民起義達到了地主。

同義詞辨析：take，fetch

His mother **took** his game machine. 她媽媽**拿走**了他的遊戲機。

Would you please **fetch** me that package. 請你幫我把行李**拿來**好嗎？

6. buy [baɪ] 買，收買

英解：to use money to exchange goods

動詞變形：bought, bought, buying

類義詞：purchase

及物動詞用法

1. buy 購買

My sister bought me *The Old Man and Sea*. 姐姐給我買了本《老人與海》。

2. buy 接受，同意，相信【俚】

I buy what he said. 我相信他說的。

不及物動詞用法

- **buy** 買

Nowadays people buy with credit cards. 現在人們通常用信用卡購物。

同義詞辨析：purchase

This company intends to **purchase** new office supplies.
公司打算**採購**一些新的辦公用品。

7. close [kloz] 關閉，合上

英解：to turn off

動詞變形：closed, closed, closing

類義詞：shut

及物動詞用法	不及物動詞用法
1. close 關閉，合上 Please close the door gently. 請輕輕地關上門。	**1. close** 關門，打烊 The Everbright Bank closes at 6 p.m. 光大銀行下午六點關門。
2. close 關（商店等），封閉（道路等） Owing to the great depression, many shops had been closed. 由於大蕭條，許多商店關門了。	**2. close** 靠攏，癒合 Don't worry. The wound will close in a week. 不要擔心，傷口在一星期內會癒合的。
3. close + down（尤指永久性地）關閉（學校、醫院等） With the development of the society, the government decided to close down the old-style private schools. 隨著社會的發展，政府決定關閉舊式的私塾。	**3. close + in + on** 包圍，接近 The masses closed in on the thief immediately. 群眾立馬把小偷圍住了。

同義詞辨析：shut

The company has to decide to **shut down** for a week because of high temperature.
由於高溫天氣，公司不得不決定**停工**一周。

8. come [kʌm] 來自，來到，開始

英解：to arrive at some place from anywhere else
動詞變形：came, come, coming
類義詞：originate, arrive

及物動詞用法	不及物動詞用法
1. come（口）擺出……的樣子，裝出 Don't come a good person. 不要裝好人了。	**1. come** 來，來到 Thank you for coming to see me. 謝謝您來看我。
2. come 將滿（……歲） What a pity! She is coming twenty.　真可惜！她就快 20 歲了。	**2. come + from** 發生，來自 Where do you come from? 你來自哪兒？

同義詞辨析：originate，arrive

Ballet **originates** from Italy.　芭蕾**起源於**義大利。

It is a train that will never **arrive at** the destination.
這是一輛永遠也**到**不了目的地的列車。

9. decide [dɪˋsaɪd] 決定，下決心

英解：to set one's mind to do
動詞變形：decided, decided, deciding
類義詞：determine

及物動詞用法	不及物動詞用法
1. decide 決定，決意 We decide to go on a picnic on Sunday. 我們決定星期天去野餐。	**1. decide + on** 決定某事 He thinks it over and decides on a further study. 經過深思熟慮後他決定繼續深造學習。
2. decide 使下決心，使決斷 This accident decided me to enjoy everyday. 經歷過那場事故後，使我下定決心要珍惜每一天。	**2. decide + against** 決定不做 Sarah decided against believing anyone else. Sarah 決定不再相信任何人了。
3. deciede 解決，裁決，判決 That case hasn't been decided. 那個案子還沒有判決。	**3. decide + for** 做出決定 Decide for yourself. 信不信由你。

同義詞辨析：determine

What you are when you're young could **determine** what you'll be in future.
小時候什麼樣樣子**決定著**你長大後什麼樣。

10. eat [it] 吃，喝

英解：to take food in order to make you full
動詞變形：ate, eaten, eating
類義詞：have

及物動詞用法	不及物動詞用法
1. eat 吃，喝 Have you eaten lunch? 你吃午飯了嗎？ **2. eat** 使煩惱，使不安（口） The failure of the exam ate him. 考試不及格讓他煩惱。	**1. eat** 吃飯 Mr. Wang invited me to eat together this noon. 今天中午王先生請我共進的午餐。

同義辨析：have

I with my brother **had** a big meal. 　我和哥哥大**吃**了一頓。

11. feel [fil] 覺得，感覺

英解：undergo an emotional sensation, perceive by a physical sensation

動詞變形：felt, felt, feeling

類義詞：perceive, think

及物動詞用法	不及物動詞用法
1. feel 摸，觸，試探 The blind girl feels the water by hand. 那個盲人小女孩用手感觸流水。 **2. feel** 感覺，感知 Can kids feel their parents' love? 小孩能感覺到父母的愛嗎？ **3. feel** 認為，以為，相信 I feel it's unnecessary to do so. 我覺得沒有必要這麼做。	**1. feel** 有感覺，覺得（聯繫動詞） He feels lucky. 他覺得很幸運。 **2. feel** 摸索著尋找 He got drunk and felt in his bag for the key randomly. 他喝醉了，在包裡胡亂地找鑰匙。

同義辨析：perceive, think

I **perceived** his praise as an encouragement. 　我把他的讚賞**認**為是一種鼓勵。

I don't **think** so. 　我不這麼**認為**。

12. find [faɪnd] 發現，找到

英解：to look for

動詞變形：found, found, finding

類義詞：seek

及物動詞用法

- **find** 找到，發現

In *Criminal Minds*, FBI agents always succeed in finding criminals.

在《犯罪心理》裡，美國聯邦調查局的探員總能成功的找到罪犯。

不及物動詞用法

- **find** 裁決

The referee found against Chicago Bulls.

裁判做出了不利於芝加哥公牛隊的判決。

同義辨析：seek

The villagers sought for the lost boy in the forest.

村民們在森林裡搜尋那個丟失的男孩。

13. finish [ˈfɪnɪʃ] 完成

英解：to put sth to an end successfully

動詞變形：finished, finished, finishing

類義詞：complete, accomplish

及物動詞用法

1. **finish + v-ing** 完成

Have you finished practicing Ping-Pong?

你完成乒乓球練習了嗎？

Bill Gates didn't finish his college course.

比爾蓋茨沒有完成他的大學課程。

2. **finish + off** 對……最後加工，潤飾，結束，完成，徹底壓倒，擊敗

Please let your teacher finish off your composition. 請讓你的老師幫你潤飾一下你的作文。

不及物動詞用法

1. **finish** 結束，終止

The long-time project finished.

這個長期項目結束了。

2. **finish**（在競賽）獲得名次

The Chinese Team finished first in the competition.

中國隊在比賽中獲得了第一名。

同義辨析：complete, accomplish

Nikita succeeds in completing every task.　Nikita 能成功完成每項任務。

I will accomplish my plan in 3 months.　三個月內我要完成我的計畫。

14. get [gɛt] 得到

英解：to acquire

動詞變形：got, gotten, getting

類義詞：obtain, acquire

及物動詞用法

1. get 獲得，贏得

He got the chance to attend Jay Chou's concert.

他獲得了參加周杰倫演唱會的機會。

2. get 捉住

Through difficult investigation, the police got the criminal.

經過艱難的盤查，員警抓住了罪犯。

3. get 為……弄到

May I get you a cup of tea?

我給您倒杯水喝好嗎？

4. get 明白，理解

Did you get me?

你知道我要說什麼吧？

5. get 難倒

This question gets me.

這個問題把我難倒了。

6. get 使工作，使運行

Can you get him to buy a book for me?　你能讓他幫我買本書嗎？

7. get 趕上

It's too late to get the regular car.

今天太遲了，不能趕上班車了。

不及物動詞用法

1. get + to 到達

When will we get to Los Angeles?

我們什麼時候能到洛杉磯？

2. get + v-ing 開始

Let's get working.

我們開始工作吧。

3. get + on + with 相處，進展

I got on well with my new roommates.

我和我的新室友相處很愉快。

4. get + off 出發

Let's get off now.

我們現在就出發吧。

5. get + on ／ off 上／下車

When we get on ／ off the bus, we should be in order.

我們上下車時，應該有序進行。

6. get + up 起床

It's time to get up!　該起床了。

7. get + through 通過

I believe I can get through every difficulty.

我想我能克服所有困難。

同義辨析：obtain, acquire

I'm glad you've **obtained** the loan from the bank. 　真高興你從銀行那**得到**了貸款。

He **acquired** a large knowledge of Chinese history. 　他**學到**了很多中國國歷史知識。

15. give [gɪv] 給

英解：to send sth to sb

動詞變形：gave, given, giving

類義詞：supply

及物動詞用法

1. give 給予，送給

My father gave me a book as a birthday gift.
我爸爸送我一本書當做生日禮物。
Give me 5 minutes and I'll handle it. 　給我五分鐘，我就能搞定。

2. give 供給，產生

This company gives help to the weak. 　這個公司為弱勢提供幫助。

3. give + for／to 獻出

This hero give his life to his position.
這位英雄為他的崗位奉獻了一生。

4. give + for 付出，出售

How much will you give for the house?
你打算花多少錢買這棟房子？

不及物動詞用法

1. give + in 屈服，交上

Faced with difficulties, we'll never give in.
面對困難，我們從不屈服。

2. give + up 停止，認輸

Are you planning to give up?
你就打算這麼放棄了？

3. give + way + to 讓位於，被替代

In ancient time, the emperor gave way to his eldest son.
在古代，皇上總讓位于自己的長子。

4. give + away 贈送，洩露

The confidential information has been given away.
機密資訊被洩露了。

同義辨析：supply

He admitted to **supply** us with anything we asked. 　他承諾**提供**我們所要的一切東西。

16. go [go] 去，走

英解：the opposite word of come, to leave

動詞變形：went, gone, going

類義詞：leave, remove

及物動詞用法	不及物動詞用法
1. go + on 拿……打賭 He went 200 thousand on it. 他為此拿 20 萬去打賭。	**1. go** 去，離去 I'll go now. 我現在就離開了。
2. go（常用於否定句）忍耐（口） That boy is quite naughty so that I can't go him any more. 那個男孩太淘氣了以至於我不能容忍他了。	**2. go + v-ing** 做，從事 This weekend I as well as my friends am going fishing. 這週末我要和朋友去釣魚。

同義辨析：leave, remove

I'll leave for Taipei.　我要離開去臺北了。

How can I remove the spot?　我怎麼能祛除污漬呢？

17. have [hæv] 有

英解：to possess sth

動詞變形：had, had, having

類義詞：possess, own

助詞用法	及物動詞用法
1. have + done 已經，曾經 I have graduated from school for 3 years. 我已經畢業離開學校三年了。	**1. have** 有，擁有 I have a bike which is the same as yours. 我有一輛和你一樣的腳踏車。
2. have（用於虛擬語氣，表示於過去事實相反的假設）假如那時……的話 If I had done my work beforehand, I should have seen Transformers Ⅲ. 如果我提前把工作做了，早就看過《變形金剛 3》了。	**2. have** 吃，喝 What do you want to have for lunch?　午飯你想吃什麼？
	3. have + to 必須，不得不 You have to respect your eldership.　你必須尊重長輩。

同義辨析：possess, own

Every country **possess** the right of sovereignty and territory integrality.
每個國家**享有**主權與領土完整的權利。

This boss **owns** 3 real estates.　這個老闆有三處房產。

18. hear [hɪr] 聽見

英解：to have a sense of listening

動詞變形：heard, heard, hearing

類義詞：listen

及物動詞用法	不及物動詞用法
1. hear 聽見 I hear a boy singing. 我聽見有個男孩在唱歌。 **2. hear + about ／ of** 聽說 I heard about some rumors. 我聽到一些謠言。	● **hear** 聽得見 It's so noisy here. I couldn't hear clearly. 這兒太吵了，我聽不清。

同義辨析：listen

Learning English should learn to **listen to** the CD.　學英語要學會聽 CD。

19. help [hɛlp] 幫助

英解：to do a favor

動詞變形：helped, helped, helping

類義詞：assist, aid

及物動詞用法	不及物動詞用法
1. help + with 幫助 Thank you for helping me with moving . 謝謝你幫我搬家。	● **help** 幫助，有用 This machine saved me a lot of time and helped a lot. 這個機器為我省了很多時間，幫助很大。

同義辨析：assist, aid

He **assisted** me in designing my diploma project.　他**幫**我設計了畢業設計。

I can **aid** him with watching his dog.　我**幫**他照看小狗。

20. keep [kip] 保持

英解：to hold on, to be the same as before

動詞變形：kept, kept, keeping

類義詞：maintain, preserve

及物動詞用法	不及物動詞用法
1. keep 持有，保有 I will keep this toy forever. 我會永遠保留這個玩具的。 **2. keep** 使……保持 Would you keep the bird silent? 你能讓那個小鳥保持安靜嗎？	• **keep** 食物保持不壞 Put the food in the fridge in order to keep in low temperature. 把食物放在冰箱是為了使其在低溫下保持不壞。

同義辨析：maintain, preserve

Until now he **maintains** his childlike innocence.　一直到現在他都**保持**著童心。

The government spent much money **preserving** this historic site.
政府花了很多錢**保存**這個歷史遺跡。

21. know [no] 知道，認出

英解：to understand

動詞變形：knew, known,（無進行時態）

類義詞：recognize

及物動詞用法	不及物動詞用法
1. know 知道，瞭解 Do you know his name? 你知道他的名字嗎？ **2. know** 認識，熟悉 I have known him for a long time. 我認識他很久了。	**1. know + about／of** 知道，瞭解，懂得 The families of the victims only want to know about the truth. 遇難者家屬只想瞭解真相。

同義辨析：recognize

I didn't **recognize** him on the street.　在街上我沒**認出**他。

22. learn [lɜn] 學習

英解：to study
動詞變形：learnt, learnt, learning
類義詞：acquire, study

及物動詞用法	不及物動詞用法
1. learn 學習 I'm learning swimming. 我正在學游泳。 Sarah learns Japanese in order to understand Japanese anime and manga. Sarah 學日語是為了看懂日本動漫。 **2. learn** 了解 We have learned that dishonesty does not pay. 我們了解到不誠實是沒有好報的。	**1. learn + from** 學習 We are supposed to learn from the good model. 我們應該向好的榜樣學習。 **2. learn + of／about** 得知，獲悉 The audience learnt of their divorce in the newspaper. 觀眾們在報紙上獲悉他們離婚了。

同義辨析：acquire, study

Through repetitive learning, I **acquired** the skills of this magic.
經過反復練習，我終於**掌握**了這個魔術的技巧。

Study hard, you'll make a great progress.　好好**學習**，天天向上。

23. leave [liv] 離開

英解：to go out of the original place
動詞變形：left, left, leaving
類義詞：depart

及物動詞用法	不及物動詞用法
1. leave 離開 Can you leave the site now? 你現在能離開現場了嗎？ **2. leave** 離開，遺棄 Don't leave me alone. 不要留下我一個人孤孤單單地。	● **leave ＋ for** 離去，動身 I'm leaving for Los Angeles. 我打算動身去洛杉磯。

同義辨析：depart

They are unwilling to **depart** from their hometown.　他們不想<u>離開</u>他們的故鄉。

24. like [laɪk] 喜歡

英解：to be fond of

動詞變形：liked, liked, 無進行時態

類義詞：adore, admire

及物動詞用法	不及物動詞用法
1. like ＋ v-ing ／ to ＋ v More and more people like playing ／ to play smartphone. 越來越多的人喜歡玩智慧型手機。 **2. like** 適合於 It seems that spicy food doesn't like me. 麻辣食品不適合我。	● **like** 喜歡，願意 Sometimes people can't do as they like. 有些時候人們不能隨心所欲。

同義辨析：adore, admire

I **adore** him for his maturity.　我因為他的成熟而<u>愛慕</u>他。

I **admire** her perseverance.　我<u>敬佩</u>她堅持不懈的精神。

25. live [lɪv] 居住

英解：to stay in a place as a habitat

動詞變形：lived, lived, living

類義詞：reside

及物動詞用法	不及物動詞用法
1. live 度過 Every child wants their parents to live a happy life in their old age. 所有子女希望父母能有個幸福的晚年。 **2. live** 實踐，經歷 I have lived an unbelievable experience. 我經歷了一個難以置信的遭遇。	**1. live** 活著 The dying mouse is still living. 那只垂死的小白鼠依舊活著。 **2. live + on** 以什麼為生 That man lives on begging. 那個人以乞討為生。

同義辨析：reside

The army troops **reside** in the Gobi desert.　這些軍隊**駐紮**在戈壁。

26. look [lʊk] 看見，看

英解：to see

動詞變形：looked, looked, looking

類義詞：watch, see, stare

及物動詞用法	不及物動詞用法
1. look 留意，注意 Look! What happened? 看！發生什麼事了？ **2. look** 用眼／臉色表示 He looked what he thought. 他的表情已經表露了他在想什麼。	**1. look + at** 看 Why are you looking at me? 為什麼你總看著我？ **2. look + after** 照顧 I will look after her. 我會照顧好她的。

同義辨析：watch, see, stare

I **watched** the train crash.　我**看到**了火車的撞擊。

When will you go with me to **see** the film?　你什麼時候和我一起去**看**電影？

Don't **stare** at me.　不要**瞪**著我。

27. make [mek] 做，製造

英解：create or manufacture a man-made product, perform or carry out
動詞變形：made, made, making
類義詞：manufacture

及物動詞用法	不及物動詞用法
1. make 製作 I like making paper crane. 我喜歡折千紙鶴。 **2. make 做** I haven't made a decision yet. 我還沒有做決定。	**1. make + to 正要做，剛要開始做** Sarah made to leave, but Flora stopped her. Sarah 剛要離開，就被 Flora 攔住了。 **2. make + up + for 補償** I will make up for the loss. 我會補償損失的。

同義辨析：manufacture
Rumors are **manufactured** by nosy parker.　謠言都是好事者捏造的。

28. meet [mit] 遇見，會見

英解：to happen to see sb or sth
動詞變形：met, met, meeting
類義詞：encounter

及物動詞用法	不及物動詞用法
1. meet 遇見，碰上 I met him at the street. 我在街上遇見了他。 **2. meet 滿足** A good service is to meet all the needs of customers. 好的服務就是要滿足顧客的所有需求。	**1. meet 相遇，相會** The couple met at the Oriental Pearl Tower. 這對情侶在東方明珠塔上相遇。 **2. meet 接觸，會和** The two circles meet at point A. 這兩個圓在 A 點相切。

同義辨析：encounter
When **encountering** difficulties, we should face difficulties squarely.
當我們**遇到**困難時，我們應該迎難而上。

29. move [mit] 搬家

英解：to change position
動詞變形：moved, moved, moving
類義詞：remove, shift

及物動詞用法

1. move 使移動
Please move the barriers in the way.
請把擋在路中間的障礙物挪開。

2. move 使感動
We are all moved by their sad but beautiful love story.
我們都被他們淒美的愛情故事感動了。

3. move（在會上）提議，動議
The manager moves that we have dinner together after the meeting.
經理提議會議後大家一起去聚餐。

不及物動詞用法

1. move 移動，離開
The train is moving from the station.
火車一點點離開了車站。

2. move＋in／out／away 遷移，搬家
We have moved away.
我們已經搬家了。
Tom's moved to Italy.
Tom 舉家搬遷到了義大利。

3. move＋on 離開，繼續前進；更換工作、話題等
Can we move on now?
我們現在能繼續開始了嗎？

同義辨析：remove, shift
Please help me **remove** the furniture.　請幫我**搬開**這些傢俱。
The foolish old man attempted to **shift** the two mountains in front of his home.
愚公企圖**移開**門前的兩座大山。

30. open [ˈopən] 打開

英解：the opposite word of "close"
動詞變形：opened, opened, opening
類義詞：unfold, unwrap

及物動詞用法	不及物動詞用法
1. open 打開 Do you mind me opening the window? 您介意我開窗嗎？	**1. open** 開，張開 The wings of the eyas are opening. 雛鷹的翅膀張開了。
2. open 開張 We plan to open a cybershop. 我們打算開一個網路商店。	**2. open** 展現 Keep on, the success opens before you. 堅持一下，勝利就在眼前。
3. open 開始 The World Expo will be open in 100 days. 世博會還有一百天就開始了。	

同義辨析：unfold, unwrap

He **unfolds** to us all his ambition. 他向大家**表露**了他的抱負。

The string is **unwrapped**. 繩子**鬆開**了。

31. play [pleɪ] 玩耍

英解：to do sth for fun or entertainment

動詞變形：played, played, playing

類義詞：disport, amuse

及物動詞用法	不及物動詞用法
1. play 演奏，放（唱片） Please play us a piece of music. 請為我們演奏一曲吧。	**1. play + with** 玩耍，遊戲 Kids like playing with the ball. 小朋友喜歡玩球。
2. play 打（球、棋牌），做遊戲，彈奏（樂器） He began to play the violin when he was 5. 他五歲時開始拉小提琴。 He plays basketball with his friends every Friday. 他每週五和夥伴們一起打籃球。	**2. play** 演奏，彈奏，吹奏，放音 The CD player is playing. CD 播放機正在播放。
	3. play + for ／ against 為……效力 He plays for Houston Rockets. 他效力於休斯頓火箭隊。

同義辨析：disport, amuse

It's so sunny today. Let's **disport** ourselves in the park.
今天陽光燦爛，我們去公園遊玩吧！

The funny clown **amused** the spectators with his exaggerated action.
那個搞笑的小丑用其誇張的行為娛樂著觀眾。

22

32. read [rid] 讀，讀書

英解：to look and understand the written materials
動詞變形：read, read, reading
類義詞：peruse, skim

及物動詞用法	不及物動詞用法
1. read 讀，閱讀，朗讀 I read newspaper every day. 我每天都讀書。 **2. read** 讀懂，覺察 Every mother can read their daughters' thoughts. 每位母親都能讀懂女兒的心思。	**1. read** 閱讀，朗讀 I'm not interested in reading. 我對閱讀不感興趣。

同義辨析：peruse, skim

The judge **perused** his testimony.　法官細讀了他的證詞。

The most frequent way of reading is **skimming**.　最頻繁的閱讀方式就是略讀。

33. run [rʌn] 跑，經營

英解：to move quickly
動詞變形：ran, run, running
類義詞：scamper, escape

及物動詞用法

1. run 開動

Can you run the advanced machine which is brought in overseas?
你會啟動這個從國外引進的先進機器嗎？

2. run 經營，管理

You'd better run your own affairs.
你最好管好自己的事情。
She runs an on-line store extremely well.
她把她的網路商店經營的非常好。

不及物動詞用法

1. run 跑，奔

Liu Xiang is the one who runs fastest in China.
劉翔是中國跑得最快的人。

2. run + after 追趕

The wolf is running after a rabbit.
狼在追兔子。

3. run + for 競選

James is going to run for the class monitor.
James 打算競選班長。

同義辨析：scamper, escape

The little girl is **scampering** happily as a rabbit.
那個小女孩開心的**蹦蹦跳跳**，像只小兔子。

No one can **escape** from the justice.　沒有人能**逃過**法網。

34. see [si] 看見

英解：to watch
動詞變形：saw, seen, seeing
類義詞：glare, stare

及物動詞用法

1. see 看見，見到

Can you see the light tower in a distance?
你能看見遠方的燈塔嗎？

2. see 目睹，經歷

The old generation saw the great transformation of our country.
老一輩切身經歷了國家的轉變。

3. see 理解，領會，發現

I see your implication.
我理解你暗示了。

不及物動詞用法

1. see 看見

My grandmother can't see without her presbyopic glasses.
我奶奶不戴老花鏡就看不清了。

2. see 看出，理解

You can't see at all if you don't put yourself in his place.
如果你不設身處地為他想，你根本不能理解。

3. see 想，考慮

A:Do you have any good idea?
B:Let me see.
A: 你有什麼好注意嗎？
B: 讓我想想。

同義辨析：glare, stare

The enemies **glared** at each other.　這兩個冤家**怒視著**對方。

It's impolite to **stare** at a girl.　**盯著**女孩看是不禮貌的。

35. send [sɛnd] 送

英解：to give sth to sb or to move sth to sb

動詞變形：sent, sent, sending

類義詞：dispatch, provide

及物動詞用法	不及物動詞用法
1. send 發送，寄 I sent a letter of complaint to the customer service department. 我給客服部門發了一封投訴信。 **2. send** 派遣，發送 He sent his daughter to a boarding school. 他把他女兒送到了寄宿學校。	• **send + for** 派遣 Please send for the doctor. 請請醫生來。

同義辨析：dispatch, provide

The manager **dispatched** an experienced staff to negotiate with him.

經理**派**了一個有經驗的員工去和他談判。

Parents **provide** their children with food and clothing but call for nothing.

父母不求回報地**提供**自己兒女吃穿。

36. show [ʃo] 表現

英解：to present sth in front of others

動詞變形：showed, showed, showing

類義詞：express, manifest

及物動詞用法	不及物動詞用法
1. show 顯示，露出 He showed great interest in singing when he was young. 他從小就表現出對唱歌的巨大興趣。	**1. show** 顯現，露面 His uneasy feeling showed in his face. 他的不安顯露在他的臉上。

21
22
23
24
25
26
27
附錄一
附錄2
附錄3

> **2. show** 陳列
> The museum shows cultural relics in Stone Age.　這個博物館陳列了很多石器時代的文物。
>
> **3. show** 證明，表明
> I'll show you that I'll succeed sooner or later.　遲早有一天我要證明給你看我會成功的。

> **2. show** 上演，放映
> When will the film show?
> 這部電影什麼時候上映？
>
> **3. show ＋ off** 賣弄，炫耀
> Some boys are always showing off their specialties in front of beautiful girls.
> 有些男生總在女生面前賣弄他們的特質。

同義辨析：express, manifest

I don't know how to **express** myself exactly.　我不知道怎麼準確地**表達**自己。

This article **manifests** the truth of the present society.　這篇文章**揭露**了當今社會的現實。

37. sit [sɪt] 坐

英解：to take a seat
動詞變形：sat, sat, sitting
類義詞：slouch

及物動詞用法

1. sit 使坐下，使就坐
Please sit your children at the seat with seat belts.
請把孩子就做，並繫好安全帶。

2. sit 騎馬
James is good at sitting horses.
James 擅長騎馬。

3. sit（車等）可坐下
This hall will sit 3 thousand people.
這個禮堂可以做三千人。

不及物動詞用法

1. sit 坐著，就坐
They sat around the table.
他們繞桌子一圈坐下。
Sit down, please.　請坐。

2. sit ＋ on 佔有席位，當委員
He sits on the Parliament.
他是國會議員。

3. sit 坐落
Sun Moon Lake sits in the middle of Nantou district.
日月潭坐落在南投縣中部。

同義辨析：slouch

He **slouched** in the sofa.　他沒精打采地**癱坐**在沙發上。

38. sleep [slip] 睡覺

英解：to close eyes and rest other organs of body at night

動詞變形：slept, slept, sleeping

類義詞：nap

及物動詞用法	不及物動詞用法
● **sleep** 可供……住宿 How many people can this tent sleep? 這個帳篷可以睡多少人？	**1. sleep** 睡覺 She likes sleeping. 她喜歡睡覺。 **2. sleep** 靜止，保持寂靜 After daytime noisy, the village came to sleep. 經過白天的喧鬧，整個村莊陷入一片寂靜。

同義辨析：nap

I **nap** on the desk every noon. 每天中午我在住上打個盹兒。

39. speak [spik] 說，講

英解：to talk a kind of language or to express ideas

動詞變形：spoke, spoken, speaking

類義詞：argue, discuss

及物動詞用法	不及物動詞用法
1. speak 說語言，說出 Hearing Miss Wang speaking French is an enjoyable thing. 聽王小姐講法語是一種享受。 **2. speak** 顯示 Her expression spoke her unwillingness. 她的表情說明她不願意。 **3. speak** 背誦（臺詞） The basic challenge of actors or actresses is to speak long lines at a sitting. 作為演員的最基本挑戰就是一口氣背下很長的臺詞。	**1. speak + to** 說話，講話 He's angry at his mother and doesn't speak to her. 他生他媽媽的氣，不願意跟她講話。 **2. speak** 發表演說，陳述意見 Pay more attention to manners when you speak in public. 在公眾面前演講時應多禮儀。

301

同義辨析：argue, discuss

They are **arguing** whether only by studying abroad can they have a brighter future.
他們就是否只有出國學習才能有更美好的未來**爭論**不休。

What are they **discussing**? 他們在**討論**什麼？

40. start [start] 開始

英解：to begin
動詞變形：started, started, starting
類義詞：commence, begin

及物動詞用法

1. **start ＋ to-v ／＋ v-ing** 使開始，開始
   When she was five years old, she started to learn Latin dancing.
   她五歲就開始學習拉丁舞了。

2. **start** 引發；發起，創辦
   He plans to start his career on the Internet.
   他打算以網路開始他的職業生涯。

3. **start** 使開始運轉，啟動
   Is there anyone else able to start the machine?
   有其他人會啟動這個機器嗎？

4. **start** 使驚跳，驚起
   The thief started the dog when forcing opening the door.
   小偷撬門時驚動了狗。

5. **start** 開始雇傭
   The company starts him as a legal adviser.
   公司啟用他作為法律顧問。

不及物動詞用法

1. **start** 出發，啟程
   When will you start?
   你們什麼時候出發？

2. **start** 開始，著手
   The film will start soon.
   電影就快開始了。

3. **start** 突然驚起，吃驚
   I started at the sound of the ambulance.
   他被救護車的聲音嚇了一跳。

4. **start** 突然出現，冒出，湧出
   The multicolored fountain starts out every night.
   五彩噴泉每晚都開放。

5. **start ＋ at ／ with** 起始於
   His speech starts with a song.
   他以一首歌開始了他的演講。

同義辨析：commence, begin

A new round of competitions will **commence** right now. 新一輪比賽馬上就要**開始**了。

The meeting will **begin** in ten minutes. 會議將在十分鐘內**開始**進行。

41. stop [stɑp] 停止

英解：to interrupt
動詞變形：stopped, stopped, stopping
類義詞：pause

及物動詞用法

1. **stop + v-ing** 停止，中止
   His heart stopped beating.
   他的心臟停止了跳動。

2. **stop + from** 阻止，阻礙
   My mother stopped me from travelling alone.
   媽媽阻止了我一個人旅行。

3. **stop + up** 塞住，堵塞
   Come to stop up the leak in the pipe.
   快來堵住水管的漏洞。

4. **stop** 斷絕，止付，扣留
   This company stopped staff's wages and was faced with bankruptcy.
   公司停發了工人工資並面臨破產。

不及物動詞用法

1. **stop** 停止，中止
   Please stop and take a rest since you have been working for 6 hours.
   由於你已經工作六個小時了，請停下來休息一下吧！

2. **stop + to + v** 停下來（做別的事）
   Would you please stop to check the machine?
   您能停下來去檢查一下機器嗎？

3. **stop** 逗留，歇宿，（偶然）過訪【口】
   On my visit to France I stopped at my friend's.
   在我去發過旅遊期間，我順便到朋友家拜訪了一下。

同義辨析：pause

She **paused** for a while before talking the exciting part of her experience.
她在講述她經歷中最令人激動部份之前**停頓**了一下。

42. study [ˈstʌdɪ] 學習

英解：to learn
動詞變形：studied, studies, studying
類義詞：learn, research

21
22
23
24
25
26
27

附錄一

附錄2

附錄3

及物動詞用法	不及物動詞用法
1. study 學習，研究 When he was an undergraduate, he studied law. 他大學期間學習法學。 **2. study** 細看，細察 You should study him longer. 你應該多查看他一段時間。	● **study** 學習，用功 Study hard and then you'll make it. 努力學習你會成功的。

同義辨析：learn, research

You should **learn** from others and make up for your shortness.
你應該多向別人**學習**，彌補自身不足之處。

He **researches** on the wild animals.　他**研究**野生動物。

43. talk [tɔk] 說，談論

英解：to say sth with others
動詞變形：talked, talked, talking
類義詞：argue, lecture

及物動詞用法	不及物動詞用法
1. talk 講，說 What he talked is nonsense. 他說的都是胡說八道。 **2. talk** 討論，商談 We are all fond of talking philosophy in his class. 我們都喜歡在他的課上討論哲學。 **3. talk** 勸說 There is no need in talking me to forgive him. 沒有必要勸我原諒他。	**1. talk ＋ to ／ with ／ about** 講話，談話 Let's talk about the current affairs. 我們一起討論一下時事。 Mr. Wang is talking with the client. 王先生正在和客戶談話。 **2. talk** 說閒話，揭人隱私 You don't need to care how others talk. 你沒有必要在乎別人怎麼談論。

同義辨析：argue, lecture

They are arguing about the policy toward America.　他們在對美政策上爭論不休。

Why you are always lecturing me like my teacher?　為什麼你總是跟老師一樣對我說教？

44. tell [tɛl] 告訴，陳訴

英解：to state sth
動詞變形：told, told, telling
類義詞：express, confess

及物動詞用法	不及物動詞用法
1. tell + about ／ off ／ to 告訴，講述 Don't tell me about your excuse for late. 不要告訴我你遲到的藉口。	**1. tell + of ／ about** 講述 This book tells of San Mao's whole life. 這本書講述了三毛的一生。
2. tell 吩咐，命令，警告 His mother told him not to swim in the lake. 她媽媽囑咐他不要在湖裡游泳。	**2. tell + on** 產生效果 His frequent lateness tells on his unemployment. 他沒完沒了的遲到最終導致了他的失業。

同義辨析：express, confess
You should **express** yourself more slowly and clearly.
你在**表述**自己想法的時候應該再慢點，再清晰點。

He **confessed** that he failed in the final exam.　他**坦白**了自己沒有通過期末考試。

45. think [θɪŋk] 思考，考慮

英解：to consider sth
動詞變形：thought, thought, thinking
類義詞：contemplate

及物動詞用法	不及物動詞用法
1. think 想，思索 You should think how it will benefit your future by studying abroad. 你應該好好思考一下出國念書對你的將來有什麼好處。	**1. think + about** 想，思索 You should think about what you've done. 好好想想你都做了些什麼。
2. think 認為，以為 I don't think you are able to competent for this job. 我認為你還不能夠勝任這份工作。	**2. think** 認為 He can't do as he think. 他不能想怎麼做就怎麼做。

同義辨析：contemplate

He **contemplated** all the consequences before making such a decision.
他在做這個決定之前**思忖**了所有的後果。

46. travel ['trævl] 旅遊

英解：to be on a trip
動詞變形：traveled, traveled, travelling
類義詞：tour, visit

及物動詞用法	不及物動詞用法
1. travel 在……旅行，遊遍 My dream is to travel the whole world. 我的夢想就是遊遍世界。 **2. travel** 經過，走過，駛過 After travelling a long distance, they finally arrived at this tropical rain forest. 經過長時間的車程，他們終於到達了這邊熱帶雨林。	**1. travel** 旅行 They are travelling in Taipei. 他們正在臺北旅遊。 **2. travel**（光、聲音等）行進，傳導 Sound can't travel in a vacuum. 真空不能傳聲。 **3. travel** 移動，掃視 His eyes traveled over her. 他雙目掃視了一下她。

同義辨析：tour, visit

He **tours** their factory for investment.　他為投資而**參觀**了他們的工廠。

He **visits** the children in the orphanage every weekend.　他每週都去孤兒院**探望**孤兒。

47. try [traɪ] 嘗試

英解：to do sth with hard-working
動詞變形：tried, tried, trying
類義詞：attempt

及物動詞用法	不及物動詞用法
1. try 嘗試，試行 You can try the new car before buying it. 你在買這輛新車之前可以嘗試試駕一下。 **2. try + out** 試驗，試用 We have tried all the solutions out to this problem. 我們已經使用了所有解決這個問題的方法。	**1. try** 試圖，努力，試驗 Don't be shy and just try. 不要害羞，只要努力嘗試一下。 **2. try + to** 試圖，努力 We should try to overcome all the difficulties. 我們應該努力克服各種困難。

同義辨析：attempt

He **attempted** to attract that girl's attention.　他企圖引起那個女孩的注意。

48. wait [wet] 等待

英解：to give sb more minutes

動詞變形：waited, waited, waiting

類義詞：bide

及物動詞用法	不及物動詞用法
1. wait 等待機會 You shouldn't always wait the chance. 你不能總是等待機會的青睞。 **2. wait + for** 為……延後(用餐等) You don't need to wait dinner for me.　你們不用等我吃飯。	**1. wait + for** 等待 Are you waiting for me? 你們在等我嗎？ **2. wait** 延緩，耽擱 We can't wait any more. 我們不能再等了。

同義辨析：bide

Please **bide** here for a moment, our manager will come soon.

請在這等一會，我們經理就過來。

49. work [wɜk] 工作

英解：to do the job
動詞變形：worked, worked, working
類義詞：implement

及物動詞用法

1. work 開動

This instruction tells us how to work the machine.
這個說明書告訴我們怎麼開動機器。

2. work 使工作

Some bosses work their staff to death. 一些老闆讓員工拼命幹活。

不及物動詞用法

1. work 工作，勞動

Many overseas students work in the restraurant.
許多留學生在國外餐館工作。

2. work 運轉

My watch doesn't work.
我的手錶壞了。

3. work 起作用，行得通

It seems this solution will work well. 似乎這個方案能行得通。

同義辨析：implement

This company will **implement** the program in a month.
公司在一個月內將要**實行**這個項目。

50. worry [ˋwɜɪ] 擔心

英解：to feel worried about others; to care about others
動詞變形：worried, worried, worrying
類義詞：concern

及物動詞用法

1. worry 使擔心

Your reaction worries me.
你的反應令我擔憂。

2. worry 擔心

You don't need to worry whether it will bother me.
你無需擔心我是否會為此煩心。

不及物動詞用法

● **worry + about 擔心**

It's unhealthy for you to worry about all the sundries.
你擔心所有的瑣事對你身體是不健康的。

同義辨析：concern

The security problem of high-speed railway **concerns** everyone.
高鐵的安全問題令每個人**擔憂**。

附錄二：名詞50個

1. action [ˈækʃən] 行動，行為

完成一項事物的過程，為某特殊目的從事某種行為。

英解：the process of doing sth. in order to make sth. happen or to deal with a situation

類義詞：movement, behavior, deed

名詞的用法	動詞的用法〈及物動詞〉
1. 行動，行為過程〈不可數名詞〉 The government has taken immediate action to prevent the news spreading. 政府立刻採取了措施來阻止消息傳播。 **2.** 所做之事〈可數名詞〉 Everyone should take responsibility for their own actions. 每個人都該為自己的行為負責。	● 採取措施 Your request will be fixed soon. 你的要求很快就可以得到處理。

同義詞辨析：movement 運動、運行，behavior 行為，deed 作事之行為

Scientists are watching the new-found star to gather data about its **movement**.
科學家們正在觀察新發現的恒星，以收集其**運行**的資料。

Under that kind of circumstance, his **behavior** was totally unwise.
在那種情況下，他的**行為**是非常不明智的。

Be true in word and resolute in **deed**. 說話要真實，**做事**要果斷。

2. actor [ˈæktɚ] 男演員

從事戲劇演出的男性演員。

英解：someone who performs in a play or film

類義詞：actress, hero, heroine, performer

名詞的用法〈可數名詞〉	常用片語
1. 演員，舞臺表演者 He was nominated as the best actor for his excellent performing. 他因演技出色獲得了最佳男演員的提名。 **2. 參與者** All the actors will face a serious punishment after the riots. 騷亂平息後，所有參與者都將面臨嚴重懲罰。	best actor 最佳男主角，最佳男演員 leading actor 主演 supporting actor 男配角 best supporting actor 最佳男配角

同義詞辨析：actress 女演員，hero 英雄，heroine 女主人公；女英雄，performer 表演者

The Titanic made Kate Winslet a famous **actress**.
《鐵達尼號》讓凱特·溫絲蕾一躍成為了著名的**女演員**。

The **hero** of this book is a man who was disabled. 這本書的**男主人公**是個殘疾人。

The death of the **heroine** at the end of the movie is really touching.
影片結尾**女主人公**的死非常感人。

He used to work as a **stunt performer**. 他曾做過**特技演員**。

3. airport [ˈɛrˌport] 機場，航空站, 航空港

飛機降落起飛及有大型建築物讓旅客等待的地方。

英解：a place where planes land and take off and that has buildings for passengers to wait in

類義詞：landing field, aeroport

名詞的用法〈可數名詞〉

- 機場，航空站

  Excuse me, how can I get to the airport? 打擾一下，請問去機場怎麼走？

同義詞辨析：landing field 飛機起降場，aeroport 機場 (英式用語)

This place used to be a landing field during WWII. 二戰期間這裡曾是飛機起降場。

They have arrived at Aeroport Orly.　他們已經到奧利機場了。

4. anger [`æŋɡɚ] 憤怒，（使）發怒

當遇到令人感到不好或不公平時，所感到的一種強烈的情緒。

英解：a strong feeling you have when something bad or unfair you think happens to you

類義詞：wrath, bile, furious, provoke

名詞的用法〈不可數名詞〉	動詞的用法〈及物動詞〉
● 怒火，怒氣，憤怒 The growing anger and frustration of young unemployed people leads to UK's recent disorder. 年輕失業者日益增長的憤怒和沮喪導致了英國近期的騷亂。	● 使發怒，激怒 Obviously, he was angered by her question. 很明顯，她的問題激怒了他。

同義詞辨析：wrath 盛怒，bile 怒氣衝天，furious 憤怒的，provoke 激起…的怒氣

Their action provoked the **wrath** of environmental campaigners.
他們的行為激起了環保人士的**盛怒**。

It gets my **bile** to be treated in such an unfair way.　如此不公的待遇叫我感到**怒氣衝天**。

She was **furious** with her son's words.　兒子的話讓她非常**生氣**。

5. answer [`ænsɚ] 回答，答案

用於回答問題、要求、批評、指控的口說或書寫的陳述。

英解：a statement (either spoken or written) that is made in reply to a question or request or criticism or accusation

類義詞：reply, response, result, meet with, accord

名詞的用法〈可數名詞〉	動詞的用法〈及物動詞〉
1. 答覆，回答 I rang the bell, but there's no answer. 我按了門鈴，但沒有人應門。	**1.** 回答 He didn't answer my question. 他沒有回答我的問題。

311

2.（試題、習題的）答案

Do you know the answer to question 2?
你知道第二題的答案嗎？

3.（問題的）解決辦法

I can't find the answer to this problem. 這個問題我沒法解決。

2. 符合，適合，比得上（可加 **that** 從句）

Does this answer your requirement?
這個符合你們的要求嗎？

同義詞辨析：reply 回答，response 反應，result 結果

Your earlier **reply** will be highly appreciated. 我們將非常感謝您的早日答覆。

His **response** was extremely strange. 他對這件事的反應很奇怪。

Their experiment leads no **result**. 他們的實驗沒出任何結果。

6. arm [arm] 臂，臂狀物

人類身體的一部分，連接肩膀和手的部分。

英解：part of human body that stick out from the top and connected the shoulders to the hands

類義詞：sleeve, rail, balustrade, branch

名詞的用法〈可數名詞〉

1. 臂，手臂

He fell from the tree and broke his arm.
他從樹上掉了下來，摔斷了胳膊。

2. 扶手

He rested himself on the arm of his father's chair.
他靠坐在他父親椅子的扶手上休息。

動詞的用法〈及物動詞〉

● 武裝，備戰

To leave her parents-in-law a good impression, she has armed herself with her most valuable jewelry.
為了給公婆留個好印象，她戴上了她最貴重的珠寶。

同義辨析：rail 扶手, balustrade 陽台欄杆

It's said that the accident was caused by a little boy who climbed outside of the escalator **rail**. 據說事故是由於一個爬到電梯扶手外側的小男孩引起的。

She leaned over the **balustrade** and shouted to the man downstairs.
她俯身在陽臺欄杆上對樓下的男人喊道。

7. bath [bæθ] 浴缸，洗澡

靠乞求救濟度日的人

長而大的容器，可放水並進而清洗全身。

英解：a large long container that you put water in and get into wash your whole body

類義詞：wash oneself，take a shower

名詞的用法〈可數名詞〉	動詞的用法〈及物動詞〉
● 沐浴，洗盆浴 Usually he will have a bath before going to bed. 通常情況下睡覺前他都會洗個澡。	● 給……洗澡 It's time to bath the baby. 該給寶寶洗澡了。

同義詞辨析：wash oneself 自己洗澡，take a shower 沖澡

My little brother is too young to **wash himself**.　我弟弟太小了，還不會自己洗澡。

It's my habit to **take a shower** before going to bed every day.

我的習慣是每天睡前沖個澡。

8. beggar [ˈbɛgɚ] 乞丐

靠乞求救濟度日的人

英解：a pauper who lives by begging

類義詞：the poor, fellow, guy

名詞的用法〈可數名詞〉	動詞的用法〈及物動詞〉
1. 乞丐 There're a lot of beggars on the Line 10 in Beijing. 北京地鐵十號線上有許多乞討者。 2. 傢伙 You lazy beggar, aren't you still undressed? 懶傢伙，還沒穿好衣服嗎？	● 使貧窮，使匱乏 Why should I beggar myself for you?　我為什麼要為你受窮？

同義詞辨析：the poor 窮人，fellow 同伴，guy 伙計

The government should take the responsibility for the poor's education.

政府應為窮人的教育負起責任。

He's my fellow.　他是我的同伴。

Hey, guys, what's up? 伙計們，怎麼了？

9. branch [bræntʃ] 樹枝，分支機構

樹木的分支；一個大型且複雜組織的分部單位。

英解：an administrative division of some larger or more complex organization

類義詞：feeder, ramification

名詞的用法〈可數名詞〉	動詞的用法〈不及物動詞〉
1. 樹枝 Some small branches of the tree have been cut down by the worker. 工人把這棵樹的一些小枝剪掉了。	● 分開，開叉 The accident happened where the road branches. 事故發生在岔道口處。
2. (公司，政府，語言等的) 分支，分部 Our Beijing Branch will deal with the matter. 北京分公司會處理這件事。	
3. 家族分支，河流支流 My uncle's branch of the family moved to the South. 我們家族中叔叔的一支搬去了南方。	

同義詞辨析：feeder 交通支線，ramification 分支

The city plans to perfect its road network, especially about the **feeder** roads.
該市計畫完善其交通網絡，尤其是加強支線道路建設。

Mathematic Programming is one important **ramification** of Operational Research.
線性規劃是運籌學的一個重要分支。

10. breakfast [ˈbrɛkfəst] 早餐，早飯

通常指每天早上的第一餐。

英解：the first meal of the day (usually in the morning)

名詞的用法〈(不) 可數名詞〉

- 早餐，早飯

  Breakfast starts at 7 o'clock in our family.

  我們家通常 7 點鐘吃早飯。

動詞的用法〈不及物動詞〉

- 吃早飯

  He hadn't had breakfasted yet when he came here.

  他來這兒的時候還沒吃早飯。

常用片語

for breakfast 當作早餐；對於早餐來說
have breakfast 吃早餐，吃早飯
at breakfast 早餐時，正在吃早飯
continental breakfast 歐式早餐（僅有咖啡和果醬麵包）
bed and breakfast 歐洲的一種簡易旅館；住宿加早餐
breakfast buffet 自助早餐；自助早餐吧

11. cake [kek] 蛋糕

由麵粉、糖和蛋為基底混合做成的食物。

英解：a kind of food which is made from or based on a mixture of flour and sugar and eggs

類義詞：clot

名詞的用法〈(不) 可數名詞〉	動詞的用法〈及物動詞〉
• 蛋糕，糕點 It's just a piece of cake. 小意思。	**1.** 覆蓋 His shoes were caked with mud. 他的鞋上全是泥巴。 **2.** 結成硬塊，膠凝 The blood was caked. 血液凝固了。

同義詞辨析：clot 凝固

The blood on the ground clotted quickly.　地上的血很快就凝固了。

12. cap [kæp] 帽子

無邊有遮簷的帽子。

英解：a tight-fitting headdress

類義詞：hat

名詞的用法〈可數名詞〉

1. 便帽，制服帽；軟帽；方帽

He likes to collect all kinds of caps.

他喜歡收集各種帽子。

2.（鋼筆、瓶子等的）蓋，帽

The baby was chocked by a bottle cap.

那個小嬰兒的喉嚨被瓶子蓋卡住了。

動詞的用法〈及物動詞〉

1. 用……覆蓋頂部

The mountains are capped with snow.

山頂白雪皚皚。

2. 勝過，超過

What an amazing story! Can anyone cap that?

故事真精彩！還有人能講得更精彩嗎？

同義詞辨析：hat 有簷的帽子

Dad wants to buy me a **hat**, but I prefer a **cap**.

爸爸想給我買個**有簷的帽子**，但我更喜歡**沒簷的**。

13. channel [ˈtʃænḷ] 電視臺，管道

一種電訊號可以傳遞的路徑。

英解：a path over which electrical signals can pass

類義詞：door, exit, route

名詞的用法〈可數名詞〉

1. 電視臺，頻道，波段

What's on channel 5 tonight?

今晚第五頻道有什麼節目？

2. 途徑，管道，系統

Complaints must be made through the proper channel.

投訴必須以正當方式進行。

動詞的用法〈及物動詞〉

1. 為……引資，引導，貫注

He channels his aggression into the sports.

他把衝勁傾注於運動之中。

2. 輸送資金，提供幫助

Money for the project will be channeled by the local government.

這個項目的資金將有地方政府提供。

3. 方式，方法，手段

Music is a great channel to release your emotion.

欣賞音樂是宣洩感情的一種有效方式。

4. 水道，海峽

They were crossing the English Channel.

他們正在越過英吉利海峽。

3. 輸送，傳送

It's hard to channel the light signal in such a bad weather.

在這樣糟糕的天氣下傳送光信號太難了。

同義詞辨析：door 門，exit 出口，route 路徑

The door to the garden was locked.　通往花園的門被鎖了。

The exit is over there.　出口在那邊。

It was the shortest route from Rome to Naples.　那是從羅馬到那不勒斯最快的路線。

14. circle [ˈsɝkḷ] 圓形，環

一種完全圓形且平面的形狀。

英解：a completely round flat shape or sth like that

類義詞：round, wheel, cycle

名詞的用法〈可數名詞〉

1. 圓形，圓周，圓圈

He drew a circle on the blackboard.

他在黑板上畫了個圓。

2. 圓形物，環狀物

The children stood in a circle.

孩子們站了一圈。

3. 圈子，階層，界

She's well known in the drama circle.

她在戲劇界很有名。

動詞的用法

1. 盤旋，環行，轉圈

Seagulls circled around his head.

海鷗在他頭頂盤旋。

2. 圍繞……畫圈，圈出

All spelling mistakes have been circled in red ink.

所有的拼寫錯誤都用紅筆圈起來了。

同義詞辨析：round 圓形的，wheel 方向盤，cycle 圓形

He has a **round** face.　他有張圓臉。

His hands were off the **wheel**.　他的手沒有握住**方向盤**。

317

Education is the only way to break this **cycle**. 教育是打破這種**循環**的唯一途徑。

15. cream [krim] 奶油，乳脂

牛奶中含有乳脂的那一部份。

英解：the part of milk containing the butterfat

類義詞：essence, elite

名詞的用法〈不可數名詞〉	動詞的用法
1. 奶油，油脂 Would you like milk or cream in your coffee? 你的咖啡是要加牛奶還是加奶油？	**1.** 把……攪成糊狀 Cream the butter and sugar together. 把黃油和糖攪成糊狀。
2. 護膚霜，潔淨劑，清洗液 She bought a hand cream in the supermarket. 她在超市買了一個護手霜。	**2.** 徹底打敗，狠揍 He was creamed in the playground. 他在操場上被狠狠打了一頓。

同義詞辨析：essence 本質, elite 精英份子

His paintings captured the **essence** of the country.
他的畫描繪出了這個國家的**神韻**。

At that time, most of the **elites** graduated from this famous university.
在那個時代，許多**社會精英**都畢業於這所著名的大學。

16. crowd [kraʊd] 人群，觀眾

一大群聚集一起的人。

英解：a large number of things or people considered together

類義詞：pile, mass

名詞的用法〈不可數名詞〉	動詞的用法〈及物動詞〉
1. 人群，觀眾 It's hard to push a way through the crowd. 在人群中擠過去很不容易。	**1.** 擠滿，塞滿，使擁擠 Thousands of people crowded the narrow street. 成千上萬的人把狹窄的街道擠得水泄不通。

2. 一夥人，一幫人
I saw some friends of the usual crowd yesterday.
昨天我見到了幾個常見面的朋友。

3. 群眾，民眾，老百姓
She's quite happy to follow the crowd.
她就願意隨著群眾。

2. 湧上（心頭），湧入（腦海）
Memories crowded his mind.
往事湧上心頭。

同義詞辨析：pile 堆，mass 大眾

They found some apples beneath a pile of leaves.
他們在一堆樹葉下發現了幾個蘋果。

Mass media play an important role in today's education.
在現代教育中，大眾傳媒起著很重要的作用。

17. dirt [dɜt] 塵土

不乾淨的微小泥塵。

英解：the state of being covered with unclean things
類義詞：dust, soil, earth

名詞的用法〈不可數名詞〉

1. 汙物，塵土，爛泥
Every time my little sister comes back home, her clothes will be covered in dirt. 小妹每次回家，都全身泥土。

2. 鬆土，泥土，散土
The little girl has been sitting in the dirt. 小女孩一直坐在泥土上。

3. 醜聞，流言蜚語
The new teacher hasn't come to the school, but the dirt about him has.
新老師還沒來學校，但有關他的流言已經到了。

同義詞辨析：dust 灰塵，soil 土壤，earth 泥土
Dust off the vase, please. 請把花瓶上的灰塵撢掉。
The **soil** here is not that rich now. 這兒的土壤不是很肥沃了。
The snow on the **earth** is becoming thicker and thicker. 地上的積雪越來越厚。

18. dust [dʌst] 塵土，沙土

粉狀物質，可被吹入空氣中，例如：乾土或花粉。

英解：fine powdery material such as dry earth or pollen that can be blown about in the air

類義詞：soil, earth, dirt

名詞的用法〈不可數名詞〉

1. 沙土，塵土
A cloud of dust rose as the truck drove off.
卡車開過時揚起一片沙塵。

2. 灰塵，塵埃
The books are all covered with dust.　書上積了很多灰。

動詞的用法

1. 擦去塵土，擦灰
Can you dust the shelf?
你能把貨架子上的塵土擦一擦嗎？

2. 撒粉末
Dust the cake with sugar.
把糖撒在蛋糕上。

同義詞辨析：soil 土壤，earth 地面，dirt 灰塵

The **soil** here is not that rich now.　這兒的**土壤**不是很肥沃了。

You can feel the **earth** shake when the train passes by.
火車經過時可以感受到**地面**的震動。

Remove the **dirt** from the surface of the vase.　把花瓶上的**灰塵**擦掉。

19. education [ˌɛdʒʊˈkeʃən] 教育

教導或教授知識的活動。

英解：the activities of educating or instructing; activities that impart knowledge or skill

類義詞：cultivation, training

名詞的用法〈不可數名詞〉

1. 教育，培養，訓練
Health education has the same importance as primary education.
健康教育同基礎教育一樣重要。

2. 教育機構，教育界人士，教育學
She used to study at a college of Education.　她曾就讀於一所教育學院。

3. 有教益的經歷

The rock concert is quite an education for my parents!
這場搖滾音樂會讓我父母大受教益！

同義詞辨析：cultivation 文明；培養，training 訓練

This school emphasizes the **cultivation** of independent thinking for students.
這所學校注重**培養**學生的獨立的思考的能力。

He hurt his ankle in the **training**.　他在**訓練**中傷了腳踝。

20. feast [fist] 盛宴

為許多人所開的典禮式晚宴。

英解：a ceremonial dinner party for many people

類義詞：enjoy, festival, banquet

名詞的用法〈可數名詞〉	動詞的用法〈不及物動詞〉
1. 盛宴，宴會 There will be a big wedding feast tomorrow. 明天將舉行一場盛大的婚宴。	● 盡情享用 Now feast your eyes on the beautiful scene. 現在請盡情欣賞這片美景吧！
2. 節日，節期 During the feast of Spring Festival, the family will go for a vacation in China. 春節時他們要去中國度假。	
3. 使人歡快的事物或活動 The evening was a real feast for music lovers. 這個晚會真是讓音樂愛好者大飽耳福。	

同義詞辨析：enjoy 享受，banquet 宴會

Hope you can **enjoy your meal**.　希望您**用餐**愉快。

There are a lot of bigwigs in that **banquet**.　**宴會**上有許多大人物出席。

21. flavor [ˋflevɚ] 味道

食物或飲料嚐起來的感覺。

英解：how food and drink tastes
類義詞：sapor, taste

名詞的用法	動詞的用法
1. 味道〈不可數名詞〉 The coffee made by her gives some strange flavor. 她煮的咖啡味道怪怪的。 **2. 某種味道〈可數名詞〉** This cake comes in 5 different flavors. 這種蛋糕有 5 種不同口味。	● 加味於 Don't flavor the soup with extra things. 湯裡不要再放東西了。

同義詞辨析：sapor 味道，taste 嚐起來

Standardization of dishes may make all dishes take on single sapor.
菜餚標準化可能會讓所有菜都變成一個味。

It tastes better after adding some soy sauce. 加醬油後嘗起來味道好多了。

22. furniture [ˋfɝnɪtʃɚ] 傢俱

陳設品以供人在房間或區域使用。

英解：furnishings that make a room or other area ready for occupancy
類義詞：equipment, facility

名詞的用法

● 傢俱，設備
Since we ran short of money, we had to buy some second-hand furniture.
由於資金不足，我們不得不買些二手傢俱。

同義詞辨析：equipment 設備，facility 設備 (常用複數形)

The adjustment of the **equipment** must be finished by Sunday.
設備調試必須在周日之前完成。

Recently this company has introduced some advanced **facilities** from abroad.
最近，這家公司從國外引進了一些先進設備。

23. game [gem] 遊戲

一種有規則以決定獲勝者的比賽。

英解：a contest with rules to determine a winner

類義詞：competition, play, tournament, match

名詞的用法〈可數名詞〉	形容詞的用法
1. 遊戲，運動，比賽項目 We're going to the ball game. 我們要去看棒球比賽。 **2.** (網球比賽等的) 一場，一局 He lost two games in the tennis match. 他在網球比賽中輸了兩場。	甘願嘗試，有冒險精神 She's game for anything. 她什麼都敢嘗試。

同義詞辨析：competition 競爭，play 玩；參與比賽，tournament 錦標賽，match 比賽

The **competition** between schools to attract students is quite intense.
學校之間為招攬生源展開了激烈**競爭**。

I can't **play** this game. It's too hard. 這遊戲我**玩**不了，太難了。

He got an excellent mark in the last golf **tournament**.
他在上次的高爾夫**錦標賽**中取得了非常好的成績。

Every year my mother will spend several days watching her favorite **matches** in Beijing. 每年我母親都要抽幾天時間去北京看她最喜歡的**比賽**。

24. glove [glʌv] 手套

帶在手上以覆蓋手與手腕。

英解：hand wear: covers the hand and wrist

類義詞：mitten

名詞的用法

- 手套
  I need a new pair of gloves for the cold winter.
  我需要一雙新手套來度過寒冷的冬天。

同義詞辨析：mitten 連指手套 (手指沒有分開)

I want a pair of **mittens** instead of gloves.　我要的是**連指手套**，不是五指分開的手套。

25. grade [gred]（分）等級

特殊產品或物質有不同級數的分級。

英解：the quality of a particular product or material

類義詞：degree, class

名詞的用法	動詞的用法
1. 等級，品級 These materials are all of high grade.　這些材料全是優質品。 **2.** 級別，職別 She's still only in a secretarial grade.　她的職別仍然是秘書。 **3.** 成績等級，評分等級 She got great grades on her exams.　她考試成績優良。 **4.** 年級 My daughter is in her fifth grade now.　我女兒正在上五年級。	**1.** 分級，分類 The students were graded by scores. 這所學校的學生是按成績分級的。 **2.** 給……評分 I spent all weekends grading papers.　我整個週末都在閱卷。

同義詞辨析：degree 學位，class 班級

He failed to get the PHD **degree** for his poor score.
他成績太差，沒有拿到哲學博士**學位**。

Which **class** are you in?　你是幾**班**的？

26. hat [hæt] 帽子

英解：headdress that protects the head from bad weather; has shaped crown and usually a brim

類義詞：cap

名詞的用法〈可數名詞〉

1.（有簷的）帽子（與無簷帽 **cap** 相對）

Take off your hat, please.　請把帽子摘了吧。

2. 職位，角色

I'm telling you this with my teacher's hat on, you know.

你知道，我是以教師的身份告訴你這些。

同義詞辨析：cap

He wore a black **cap** on that day.　那天他戴了一頂黑色鴨舌帽。

27. home [hom] 家，住所

英解：where you live at a particular time，especially with your family

類義詞：residence，family

名詞的用法	形容詞的用法
1. 家，住所〈(不)可數名詞〉 Hold on, we are heading home now. 堅持住，我們就要回家了。	**1. 家的，家庭的** We offer free home delivery service. 我們提供免費宅配服務。
2. 房子，住宅，寓所〈可數名詞〉 A lot of new homes are being built at the edge of the town. 小鎮週邊正在興建很多新房屋。	**2. 在家裡做的，家用的** This company sales all kinds of home appliance. 這家公司銷售各種家電產品。
3. 家鄉，故鄉，定居地〈(不)可數名詞〉 It's ten years since I went home last time. 我已經 10 年沒回家鄉了。	**3. 本國的，國內的** There's nothing new in today's home news. 今天的國內新聞沒什麼新鮮事。
	4. 主場的 The team lost the game at their home match. 這支隊伍在主場比賽中失敗了。
副詞的用法 **1. 到家，向家，在家** What time did you get home last night? 你昨晚幾點到家的？	**常用片語** at home 在家；在國內；熟悉 home and abroad 國內外，海內外 home appliance 家電產品；家用電器 home page 主頁；第一個介面

| **2.** 到正確的位置
He leaned on the door and pushed the bolt home.
他倚在門上，上好了門閂。 | at home in 熟悉；精通…
home country 祖國；原籍國
feel at home 在家中般輕鬆自在；感覺自在
home office（英國）內政部 |

同義詞辨析：residence，family

This is not his permanent **residence**.　這並不是他的常住地址。

After graduation from college, he moved back to live with his **family**.

大學畢業後，他又搬回去和家人同住了。

28. joke [dʒok] 笑話；戲謔；玩笑

英解：a humorous anecdote or remark intended to provoke laughter

類義詞：fun,play trick on,fool, kid around

名詞的用法〈可數名詞〉	動詞的用法〈不及物動詞〉
1. 笑話，玩笑 I can't get the joke. 我不懂這有什麼可笑的。 **2.** 笑料，笑柄 Taking this job is a joke for her. 選擇這份工作對她來說簡直就是個笑話。	● 說笑話，開玩笑 You must be joking! 你是在開玩笑吧！

同義詞辨析：fun,play trick on,fool，kid around

I study English just for **fun**.　我學英語只是因為好玩。

Don't **play tricks** on others.　不要捉弄別人。

I'm not that easy to **fool**.　我不是那麼容易就會上當受騙的。

He is just **kidding around**.　他只不過鬧著玩兒罷了。

29. kite [kaɪt] 風箏，塗改（支票）

英解：a toy consisting of a light frame covered with tissue paper; flown in wind at end of a string

類義詞：alter, obliterate

名詞的用法〈可數名詞〉	動詞的用法〈及物動詞〉
1. 風箏 Sometimes I wish I were a kite——with one string I could fly into the sky. 有時候我希望自己是只風箏——憑一根線就可以飛上藍天。	● 塗改（支票） It's illegal to kite the checks. 用塗改支票是違法的。

同義詞辨析：alter，obliterate

The dress needs to be **altered** since it didn't fit for the bride.

這件裙子新娘穿不合身，需要**修改**一下。

The painting on the wall was **obliterated** by the rain.　牆上的畫被雨水**沖**掉了。

30. layout [ˈleˌaʊt] 佈局，安排

英解：the way in which the parts of sth are arranged

類義詞：design, plan

名詞的用法〈可數名詞〉

1. 佈局，佈置

The layout of the streets in this city is not that logical.

這個城市的街道佈局不是很合理。

2. 安排，設計

They will come here to talk about the layout of the book tomorrow.

明天他們會來這兒跟我們討論該書的情節安排。

同義詞辨析：design, plan

His **design** was quite famous.　他的**設計**當時非常有名。

My family **plans** to go for a holiday before the summer ends.

我們家**計畫**在夏季結束之前去度假。

31. mask [mæsk] 面具，掩飾

英解：a covering for part or all of the face, worn to hide or protect it

類義詞：dissimulate, make sb up, disguise, hide

21 22 23 24 25 26 27

名詞的用法〈可數名詞〉	動詞的用法〈及物動詞〉
1. 面具，面罩 It must be very hot to wear masks in such weather. 在這種天氣下戴面罩肯定很熱。 **2. 掩飾，偽裝** It's time to throw off the mask and show the real you. 是時候丟掉偽裝，展現真正的你吧！	● **掩飾，掩藏** Stop laughing! It can't mask your foolishness! 別小了！再笑也掩蓋不了你的愚蠢！

同義詞辨析：dissimulate，make sb up，disguise，hide

He's a man who's good at **dissimulating** his true thoughts.
他是個善於**隱藏**自己真實想法的人。

She's **making herself** up.　她正在**化妝**。

His **disguise** was soon penetrated.　他的**偽裝**很快就被識破了。

They **hid** themselves in a cave and survived the war.
他們**藏**在一個山洞裡，從戰爭中倖存了下來。

32. money [ˋmʌnɪ] 錢，財富

英解：what you earn by working or selling things and use to buy things
類義詞：currency, wealth, treasure, fortune

名詞的用法〈不可數名詞〉

1. 錢，薪水，收入

Our program can ensure that you get your money's worth.
我們的項目一定會讓您覺得物有所值。

2. 紙幣，鈔票

Where can I change my money into dollars?
到哪兒可以把我的錢換成美元？

3. 財富，財產

He believes in that money talks.　他相信財大才能氣粗。

4.（律）款項

All money has been transferred into his own account.
所有的款項都被轉到了他自己的帳戶上。

同義詞辨析：currency，wealth，treasure，fortune，underline

The **currency** of foreign investors shall be changed into RMB.
外國投資者須將**貨幣**換成人民幣。

His **wealth** has shrunk seriously because of the crisis.　由於經濟危機他的**財富**大幅縮水。

This is the treasure of my memory.　這是我記憶的珍寶。

God sends **fortun**e to fools.　上帝將**財富**送給愚者。

33. number [ˈnʌmbɚ] 數字，數量

英解：a word or symbol that represents an amount or a quantity
類義詞：figure, arithmetic, digital

名詞的用法	動詞的用法〈及物動詞〉
1. 數位，數，數量〈可數名詞〉 You own me 28, right? Make it 30. That's a good round number. 你欠我 28 元，對吧？湊到 30 吧，討個整數好記。 **2.** 編號，序數〈可數名詞〉 Number 23, it's you turn! 23 號，該你了！	**1.** 標號，給……編號 All athletes were numbered. 所有的運動員都編了號。 **2.** 總計 We numbered 45. 我們總共有 45 人。

同義詞辨析：figure，arithmetic，digital

The **figures** of casualties in China's official report are always 35 or so.
中國的官方傷亡**人數**總是在 35 左右。

This **arithmetic expression** is not complete.　這個**算術運算式**是不完整的。

Today's **digital camera** is pretty advanced.　現在的**數碼相機**已經非常先進了。

34. plastic [ˈplæstɪk] 塑膠，可塑的

英解：generic name for certain synthetic or semi synthetic materials that can be molded or extruded into objects

名詞的用法	形容詞的用法
1. 塑膠（可數名詞，常用單數） This pipe was made of plastic. 這種管子是用塑膠製成的。	**1.** 塑膠製的，塑膠的 Plastic toys are not safe for baby to play. 塑膠玩具對嬰兒來說不是很安全。

21 22 23 24 25 26 27 附錄一 附錄 2 附錄 3

| 2. 信用卡（不可數名詞）
Do they take plastic?
他們收信用卡嗎？ | 2. 可塑的，可塑性的
We need some plastic materials such as the clay.
我們需要一些具有可塑性的物質，比如說黏土。 |

同義詞辨析：moldable，malleable

This is the exactly **moldable** and low-cost insulator we are looking for.
這就是我們正在找的**易模塑**、又廉價的絕緣體。

Please find me some **malleable** metal.　請給我找一些**延展性好的**金屬來。

35. pocket [`pakɪt] 口袋，把……放進口袋

英解：a small pouch inside a garment for carrying small articles
類義詞：container, bag

名詞的用法〈可數名詞〉

1. 口袋
Turn out your pockets.
把你口袋裡的東西都掏出來。

2.（附在車門上、提包內的）小口袋
The information you want is in the pocket of your handbag.
你要的信息在提包的口袋裡。

3. 錢財，財力，資金（常用單數）
This travel agency has many ways for holidays to suit every pocket.
這家旅行社有適合各種程度消費的度假方式。

4.（與周圍不同的）小組織，小區域
There's still a pocket of criminals not arrested.
還有一小股犯罪分子未被抓獲。

動詞的用法〈及物動詞〉

1. 把……放進衣袋
She paid for the drink and pocketed the change without counting it.
她付了飲料錢，找回的零錢數都沒數就放進了口袋。

2. 揩油
What I hate the most is pocketing things that do not belong to oneself.
我痛恨的就是中飽私囊。

3. 賺下
Last year he pocketed $10million in publishing industry.
去年他從出版業掙了 1000 萬美金。

同義詞辨析：container，bag

Cover the **container** with a clean piece of wood.　在容器上蓋上一塊乾淨的木板。

She lost her **bag** in the big crowd.　她在人群中丟了包。

36. quiet [ˈkwaɪət] 安靜（的），（使）安靜

英解：a state of being calm and without much noise

類義詞：peace, calm, still, tranquil

名詞的用法〈不可數名詞〉

● 安靜，寧靜，平靜

I like to enjoy the quiet of my room.　我很享受房間裡的寧靜。

動詞的用法

1. 使平靜〈及物動詞〉

She's quite good at quieting down the kids.　她很有辦法讓孩子們安靜下來。

2. 安靜〈不及物動詞〉

Quiet! Quiet! Let's welcome our leader——Jim!
安靜！安靜！讓給我們歡迎我們的領袖——吉姆！

形容詞的用法（quieter，quietest）

1. 僻靜的，寂靜的，清靜的

Business is usually quieter at this time of year.
每年的這個時候，生意都很清淡。

2.（人）寡言少語的，文靜的

She's a quiet girl.　她是個文靜的女孩。

3.（感情或態度）穩重的，不張揚的

He had an air of quiet authority.　他神態威嚴凝重。

同義詞辨析：peace，calm，still，tranquil

Reading can make her heart **in peace**.　讀書可以讓她保持心靈平靜。

Calm down. We can make it.　鎮靜。我們一定可以成功。

Don't stay **still**.　不要一動也不動的。

They led a **tranquil** life in the country.　他們在鄉村裡過著一種平靜的生活。

37. rain [ren] 雨，下雨

英解：water falling in drops from the clouds

類義詞：wet, monsoon

名詞的用法	動詞的用法〈及物動詞〉
1. 雨，雨水〈不可數名詞〉 It's pouring rain outside. 外面正在下瓢潑大雨。 **2.** 熱帶地區的雨季（常用複數） 〈可數名詞〉 The rains come in September. 雨季九月份開始。	**1.** 下雨 It's raining cats and dogs. 天正在下傾盆大雨。 **2.** 雨點般落下 Bombs rained down on the streets. 炮彈雨點般地落在街道上。

同義詞辨析：wet

Tomorrow will be **a wet day**.　明天是個雨天。

38. reward [rɪˈwɔrd] 報酬；獎勵

英解：a recompense for worthy acts or retribution for wrongdoing

類義詞：compensation, payment, consideration, return

名詞的用法〈可數名詞〉	動詞的用法〈及物動詞〉
1. 獎勵，回報，報酬 You deserve this reward since you've done me such a great favor. 你幫了我這麼大的忙，這是你應得的報酬。 **2.** 懸賞金 A $10000 reward has been offered for the information of the criminal. 已懸賞 10000 元尋找罪犯的消息。	● 獎勵，獎賞，給以報酬 He rewarded us handsomely for helping him. 對於我們的幫助，他大加酬謝。

同義詞辨析：compensation，payment，consideration

No matter how large the **compensation** is, it won't bring back those lives lost in the accident.　不管**賠償**金額有多高，都帶不回事故中逝去的生命。

What are your **terms of payment**?　你們的**付款條件**是什麼？

Here's a small sum of **consideration** for your services.　這是酬謝你服務的**報酬**。

39. scale [skel] 規模

英解：the size or extent of sth.

類義詞：dimensions, ratio, calibration

名詞的用法

1. 規模，範圍，程度〈不可數名詞〉
Corruption here is on a grand scale.
這裡的腐敗現象很嚴重。

2. 等級，級別，等級體系〈可數名詞〉
The society scale in ancient China was quite severe.
古時候中國的社會等級體系非常嚴格。

3. 秤，天平
There's a scale in her bathroom.
她的浴室裡有個磅秤。

動詞的用法（及物動詞）

1. 攀登，到達頂點
He has scaled to the peak of his career.
他登上了事業的頂峰。

2. 去鱗
I hate to scale the fish.
我討厭給魚去鱗。

3. 改變大小
They are thinking of scaling down their living expenses.
他們正在考慮縮減生活開支。

同義詞辨析：dimensions，ratio

This issue covers many **dimensions**.　這個問題涉及許多**方面**。

Now the sex **ratio** in Taiwan is becoming bigger and bigger.
現在台灣的性別**比例**變得越來越大了。

40. shop [ʃap] 商店，購物

英解：a mercantile establishment for the retail sale of goods or services

類義詞：store, market, purchase, buy

名詞的用法〈可數名詞〉

1. 商店，店鋪
He bought a piece of meat in the butcher shop.
他在肉鋪買了一塊肉。

動詞的用法

1. 去商店賣，到商店購物（不及物動詞）
He likes to shop in big malls.
他喜歡在大商場購物。

2. 工廠，作坊

He used to work in a repair shop.
他曾經在一家修理廠上班。

3. 購物，採買（常用單數）

I do my weekly shop in the supermarket.
我一星期到超市採購一次。

2. 逛商店（不及物動詞）

There's still some time for us to go shopping before we leave.
離開之前 我們還有點時間去逛商店。

3. （向員警等）告發（及物動詞）

The landlady shopped the stranger to the police.
房東太太向警方告發了那個陌生人。

同義詞辨析：purchase，buy

If you're not satisfied with your **purchase**, we can offer you a full refund.
如果你們對**購買**的東西不滿意，我們可以提供全額退款。

He **bought** a lot of things to please his old mother.　為了讓母親高興，他**買了**許多東西。

41. team [tim] 隊，組

英解：a cooperative unit
類義詞：group, crew, suit

名詞的用法〈可數名詞〉

1. （遊戲或運動的）隊

The team plays very well this season.　球隊這個賽季表現極佳。

2. （一起工作的）組，班

A team of police have been sent to the spot.
一隊員警已經派駐現場了。

動詞的用法〈及物動詞〉

結成一隊，協作，合作

He was teamed up with his brother in the doubles.
他被安排和哥哥搭檔打雙打。

同義詞辨析：group，crew

A large group of trees have been cut down in the past three days.
過去三天裡已經有**一大片**樹林被砍倒了。

None of the passengers or **crew** has been injured.　沒有一個乘客和機組**人員**受傷。

42. territory [ˈtɛrəˌtorɪ] 領土

英解：land that is under the control of a particular country or ruler

類義詞：boundary, region, kingdom

名詞的用法〈（不）可數名詞〉

1. 領土，領地；領海；版圖

They thought it was a great shame to let other troops stationed in their territory.
他們覺得讓別國軍隊駐紮在自己的國土上是種恥辱。

2.（個人、群體、動物等佔據的）領域，地盤

Legal problems are Andy's territory. 法律問題由安迪負責。

3.（某人負責的）地區

This company's representatives cover a large territory.
這家公司的代理人負責的地區很廣。

4.（美國）准州，（加拿大）地方，（澳大利亞）區

Guam and American Samoa are US territories.
關島和美屬薩摩亞是美國的准州。

同義詞辨析：boundary，region，kingdom

The **boundary** demarcation works between the two countries finally came to an end after 40 years' negotiation. 經過 40 年的談判，兩國間的邊界劃分問題終於有了結果。

Alsace is a **region** that now belongs to France. 阿爾薩斯現在是法國的一個地區。

They have been struggling for ages to build their own **kingdom**.
為了建立自己的王國，他們已經掙紮了幾個世紀了。

43. thread [θrɛd] 線，穿過

英解：a fine cord of twisted fibers (of cotton or silk or wool or nylon etc.) used in sewing and weaving

類義詞：string, line, route

名詞的用法〈不可數名詞〉	動詞的用法〈及物動詞〉
1. 線，絲線	**1.** 穿（針），穿過
"Bring me some threads next time you come here," she whispered in his ears.	Granny's eyesight was so poor that she had to find someone to thread the needle.
「下次來的時候給我帶點線來。」她在他耳邊低語道。	奶奶的眼神不好，不得不讓別人給她穿針。

> **2.** 線索，脈絡，思路
> The thread of the paper is too complicated to be sorted out.
> 這篇論文的線索太複雜了，沒法理清楚。
>
> **3.** 線狀物
> A thread of light finally emerged at the end of the road.
> 終於，路的盡頭出現了一絲光線。
>
> **2.** 穿過，穿行
> It took me an age to thread my way through the crowd.
> 我花了很長時間才從人群中擠過去。
>
> **3.** 穿成串，穿在一起
> She threaded the beads onto a string and made a beautiful necklace. 她把珠子串成一串做了一條漂亮的項鍊。

同義詞辨析：string，line，route

All her luggage was tied with **strings**. 她的行李都拿繩子**捆**好了。

Please stand in **line**. 請排隊。

The **route** he gave you is totally wrong. 他給你的路線全錯了。

44. toothpaste [ˋtuθˌpest] 牙膏

英解：a dentifrice in the form of a paste

類義詞：dentifrice

名詞的用法〈不可數名詞〉

- 牙膏
  The young mother hurried to the hospital for her baby ate some toothpaste accidently.
  年輕的母親匆匆忙忙趕往醫院，因為她的寶寶吃不小心把牙膏吃下去了。

同義詞辨析：dentifrice

Ma'am, do you have any **dentifrice** in your shop? 女士，您店裡有**牙粉**賣嗎？

45. treatment [ˋtritmənt] 治療，療法；處理；對待

英解：care by procedures or applications that are intended to relieve illness or injury

類義詞：settlement, disposal

名詞的用法〈不可數名詞〉

1. 治療；療法；診治

Treatment depends on her physical condition. 治療方案取決於她的身體狀況。

2. 待遇；對待

Some areas of the city need special treatments.
這個城市的某些地方需要特別治理。

3. 處理；論述；討論

The treatment of madness in this article is quite impressing.
本文中對瘋癲的處理給人印象十分深刻。

同義詞辨析：settlement，disposal

He showed great leadership in the **settlement** of the problem.
他在這件事情的**處理**上表現出了傑出的領導才能。

The **sewage disposal system** in this city is not that efficient.
這個城市的**汙水處理系統**不是很有效。

46. vocation [voˋkeʃən] 職業

英解：a type of work or way of life that one thinks is specially suit for himself
類義詞：profession, employment, career, occupation

名詞的用法〈可數名詞〉

1. 工作，職業，生活方式

He took teacher as his lifelong vocation. 他把教師當做他畢生的職業。

2. 信心，使命感〈（不）可數名詞〉

His father is an engineer with a strong sense of vocation.
他父親是一個具有強烈使命感的工程師。

同義詞辨析：profession，employment，career

After graduation from college, she entered **the caring profession**.
大學畢業後，她進入了**護理行業**。

The employment issue can have great effect on a nation's stability.
就業問題對於一個國家的穩定有重要影響。

Be careful when choose a **career**. 選擇**職業**道路時要認真。

47. water [ˈwɔtɚ] 水，澆水

英解：a liquid without color, smell or taste that falls as rain, is in lakes, rivers and seas, and is used for drinking, washing, etc.

類義詞：seawater, shed tears, pipe one›s eye

名詞的用法	動詞的用法
1. 水〈不可數名詞〉 There's no hot water in the room. 房間裡沒熱水了。	**1.** 澆水，灌溉 Mother loves to water the flowers on the balcony. 媽媽喜歡給陽臺上的花澆水。
2. 大片的水域，（尤指）江河湖海〈不可數名詞〉 She drowned in the deep water. 她在深水區溺水了。	**2.**（眼睛）充滿眼淚 The onion makes my eyes water. 洋蔥讓我眼睛直流淚。
3. 水面〈不可數名詞〉 There floats a huge plastic bag on the water. 水面上漂浮著一隻大塑膠袋。	**3.**（嘴）流口水 The smells from the kitchen made our mouths water. 廚房的香味饞得我們直流口水。
4. 領海，領域（常用複數） The enemy has invaded in our nation's waters. 敵人已經入侵到我們的領海了。	**4.** 給……喝水 You go to water the horses there. 你去那邊給馬飲水。

同義詞辨析：shed tears，pipe one's eye

I want to cry but I just can't **shed** any **tears**.　我想大哭一場，但就是**流**不出**眼淚**。

Her mission in this scene was to **pipe her eye** when the leader died.
在這一場戲裡，她的主要任務是主角死時**流眼淚**。

48. wealth [wɛlθ] 財富, 富有

英解：a large amount of money, property, etc.

類義詞：rich, well off

名詞的用法〈不可數名詞〉

1. 錢財，財產，財物
The imbalance of the distribution of wealth may lead to sever social problems.
財富分配不均會導致嚴重的社會問題。

2. 富有，富裕

Good education often depends on wealth.
良好的教育與良好的經濟條件通常是分不開的。

3. 大量許多

Everyday a wealth of information would come into our mind.
每天都有大量資訊湧入我們腦海。

同義詞辨析：rich，well off

Green vegetables are **rich in vitamins**. 綠色植物**富含維生素**。

She married **a well-off man**. 她嫁給了一個**有錢人**。

49. writer [ˋraɪtɚ] 作家，作者
英解：a person whose job is writing books, stories, articles, etc.
類義詞：author, composer, drafter

名詞的用法〈可數名詞〉

1. 作家，作者，著者

He wants to be a wirter of children's stories. 他想成為兒童故事的作者。

2. 執筆人，撰稿人

He was known as the writer of the computer program.
他在寫電腦程式方面很有名。

3. 寫字……的人（與形容詞連用）

He's a messy writer. 他是個寫字潦草的人。

同義詞辨析：author，composer，drafter

Yu Hua is one of my favorite **authors**. 餘華是我最喜歡的**作家**之一。

Taylor is a famous country singer and **composer**.
泰勒絲是一位著名的鄉村歌手兼**作曲家**。

Apart from the US president, Thomas Jefferson is also known as the chief **drafter** of the Declaration of Independence.
除了美國總統的身份，湯瑪斯·傑弗遜還因是《獨立宣言》的主要**起草者**而著名。

50. year [jɪr] 年，年度
英解：a period of time containing 365 (or 366) days

類義詞：age, old, long time

名詞的用法〈可數名詞〉

1. 年，日曆年

The war finally came to an end in the year 1945.　1945 年，戰爭終於結束了。

2. 一年時間

Our spending is increasing year on year.　我們的開銷在逐年增加。

3. 年度，與某事有關的一年

He failed 4 exams in the second school year.　他第二學年被當了四門課。

4. 年級，某一年級的學生

We are all students of year seven.　我們都是七年級的學生。

5. 年紀，年齡

The witness is a twelve-year-old boy.　目擊證人是一個 12 歲的小男孩。

6. 很久，很長時間（常用複數）

It's been years since we last met.　我們很長時間沒見面了。

同義詞辨析：year，age，old

He's **getting on in years**.　他已經上了年紀了。

At **the age of five**, he knew what love meant for the first time.
五歲那年，他第一次懂得了愛的含義。

She's too **old** to run.　她已經老得跑不動了。

附錄三：形容詞50個

1. afraid [əˋfred] 害怕，恐怕

《 afraid 主要有兩大意思，一是擔心害怕，另一是轉換語氣的恐怕》

英解：worried about what might happen, or that something bad will happen

比較級最高級：more afraid, most afraid

類義詞：scared, worried, frightened

形容詞的用法

1. 害怕的，怕的〔（＋ of-n ／ v-ing）〕〔＋ to-v〕〔＋（that）〕

She was afraid that she might lose her job.　她擔心會丟掉工作。

2. （用於提出異議，告訴不好的消息等場合，使語氣婉轉）恐怕，遺憾〔＋（that）〕

I'm afraid that you can't leave.　對不起，恐怕你不能走。

同義詞辨析：scared，worried，frightened

I'm not **scared** of spiders at all.《主要用於害怕某事物》　我一點都不**怕**蜘蛛。

The mother is **worried** about her son's safety.《主要形容擔心的情緒》
這位母親**擔心**她兒子的安全。

She was **frightened** by a dog.《經常用於被與榻，表示被受到驚嚇》　她被一條狗**嚇壞**了。

2. agreeable [əˋgriəbl̩] 愉快的，欣然同意的，一致的

《由動詞 agree 加形容詞字尾 -able》

英解：quite enjoyable and pleasurable; pleasant

比較級最高級：more agreeable, most agreeable

類義詞：enjoyable, pleasant ,comfortable

形容詞的用法

1. 令人愉快的，宜人的

Here we got an agreeable weather.　那天天氣宜人。

2. 欣然贊同的，準備同意的 [（＋**to**）][＋**to-v**]

I'm not sure whether she is agreeable to my suggestion.
我不確定她是否會接受我的建議。

3. 符合的，一致的 [（＋**to**）]

This decision is agreeable to the interest of our nation.
這項決定是符合我國利益的。

延伸用法

來源名詞 → agreeableness [əˋgrɪrblnəs] 適合；一致
Agreeableness means the tendency to get along well with other people.
親切是指和他人愉快相處的個性傾向。

同義詞辨析：pleasant，lovely，grateful

It had been a **pleasant** evening.《指令人感到愉悅或愉快》 那是一個很**愉快**的夜晚。

She is a **lovely** girl.《同義字 adorable》 她是一個**可愛**的女孩。

3. amused [əˋmjuzd] 被逗樂的，愉快的

《分詞形容詞由動詞 amuse 變化而來》

英解：cause (someone) to find something funny

類義詞：good, bright, cheerful

形容詞的用法

1. 被逗樂的

He's a man hard to be amused. 要取悅他很難。

2. 愉快的，頑皮的

Dr. Li's reply is slightly amused. 李博士的回答略帶詼諧。

延伸用法

1. 延伸副詞 → amusedly [əˋmjuzɪdlɪ] 愉快地；好玩地；表開心地；被逗樂地

"I got the ticket!" he told me amusedly.
「我買到票了！」他樂呵呵的跟我說。

2. 來源動詞 → amuse [əˋmjuz] 逗樂，逗笑；給…提供娛樂

I am glad to amuse you. 很高興逗笑你了。

同義詞辨析：good，bright，cheerful

It's a **good** day.《 good 在此指天氣》 天氣**很好**。

He is a **bright** man.《bright 形容人意思為機靈或聰明》 他是一個**機靈**的人。

Whether sick or fine, she is always **cheerful**.《cheerful 一般指心情的愉悅》
不管她生不生病，她總是**開開心心**的。

4. brave [brev] 勇敢的

《分詞形容詞由動詞 amuse 變化而來》

英解：ready to face and endure danger or pain; showing courage

比較級最高級：braver, bravest

類義詞：magnificent

形容詞的用法

1. 勇敢的，英勇的

Dear, You must be brave. 你一定要勇敢。

2. 勇猛的，壯觀的

He was as brave as a lion. 他勇猛如雄獅。

名詞的用法

勇士，（北美印第安人的）武士

Let us remember the brave who died in the last war.
讓我們記住在上次戰爭中犧牲的勇士們。

動詞的用法

1. 勇敢地面對

They braved the rain of bullets to get the wounded back.
他們冒著槍林彈雨把傷員帶了回來。

2. 不把…放在眼裡，敢於冒犯

Rose braved her parents' wrath by running away with her beloved man.
Rose 不顧父母的憤怒與心愛的人私奔了。

延伸用法

1. 延伸副詞 ➡ **bravely** [ˈbrevlɪ] 勇敢地

He bravely held back his tears. 他強忍著不讓眼淚流出來。

2. 源於名詞 ➡ **bravery** [brevrɪ] 勇敢，大膽，剛毅

He gave an example of bravery and wisdom. 他是個智勇雙全的典型。

343

同義詞辨析：magnificent，warrior
The scenery there is really **magnificent**.《大部分指景觀的壯麗》
那裡的景色實在是太**壯麗**了。

5. broken [ˋbrokən] 弄壞的，破碎的

《分詞形容詞由動詞 break 變化而來》

英解：having been broken

類義詞：damaged, fragmentized

形容詞的用法

1. 破碎的，損壞的

My watch is broken.　我的手錶壞了。

2. 被破壞的，遭違背的

She was deeply hurt by the broken engagement.　解除婚約對她的打擊很大。

3. 不連續的，中斷的

After a night of broken sleep, I felt more tired.
睡得極不踏實的一夜過後，我感覺更累了。

4. 衰弱的，沮喪的，低沉的

The failure of the game made him a broken man.　比賽失敗後他變得心灰意懶。

5.（語言）拙劣的，不流利的

I really hate to speak in broken English.　我不喜歡自己結結巴巴的英語。

延伸用法

1. 延伸副詞　→ **brokenly** [ˋbrokənlɪ] 斷斷續續地；不規則地

I used to learn drawing brokenly.　我斷斷續續地學過一點素描。

2. 延伸動詞　→ **break** [brek] 打破，弄壞，破碎，破曉

The car broke down on half way.　汽車半路拋錨了。

同義詞辨析：damaged，fragmentized

Nobody wants to pay for the damaged goods.《主要是指被損毀》
沒人願意買被損壞的貨物。

Watch out for the fragmentized scraps, or you may be hurt.《主要是指被壞成碎片》
小心金屬碎片，否則可能會被劃傷。

6. charming [ˈtʃɑrmɪŋ] 迷人的，可愛的

《分詞形容詞由動詞 charm 變化而來》

英解：very pleasant or attractive
比較級最高級：more charming, most charming
類義詞：lovely, pretty, engaging

形容詞的用法

令人高興的，迷人的，有魅力的
Here comes a charming young lady.　一位迷人的年輕女士走過來了。

延伸用法

- 延伸副詞 → **charmingly** [ˈtʃɑrmɪŋlɪ] 迷人地，愉悅地
  The little girl's dream is that oneday she could talk charmingly with her beloved prince.
  這個小女孩的夢想是有一天能和自己心愛的王子娓娓而談。

同義詞辨析：lovely，pretty，engaging

She is a **lovely** girl.《注意 -ly 並非一定是副詞結尾》　她是一個**可愛的**女孩。

The **pretty** boy is my brother.《pretty 也可作程度副詞使用》　這個**漂亮**男孩是我弟弟。

He **waved** his hand at the girls with an engaging smile on his face.《engage 有吸引人的意思》　他朝女孩們揮了**揮手**，臉上帶著迷人的微笑。

7. comfortable [ˈkʌmfɚtəbl̩] 舒適的，充裕的

《可形容任何讓人感到舒服的人事物》

英解：providing physical ease and relaxation
比較級最高級：more comfortable, most comfortable
類義詞：pleasant, easy, cozy

形容詞的用法

1. 使人舒服的，舒適的
You gonna love the comfortable climate here.　你會愛上這兒宜人的氣候的。

2. 寬裕的，豐富的
They are not millionare, but they are quite comfortable.
他們雖然不是百萬富翁，但還是相當富有的。

3.（人）舒服的，自在的，安逸的
The aim of our hotel is to make the guests feel as comfortable as at home.
我們酒店的宗旨是讓客人感到像在家一樣舒服。

延伸用法

1. 源於名詞 ➞ **comfort** [ˈkʌmfət] 舒適；安慰

Acording to the latest survey, it seems that Canada is the best comfort country.

最新調查顯示，加拿大似乎是最宜居的國家。

2. 延伸副詞 ➞ **comfortably** [ˈkʌmfətəblɪ] 舒適地

With the money, you can live comfortably in your rest life.

有了這些錢，你下半輩子就可以舒舒服服地生活了。

同義詞辨析：pleasant，easy，cozy

The climate in Australia is generally **pleasant**. 《令人感到愉悅的》

一般來説，澳大利亞氣候宜人。

Easy life will sap one's will to fight. 《easy 除了簡單的，還有安逸的解釋》

安逸的生活會消磨人的鬥志。

They asked me to find them a **cozy** hotel. 《指環境的舒適》

他們讓我給他們找一家**舒適溫馨的**酒店。

8. confused [kənˈfjuzd] 困惑的，混亂的

《分詞形容詞由動詞 confuse 變化而來》

英解：(of a person) unable to think clearly

比較級最高級：more confused, most confused

類義詞：troubled, chaotic, puzzled

形容詞的用法

1. 混亂的，亂七八糟的，雜亂的

A jumble of confused ideas has piled his mind.　他腦子裡一團亂麻。

2. 困惑的，惶惑的

I am a confused and stressed-out pregnant woman.

我是一個困惑的並且壓力重重的孕婦。

延伸用法

1. 延伸動詞 ➞ **confuse** [kənˈfjuz] 使困惑，把⋯弄糊塗；混淆；混亂，搞亂

These two words are easy to be confused.　這兩個詞很容易弄混。

2. 延伸副詞 ➞ **confusedly** [kənˈfjuzɪdlɪ] 受困惑地，慌亂地，混亂地

"Where's my purse?" she asked confusedly.　"我的錢包呢？"她慌亂的問道。

3. 源於名詞 → **confusion** [kənˈfjuʒən] 困惑，糊塗；混淆；混亂，騷亂

The city fell into confusion after the war began.

戰爭開始後，這個城市陷入了混亂。

同義詞辨析：troubled，chaotic，puzzled

The UN says that more people are now being killed in the south than in Darfur, Sudan's **troubled** western region.《指混亂的環境或心理狀態》

聯合國宣稱，南蘇丹所喪生的人口數目，比蘇丹西部<u>混亂的</u>達爾富爾地區還要多。

The **chaotic** situation in London has lasted for a long time.《由名詞 chaos 變化來》

倫敦的<u>騷亂</u>態勢已經持續了很長時間了。

His action made me **puzzled**.《主要是指無法想透或想通答案》

他的行為令我<u>百思不得其解</u>。

9. courageous [kəˈredʒəs] 勇敢的；無畏的

《注意名詞 courage 與形容詞 courageous 重音在不同音節》

英解：not deterred by danger or pain

比較級最高級：more courageous, most courageous

類義詞：brave, manful, fearless

形容詞的用法

英勇的，勇敢的

You were courageous to tell the truth.　你說了實話，真勇敢。

延伸用法

1. 延伸副詞 → **courageously** [kəˈredʒəslɪ] 勇敢地

Courageously he opened the door but only to find nothing.

他鼓起勇氣打開了門，卻發現裡面什麼都沒有。

2. 源於名詞 → **courage** [ˈkɝɪdʒ] 勇氣，膽量

What he lacks now is courage.　他現在缺乏的就是膽量。

同義詞辨析：brave，fearless

Jane is a **brave** girl.《形容無所懼怕的》　簡是個<u>勇敢的</u>女孩。

Only those who are **fearless** can succeed.《由名詞 fear 變化而來》

只有那些<u>勇敢無畏的</u>人才會成功。

10. crazy [ˋkrezɪ] 瘋狂的，狂熱的，著迷的

《主要除了瘋狂的解釋之外，經常用在形容對事物的熱衷》

英解：mad, especially as manifested in wild or aggressive behaviour

比較級最高級：crazier, craziest

類義詞：wild, insane

形容詞的用法

1. 瘋狂的，蠢的，古怪的 [+to-v]

Are you crazy? It's too dangerous.　你瘋了嗎？這樣做太危險了。

2. 【口】著迷的，熱衷的，狂熱的 [（+about/for/on）]

He's crazy about collecting stamps.　他非常熱衷集郵。

延伸用法

1. 源於名詞 ⇒ **craziness** [ˋkrezɪnɪs] 瘋狂

At first we are very much interested in him, but now we are afraid of his craziness.　最初我們對他很感興趣，可現在我們對他的瘋狂感到恐懼。

2. 延伸副詞 ⇒ **crazily** [ˋkrezɪlɪ] 瘋狂地，狂熱地

To get that job, he's practising English crazily.
為了得到那份工作，他正在瘋狂的練英語。

同義詞辨析：wild，mad，insane

He has the talent to make his fans go **wild**.《形容陷入瘋狂狂野狀態》
他有讓歌迷為他瘋狂的天分。

Are you **insane**? Why did you do that?《比較是指精神狀態的失常》
你瘋了？為什麼要那麼做？

11. creepy [ˋkripɪ]（使人）毛骨悚然的，怪異的

《口語中常用來形容令人不舒服的人事物》

英解：causing an unpleasant feeling of fear or unease

比較級最高級：creepier, creepiest

類義詞：weird, horrified, horrid

形容詞的用法

1. 令人毛骨悚然的，不寒而慄的

I get a creepy feeling when he stares at me.　當他盯著我的時候, 我覺得不寒而慄。

2. 蠕動的，緩行的

It's really scary when you saw a man crawl on the ground like a creepy crawlies. 當你看到一個人像緩緩蠕動的爬蟲一樣在地上爬時，真的是太嚇人了。

同義詞辨析：weird，horrified

It's so weird. Why is he here?《口語中經常使用》 **太奇怪了**，為什麼他會在這兒？

Horrified by the mess in her house, she decided to call the police.《形容被受到驚嚇》
她被房間裡的混亂**嚇了一大跳**，她決定報警。

12. dangerous [ˋdɛndʒərəs] 危險的

《經常誤用的狀況是直接拿 dangerous 形容人事物陷入危險的情境，此時應用 in danger》

英解：able or likely to cause harm or injury
比較級最高級：more dangerous, most dangerous
類義詞：unsafe, risky, threatening

形容詞的用法

- 危險的
  I think it is dangerous to play the knife. 我認為玩小刀很危險。

延伸用法

1. 延伸副詞 ⇒ **dangerously** [ˋdɛndʒərəslɪ] 危險地；不安全
The drunk man is driving dangerously. 醉漢正在危險地駕車。

2. 源於名詞 ⇒ **danger** [ˋdɛndʒɚ] 危險；危險事物，威脅
The police find this boy, so he is out of danger now.
員警找到了這個孩子，現在他脫離了危險。

同義詞辨析：unsafe，risky，threatening

Don't let the children play in the **unsafe area**.《safe 的反義詞》
不要讓孩子們在**非安全區內**玩耍。

The doctor rejected her operation request since it was too risky for her.《指有風險的》
醫生拒絕了她的手術請求，因為這樣她的身體冒的**風險**太大了。

Now any mistake will be **life-threatening** for him.《形容危及某事物》
現在任何錯誤都會**危及**他的**生命**。

349

13. delightful [dɪˋlaɪtfəl] 令人愉快的，有意思的，討人喜歡的

《由名詞 delight 變化而來》

英解：causing delight; charming

比較級最高級：more delightful, most delightful

類義詞：lovely, pleasant, grateful

形容詞的用法

● 令人愉快的，令人高興的，可愛的

Why are you so delightful? 什麼事這麼高興啊？

延伸用法

1. 延伸副詞 → **delightfully** [dɪˋlaɪtfəlɪ] 欣然地，大喜

 He could still talk delightfully about movies. 他還是很能談笑風生地談論電影的。

2. 源於名詞 → **delight** [dɪˋlaɪt] 高興；使人高興的東西（或人）

 "She says she is sorry, but her eyes betray her secret delight."

 她說她很難過，但從她的眼神裡卻流露出她內心的高興。

3. 延伸形容詞 → **delighted** [dɪˋlaɪtɪd] 高興的，快樂的

 We are delighted to confirm your reservation. 很高興跟您確認您的訂單。

同義詞辨析：lovely，pleasant，grateful

She is so **lovely** that everyone loves her.《同義字 adorable》

她如此**可愛的**，大家都愛她。

It's so pleasant today. We really should have gone climbing.《指令人感到愉悅或愉快》

今天**天氣真好**，我們真應該去爬山。

14. depressed [dɪˋprɛst] 沮喪的，消沉的

《分詞形容詞由動詞 depress 變化而來》

英解：(of a person) in a state of unhappiness or despondency

比較級最高級：more depressed, most depressed

類義詞：blue, gloomy

形容詞的用法

1. 沮喪的，消沉的，憂鬱的

 The cruel reality made him depressed. 殘酷的現實讓他意志消沉。

2. 蕭條的，不景氣的，貧困的

They used to visit a depressed area.　他們曾到過一個貧困地區。

延伸用法

1. 延伸動詞 ➡ **depress** [dɪˋprɛs] 使沮喪，壓下，使蕭條，降低，壓抑

The bad news depressed us for a long time.
這個壞消息讓我們情緒低落了很長時間。

2. 源於名詞 ➡ **depression** [dɪˋprɛʃən] 抑鬱，沮喪；不景氣，蕭條期

Lots of enterprises went bankrupt during the Depression.
大蕭條時期有無數家企業倒閉。

同義詞辨析：blue，gloomy

I'm feeling **blue** today.《形容心情的憂鬱》　我今天的**心情不好**。

Don't be so **gloomy** about your future. It's not that bad.《像天氣的一般陰暗》
不要對你的未來這麼**悲觀**。事情沒那麼糟。

15. empty [ˋɛmptɪ] 空的，空虛的，空閒的

《除了形容空無一物的狀態，也常用來形容缺乏的》

英解：containing nothing; not filled or occupied

比較級最高級：emptier, emptiest

類義詞：hollow, bare, vacant

形容詞的用法

1. 空的，未佔用的，無人居住的

He got there rushly but only to find an empty house.
他匆匆忙忙趕到那兒，結果卻發現那兒早已人去樓空。

2. 無，沒有，缺少 [（+of）]

His mind is empty of knowledge.　他腦袋空空，沒什麼學識。

3. 空洞的，無意義的，徒勞的

We will get nothing if we continue this empty talk.
繼續空談的話，我們什麼都不會得到。

同義詞辨析：hollow，bare，vacant

People used to cook meal in the **hollow** of the bamboo.《形容中空的物體》
過去人們用**中空的**竹子來煮飯。

The top of the montain is **bare** now since all the trees has been cut down.《形容光禿的
表面》　現在山頂**光禿禿的**，因為人們把所有的樹都砍倒了。

I have a **vacant** room left. You can live in it if you like.《形容空間無人占用使用 》
我還有間房**空著**，你願的話可以住那兒。

16. encouraging [ɪnˋkɝɪdʒɪŋ] 令人鼓舞的
《分詞形容詞由動詞encourage變化而來》

英解：giving someone support or confidence; supportive

類義詞：promotional, stimulant

形容詞的用法

鼓勵的，贊助的，促進的
A encouraging news has come from the frontline.
前線傳來了一條鼓舞人心的消息。

延伸用法

1. 源於名詞 → **encouragement** [ɪnˋkɝɪdʒmənt] 鼓勵；贊助；引誘
Parents' encouragement is quite important to the kid's success.
父母的鼓勵對於孩子的成功非常重要。

2. 延伸動詞 → **encourage** [ɪnˋkɝɪdʒ] 鼓勵，促進，支持
Wars often encourage poverty.　戰爭經常助長貧窮。

同義詞辨析：promotional，stimulant

These old **promotional** materials are really very precious.《由名詞promotion變化而來》　這些古老的**廣告宣傳**材料非常珍貴。

Taking **stimulants** is against the rule of the game.《指有刺激作用的物質》
使用**興奮劑**是違反比賽規則的。

17. energetic [ˌɛnɚˋdʒɛtɪk] 精力充沛的，充滿活力的
《注意名詞energy與形容詞energetic重音位置不同》

英解：showing or involving great activity or vitality

比較級最高級：more energetic, most energetic

類義詞：active, positive

形容詞的用法

1. 精力旺盛的，精神飽滿的
He felt very energetic after a good sleep.
飽飽地睡了一覺後，他感覺精神非常飽滿。

2. 有力的，積極的

He's an energetic supporter of our policy. 　他是我們政策的大力支持者。

延伸用法

- 源於名詞 → **energy** [ˈɛnədʒɪ] 精力，活力，能源
  Don't waste your energy. It's not worthy. 　別再浪費精力了，不值得。

同義詞辨析：active，positive

He's still quite **active** in the stage of politics, though he's 60.《指很有活動力的》
儘管他已經有 60 歲了，但他在政壇上依然很**活躍**。

We must take **positive** steps to protect the endangered species.《時常也使用在形容人或
個性的正向》 我們必須採取**積極**措施保護瀕危物種。

18. few [fju] 很少的，少數的，不多的

　　　《用在可數名詞》

英解：used to emphasize how small a number of people or things is

比較級最高級：fewer, fewest

類義詞：little

形容詞的用法

1. 很少數的，幾乎沒有的
  There are fewer girls than boys in my class. 　我班上女生比男生少。

2.（與 **a** 連用）有些，幾個
  He has a few friends in this city. 　他在這個城市裡有幾個朋友。

同義詞辨析：little

There is **little** water in the cup.《用在不可數名詞》 杯子裡有**很少**的水。

19. gentle [ˈdʒɛntl̩] 和善的，仁慈的

　　　《除了形容和善的特質外，有經常形容動作的溫和》

英解：having or showing a mild, kind, or tender temperament or character

比較級最高級：gentler, gentlest

類義詞：cultured, friendly, soft

形容詞的用法

1. 溫和的，和善的，仁慈的

No matter how gentle a man is, he would has his own temper.
一個人，無論多麼溫和，也總有發脾氣的時候。

2. 輕柔的，和緩的

Cook the food with a gentle heat and then we can get some super soup to drink.　用文火煮這些食物，這樣就可以有上好的湯喝了。

3. 馴服的，溫順的

Our pet is a gentle dog.　我們的寵物是條溫順的狗。

4. 有教養的，文靜的

I can't believe a man gentle in manner would say things like this.
我真不敢相信一個舉止文雅的人居然會這樣說。

延伸用法

1. 延伸副詞　→ gently [ˋdʒɛntlɪ] 溫柔地，輕輕地，溫和地，和緩地

"Don't cry", he said gently.　"別哭了"，他溫柔地說道。

2. 源於名詞　→ gentility [dʒɛnˋtɪlətɪ] 高貴的出身，高雅的風度

They were talking with discreet gentility.　他們在溫文儒雅地交談。

同義詞辨析：cultured，friendly，soft

A friend of mine is a **cultured** lady.《有文化修養的》
我有一個朋友，是一位**有修養的**女士。

Most of Chinese people are all **friendly**.《由名詞 friend 變化而來》
大多數的中國人很**友善**。

He has the **soft** voice.《指柔和的特質》　他有著**柔和的**嗓音。

20. giant [ˋdʒaɪənt] 龐大的，巨大的

《也可當名詞使用》

英解：of very great size or force; gigantic
比較級最高級：more giant, most giant
類義詞：enormous, gigantic

形容詞的用法	名詞的用法
巨人般的，巨大的 This is a giant step to success. 這是邁向成功的一大步。	（力量、智力超群的）偉人 He thinks nobody in China can be called a literary giant. 他覺得在中國沒人稱得上文豪。

同義詞辨析：enormous ,huge

Their house is so **enormous**.《指物體的龐大》 他們的房子這麼<u>大</u>。

There is a **huge** hole in the tree.《另一常見的同義字為 big》 樹上有個<u>巨大的</u>洞。

21. handsome [ˈhænsəm] 英俊的，慷慨的，大方的

《主要形容男性》

英解：(of a man) good-looking

比較級最高級：more handsome, most handsome

類義詞：attractive, good-looking

形容詞的用法

1.（男子）英俊的；（女子）端莊健美的

He looks so handsome. 他看上去那麼英俊。

2. 相當大的，可觀的

As long as you finish the job, this handsome tip will be yours.
只要你把活干完，這筆可觀的小費就是你的了。

3. 漂亮的，美觀的

What a handsome room! 多漂亮的房間啊！

延伸用法

1. 延伸副詞 → **handsomely** [ˈhænsəmlɪ] 漂亮地，可觀地

They has a handsomely sized room. 他們房間大得有氣派。

2. 源於名詞 → **handsomeness** [ˈhænsəmnɪs] 英俊，慷慨，大方，數目可觀

His handsomeness attracts a lot of ladies. 他的英俊吸引了很多女性。

同義詞辨析：attractive，good-looking

The price of this car is very **attractive** to us.《由動詞 attract 變化而來》
這輛車的價格對我們具有很大<u>吸引力</u>。

Amy is a **good-looking** girl.《複合形容詞指 Amy is a girl who looks good》
Amy 是一個<u>漂亮的</u>女孩。

22. hard [hɑrd] 硬的；困難的

《除了形容物體的堅硬外，也可指事物的困難》

英解：solid, firm, and rigid; not easily broken, bent, or pierced:

比較級最高級：harder, hardest

類義詞：difficult,tough,heavily, strong

形容詞的用法

1. 硬的，堅固的

The wood is so hard.　這塊木頭真硬。

2. 困難的，費力的[＋ **to-v**]

Tom is hard to get along with.　湯姆很難相處。

3. 刻苦的，努力的

She is a hard worker.　她是一個工作十分勤奮的人。

4. 艱難的，難受的

I know that he has a very hard life.　我知道他日子過得很艱難。

5. 冷酷無情的，嚴厲的，嚴格的[（**+on**）]

She is too hard on her students.　她對學生太嚴格了。

6. (氣候) 嚴寒的，難捱的

It was a hard winter.　那是一個嚴寒的冬天。

副詞的用法

1. 努力地，艱苦地

She works very hard.　她工作很努力。

2. 猛烈地，重重地

It's raining hard.　雨下得很大。

3. 困難地，困苦地

The old man is breathing hard.　這位老人呼吸困難。

4. 牢固地，緊緊地

She held her purse so hard.　她緊緊地抓著她的錢包。

延伸用法

● 延伸動詞　➡ **harden** [ˋhardn] 使變硬，使變堅強

Life in the army hardened me.　部隊裡的的生活使我堅強起來。

同義詞辨析：difficult，tough，strong

It's so **difficult to** learn Chinese.《形容難達成的目標》　中文太難學了。

She is a **tough** mother.《形容人的嚴苛》　她是一個**嚴苛的**母親。

In Beijing, the winds so **strong** in the winter.《形容程度的劇烈》
在北京，冬天的風**太猛烈**了。

23. lazy [ˈlezɪ] 懶散的，怠惰的

英解：moving slowly; disinclined to work or exertion
比較級最高級：lazier, laziest
類義詞：idle, sluggardly

形容詞的用法

1. 懶散的，怠惰的

I hate lazy people.　我不喜歡懶散的人。

2. 使人倦怠的，懶洋洋的

Don't be so lazy. Let's go shopping!　別無精打采了。我們去買東西吧！

3. 緩慢的，慢吞吞的

A lazy old man is walking on the street.　一位老人在大街上慢吞吞地走著。

同義詞辨析：idle

The cowboy lives an **idle** life.《形容閒置的狀態》　牛仔過著**悠閒的**生活。

24. light [laɪt] 明亮的，輕便的

英解：of comparatively little physical weight or density
比較級最高級：lighter, lightest
類義詞：shining, brighten

形容詞的用法

1. 明亮的

It's getting light at about 5 o'clock.　差不多 5 點鐘的時候天就亮了。

2. 淺色的

There once was a period time when I just liked light clothes.
有一段時間我只喜歡淺色衣服。

3. 輕便的

This suitcase is not as light as it looks.　這個箱子可不像它看起來那麼輕巧。

4. 輕柔的，柔和的

I really enjoy the light music in this shop.　我真的很喜歡這家店播放的輕音樂。

5. 輕鬆的，容易做的

Proper light exercise can help you to relax.　適量的簡單運動可以幫助你放鬆。

6. 清淡的

The food is pretty light for him.　這些食物對他來說太過清淡了。

7. 酒精濃度低的

Even a light beer can put him down.
即使是一杯酒精濃度很低的啤酒也可以把他灌醉。

8. 睡眠淺的

I am a light sleeper.　我睡眠很淺。

動詞的用法

〈及物動詞 lighted-lighted ／ lit-lit〉

1. 點燃，點火

He lighted a candle.
他點亮了一根蠟燭。

2. 照亮，使明亮

He lighted my life again with love.　他用愛重新點亮了我的生活。

3. 用光指引

He lighted my way to the future by love.　他用愛照亮了我前行的道路。

名詞的用法

1. 光線，光亮

Bring it into the light so that I can see it.　把它拿到亮一點的地方，這樣我才看得見。

2. 發光體，光源（尤指）電燈

Would you please turn on the light? It's too dark here.
你能把燈開一下嗎？這兒太暗了。

3. 火柴，打火機，點火器

Do you have a light?
你有打火機嗎？

4. 眼神

There was a soft light in her eyes when she looked at him.
她看他時，眼神非常溫柔。

5. 淺色，亮色

The use of light and shade can create beauty.
色彩的明暗對比運用可以創造美。

6. 窗戶

Eyes are the lights of minds.　眼睛是心靈的窗戶。

延伸用法

1. 延伸動詞　→ **lighten** [ˈlaɪtn̩] 減輕，減少，緩和

Her smile lightened my nervousness.
她的微笑使我不那麼緊張了。

2. 延伸副詞　→ **lightly** [ˈlaɪtlɪ] 輕柔地，漫不經心地，草率地

He kissed the baby lightly on the face.
他在寶寶的臉上輕輕吻了一下。

同義詞辨析：shining，brighten

They got married on a **shining** day.　他們在一個陽光**燦爛**的日子裡結婚了。

The dark sky was **brightened** by the lightening.　閃電**照亮**了夜空。

25. lively [ˈlaɪvlɪ] 活潑的，精力充沛的

英解：full of life and energy
比較級最高級：livelier, liveliest
類義詞：alive, vivid

形容詞的用法

1. 精力充沛的，活潑的，生機勃勃的

He married a lively young girl.　他娶了一個充滿活力的年輕女孩。

2. 充滿趣味的，令人興奮的

There's a lively bar around my house.　我家附近有一家充滿樂趣的酒吧。

3. 濃的，鮮豔的

He likes to wear in lively color.　他喜歡穿顏色鮮豔的衣服。

延伸用法

1. 來源動詞　→ **live** [lɪv] 生活，享受生活

"Do you want to live with me and be my child?"asked the man.
男人問道："你想和我一起生活，做我的孩子嗎？"

2. 延伸名詞　→ **liveliness** [ˈlaɪvlɪnɪs] 活潑，熱烈，鮮明

His liveliness and humor impressed me.　他的活潑幽默給我留下了深刻印象。

同義詞辨析：alive，vivid

I'm **still alive**, so stop yelling!　我還沒死呢，別叫了！

This is a **vivid** description of our present life.　這是對我們當前生活的生動描述。

26. lonely [ˋlonlɪ] 寂寞的；偏僻的

英解：lacking companions or companionship

比較級最高級：lonelier, loneliest

類義詞：alone

形容詞的用法

1. 孤獨的，寂寞的

He feels lonely.　他感到非常孤獨。

2. 在孤單中度過的

I spent 5 lonely nights at home.　我在家度過了 5 個孤寂的夜晚。

3. 偏僻的，人跡罕至的

The car broke down on a lonely road.　汽車在一條人跡罕至的小道上拋錨了。

延伸用法

- 延伸名詞 ➡ **loneliness** [ˋlonlɪnɪs] 寂寞，孤獨

My life has been marked by loneliness.　我的生活充滿了孤獨寂寞。

同義詞辨析：alone

Did you come here **alone**?　你是一個人過來的嗎？

27. lovely [ˋlʌvlɪ] 可愛的，令人愉快的

英解：appealing to the emotions as well as the eye

比較級最高級：lovelier, loveliest

類義詞：pleasant, cute

形容詞的用法

1. 美麗的，迷人的

She has a lovely voice.　她的嗓音非常迷人。

2. 令人愉快的，極好的

What a lovely surprise!　真讓人感到驚喜！

3. 親切友好的，慷慨大方的

My mother is a lovely woman.　我母親是個心地善良的人。

延伸用法

- 來源動詞 ➡ **love** [lʌv] 喜愛，熱愛

I love my life here.　我很喜歡這裡的生活。

同義詞辨析：pleasant，cute

It's a **pleasant** day today.　今天的天氣非常<u>宜人</u>。

What a **cute** baby!　好<u>可愛的</u>寶寶啊！

28. low [lo] 低的，矮的

英解：less than normal in degree or intensity or amount

比較級最高級：lower, lowest

類義詞：short, shallow

形容詞的用法

1. 低的，矮的，離地面近的

They are eating on a low table.　他們正在一張矮桌上吃飯。

2. 在底部的，近底部的

There is a big forest at the lower slopes of the mountain.
在山麓斜坡上有一大片樹林。

3. 低於正常或平均水準的

To lose weight, she only drinks lower-fat yogurt.　為了減肥，她只喝低脂優酪乳。

4. 低下的，次要的，低等的

We should pay more attention to the lower classes of society.
我們應該更加關注下層社會。

5. 虛弱的，消沉的，沮喪的

I feel really low now because of the endless overtime working.
由於無休止的加班，我現在很消沉。

副詞的用法

1. 在靠近底部的位置

The candle is burning low.　蠟燭快燒完了。

2. 低於常值地

The low-priced goods are not always of good quality.
低價商品通常品質不是很好。

名詞的用法

1. 低點，低數目

The government's popularity has hit a new low.
政府的聲望降到了一個新的低點。

2. 低谷

She was in all-time low because she was fired.
她正處於人生的低谷，因為她被炒魷魚了。

同義詞辨析：short，shallow

The sleeves of this shirt were too **short**.
這件襯衫的袖子**太短**了。

The kids are playing water in a **shallow** river.
孩子們在一條**淺淺的**小河裡玩水。

29. magnificent [mæg`nɪfəsnt] 壯麗的，宏偉的

英解：characterized by grandeur
比較級最高級：more magnificent, most magnificent
類義詞：grand, massive

形容詞的用法

- 壯麗的，宏偉的，值得讚揚的

  I'm sure you will enjoy the magnificent scenery there.
  你們肯定會喜歡那兒的壯麗美景的。

延伸用法

1. 延伸名詞 → **magnificence** [mæg`nɪfəsns] 壯麗，宏偉，富麗堂皇

I'm deeply impressed by the magnificence of Versailles.
凡爾賽宮的宏偉壯麗給我留下了深刻印象。

2. 延伸副詞 → **magnificently** [mæg`nɪfɪsəntlɪ] 壯麗地，宏偉地，壯觀地

We stayed in a hotel which was magnificently decorated.
當時我們住在一家裝潢華麗的酒店裡。

同義詞辨析：grand，massive

Their wedding ceremony was **grand**. 他們舉辦了<u>盛大的</u>婚禮。

He's still awake after drinking a **massive** amount of alcohol.
他喝了<u>大量的</u>烈酒但依然很清醒。

30. many [ˋmɛnɪ] 許多，大量

英解：amounting to a large but indefinite number

比較級最高級：more, most

類義詞：much, a lot of

形容詞的用法

1. 許多的，大量的

How many books have you read? 你讀了多少本書了？

2. 大多數人

The government must improve conditions for the many.
政府必須為大多數人改善生活。

3. 許多，大量

Many a singers has been invited to the concert. 演唱會邀請了許多歌手。

同義詞辨析：much，a lot of

I ate **too much** at supper. 我晚飯吃<u>太多了</u>。

A lot of children who are in school age have dropped out in the country.
在農村，<u>許多</u>適齡兒童都輟學了。

31. modern [ˋmadən] 現代的

英解：relating to a recently developed fashion or style

比較級最高級：more modern, most modern

類義詞：recent, fashionable

形容詞的用法

1. 現代的，當代的，近代的

In modern society, communication is very important.
現代社會中通信是非常重要的。

2. 新式的，有別於傳統的

Do you like modern arts? 你喜歡現代藝術嗎？

363

3. 時新的，現代化的

The modern methods of farming can help to increase products.
現代化耕作方式有助於提高產量。

延伸用法

1. 延伸名詞 → **modernism** [ˋmɑdɚˏɪzəm] 現代主義

Modernism has affected a generation.　現代主義已經影響了一代人。

2. 延伸動詞 → **modernize** [ˋmɑdɚˏɑɪz] 現代化

We need 9 million dollars to modernize the facilities.
我們需要 9 百萬美元來將設備現代化。

同義詞辨析：recent，fashionable

His **recent** trip to America was last month.　他**最近**一次去美國是在上個月。

She likes all kinds of **fashionable** clothes.　她喜歡各式各樣**時髦的**衣服。

32. nervous [ˋnɝvəs] 焦慮的

英解：causing or fraught with or showing anxiety
比較級最高級：more nervous, most nervous
類義詞：anxious, worried

形容詞的用法

1. 焦慮的，擔心的，惶恐的

People are now nervous about the safety of food.　現在人們非常擔心食品安全。

2. 神經質的，易緊張的

She is a nervous girl.　她是個膽怯的女孩。

3. 神經系統的

There's something wrong with her nervous system.　她的神經系統出了點問題。

延伸用法

1. 來源動詞 → **nerve** [nɝv] 鼓起勇氣，振作精神

He nerved himself to propose to her.　他鼓起勇氣向她求婚了。

2. 延伸名詞 → **nervousness** [ˋnɝvəsnɪs] 神經質，神經過敏，緊張不安

He tried to hide his nervousness, but he failed.　他試圖掩飾他的不安，但沒有成功。

3. 延伸副詞 → **nervously** [ˋnɝvəslɪ] 不安地，緊張地

He nodded his head nervously.　他緊張地點了點頭。

同義詞辨析：anxious，worried

She is **anxious** for their safety.　她**很擔心**他們的安全。

What I'm really **worried** about is when you can get married.
我真正**擔心**的是你到底什麼時候結婚。

33. odd [ɑd] 古怪的

英解：beyond or deviating from the usual or expected
比較級最高級：odder, oddest
類義詞：extraordinary, strange

形容詞的用法

1. 奇異的，古怪地

　There are some odd people in this community.　這個社區住著幾個古怪的人。

2. 偶然出現的（無比較級、最高級）

　I make odd mistakes, but not serious.　我偶爾會犯錯誤，但不嚴重。

3. 奇形怪狀的，各種各樣的（無比較級、最高級）

　The room was decorated with odd flowers.　房間用各種各樣的鮮花裝飾過了。

4. 奇數的（無比較級、最高級）

　1, 3, 5 and 7 are odd numbers.　1,3,5,7 是奇數。

延伸用法

1. 延伸名詞　→ **oddness** [ˋɑdnɪs] 奇怪，反常

　Look at the oddness her appearance！　瞧她那怪樣子！

2. 延伸副詞　→ **oddly** [ˋɑdlɪ] 古怪地，反常地，令人驚奇地

　Oddly enough, she thought she met him before at the first sight.
　奇怪的是，她第一眼看到他就覺得他們之前見過面。

同義詞辨析：extraordinary，strange

This book is about an **extraordinary** story.　這本書講述了一個**離奇的**故事。

His behavior is quiet **strange**.　他的行為**很反常**。

34. old [old] 老的，年紀大的

英解：(used especially of persons) having lived for a relatively long time or attained a specific age

比較級最高級：older ／ elder, oldest ／ eldest
類義詞：ancient, aged

形容詞的用法

1. 具體年齡，……歲

She went to school at 7 years old.　她七歲上的學。

2. 老的，年紀大的

We should care more about the old.　我們應該多關心一下老人。

3. 過去的，從前的

For old time's sake, please forgive me.　看在往日的情分上，你原諒我吧。

4. 原來的，原先的

I think the old house has more room.　我覺得原來的房子更寬敞。

5. 表示親昵或不拘禮節

God bless you, old fellow!　上帝保佑你，老夥計！

同義詞辨析：ancient，aged

China has many **ancient** cultures.　中國有許多**古老的**文化。

Many western countries have stepped into **aged society**.
許多西方國家已經進入**老齡化社會**。

35. patient [ˈpeʃənt] 有耐心的

英解：enduring without protest or complaint
比較級最高級：more patient, most patient
類義詞：endurable, tolerant

形容詞的用法

- 有耐心的，能忍耐的

He's not very patient with the old.　對於上了年紀的人，他不是很有耐心。

名詞的用法

- 病人，患者

How do you calm your patients down when they are extremely frightened by their illness?
當病人被自己的病情嚇壞了的時候，你會採取什麼辦法讓他們冷靜下來？

延伸用法

1. 延伸名詞 → **patience** [ˈpeʃəns] 耐心，忍耐力，毅力

It takes time and patience to take care of the newborn baby pandas.
照顧新生的熊貓寶寶既需要時間，也需要毅力。

2. 延伸副詞 → **patiently** [ˈpeʃəntlɪ] 耐心地，有毅力地

Please wait patiently. Soon it will be your turn.
請耐心等待，很快就到您了。

同義詞辨析：endurable，tolerant

This packing is environmental and **endurable**.　這種包裝既環保又<u>耐用</u>。

She has a **tolerant** attitude toward gays.　她對同性戀者抱有一種**寬容的**態度。

36. perfect [ˈpɝfɪkt] 完美的，完善

英解：being complete of its kind and without defect or blemish
類義詞：ideal, best

形容詞的用法

1. 完備的，完美的，萬全的

He gave us a perfect set of solution.　他給我們提供了一套完美的解決方案。

2. 完全正確的

You are a perfect match!　你們真是天作之合！

3. 最佳的，極好的

Your performance today was perfect!　你今天的表演棒極了！

4. 完成式的

"I have finished my job" is the present perfect tense of "finish".
"I have finished my job" 是 "finish" 的現在完成時。

動詞的用法

使完善，使完美，使完備
Their love was perfected after the baby's birth.
寶寶的出生使他們的愛情更完美了。

延伸用法

1. 延伸名詞 → **perfection** [pɚˈfɛkʃən] 完善，完美，圓滿

His performance was perfection.　他的演技已經登峰造極了。

2. 延伸副詞 → perfectly [ˋpɝfɪktlɪ] 萬全地，非常，十分

I know perfectly what he meant.　他是什麼意思我知道得一清二楚。

同義詞辨析：ideal，best

He's an **ideal** boy friend.　他是個**理想的**男友。

They are my **best** friends.　他們是我**最好的**朋友。

37. pleasant [ˋplɛzənt] 令人愉快的，舒適的

英解：enjoyable, pleasing or attractive
比較級最高級：pleasanter, pleasantest
類義詞：lovely, favorable, comfortable

形容詞的用法

1. 令人愉快的，可喜的，宜人的，吸引人的

This is a pleasant city to live.　這是一個宜居的城市。

2. 友好的，和善的，文雅的

I opened the door and saw a pleasant young man.
我打開門，看到了一個彬彬有禮的年輕人。

延伸用法

1. 來源動詞 → please [pliz] 使滿意，使愉快

He's hard to please.　他是個難以取悅的人。

2. 延伸名詞 → pleasantness [ˋplɛzntnɪs] 愉快，快樂，和藹可親

I still remember the pleasantness of that weekend.
我對那個愉快的週末記憶猶新。

3. 延伸副詞 → pleasantly [ˋplɛzntlɪ] 愉快地，親切地，友好地

I was pleasantly surprised by her president.　對於她的禮物我感到喜出望外。

同義詞辨析：lovely，favorable，comfortable

I bought a flower from **a lovely** girl.　我從一個**可愛的**女孩那兒買了一朵花。

I will give you a **favorable** reply.　我會給你一個**滿意的**答覆的。

It's really **comfortable** to stay with you.　和你在一起很**舒服**。

38. proud [praʊd] 自豪的，自負的

英解：feeling self-respect or pleasure in something by which you measure your self-worth; or being a reason for pride

比較級最高級：prouder, proudest

類義詞：complacent

形容詞的用法

1. **驕傲的，自豪的，得意的，滿足的**
   He's proud of his achievements.
   他為自己取得成就感到自豪。

2. **引以為榮的，令人自豪的**
   This is the proudest moment in the country's history.
   這是我國歷史上最令人自豪的時刻。

3. **傲慢的，自大的**
   She was too proud to accept others' suggestion.
   她自視甚高，不屑接受他人的建議。

4. **自尊的，自重的**
   We are a proud and independent people.
   我們是一個獨立自主的民族。

副詞的用法

1. **盛情款待**
   They hope we can do them proud.
   他們希望我們能盛情款待他們。

2. **做令自己風光的事**
   I won't do myself proud on purpose.
   我不會特意去做令自己風光的事。

延伸用法

1. 延伸名詞 → **pride** [praɪd] 驕傲，自豪，自尊心
   The teacher took pride in his students.　老師為他的學生感到自豪。

2. 延伸副詞 → **proudly** [ˈpraʊdlɪ] 驕傲地，自負地，得意洋洋地
   He winked at me proudly.　他得意洋洋地朝我眨了眨眼睛。

同義詞辨析：complacent

She's quite **complacent** after succeeding.　她成功後變得**驕傲自滿**了。

39. ripe [raɪp] 成熟的

英解：fully developed or matured and ready to be eaten or used

比較級最高級：riper, ripest

類義詞：mature, adult

形容詞的用法

1. 成熟的

The grapes are ripe now.　現在葡萄已經成熟了。

2. 味道濃鬱的

This wine is quite ripe.　這種酒味道非常醇厚。

3. 時機成熟的

This land is ripe to development.　這片土地適宜開發。

延伸用法

1. 延伸動詞　→ **ripen** [ˋraɪpən]（使）成熟

Disaster can ripen us.　困難可以催我們成熟。

2. 延伸名詞　→ **ripeness** [ˋraɪpnɪs] 成熟，老練

His ripeness showed his ability to handle such kind of things.
他的老練顯示出了他處理這方面事情的能力。

同義詞辨析：mature，adult

He **matured** fast after the thing.　那件事後他**成長**的很快。

You are an **adult** now, so don't be so immature!
你現在已經是**大人**了，不要再這麼幼稚了！

40. scary [ˋskɛrɪ] 提心吊膽的；引起驚慌的；膽小的

英解：frightening

比較級最高級：scarier, scariest

類義詞：timid, tremulous

形容詞的用法

1. 恐怖的，引起驚慌的

He told me a story that was really scary.　他給我講了個很恐怖的故事。

2. 提心吊膽的

He is scary that his father will punish him for his lying.
他擔心自己說謊會遭到爸爸的懲罰。

3. 膽小的

Lucy is so scary that she never sleeps alone.
Lucy 膽子特別小，從來不敢一個人睡覺。

延伸用法

- 來源動詞 → **scare** [skɛr] 使害怕，使恐懼，驚嚇
  Monica, you scared me. Monica，你嚇到我了。

同義詞辨析：timid，tremulous

The punishment to the rebels looks too **timid**. 對這些叛黨的懲罰似乎太過**怯懦**。

John gave a presentation in class with a **tremulous** voice.
John 在班上做了發言，聲音一直在**顫抖**。

41. selfish [ˈsɛlfɪʃ] 自私的；利己主義的

英解：concerned chiefly or only with yourself and your advantage to the exclusion of others

比較級最高級：more selfish, most selfish

類義詞：self-centered, asocial

形容詞的用法

1. 自私的

He is a selfish, greedy and vain crook. 他是一個自私的，貪婪的，虛榮的騙子。

2. 利己主義的

My father always educates me not to be selfish.
父親經常教導我不要成為利己主義的人。

延伸用法

1. 延伸名詞 → **selfishness** [ˈsɛlfɪʃnɪs] 自私自利；自我中心；任性
  He has no real friends as a result of his selfishness, deceit and money worship.
  他的自私，欺騙和拜金使他沒有真正的朋友。

2. 延伸副詞 → **selfishly** [ˈsɛlfɪʃlɪ] 自私地
  I selfishly think that everyone around me should obey me.
  我自私地認為身邊的每個人都應該服從於我。

同義詞辨析：self-centered，asocial

I shouldn't have been so selfish and **self-centered**. 我不應該這麼自私和以**自我為中心**。

She's an **asocial** girl. 她是個**不合群的**女孩。

42. shallow [ˈʃælo] 淺的

英解：not deep or strong; not affecting one deeply
比較級最高級：shallower, shallowest
類義詞：surface

形容詞的用法

1. 淺的
Just play in the shallow water; don't go further.　就在淺水區玩吧，不要走遠了。

2. 淺薄的，膚淺的
It's shallow of you to do such a thing.　你真膚淺，還做這種事！

3. 淺的，弱的
She has a shallow breathing.　她的呼吸很微弱。

延伸用法

1. 延伸名詞 ➜ shallowness [ˈʃælonɪs] 淺，膚淺
I can feel the shallowness of my knowledge. I just don't know how to change it.
我可以感覺得到自己只是方面的淺薄。但我就是不知道要怎麼改變這一狀況。

2. 延伸副詞 ➜ shallowly [ˈʃæloɪ] 淺淺地，膚淺地
She sipped shallowly.　她淺淺嘗了一口。

同義詞辨析：surface

They found something uncommon on the **surface** layer of the cell.
他們在**細胞**表層發現了一些不常見的東西。

43. short [ʃɔrt] 短的，矮的

《經常做缺少的使用》
比較級最高級：shorter, shortest
類義詞：insufficient, deficient, lacking

形容詞的用法

1. 短的，短期的，短暫的
We will go on a short holiday on the weekend.　我們週末要去做短途旅行。

2. 矮的
I was short and dummy.　那時候我又矮又胖。

3. 不足，短缺

We are short of food now.　我們現在缺少食物。

4. 缺乏，缺少

He was a stapping man but short on brain.　他是個魁梧的人但缺乏頭腦。

5. 簡略的，縮寫的

Call me Tom—it's short for Thomas.　叫我 Tom 好了──這是 Thomas 的簡稱。

6. 粗暴，簡慢無禮

I'm sorry for being short with you earlier.　很抱歉，剛才失禮了。

副詞的用法

- 缺少，不足

They had run short of water.　他們的水不夠用了。

延伸用法

- 延伸名詞 → **shortness** [ˈʃɔrtnɪs] 不足

He has suffered from shortness of breath for years.
他那氣急的毛病已經有許多年了。

同義詞辨析：insufficient，deficient，lacking

We have to give up the plan due to <u>**insufficient**</u> funds.《sufficient 足夠的反義詞》
由於資金**不足**，我們不得不放棄這個計畫。

He's <u>**deficient**</u> in common sense.《名詞 deficiency 經常用於疾病名稱》　他**缺少**常識。

He was blamed for <u>**lacking**</u> ambition.《片語 being lack of sth》　他被指責**缺乏**雄心壯志。

44. sour [ˈsaʊr] 酸的，餿的

《形容詞味道的酸味及不愉悅的態度》

比較級最高級：**sourer, sourest**

類義詞：**acid, go bad**

形容詞的用法

1. 酸的，有酸味的

I like sour apples.　我喜歡吃酸蘋果。

2. 酸腐的，餿的

The rice has gone sour.
米飯已經餿了。

動詞的用法

1.（關係、人等）變壞，惡化

Their relationship has soured because of this thing.
因為這件事他們之間的關係惡化了。

2. 變酸，變味

The milk soured.　牛奶變味了。

延伸用法

1. 延伸名詞 ➡ **sourness** [ˋsaʊrnɪs] 酸味，性情乖僻

I can't stand his increasing sourness any more.
我再也忍受不了他那日益乖張的脾氣了。

2. 延伸副詞 ➡ **sourly** [ˋsaʊrlɪ] 酸酸地，壞脾氣地，性情乖張地

"How could I know?" he said sourly. 「我哪知道？」他沒好氣地說。

同義詞辨析：acid，go bad

Acid rain can do great harm to the agriculture.《指酸鹼值中的酸性》
酸雨對農業生產有巨大的破壞作用。

This cup of yoghourt has **gone bad**. You'd better throw it away.《指物品品質變壞過期》
這杯優酪乳已經變質了。你最好把它丟掉。

45. splendid [ˋsplɛndɪd] 輝煌的，極好的

《一般用來形容景色》

比較級最高級：more splendid, most splendid
類義詞：brilliant, excellent, wonderful

形容詞的用法

1. 極佳的，非常好的

The scenery here is splendid.　這兒的風景非常好。

2. 壯麗的，雄偉的，輝煌的，豪華的

They plan to celebrate their marriage in a splendid castle.
他們打算在一座雄偉的城堡裡舉行婚禮。

延伸用法

● **延伸副詞** ➡ **splendidly** [ˋsplɛndɪdlɪ] 華麗地，豪華地，壯觀地

The girls of the volleyball team have done their job splendidly in this game.
這次排球比賽，女生隊員們表現非常出色。

同義詞辨析：brilliant，excellent，wonderful

He was highly spoken of his **brilliant** performance.《指聰明出色的想法》
他的出色表演受到了非常高的讚揚。

We can offer you **excellent** service during your stay here.《指優秀出眾的特質》
您在此停留期間，我們可以為您提供優質服務。

It's so **wonderful**! How did you do that?《指美好的事物》
太不可思議了！你是怎麼做到的？

46. straight [stret] 直的

《除了形容如直線般的特質外，也常使用在描述不間斷的事物》

比較級最高級：straighter, straightest

類義詞：continuing, endless

形容詞的用法

1. 直的

I like your straight hair. Maybe someday I will do mine, too.
我喜歡你的直髮。說不定哪天我也去做成直的。

2. 準的，正中目標

I gave him a straight punch to his face. 名詞的用法

● 異性戀者

Gays should have equal rights with straights.
同性戀者應與異性戀者擁有同等權利。我一拳不偏不倚正好打在他臉上了。

3. 坦誠的，直率的

You are not straight with me. 名詞的用法

● 異性戀者

Gays should have equal rights with straights.
同性戀者應與異性戀者擁有同等權利。你沒跟我坦白。

4. 不間斷的

I've got five straight wins in the game.　比賽中，我已經五連勝了。

5. 異性戀的

Don't hit on her. She's not straight.　不要勾引她了。她是同性戀。

副詞的用法

1. 筆直地

Keep straight on for two blocks and you will find the mall on your right side.
一直往前走 2 個街區，你就會發現購物商場就在你的右邊。

2. 直接，立即

The mother told her son to come straight home after school.
母親告訴兒子放學後直接回家。

3. 正，直

Stand straight!　站直了！

4. 坦率地，直截了當地

I told him straight that I fell in love with him.　我直截了當的跟他說我愛上他了。

5. 連續不斷地

He has been walking for 5 hours straight.　他已經連續走了 5 個小時了。

名詞的用法

● 異性戀者

Gays should have equal rights with straights.

同性戀者應與異性戀者擁有同等權利。

延伸用法

● 延伸動詞 → **straighten** [ˋstretn]（使）變直，變正

When he started to murmur, I would wish him to straighten his tongue.

每當他說話含含糊糊的時候，我都希望他能把舌頭捋直了。

同義詞辨析：continuing，endless

The **continuing** horrific violence has seriously weakened the public confidence for the government.《由動詞 continue 變化而來》

持續不斷的恐怖暴力事件嚴重削弱了公眾對政府的信任。

I was tired of their **endless** quarrelling.《指無止盡的狀態》

我厭倦了他們**無休止的**爭吵。

47. strange [strendʒ] 奇怪的，陌生的

《主要用在形容陌生的事物與奇怪的特質》

比較級最高級：stranger, strangest

類義詞：unfamiliar

形容詞的用法

1. 奇怪的，奇特的，異常的

That's strange—I remember I locked the door.　奇怪，我記得我鎖門了。

2. 陌生的，不熟悉的

This place was totally strange to me.　我對這個地方完全不熟悉。

延伸用法

1. 延伸名詞 → strangeness [ˋstrendʒnɪs] 陌生，冷淡

It's really hurt when your close friends look at you in strangeness.

當你的朋友用冷淡的眼神看著你時，那種感覺真的很痛苦。

2. 延伸副詞 → **strangely** [ˋstrendʒlɪ] 奇怪地，奇妙地，不可思議地
Strangely enough, I didn't feel hurt when he beat me.
真奇怪，他打我的時候我居然感覺不到疼痛。

同義詞辨析：unfamiliar

I am as **unfamiliar** with the city as you are.《形容詞 familiar 的反義詞》
我和你一樣**不熟悉**這個城市。

48. strong [strɔŋ] 堅強的，強壯的

《經常用在形容個性與意念的堅定》
比較級最高級：stronger, strongest
類義詞：tough, firm

形容詞的用法

1. 強壯的，強勁的
He's strong enough to pull out a big tree!　他力氣大得可以拔起一棵大樹！

2. 堅決的，堅定的
She had a strong will that her husband would come back to her someday.
她堅定的相信，總有一天她的丈夫會回到她的身邊。

3. 堅固的，結實的
Be careful! This ladder is not that strong.　小心點！這個梯子可沒那麼結實。

4. 堅挺的，行情看漲的
The British pound is still stronger against the RMB.　英鎊對人民幣走勢依然強勁。

5. 濃烈的
He likes to use strong colors in his painting.　他喜歡用濃烈的色彩作畫。

延伸用法

1. 延伸名詞 → **strength** [strɛŋθ] 力量，力氣
Show me the strength of your muscles.　給我展示一下你肌肉的力量。

2. 延伸副詞 → **strongly** [ˋstrɔŋlɪ] 強有力地，堅強地，氣味濃厚地
In the meeting, his idea was strongly against.　會上他的想法遭到了堅決反對。

同義詞辨析：tough，firm

American threatened to take a **tough** attitude.《形容人的嚴苛》
美國威脅說要採取**強硬**態度。

You can rely on me. I'm your **firm** and loyal follower.《形容不輕易改變的態度》
你可以相信我，我是你**堅定**、忠實的追隨者。

49. terrible [ˈtɛrəbl̩] 可怕的，討厭的

《形容詞主要是可怕的，但是副詞 terribly 卻是經常使用為程度副詞》

比較級最高級：more terrible, most terrible
類義詞：horrible, fearful

形容詞的用法

1. 非常討厭，令人極不快的，可怕的

That's a terrible nightmare for me.　那件事對我來說簡直就是個可怕的噩夢。

2. 非常嚴重的，危害極大

A terrible accident happened because of the bad weather.
糟糕的天氣狀況導致了一場嚴重事故。

3. 極度的，嚴重的

He's in terrible pain.　他正處於極度痛苦之中。

延伸用法

● 延伸副詞　→ **terribly** [ˈtɛrəblɪ] 很，非常

I'm terribly sorry for the inconvenience.　為您造成不便，我感到非常抱歉。

同義詞辨析：horrible，fearful

She was shocked by the **horrible** news.《令人覺得可怕的》
她被這個**聳人聽聞的**消息嚇到了。

Your fault may bring **fearful** consequences, do you understand?《由名詞 fear 變化而來》
你的錯誤可能會引起**可怕的**後果，你明白嗎？

50. thirsty [ˋθɝstɪ] 口渴的

《除了形容口渴之外，也經常用在形容對於事物的渴望》

比較級最高級：thirstier, thirstiest

類義詞：eager

形容詞的用法

1. 渴的，口渴的

I'm thirsty now. Can you get me some water?　我現在很渴，你能給我點水嗎？

2. 渴望，渴求，熱望

He's thirst for power.　他拼命想掌權。

3. 乾旱的，缺水的

The field is thirsty and needs water.　田地乾旱，需要澆水灌溉。

延伸用法

1. 來源動詞 ➞ **thirst** [θɝst] 口渴，想喝水

She thirsts for famous brand.　她渴望擁有名牌。

2. 延伸副詞 ➞ **thirstily** [ˋθɝstɪlɪ] 口渴地，如饑似渴地

He's been studying thirstily recently.　他最近在如饑似渴地學習。

同義詞辨析：eager

He's **eager** to know what would happen next.《形容急迫的期待》

他<u>很想</u>知道接下來會發生什麼事。

好書報報 —生活系列

Best Publishing

愛情之酒甜而苦。兩人喝，是甘露；
三人喝，是酸醋；隨便喝，要中毒。

精選出偶像劇必定出現的**80**個情境，
每個情境－必備單字、劇情會話訓練班、30秒會話教室
讓你跟著偶像劇的腳步學生活英語會話的劇情，
輕鬆自然地學會英語!

作者：伍羚芝
定價：新台幣349元
規格：344頁 / 18K / 雙色印刷

全書中英對照，介紹東西方節慶的典故，
幫助你的英語學習－學得好、學得深入!

用英語來學節慶分為兩大部分－東方節慶&西方節慶

每個節慶共**7**個學習項目：
節慶源由－簡易版、精彩完整版＋實用單字、閱讀測驗、
習俗放大鏡、實用會話、常用單句這麼說、互動單元...

作者：Melanie Venekamp、陳欣慧、倍斯特編輯團隊
定價：新台幣299元
規格：304頁 / 18K / 雙色印刷

用現有的環境與資源，為自己的小寶貝
創造一個雙語學習環境；讓孩子贏在起跑點上!

我家寶貝愛英文，是一本從媽咪懷孕、嬰兒期到幼兒期，
會常用到的單字、對話，必備例句，
並設計單元延伸的互動小遊戲以及童謠，
增進親子關係，也讓家長與孩子一同學習的參考書!

作者：Mark Venekamp & Claire Chang
定價：新台幣329元
規格：296頁 / 18K / 雙色印刷 / MP3

好書報報

Best Publishing

心理學研究顯示，一個習慣養成，至少必須重複21次！
全書規劃30天學習進度表，搭配學習，
不知不覺養成學習英語的好習慣！

▲圖解學習英文文法 三效合一！
◎刺激大腦記憶◎快速掌握學習大綱◎複習迅速

▲英文文法學習元素一次到位！
◎20個必懂觀念 ◎30個必學句型 ◎40個必閃陷阱

▲流行有趣的英語！
◎「那裡有正妹！」
◎「今天我們去看變形金剛3吧！」

作者：朱懿婷
定價：新台幣349元
規格：364頁 / 18K / 雙色印刷

要說出流利的英文，就是需要常常開口勇敢說！

國外打工兼職很流行，如何找尋機會？
怎麼做完整的英文自我介紹，成功promote自己？
獨自出國打工，職場基礎英語對話該怎麼說？
不同國家、不同領域要知道那些common sense？
保險健康的考量要更注意，各國制度大不同？

6大主題 30個單元 120組情境式對話 30篇補給站！
九大學習特色：
■主題豐富多元　■多種情境演練　■激發聯想延伸
■增強單字記憶　■片語邏輯組合　■例句靈活套用
■塊狀編排歸納　■舒適閱讀視覺　■吸收效果加倍

作者：Claire Chang & Melanie Venecamp
定價：新台幣469元
規格：560頁 / 18K / 雙色印刷

英文文法超理解

作者	倍斯特編輯部◎著
封面設計	高鍾琪
內頁構成	華漢電腦排版有限公司
發行人	周瑞德
企劃編輯	倍斯特編輯部
印製	世和印製企業有限公司
初版	2013 年 11 月
定價	新台幣 399 元

出版　　倍斯特出版事業有限公司

電話／（02）2351-2007 傳真／（02）2351-0887

地址／100 台北市中正區福州街 1 號 10 樓之 2

Email ／ best.books.service@gmail.com

總經銷　商流文化事業有限公司

地址／新北市中和區中正路 752 號 7 樓

電話／（02）2228-8841 傳真／（02）2228-6939

版權所有　翻印必究

國家圖書館出版品預行編目（CIP）資料

英文文法超理解／倍斯特編輯部著．
-- 初版 . -- 臺北市：倍斯特，2013.11
面；　公分
ISBN：978-986-89739-5-4　（平裝）
1. 英語　2. 語法
805.16　　　　　　　　　　　　102022366